The Impending Night

Jon Monson

Castle Peak Publishing

Cover and map design by Kimberly Monson

ISBN-13 (Print): 978-1728792774

ASIN (E-Book): B07KLZM5D7

For Cade, Ryan, Megan, Mike, David, and everyone else who read through the inferior iterations in an attempt to make this book something worth reading.

For Mom, who has always believed in me, even when she probably shouldn't have.

And for Kim and Adelaide—without you, there would be no point in writing anything.

Works by Jon Monson

The Sun and the Raven
Rise of the Forgotten Sun
The Impending Night
The Return

The Final Heir Trilogy
The Final Heir
The Fallen Usurper (Coming Soon)
The Eternal Bond (Coming Soon)

From the Author

First of all, I want to thank you for picking up and reading this book. Your support, even if you just downloaded the e-book on a free weekend, is more appreciated than you could ever know. The story has been years in the making, and I'm so pleased to be able to share it with you.

As the author, the places and characters within these pages are real to me, and I really want at least a portion of that reality to materialize in your mind. To help with that, there is a glossary at the back of the book, complete with a pronunciation guide and helpful facts. So, if you are ever confused about how to pronounce a name or you've forgotten about a character, please take a look.

NAERDON

Naerd

ALBONA

Somerset

Silvino

MARGELLA

Lusita

LUSITA

Ghindi

GHINDI

the Soulless Desert

SALATIA

Maradon

Gulf of Gorteo

GORTEO

PILSA

Mt. Pietra

Palmas

GENODRA

N

Prologue

Alarun stood at the edge of his garden, the smile on his face fading along with the sunlight that bathed the vegetation in an array of oranges and reds. Shadows danced through the trees and hedges, signaling the impending night. The Sun God hoped he would live to see the morning.

The day had been perfect. A few small clouds had threatened in the morning, but a sliver of power had pushed them away. Instead, the daylight hours had been spent sipping wine and cultivating the vegetation that now surrounded him.

His eyes began to adjust as the light faded, the sun fleeing behind the western mountains. His heart sank along with the giant orb. Even the best of days had to end.

"I thought today would never end—the sunlight is just so harsh," a feminine voice whispered from the shadows behind Alarun, and the Divine turned to face the only woman in existence who would utter such words.

A face sculpted from flawless white marble and framed by long raven hair greeted him. High cheeks and a sharp jaw were complemented by dark, full lips. Those lips spread into a smile, displaying a set of teeth even brighter than her alabaster skin.

"You must have missed me terribly," the woman said, stepping out of the shadows. "I know I would."

Alarun stood in silence, refusing to respond. He had agreed to this little meeting—that didn't mean he was happy about it. The less he said, the sooner it would be over.

"Don't you love my new dress?" the woman asked, lifting her arms and rotating for Alarun to get a complete view. Her body curved under the thin fabric, leaving very little to the imagination. He tried to keep his eyes focused on her face, but there was something about the way the fabric shimmered and danced in the sunset.

"I made it myself," the woman continued, moving closer to Alarun. "Woven from the finest darkness I could create—it's a very special raiment for a very special night."

"What makes you think this night is special?" Alarun asked, the words sticking in his throat.

"It's the night I return to your arms," the woman replied, covering the remaining distance between them and placing a delicate hand on Alarun's chest. "Or more accurately, it's the night you return to mine."

"Just because I agreed to meet doesn't change what you've done," Alarun said, stepping backward to escape the woman's touch. "And it most certainly doesn't change how I feel about it."

"Those were just some misunderstandings," she said, pushing out her lips and widening her eyes, giving Alarun the impression of a penitent puppy.

For the first time, Alarun allowed himself to look into the woman's large, black eyes. The orbs were filled with raw desire, both for him and for power. A knot formed in Alarun's stomach, and he moved to turn away from the woman's gaze.

Yet he found himself unable to do so. The eyes were far more than an organ used to capture images—they were finely crafted works of art. At that moment, turning away from them would be sacrilege bordering on cursing the name of the Sender.

"Now there, that's more like it," the woman cooed, her voice ringing out like fine crystal. "The two of us should just talk. That sounds pleasant, now doesn't it?"

Alarun found himself nodding his head, although there was something in the back of his mind telling him that talking would be a terrible idea. Yet another part of him—a much stronger part—could pass the entire night listening to that voice. In fact, he could spend the rest of eternity in any state, as long as he was accompanied by the creature before him.

"I think it's long past time for this little war to end," the woman said, again placing a hand on Alarun's chest. This time, he didn't move to avoid her touch. "Too many have already fallen, and for nothing. Besides, you can't really say that fighting for these mortals is better than spending eternity with me at your side."

Alarun again only nodded his head, and a few words tried and failed to escape his throat. This woman spoke the truth—spending eternity with perfection was vastly superior to a life cut short in the defense of a base and ungrateful creation.

"I'm so glad you agree," she said, nuzzling her head into Alarun's chest. "Now, come—an agreement such as this requires a fitting celebration."

As she grabbed his hand to lead him away from the garden, a voice began shouting in the back of his mind. He knew that fighting for the mortals was important, but he couldn't remember exactly why. It really did seem silly—he was spending his days fighting his fellow Creators when he could be spending that time engaged in much more pleasant endeavors.

A rustling in the bushes grabbed his attention, and a small child emerged, her face covered in both dirt and a wide smile. The young girl looked up at the scene she had interrupted, and the smile faded. Alarun looked over to see a snarl marring his visitor's perfect mouth.

"Get out of here, you wretched thing," the woman's voice snapped as she spun toward the child.

The young girl's eyes grew wider than saucers, and tears began to well up. Yet, she didn't move, as if she had been frozen to that spot.

"Perhaps your ears aren't working," the woman snarled, letting go of Alarun's hand as she moved toward the intruder. "Don't worry, I'll loosen whatever is plugging them up."

A loud crack reverberated through the garden as an alabaster hand connected with the child's dirt-smattered face. The girl screamed as the force of the blow knocked her to the ground. A soft whimper escaped the girl's lips as she curled up into a ball.

"I told you to leave," the woman shrieked, grabbing the child by the hair. The girl's screams reverberated in Alarun's ears, yet he found himself unable to do anything about it. If the woman wanted to hurt the child, then who was he to stop her?

You are the God of Gods, a voice called out, escaping from the back of his mind. *That woman has no real power over you. You know that she is not what she appears.*

"Let the girl be," Alarun croaked, his voice breaking through whatever had bound it. The woman stopped, her hands still clinging to the hair of the struggling child.

"Don't worry, sweetness," she cooed, turning her gaze back on Alarun. "I'll be right back after I dispose of this creature. Then we can be alone."

"Let her go," Alarun growled, strength again returning to his throat. "This meeting is over—it's time for you to return home."

"You fight for a lost cause," the woman said, the honey gone from her voice. "You can either join me tonight, or you can say goodbye to your pathetic existence."

"You almost had me," Alarun growled, moving forward and picking up the young child in his arms. "Yet your true nature always comes out."

"You are a fool," the woman hissed, again drawing closer in the twilight. "Don't forget that, for the moment, you are in my domain."

The woman held up a hand, and tendrils of black mist began to swirl in the air. Like a serpent, the darkness coiled around her, ready to do the bidding of its mistress.

A smile crept onto Alarun's face as the Sun God called on the power within his chest. Like a raging river held back by the strongest of dams, he could feel the force begging to be released. His smile only grew wider as he obliged its request.

The woman's eyes widened as purple twilight faded, transitioning to a bright azure. White clouds popped into view, floating lazily in the sky. The shadows surrounding the woman disappeared, like a morning fog burning in the afternoon sun.

Yet the sun was absent. The massive ball of fire was still in its proper orbit, giving light and warmth to the other side of the planet. Alarun didn't need the sun to bring light and life to his creations.

"This is far from over," the woman hissed, shooting him a glare that could pierce armor. Instead of attacking, she closed her eyes and disappeared.

1

Barrick rifled through a shelf of cheap, dust-covered bottles, squinting in the low light of his dying lantern. The cool air of the cellar felt good in his lungs, especially compared to the hot summer he was forced to battle above ground. Taking a deep breath, he focused his eyes back on his search.

"Oi, Worm!" a voice bellowed from upstairs. "Hurry up down there."

"I'm comin', quit yer whinin'," Barrick shouted back, his eyes scanning the cellar.

It wasn't a particularly large storage room, especially when compared to the wine cellars of his late father's estate. Yet, what it lacked in size, it more than compensated for with cluttered shelves and cheap spirits. How was it possible for an entire case of wine to go missing in such a small space?

"If yer not up here in ten seconds..." the voice again shouted, trailing off and leaving the consequences of tardiness up to Barrick's imagination.

"Stones," Barrick cursed before grabbing a dusty bottle and wiping it off with a cloth. It was a cheap red from the southern foothills of Albona—terrible stuff that he'd feel sorry giving to a dog, but it was probably among the finest in the entire cellar.

Grabbing the lantern, Barrick headed for the sagging wood stairs that would take him back into the dusty heat currently suffocating Naerd, the industrial and—less importantly—political capital of Naerdon. With a glare at the rotting wood, Barrick lurched to the landing at the top and steeled himself for the wave of hot air as he pushed open the trap door leading outside.

"I thought Naerdon was supposed to be some sort of freezin' tundra," Barrick said as he emerged behind the bar of the seediest tavern he could imagine.

"Oh, just wait 'til winter," a large man in a dirty apron responded, grabbing the dusty bottle from Barrick's grasp. "Yeh'll get so much rain and snow that you'll look back on the dog days of summer like she was a beautiful woman."

"Is there any good time to be here, Galo?" Barrick asked, grabbing a rag to wipe down the bar.

"Not really," Galo said, dressed in his worn brown shirt and pants topped with a dirty apron. He looked at the wine, inspecting the bottle. "Hey, this isn't what I asked for."

"Well, I couldn't find the good stuff," Barrick grunted back, mimicking the Naerdic bartender's gruff mannerisms. He tried to not lace his words with too much sarcasm. The "good stuff" Galo had requested was barely worth more than the bottles used to hold it.

"Yeh must be bloody blind as a bat," Galo shouted as he grabbed the lantern to head down into the cellar to look for himself.

With a sigh, Barrick kept wiping at the filthy bar, despite the fact that his rag wasn't clean enough to do much good. As the sweat beaded on his forehead, his thoughts turned to an image of Aydiin and Byanca likely trudging through the rain of a Genodran winter on the far side of the world, and he suddenly found himself grateful to be in Naerdon. He just hoped he could wrap things up before winter hit.

"Oi, new guy," one of the two patrons currently occupying the tavern called out, waving for Barrick. "Another mead, if yeh please."

Barrick grabbed a relatively clean pewter tankard and moved over to the large keg filled with the amber liquid. He sighed as the alcohol gushed out, and he took a moment to look around *The Drunken Maiden*.

It was by far the dirtiest, seediest establishment he'd ever had the pleasure of knowing. The plaster walls were peeling, the original color indecipherable after decades of soaking up tobacco smoke and splattered mead. Rotting shutters covered windows that Barrick had never seen opened in the month he'd spent here, which probably helped customers to ignore the filth. The wood floor creaked and groaned with practically every step, and he had little desire to know what currently made its home underneath their feet.

Barrick picked up the full tankard and brought it over to the small corner table occupied nearly full-time by the two drunkards. The man smiled at Barrick, revealing a mass of brown, rotting teeth as he slipped a small coin across the table. Holding back a sigh, Barrick picked up the coin and strode back to the bar.

The squeal of rusted hinges filled the room as the tavern's front door opened, bathing the scene in the orange glow of sunset. Barrick squinted against the light as a group of dockworkers filed through, their conversation already giving him a headache.

"Hey, *skitkarl*," one of the men called out, the others laughing at his profanity, "meads all around—it's been a rough day for those of us who actually work."

As Barrick began filling pewter tankards of mead, the *Maiden's* usual customers began to trickle in. Dock laborers, factory workers, and a collection of tradesmen came through the front door in small groups, ready to drink off the effects of a hard day's labor. Nearly all smelled of hard work, which was something Barrick had learned to tolerate over the past weeks.

"I can' find the good stuff anywhere," Galo bellowed, climbing out of the cellar. "I'll be takin' it out of yer wages."

"I don't even drink wine," Barrick shot back, stifling a smile at the thought of the roll of banknotes hidden in his bag. If Galo only knew that his lowly server had enough money to buy the *Maiden*, tear it down, and build a mansion, he'd probably wet himself.

"We ran out ages ago, Uncle," a voice piped up, and Barrick looked over to see a young woman enter through the front door.

Lilah—Galo's niece and the only serving girl working at the *Maiden*—gave Barrick a wink as she bent down behind the bar in her nightly search through the collection of dirty aprons. Her hair, so blonde it was almost white, was pulled into a ponytail, and her plain grey dress did little to dissuade Barrick from admiring her. If Galo ever found out about the after-hours activities Barrick so enjoyed with the girl, he wouldn't be safe until the entire island was well beyond the horizon.

"Now, I'm sure I ordered some just a few weeks ago," Galo stammered. "I've got a very important customer coming in tonight."

Lilah's response was lost to Barrick's ears as he took a half-dozen tankards to a table of dockworkers. The men didn't even look up as he approached, completely engrossed in their conversation.

"I ain't never seen nothing like it," one of the men said to the group. "Over a hundred bushels of Salatian cotton—gone, right from under our noses."

"Bah, the guards were probably in on it with the thieves," one of the other men shot back. "Tha's what the boss gets fer hirin' *strangers* to watch the ship."

Barrick set the drinks down, and the men stopped their conversation long enough to slip him a few coins. He backed away to grab more mead, and the men immediately went back to a huddled whisper. The door again opened, and a hush rippled through the *Maiden*.

An aging aristocrat with silver hair and a brown three-piece suit walked in, flanked on either side by men large enough to sink a ship. He pulled out a pocket watch crafted from pure gold and sniffed as he checked the time.

"Ah, my dear sir," Galo stammered, running out from behind the bar. "It is an honor to have you in my humble establishment."

"Yes, I'm sure it is," the gentleman replied, a scowl plastered to his face. "Has the room I requested been prepared?"

"Of course, m'lord," Galo responded with a bow. "Lilah, please show our esteemed guest to his private dining chamber."

"I don't like the looks of that girl," the man sniffed. "My maid is still trying to scrub out the stain from the last time I trusted a pretty little thing like that with a glass of wine."

Lilah's face turned a beautiful shade of pink, and she spun around to grab a set of tankards for a fresh pair of laborers entering behind the aristocrat.

"That man right there, he'll have to do," he said, gesturing to Barrick. "Galo, make sure my men get some refreshment—nothing too strong, of course."

"Without delay," Galo squeaked, grabbing the two tankards from Lilah and handing them to the brutes. With eyes never ceasing to scan the room, the two men moved toward an empty table on the far side of the tavern.

"Come now, boy," the gentleman snapped at Barrick. "I don't have all night."

"Yes, sir," Barrick said with a bow before grabbing the bottle of wine he'd brought up from the cellar. He led the aging aristocrat down a back hallway to the *Maiden's* only private dining room.

Dominated by an ancient table cobbled together from various hardwoods complemented by five chairs of both different styles and colors, the room was technically large enough for a private dinner. However, Barrick had only seen the room used for his after-hour dalliances with Lilah.

"Here you are, m'lord," Barrick said with a bow, placing the bottle of wine and a glass onto the flimsy table. "I hope this is satisfactory."

"It's not," the man sniffed, taking a seat as Barrick uncorked the bottle and poured a few drops into the glass. With a bow, Barrick turned to leave the room for whatever purpose this pompous *skitkarl* had reserved it.

"The Return comes swiftly," the aristocrat stated, his eyes never leaving his glass. Barrick's heart leapt into his throat—after weeks of toiling in the heat for that idiot tavern keeper, he was about to be free.

"The Elect await the Return," Barrick responded, the words rolling off his tongue.

The phrase was common among disciples of the Raven, and he'd said it countless times over the past decade. The response Barrick had given indicated that he was still an Initiate, not even ready to wear the black robes of a Squire, let alone the violet robes of a Knight.

"Come, my young friend. Sit and enjoy this...perfectly mediocre wine with me," the old man said, waving his hand at one of the empty chairs.

"Thank you, m'lord," Barrick responded, grabbing a simple wooden cup that had been left on the table and pouring some of the ruby liquid into it.

"Please drink," the man said, taking a sip from his own glass with a grimace. "I'm assuming that even this swill is a step up from whatever it is you are accustomed to consuming."

Barrick took a sip, holding back a grimace of his own. The wine was little better than vinegar, a far stretch from the fine Salatian brandy to which he had grown accustomed.

"So, I hear you have been searching for us," the grey-haired man said, placing his glass back on the table.

"Very diligently, sir," Barrick replied.

"Indeed," the man smiled. "You may call me Boral. I must warn you, however, that it will not be easy to join our ranks."

"I hear and obey, master," Barrick said, bowing his head. "I was to be initiated into the ranks of the Squires in Maradon when I heard about the...rumors. All my contacts went silent, and so I fled. I've been in Naerd for weeks now, trying to contact the Elect."

"You have done well, my son. Tell me, do you know what happened to our brethren in Salatia?"

"Just rumors, m'lord," Barrick stammered. "All news that I heard through Maradon's underground places the blame on rebellious tribesmen."

"Interesting," Boral replied. "Why did you feel it necessary to flee? Why did you not stay to help your brethren rebuild?"

"I...I didn't know what to do," Barrick stammered, and he felt the blood drain from his face. "I'd only met a few Squires, and they had always given me code names. How was I supposed to help rebuild when all my contacts were dead?"

"I can understand your logic," Boral said with a nod, pulling out his pocket watch to check the time. "Tell me, is there anything you wouldn't do for the Great Lord?"

"Of course not," Barrick responded, doubting that his previous response had provided the intended reassurance. "I am willing to give my soul so that the Raven may be freed."

"Ah, children—so eager to show grand demonstrations of devotion," Boral sighed, slipping his watch back into his pocket. "What if the task I give you is to wait? A year, maybe two? Would you be willing to continue to serve as an Initiate, not even knowing the fruit of your labors?"

"Absolutely," Barrick responded. "There is no task too menial when in service of the Raven. Of course, I rather thought that the work I had done in Maradon would be enough to—"

"Work that we cannot verify," Boral snapped. "Do you think we are stupid? Do you think we are disorganized? There is no record of you having done *anything* for us. I cannot even find your name on the Initiate rolls, Mr. James."

"That's impossible," Barrick gasped, mentally slapping himself on the forehead. He hadn't thought about the possibility of his fake name not showing up on the rolls in Maradon—they had, after all, been destroyed by his own hand. Was this man bluffing, or were there really copies sent to the various cells throughout the world?

"Oh, I'm afraid it's quite possible," Boral responded. "I was hoping to receive some honesty from you tonight, but apparently my hopes were unfounded. You may go."

Boral dismissed Barrick with a wave, and the man returned to his wine. Mouth agape, Barrick stood, not having to pretend to look crestfallen.

He'd gone to so much effort to infiltrate the Order in Naerdon. He'd spent weeks working in this trash heap, putting up with the worst sort of people ever to walk the planet. He walked slowly toward the door.

Well, time for plan B.

He lurched, appearing less than a span behind Boral's back. His hand latched onto the man's silver hair, slamming his head into the wooden table. Boral let out a grunt as blood began to pour out of his nose and onto his clothing.

"Listen here, young man," Boral sputtered, grabbing his nose with one hand and slapping at Barrick's arm with the other, "that was the last thing—"

"No, you listen," Barrick snapped, again slamming the man's face into the table. "You honestly think I'm only an Initiate? I know every intimate detail of the Order."

"That's imposs—"

"For starters," Barrick hissed, "how do you think King Frederick will react when I tell him that Mr. Boris Tamden, Minister of Finance, is part of a secret group he both fears and hates?"

The old man's eyes widened in shock as Barrick ripped off a silver wig and fake mustache, revealing a much younger mess of jet-black hair and a clean-shaven face. Barrick tossed the convincing agents of disguise into a corner of the room.

"I gave you a chance to take me in, but now we are going to do this the hard way, mate," Barrick drawled. "I am Barrick Fortescue, son of the late Grand Master. I am a full Knight of the Raven, and you *will* obey my commands."

The man nodded, wiping the blood from his nose onto his fine suit jacket. Barrick sat back down, grabbed Tamden's nose and set it back into place with a snap.

"You monster," Tamden howled, placing a hand to his crooked nose.

"Oh, you don't even know the half of it," Barrick said with a smile. "Now, tell me nicely this time—how may I be of service to the Great Lord?"

2

Despite the cold wind battering his face, despite the waves lapping against his small boat, despite the dull ache beginning to settle in his shoulders, Aydiin couldn't help but smile. Breathing in the salty air, he dipped the ash paddles into the choppy waters before pulling the handles toward his chest. The rough wood dug into his hands, and he ignored the blisters that were beginning to form as the boat crept closer to shore.

A crescent moon illuminated the world in a soft glow, its light filtered by thin clouds meandering through the sky. Facing the stern of the boat, Aydiin couldn't see the approaching beach or navigate the unfamiliar waters. For that, he trusted in the most beautiful pair of green eyes to ever grace his presence.

Byanca sat on the boat's stern, her neck craning, eyes scanning the approaching shore. The fiery hair he so adored was now tucked under the heavy wool hood protecting her from the cold. Aydiin maintained his gaze steady on her, the sight giving him strength as he rowed the small boat through the waves.

Clothed in a simple grey dress covered by a black cloak, Byanca looked beautiful as ever. Aydiin pictured his own simple clothing—a yellowing cotton seaman's shirt and tattered brown pants—and hoped she thought the same of him. Even while rowing a boat in the middle of the night, he still felt uncomfortable out of his customary robes and loose-fitting trousers.

In the moonlight, he could see Byanca's face relax, followed quickly by the rest of her posture. While still straight, her back and neck released some of the tension they had been holding for the past hour. Her eyes turned from their vigil and found Aydiin's own before a smile spread across her face.

"Thank the Divines," Byanca muttered, the words only audible to Aydiin.

"You're welcome," Aydiin grunted, pulling the oars against a particularly strong wave trying to hold him back.

"You may be the most powerful man in the world, but you're not divine," she said, leaning forward and slapping his shoulder. "Not yet, at least."

"I guess you're right. Whoever heard of a Divine rowing a boat in the middle of winter?" Aydiin said, his voice growing louder than it should.

"Just because we've been given the all-clear doesn't mean we don't need to be careful," Byanca chided in a whisper, lifting a finger up to her lips. "You never know who could be listening."

"Isn't that why we're on this dingey, rowing toward a deserted beach in the middle of the night?" Aydiin asked, returning his own voice to a whisper. "It's hard to imagine running into anyone dangerous out here."

"Oh, so now you're an expert on the Order?" Byanca asked with a smile in her voice, gesturing for Aydiin to straighten out their path. "A group that secretive and powerful could have eyes and ears anywhere."

"I do appreciate your caution," Aydiin said, his muscles beginning to protest at the continuous rowing. "Although, if you really wanted to be careful, we could be hundreds of leagues from here instead of running headlong into danger."

Byanca only responded with a smile as the boat crashed into sand underneath the water. Without waiting for a response, Aydiin leapt over the side, gasping for air as freezing water covered his legs and nether regions. The cold racked his entire body as he grabbed the front of the boat and began dragging it toward shore.

His waterlogged boot caught on a loose stone, and Aydiin stumbled headfirst into the waist-deep water. His left hand grasping the bow, he quickly pulled himself up and gasped for air. Digging his feet into the sand, he used all his strength to pull the boat through the waves.

A pair of gloved hands grabbed the boat to his right, and Aydiin felt the tiny craft move under the combined effort. Aydiin looked to see a dark-clad figure grunting with the effort of fighting the waves, face obscured by a hood. He couldn't help but think of the cowls donned by followers of the Undergods—men and women who would be only too happy to bring about his destruction.

Yet he knew that Byanca wouldn't bring any such individuals into her confidence, and he focused on pulling the small craft into the shallows. Byanca leapt into the surf, and her hands joined in the task of pulling the boat onto the sand.

As their feet made contact with dry ground, all three figures collapsed. Aydiin crawled on his knees, coughing up enough salt water to fill a vase.

Looking up from his vomit, Aydiin began taking stock of their surroundings. To his left and right, a black sand beach extended into the darkness. Ahead, a sheer cliff separated the sand from what maps told Aydiin to be several leagues of flat, coastal plain.

The hooded figure sat up with a coughing fit, and Aydiin quickly turned his gaze away from the cliff. The coughing grew worse until it turned suddenly into laughter.

"You two sure know how to make an entrance," a boyish voice wheezed. Aydiin didn't know how, but he knew the voice—not well, but it rang a small bell in the recesses of his mind.

The hood dropped back to reveal a handsome face topped with tight, brown curls. Dark stubble dotted a strong chin, and a wide smile splayed out under a large nose. Brown eyes sparkled in the moonlight, adding to the mirth already expressed by the man's laughter.

"It's good to see you, Luka," Byanca said, rising to her feet and offering her hand to the young aristocrat. "But we should probably finish hiding the boat before catching up on old times."

As he arose to help with the dingey, Aydiin's memory stretched back months to the one and only ball he'd attended with Byanca during their official courtship in Palmas. The man now helping them ashore was none other than Luka Marzio, the only friendly face in a group of young aristocrats he'd met that night.

"I have to admit," Aydiin said as the three began dragging the dingey through the dry sand. "You're the last person I expected to see tonight."

"Byanca didn't tell you about our correspondence?" Luka asked, genuine surprise in his voice.

"I told him about the letters," Byanca said with laughter in her voice. "I just didn't tell him who they were from."

"Only newlyweds, and already keeping secrets from each other, eh?" Luka laughed.

"Byanca was raised on secrets," Aydiin chuckled. "I'm just glad to see a friendly face."

"Mine's probably the friendliest you can expect to see for a while," Luka said, gesturing to a small alcove in the cliffs. "There's a good hiding spot just in there."

Leaving the boat in the small cave, Luka gestured to a narrow trail winding up the cliffside. It looked nearly washed out from a recent storm, and Aydiin wouldn't be surprised if one more deluge would be its undoing. But tonight, the weather was clear, and it looked safe enough.

"Let me be the first to say it," Luka said, patting Aydiin on the shoulder. "Welcome back to Genodra."

"I can't express how good it feels to be home," Byanca said as the trio began climbing up the cliff. Aydiin couldn't say he shared those sentiments—this adventure was Byanca's idea, against his most ardent of protests.

"You should wait until we're in the car—no use talking too much where unfriendly ears might hear us," Luka replied. Byanca nodded, and a silence settled in among the group.

With only the sound of his soggy boots crunching on the sandy soil mixed with the crashing of waves, Aydiin allowed himself again to doubt their reason for being here. He thought back to his prior conversations—bordering on arguments—with his wife regarding their next steps. Somehow, she'd won, yet Aydiin wasn't sure exactly how.

As they reached the top, Aydiin smiled at the sight of an inconspicuous automobile waiting for them, engine running. The rickety machine seemed fresh from the factories of Naerdon, the island nation far to the north that had single-handedly started an industrial revolution. Just a short time ago, Byanca had driven a beautiful piece of art into the Palmas harbor in order to escape agents of the Order. That automobile was the stuff dreams were made of.

Their current transportation was the exact opposite. His hand grabbed the handle opening the back door—the metal felt as if it wanted to break in his grip, and a loud squeak accompanied the action. As he bounced on the seat, he could tell the cheap suspension would pass every bump onto its passengers. Byanca slid onto the back bench at his side, while Luka leapt into the front passenger seat. Aydiin was surprised to see a second figure—face shrouded by a hood similar to Luka's—in the driver seat.

"Genodra's a very different place than it used to be," Luka said, turning around in his seat to face Aydiin and Byanca. "A lot has changed in just a few months."

"I know," Byanca said, her voice dark. "I saw Palmas after the riots."

The car began moving, the driver still silent. Aydiin had to stop himself from tensing up as the car moved through the darkness. The headlights were cheap, and he could barely see where they were going. However, the driver seemed to be in control, and he focused back on the conversation with Luka.

"I'm not just talking about the destruction in the city," Luka responded. "I'm talking about everything—the Republic's dead. Stones, even Genodra as a country might be dead."

Aydiin only nodded in the darkness. He knew—probably better than Luka did—the dangers facing Genodra. The young man probably knew more details about what the army headed by Field Marshal Diaz had done to Palmas, but he almost certainly had no idea just how sinister the plot was. It wasn't just a coup by an overly ambitious military leader—it was a plot by members of the Order to bring back the Undergods.

"What exactly has been happening?" Byanca asked, and Aydiin could hear the hesitance in her voice. Getting reliable news had been difficult, with rumors mixing with fact until the two became inseparable.

"Well, King Bertrand controls Palmas and some of the surrounding area, but other than that, the country is in chaos," Luka sighed.

The name struck Aydiin as familiar, and he couldn't quite remember where he had heard it. Something about it made him feel queasy; of course, it could just be motion sickness from the windy road. As he turned to look at Byanca, her wide eyes told him he wasn't imagining things.

"Bertrand?" Byanca exclaimed. "You mean our Bertrand? Your friend? The annoying little twit who spent the better part of a decade courting me?"

"The very same," Luka chuckled, shaking his head. "I still don't know how he did it. That rebel army came marching up from the south, taking what was left of the city without firing a shot. I got scared and ran to my estates up here in the north."

"Can't say I blame you," Aydiin responded. "That's a rather natural reaction to a marauding army."

"So glad you agree," Luka said. "From what I can tell, I'm in the majority—at least, the majority of the aristocracy. Part of me wonders if Bertrand got the job just because he was the highest-ranking citizen left in the city."

Byanca grabbed Aydiin's hand, squeezing it hard. Beyond the squeeze, she sat in silence for a moment, chewing on her cheek. In the silence, the driver took the opportunity to remove the dark hood, and Aydiin was even more shocked than when Luka had been revealed.

"Maybe that's how you can take the throne of the little backwater you call home," a woman's voice said without taking her eyes off the road, and Aydiin poked his head forward to see a petite, sharp face. Alise Marzio—with the same dark hair and pouty mouth he remembered from the ball—sat next to her brother, driving calmly through the narrow dirt roads of the Genodran countryside.

Aydiin shouldn't have been surprised—after all, the two were siblings. Yet while it wasn't an absolute shock to find that Luka truly cared for the Republic, it was even harder to fathom the idea that Alise held those same convictions. The only words she had ever spoken to Aydiin were to deride his homeland, questioning why they should be impressed with the "son of the dictator of some backwater country to the north." Apparently, she hadn't forgotten their little exchange either.

"Oh, don't listen to her," Luka said as he rolled his eyes, but Aydiin could see Alise's red lips turning up slightly at the corners as she focused on the road. The girl must have *some* sense of humor after all.

"In all seriousness," Alise began, pausing to take a particularly sharp turn, "it's great to have you two back. Byanca, you're probably the only one who can...persuade Bertrand to see reason. He always did have a soft spot for you."

"Oh, that insufferable boy," Byanca said. "Any chance the mantle of leadership has changed him?"

"I'd be surprised if he has any actual duties," Aydiin said. "It sounds like Diaz is probably the real power in Palmas."

"That's what I thought for a while," Luka replied. "But from the little news trickling out of the city, it really does seem like Bertrand is in control."

"Or everyone is at least trying to make it look like he's in charge," Byanca interjected. "This is all so complicated."

"You're practically licking your lips," Luka said, laughing at Byanca's eagerness. "Oh, Aydiin, I'm afraid you married a woman completely incapable of staying away from the political game."

"I'm only here to help my homeland," Byanca responded. "I have no desire to become Queen or Doge or anything like that."

"Nobody ever said you did," Aydiin responded. "It's not the ruling that you love, but the scheming, the game."

"So, what is your plan, anyway?" Luka asked, turning back around to face the couple. "I understand not wanting to write it out in a letter, but we can't wait to get started."

"Well, it's not so much a plan as a jumble of ideas," Byanca began slowly. "It's difficult to make a firm plan when you have little to no intelligence on your enemy."

"I'm not sure we'll be of much help in that department," Alise said, the car bouncing as the road became especially rough. "My eyes and ears in Palmas haven't reported in ages, and I don't think Luka's have been much better."

"We'll just need to redouble our efforts," Luka said, his smile never wavering, even with the jostling ride. "And we can start holding some meetings at our estate—there are a few barons and counts nearby who may be interested in restoring the Republic."

"And a certain red-headed mother who would be absolutely delighted to see our dear Byanca," Alise said.

"My mother's here?" Byanca asked, a mixture of hope and anxiety—mostly anxiety—in her voice.

"And Cael," Alise said. "Your father sent them up to one of his estates before things got too bad. When the government broke down, they moved in with us. Cael practically lives in our library, hiding from his mother."

"I can't imagine why," Luka said with a grin on his face, which Aydiin returned. He'd only known the Lady Lissandra a short time, but something told him he wouldn't last long if his mother-in-law were his only company. Byanca's younger brother must have been losing his mind and was probably grateful to be living with the Marzios.

"I'm not so sure hiding out in the north is the best way to meet our goals," Byanca said, biting her lip. "Is there any way we could get to Palmas sooner rather than later?"

"That won't be easy," Luka said, his smile fading as his own words came out slowly. "The railroads haven't been operating for months."

"What about normal roads?" Byanca asked. "This car isn't great, but it could get us to Palmas."

"Even in the best of times, the winter rains turn the old dirt roads out here into nothing but a muddy mess," Luka said.

"And in these worst of times, they're filled with either refugees or marauding armies," Alise added. "They have no choice but to deal with the quagmire."

"People are fleeing the city?" Byanca asked.

"The opposite, actually," Luka said. "Bertrand—or possibly Diaz—is harsh, but he's done a pretty decent job at providing food and protection. In times like these, that's more than enough for the average farmer to forget all about republican ideals and pledge his loyalty to a king."

"Bertrand has only secured Palmas and some of the surrounding areas," Alise added. "The rest of the country is divided up among too many warlords to count. My guess is he's waiting until spring to take back the rest of the country. Until then, it's everyone for themselves."

"If things are really that chaotic, can we be safe at your estates?" Aydiin asked.

"Of course—I'm one of those marauding warlords," Luka responded with a grin. "Just without the pillaging and plundering."

"Well, for the most part," Alise cut in. "A girl's gotta eat, after all."

"We control just shy of a thousand soldiers," Luka said. "Mostly the local militias—by no means enough to do anything about Bertrand but enough to protect our lands."

Alise swore under her breath, and Aydiin braced himself as the car began to slow. The girl's posture stiffened, her hands gripping the steering wheel with renewed vigor.

"What's happening?" Aydiin whispered.

"It looks like a checkpoint," Alise growled. "Luka, I thought you told me this route would be safe."

"I'm not the only warlord in town, sis," Luka said, turning around to look out the windshield.

The white light of the crescent moon—mixed with the yellow headlights—revealed a group of soldiers huddled around a makeshift guardhouse. At the edge of his vision, Aydiin could also see a small farmhouse with warm light flickering from the windows. As they drew closer, one of the soldiers waved for Alise to stop.

"I knew we should have brought some soldiers with us," Alise hissed.

"What good would that have done?" Luka shot back. "There's at least a dozen of them, maybe more. It's too dark to tell for sure."

Aydiin looked closer at the farmhouse near the road. Created from rough-hewn grey stone and topped by a thatched roof, the home looked like it had been commandeered by the soldiers. It was difficult to say if there were more men inside.

"Still, I don't like the feeling that they can do whatever they want just because they have guns," Alise said, moving the steering wheel to get off the road.

"I've got a roll of bank notes," Luka replied, fishing out a wad of papers and handing them to his sister. "They're a little wet, but they'll do. We'll be fine."

Alise brought the car to a stop only a few spans away from the grey-clad soldier waving them down. With the engine rumbling, the man approached the girl's window. Grasping the hand crank, Alise rolled down the glass.

Even in the moonlight, Aydiin could tell they were dealing with a seasoned veteran. His face bore several scars, including one that ran through his entire right cheek, creating a gash in an otherwise thick brown beard. From the way he held his rifle, it was apparent he'd fired it hundreds of times in the heat of battle.

"What seems to be the problem?" Alise asked, her voice dripping with honey. She poked out her lips and opened her eyes a bit more than usual. The man's face illuminated with a grin, and his eyes strayed from Alise's countenance and toward other parts of her body.

"We're just looking for trouble-makers in the area. Can't be too careful," the soldier drawled in a country accent, reveling in his visual inspection of Alise. "Do you have your papers?"

"Why of course," Alise responded, fluttering her eyelashes slightly. With the roll of banknotes between her fingers, she extended her hand toward the soldier with more money than he would likely see in a year.

The soldier looked down at the money in his hand and frowned. Aydiin held his breath—was this man a rare idealist who didn't take bribes? Was he too simple to know what was expected of him here? Aydiin's heartbeat began to pound in his ears.

Then, the soldier stuffed the notes into his pocket, and his frown disappeared.

"Thank you, miss," the soldier drawled, and Aydiin had to stop himself from letting out an audible sigh of relief. Then the man lifted his rifle, pointing it directly at Alise. "I'm going to have to ask you to get out of the automobile."

Alise took her hands off the steering wheel, her mouth dropping open. She opened the door, exiting the vehicle.

"You too, pretty boy," the soldier barked, gesturing toward Luka before turning his attention toward Aydiin and Byanca. "You two, in the back, put your hands up and get out here."

The soldier whistled for his companions to join him, and within moments a dozen rifle-armed soldiers surrounded the group as they exited the automobile. As Aydiin opened the door, he noticed the soldiers were dressed in matching, light-grey uniforms—not exactly what he expected from a local warlord. One of the soldiers grabbed Aydiin by the shoulder and pushed him to his knees.

Barely discernible in the night, Aydiin saw a patch sewn onto the soldier's uniform—the national flag of Genodra. Two swords crossing over a field of blue filled Aydiin's vision, and his heartbeat grew stronger in his ears. These men were obviously not some roving militia; they were the rebel soldiers that had marched on Palmas under Field Marshal Diaz. Apparently, King Bertrand wasn't waiting for spring to start taking control of the country.

Aydiin, with his hands still on his head, summoned a marble-sized ball of fire and held it in the palm of his hand. The contained energy warmed his freezing skin, although it just made him wish for a proper fire and dry clothing. Yet there was about to be more than enough heat to banish the cold from his bones.

He scanned through the memories that were not his own, the memories he had inherited from the Great Stone of Surion. While the raw power from the Great Stone was certainly helpful, the fuzzy memories gleaned from the life of the fire god were what made Aydiin the most formidable Fire-dancer in existence. Those memories from the Stone's creator allowed him to use the power in ways he had never even imagined.

Byanca seemed to sense what he was doing and gave him a sharp look. Aydiin felt himself blush at the thought of using his powers so rashly.

She was right—just as always. There was a chance these soldiers had only taken them because of Alise's bribe. As far as he knew, the Order had no idea he was back in Genodra, and he would like it to stay that way if possible. Unleashing a firestorm on a group of soldiers was not the most discreet way of exiting this situation.

An officer approached the group, the epaulettes on his shoulders marking him as a colonel. Pure blond hair sat atop a pale face with a strong chin and high cheekbones. The man's fierce black eyes scanned his prisoners, and Aydiin shifted his gaze away from those terrifying orbs.

"We're on the lookout for a pair of criminals—traitors to the crown, in fact," the officer said, his voice deeper and more melodic than Aydiin had been expecting. He paced back and forth, hands behind his back. "Honorable, outstanding citizens like you wouldn't know anything about that, would you?"

Alise shook her head, as did Luka. Byanca kept her eyes on the ground, refusing to look up. Aydiin brought his gaze back up to stare at the officer. There was something strangely familiar about that face, but he couldn't even come close to figuring out how.

"No?" the officer asked. "The question then needs to be asked—what would law-abiding citizens be doing out here in the middle of the night? I'll admit that it's a beautiful night for a drive, but something tells me that you wouldn't be willing to bribe one of my soldiers with enough cash to feed him for a year if there was nothing to hide."

The man's words were met by silence. Aydiin knew that anything they said would only make the situation worse—it was obvious by the man's tone.

"Have we all suddenly grown mute?" the officer asked, pulling out a revolver and stepping toward Alise. "What if I threatened to shoot this young prostitute in the head? Would that make you talk?"

While gunpowder hadn't been a part of the memories he'd taken from Surion, the ability to sense flammable objects had been one of the god's favorite abilities. Aydiin stretched out his mind to the man's gun, feeling for the powder held inside of the bullets. There were six—one in each chamber. It was somehow a relief to know the gun hadn't been fired recently.

"We thought this was merely some roadblock set up by a local warlord," Luka finally said, his voice shaking. "We didn't know it would be manned by soldiers of His Majesty."

"And you willfully handed funds to what you thought to be rebel forces?" the officer asked, mock surprise in his voice. "Well, well, that's what we call 'aiding and abetting rebels'—an offense punishable by death."

"You know that's not what I meant," Luka shouted.

"Tsk, tsk—it's not polite to shout at one of His Majesty's officers," the man chided, cocking the hammer of his revolver. "For that, I'll kill you first."

As the colonel brought the revolver away from Alise's head, Aydiin reached out to the powder contained within the firearm. He commanded it to ignite, and the black grains leapt to obey.

The gun exploded, separating the man's hand from the rest of his body in a spray of blood and bone. Howling in pain, the officer fell to the ground, red liquid pouring out onto the grass. Aydiin leapt to his feet, launching the fire marble straight into the man's head, ending his screams of agony.

Aydiin launched a thin stream of white-hot fire at another soldier leveling his rifle. The fire burned a hole right through the man's chest. Luka pulled out his own revolver from a side holster, quickly downing another surprised soldier. Alise pulled out a small knife from her boot, launching it into the chest of a charging soldier.

Byanca brandished her own revolver and began firing. A grey-clad brute tackled her from behind, knocking it from her hands. Summoning water from the air, Aydiin created a whip. The thin stream of water sailed through the air, and a crack rang through the night as it collided with the man's face. Byanca scrambled to her feet, giving Aydiin an appreciative nod.

Grey uniforms fell quickly, yet more kept coming—from where, Aydiin had no idea—as the noise of battle grew louder. Aydiin smiled to see that each of the approaching soldiers was armed with a rifle—both their greatest weapon and their ultimate undoing. Aydiin again reached out his mind, probing the night air for the tiny pockets of flammable powder. With a wave of energy from the seemingly endless well of power deep within his chest, Aydiin commanded the rifles to explode.

Pain beyond anything he had ever experienced overtook his entire body, and Aydiin collapsed to the ground. Screaming, he rolled onto his back to see the pale officer standing over him, a fire in his dark eyes. The hole in his head was gone as if it had never existed. His hand had reformed, showing no sign of the explosion that had sent him to the ground.

In that hand, he held a single black stone. Although inanimate, Aydiin could feel the object pulse with power.

"Oh, mortals," he laughed. "You learn a few tricks and think you understand divinity. I'm going to enjoy making you suffer."

3

A sound in the night—like stone grating on stone—roused Aydiin from his uneasy slumber. An involuntary groan escaped his lips, the croak echoing in the stillness. The moment consciousness took him, he wished it hadn't.

Every muscle in his body complained loudly at his treatment, although he knew there would be few physical bruises. His shoulders and arms were stiff from rowing, while a sharp pain in his back drew its fair share of attention. The skin on his wrists and ankles was completely raw, and as he moved, rough cords made their presence known.

The smell of old straw and manure permeated the air, an almost pleasant scent—were it not mixed with mold from the winter rains. It was a far cry from the well-kept stables at his father's palace or even the hearty aroma found in the streets of Maradon. Those memories were filled with life and hope—this moment smelled only of death and decay.

Aydiin forced his eyes open to find himself leaning against the rough stone wall of what looked to be a rather dingy barn. The awkward sitting position he'd been forced into explained the pain in his back, yet there wasn't enough strength left in him to move into a more comfortable situation. Instead, he focused on letting his eyes adjust without vomiting.

The grey light of dawn filtered in between holes in the thatched roof, providing just enough illumination to make out his basic surroundings. Rust-covered tools hung on hooks along the far wall and several stalls that had once provided shelter for various animals now stood empty. The unfortunate farmers who had worked this land for generations were probably now either dead or making their way toward the capital.

As his brain shed the fog of sleep and his stomach began to settle, memories of the pain that had preceded his uneasy slumber in this dilapidated barn flooded back. A shiver ran down his spine and his muscles began to tremble as he began thinking of the officer who had been unscathed by a hole blown through his head. The man's laughter—hoarse and yet somehow high-pitched—rang in his ears. Those eyes had practically glowed with the joy of victory, knowing that he'd captured the Heir of Alarun.

The sensations only grew stronger as his mind drifted to the vile black stone. Pulsing with darkness, it had somehow stopped him from using his powers—the very powers given to him by Surion and Katala. This was something new, something incomprehensible.

Out of habit more than anything, Aydiin reached within himself to feel the wells of power. That of Surion emanated heat, indicating a force that almost resented containment. The heat contrasted sharply with the soothing water powers of Katala.

It had only been a few months since these powers had become a part of him. Yet, after such a short time, he found himself reaching for the energies without effort. Just as some men might touch a lucky talisman or the hand of a loved one in search of comfort, Aydiin reached for divine powers. Tonight, there was a distinct difference.

Something—a force certainly associated with that dark stone—stood between him and unleashing those wells of energy. They were there, unchanged, yet it was as if a dam had been suddenly erected to block the path of a raging river. The water still flowed, pushing against the obstruction. However, that obstruction stood solid and unmovable.

It was different from that third well of power within him—the power of Alarun. That energy was vague, almost distant like a dream he could half remember. The more he reached for it, the harder it was to find. His connection with that particular, distant power was unaltered.

Things are changing, he thought. He had been warned that as he grew in strength, the prison binding the Undergods would grow weak. Aydiin was the most powerful man to walk the land in a thousand years, yet he sat bound by ordinary rope, unable to access that power in the face of something new and terrible. Just because he held the power of two Divines didn't mean that caution shouldn't rule the day.

Of course, it might be too late for caution. The thought came unbidden, but he knew it to be true. He was now a captive of the Order for a third time. Today, there would be no Seb or Barrick to rescue him. Barrick was off in Naerdon, stirring up trouble for the Order. Seb—well, he had no idea what had happened to the old soldier. All he could do now was hope for a miracle.

The sound of shifting stone again caught Aydiin's attention, reminding him of what had awoken him in the first place. The noise was faint, almost imperceptible—yet it was directly behind him. He could almost feel the vibrations coming through the stone more than he could actually hear anything.

Those vibrations grew stronger, even as the noise remained low. His teeth began to chatter with the movement, and he wriggled to move away from the sensation. A small section of the wall disappeared into dust, and Aydiin toppled backward.

His skull made a loud crack as it slammed into the hard-packed dirt, adding a headache to the list of ailments afflicting his body. He took in a deep breath, and his lungs filled with dust. Coughing, Aydiin opened his eyes to see a familiar face hovering over his own.

Red, unruly hair sat on top a face filled with white skin and freckles. Large ears stuck out to the side, and a nose that had grown faster than the rest of the head dominated Aydiin's field of vision. Yet it was the presence of large, green eyes that stuck out most. The eyes matched Byanca's.

"Hi, brother," Cael whispered, a wide grin spreading over his face. "It's sure good to see you."

Still smiling, Byanca's brother crawled in through the hole in the wall before helping Aydiin to sit up. The young man pulled a knife out of his belt and began working on the rope that bound Aydiin's feet.

"It's good to see you too, Cael," Aydiin whispered in response, holding in a cough. "But may I ask what you're doing here?"

"Rescuing you—I thought that was obvious."

"Well, yes," Aydiin chuckled. "I guess you're right. Where are the others?"

"Tied up outside the farmhouse these soldiers took over."

"They're being kept outside? It's the middle of winter," Aydiin exclaimed, struggling to keep his voice to a whisper.

"Can't imagine this lot cares too much about that," Cael responded as his knife finished off the cords around Aydiin's ankles before moving onto those binding his wrists. "From what I can tell, they're alright. Alise looks miserable, but nobody looks to be seriously harmed."

"Well, that's a plus," Aydiin said. "I'm glad to see you and all, but how did you know we needed rescuing?"

"Well, I overheard Luka and Alise talking before they left, so I decided to wait up for you guys. When it got to be almost morning, I knew something was wrong," Cael said, his knife severing the cords around Aydiin's wrists. "When I came across the checkpoint that the soldiers had set up, I started sneaking around and saw they'd taken you lot."

"That's rather impressive," Aydiin said, rubbing his wrists where they had been bound.

"Make sure to tell my mother that," Cael said, a worried smile in his voice. "I hate to imagine the tongue-lashing she'll have for me when I come home."

"We can worry about your mother later," Aydiin said, rising to his feet. He had no desire to think about his mother-in-law at this point. Lissandra was certainly opinionated, and she rarely saw the need to keep those opinions to herself. "Right now, we just need to focus on getting out of here alive. What's your plan?"

"Why do you think I came for you first?" Cael asked with a laugh. "I'm a teenager hoping his mother won't be too angry with him for running away. You're the great military strategist—strategize a way out of this."

Aydiin stifled a laugh in response. The boy must know about Aydiin's title of Prince-General, but he probably didn't realize how little that actually meant. Still, Cael had already gone above and beyond anything that could be expected of him, and Aydiin felt lucky just to be free of his bonds. If he were in the young man's situation, he would also expect the older and more experienced one to take over.

"You're greatly overestimating my abilities," Aydiin finally responded. "But I'll see what I can do. What can you tell me about the soldiers?"

"On the other side of the farmhouse is a camp with enough tents for almost a thousand men," Cael began, biting his bottom lip in thought. "Some of the officers are staying in the farmhouse, but almost everyone is camped out in the fields."

"Why would Bertrand send an entire regiment out here?" Aydiin asked, more to himself than to Cael. "It's not exactly enough to take down any of these warlords, but it's a large enough force to cause quite a commotion."

"How am I supposed to know what's going on in that jerk's head? Even if Bertrand hadn't been stalking Byanca for years, I'd still think he's a creep."

"Let's not get too caught up in why these soldiers are here," Aydiin said, trying to steer the conversation into a new direction. "Let's just focus on getting away from them. Did you see anybody guarding the others?"

"Unfortunately, yes. Five rifle-armed goons—some of the biggest guys I've ever seen."

"We'll need to figure out some sort of distraction then," Aydiin said, rubbing his chin in thought.

"I'm sure happy those fellows decided to keep you separated from the group. Are they hoping to ransom you back to the Sultan or something?"

Aydiin opened his mouth to respond, but it dawned on him that the young man had no idea what had taken place over the past months. He would have no idea that Aydiin was the greatest enemy of the Undergods. He would have no way of knowing that Aydiin's status as a prince had little meaning these days. Somehow, now didn't seem to be the time to explain.

"Something like that," Aydiin finally said, and his words were met with a raised eyebrow from the young man. "Have you seen anything we could use to our advantage?"

"Well, there's a supply tent on the other side of camp," Cael said, rubbing his chin just as Aydiin had done. "There's still only two of us though. I can't imagine more weapons would really help."

"Where there are weapons, you'll find explosives," Aydiin said, ideas rushing into his mind. "I think I'll have some fun making a little noise while you get Byanca and the others."

"With all due respect, sneaking into places is one of my specialties," Cael responded with a grin.

"I can see that," Aydiin said, wondering for the first time exactly how the young man had made his way into the barn without being seen. "Would you mind sharing how that is?"

"You've obviously got your secrets—let me have mine," Cael said with a grin before changing the subject. "I've got a truck just north of here. It's in a little grove of pine trees. If you can't find it, just tell Luka it's where we bagged that white stag. He'll know the spot."

"I don't know how Byanca will feel about me putting you in harm's way," Aydiin replied. "Getting into the armory, setting off an explosion, and getting out won't be easy."

"If I'm not to worry about my mother's wrath, then you aren't allowed to be afraid of Byanca," Cael said. "Now let's get going—I'll meet you at the truck."

The boy climbed through the hole in the wall and Aydiin followed. Now that he was going through the wall, he couldn't help but wonder how Cael had dug through. His brother-in-law certainly did have some secrets. Before he could try to pry them out again, the boy was already running through the camp, darting in and out between tents.

Bringing his mind away from the hole, Aydiin crawled on hands and knees through the freezing grass around the barn until he caught sight of the farmhouse. Built of rough grey stone, leaded windows, and a thatched roof, the structure looked to be a few hundred years old. It was well-maintained, or at least, it had been up until a few months ago. The gentleman farmer living here apparently had the means to keep up a rather stately life, a life that had been completely turned upside down along with everything else.

Just as Cael had said, five brutes stood guard in front of a covered porch—a relatively new addition to the house, made of white-washed wood. From the look of things, what these men had in size, they sacrificed in brains.

One man's eyes were drooping, on the verge of closing. One of the others looked even less interested, his gaze drifting off at the grey light peaking over the horizon. The other three were actually asleep, curled up on the ground. Aydiin's eyes scanned the area for any sign of additional guards—or worse, the young officer with the black stone.

JON MONSON

Instead, he found Byanca and the Marzios gagged and bound with rough cords to the balusters. Cael hadn't been lying when describing Alise as looking miserable, although the same could be said for all three. While none of them sported terrible wounds, Luka's shirt was ripped, and a wicked bruise was forming around his left eye.

Byanca looked relatively untouched—her hair was a mess, and her face was covered in dirt. Beyond that, she seemed to have avoided any physical harm. Even in such a state, Aydiin couldn't help but notice that she looked beautiful in the soft light. Leaning against the porch's balusters, she'd miraculously drifted off to sleep, a serene expression on her face.

The ground shook, and Aydiin fell backward as a wave of air slammed into him. Half a second later, an explosion met his ears as a ball of fire erupted into the sky. The two conscious guards jumped, all traces of their exhaustion erased in the orange light of the distant flames. The other three were ripped from their slumber, and the brutes looked at each other with wide eyes.

Shouts filled the camp along with the pounding of feet on mud as the soldiers ran toward the flaming supply tent. Aydiin returned to his crouched position, waiting for his opportunity to strike.

"Should we go see what happened, sir?" one of the soldiers asked another wearing the insignia of a sergeant on his chest.

"Morris, you go check it out," the man grunted, rubbing the sleep from his eyes. "No use in leaving these traitors unguarded."

Shouts across the camp grew louder, and Aydiin could see more flames in the semi-darkness—a clear sign that the explosion had spread to the tents.

"Stones," the sergeant cursed, pointing to three of the men. "Go with the bucket brigade—I have a feeling they're going to need all the help they can get."

Well, two is better than five, Aydiin thought to himself as three of the soldiers ran off toward the camp. Still, he was outnumbered two to one without being able to reach his powers—he didn't love those odds. Not to mention that the men were armed to the teeth, while he had nothing but his bare hands.

And the element of surprise. It was his only real advantage. From his current position, only ten spans separated Aydiin from his foes.

At a full sprint, he just might be able to reach them before they could react.

Taking a breath, Aydiin sprang to his feet. The small of his back protested the quick transition, but years of training had conditioned his muscles to respond without too much defiance. The farmhouse drew closer, the two soldiers failing to take notice of the dirty apparition approaching them at full speed.

With a few spans to go, the sergeant spotted Aydiin and began lifting his rifle. Aydiin leapt, crashing headlong into the man's broad chest, knocking him against the porch. Wood splintered as their combined weight slammed into the balusters, and Aydiin quickly shoved himself away from the shocked sergeant.

The other soldier pulled out a knife, his rifle likely to hit his wounded comrade or prisoners in such close combat. Aydiin dodged a quick slash and laid his fist into the man's stomach. The move was about as effective as punching stone, and the soldier leapt onto Aydiin.

The man's weight nearly crushed him as the two fell to the ground. Aydiin managed to roll onto his back as the soldier's knife inched closer to his neck. Placing both hands on the man's wrist, Aydiin twisted, and a shout of pain mixed with the cracking of bone met his ears.

Aydiin pushed the howling soldier off him—the man clutching his fractured wrist—and shot up to his feet. Vision still spinning, Aydiin felt a fist slam into his temple, and the prince fell to the ground.

Above him stood the sergeant, one arm dangling to the side while the other secured a revolver. A grim smile spread over his face as he cocked the hammer. Aydiin's vision swam, and he found himself unable to do anything.

A shot cracked from the porch, and the sergeant howled in pain. He dropped his revolver and fell to his knees to reveal Alise standing on the porch, her trembling hand clutching a tiny, single-shot pistol.

"You little whore," the sergeant yelled, his hand pressing into the wound in his hamstring. "I should have killed you while I had the chance."

The shot had slammed into his leg, the bullet embedding in the muscle. It wasn't powerful enough to bring the man down, but it was enough to cause a severe amount of pain.

Aydiin's vision began to steady, and he leapt onto the sergeant's discarded revolver. The hammer already cocked, Aydiin leveled the barrel at the man's head. His finger squeezed the trigger, and a sharp crack rang in his ears. The brute fell to the ground.

Looking up toward the porch, he saw Alise—her hands still bound together—working to untie the ropes still binding Luka and Byanca. Grabbing a knife from the unconscious sergeant, Aydiin ran to help.

"How did you get free?" Aydiin asked as he began severing Alise's cords.

"You should really look where you're going the next time you rescue me," Alise said with a light chuckle. "That man's thick skull almost crushed my hands—fortunately, it only damaged the baluster those morons tied me to. I was able to break it all the way and get free."

"And what about the pistol, sis?" Luka chimed in as Aydiin severed the ropes binding him to the porch, a smile on his bruised face.

"These are uncertain times," Alise said with a shrug before smiling. "And a lady never reveals her secrets."

Aydiin moved to cut Byanca free. The moment her cords were severed, he felt her body in his arms. He could feel the warmth of her tears against his face, and he kissed her on the forehead before helping her up.

"Aydiin, how did you get free?" Byanca asked, wiping the tears from her eyes.

"It was Cael," Aydiin replied, turning to Luka. "Luka, do you remember where you two caught a white stag?"

"Of course—that's not something you forget," Luka said, his eyebrow raised.

"Can you get us there from here?" Aydiin asked. "Cael said he's brought a truck, and that's where he wants us to meet him."

"Wait, where's my brother?" Byanca interjected.

"We needed a distraction," Aydiin began.

"You sent my brother out there? Alone?" Byanca said, her eyes growing wide and her voice growing hoarse.

"I didn't send him anywhere—he just ran off," Aydiin said, moving some hair out of Byanca's face. "Trying to stop him would have been like convincing you to not come back to Genodra."

"You two can fight about this later," Luka said, stepping in between them. "For now, we've got to get going. That fire won't keep them occupied for long."

Aydiin nodded, and the trio moved off the porch. Luka led the way north toward the meeting point with Cael. Aydiin hoped the young man would be okay and that he hadn't stuck around too long to admire his pyrotechnic display.

A shot rang out, and Aydiin felt a bullet brush past his right arm. He looked down and saw blood through a hole in his shirt sleeve. Bringing his gaze back toward the camp, he saw six grey-clad men raising their rifles.

Aydiin again reached out tentatively for his powers and felt a twinge of pain. He stopped immediately, recent memories of exquisite suffering rushing back to him. There was nothing he could do.

One soldier dropped to his knee and leveled his gun, pointing it straight at Aydiin. The soldier pulled the trigger, and Aydiin closed his eyes in expectation of the pain.

The sound of an exploding rifle rang in his ears.

Aydiin opened his eyes to see the soldier lying on the ground, screaming in agony. A second soldier pulled the trigger on his own rifle, and Aydiin's eyes were met by another explosion. The remaining grey-clad men looked at each other in confusion.

"Run," a voice sounded from behind, and Aydiin turned to see Cael.

Aydiin grabbed Byanca's hand, and together, the group ran off into the forest amidst shouts from their pursuers.

4

Aydiin sat with his back against the wooden frame of the truck bed, trying to control the jostling as Alise guided the vehicle through a narrow path in the dense woods. Byanca sat at his side, her head resting on his shoulder and eyes closed as if she were asleep. Yet her breathing told him that his wife's mind was actively calculating their next steps.

Across the bed sat Cael. The young man was wrapped in a blanket, his eyes staring off into nothing. With Luka and Alise up in the cab, not a word had been said since making their escape.

"How long have you been a Stone-weaver?" Aydiin asked Cael, breaking the monotony of the engine's whine and the rustle of branches hitting the truck.

"How did you know?" Cael replied, his eyes snapping into focus.

"You made a section of stone wall disappear in that barn," Aydiin said. "That's not exactly being subtle. Nice trick with the rifles, too."

"Thanks," Cael said with a smile. "I just stuffed the barrels with dirt—nothing special."

"Well, it saved our lives," Aydiin said. "That seems pretty special to me."

Cael nodded, and his eyes returned to staring at nothing. Aydiin couldn't really blame him for not wanting to talk. He'd been through a lot these past months, and he'd shown incredible bravery well beyond his years. Plus, the truck was noisy, making conversation less than enjoyable.

Aydiin braced his body as Alise made a sharp turn. Looking out, he could see that the truck had veered onto a much larger road. While still nothing more than dirt, it was wide enough for a vehicle moving in each direction—practically a luxurious boulevard compared to the narrow forest trail they had been using.

"Home sweet home," Luka shouted through his open window, and Aydiin looked ahead to see the manor off in the distance.

The term "manor" was a little modest, and Aydiin had been expecting a comfortable stone building. At best, he had hoped to see something like the stately home occupied by Count Visconti. Instead, the massive structure looming ahead could more accurately be described as a castle or fortress.

"I think we'll be safe here," Luka called back, a smile in his voice.

The fortress sat atop a hill with sheer stone cliffs on three sides, with the only access being a steep road that switched back and forth a dozen times before reaching the top. After making the ascent, an invading army would slam into a thick, ancient stone wall complete with towers providing cover for the castle defenders. Behind the fortifications, a keep made of white marble rose into the sky.

At the base of the hill, hundreds of buildings on wide streets marked a clean and prosperous town. This wasn't some simple country estate—Luka's family likely controlled more land, wealth, and population than some of the petty kingdoms in Pilsa.

"Welcome to Monterosso," Cael said, referring to the town. "A lot smaller than Palmas, but not a bad place to live."

"The Marzios own this whole town?" Aydiin asked, craning his neck to look outside the truck bed.

"No, just the castle," Luka called back. "Well, and maybe about a third of the town."

Alise didn't slow as the truck reached town, and the rumble of the engine somehow grew louder among the buildings. Several pedestrians stopped to stare or point, but Alise didn't seem to notice.

The truck's engine began to whine as Alise took them up the steep, winding road. Aydiin forced his gaze to his feet and focused on not vomiting. Careening through the open gate of the fortress walls, Alise slammed on the breaks. Aydiin let out a sigh, and he could feel Byanca's grip on him loosen. He hadn't even realized she'd been hanging onto him that tightly.

"Lord Marzio," an aging gentleman called out, running toward the truck. "Thank the Divines you've returned."

He wore the light green uniform of Genodra's militia and carried a saber at his side. While his mustache looked to be meticulously groomed, his greying hair was windswept, and his uniform looked as if it had been slept in.

"It's good to see you, Colonel Davi," Luka called out, exiting the truck. "What's the matter?"

"Scouts are reporting a royalist army heading this way," Davi said, out of breath. "All indications point to hostile intent."

"Did the scouts say how many there were?" Luka asked.

"Looks to be around a thousand," Davi sighed. "I don't know how we didn't see them sooner—moving that large of a force isn't exactly something that can be kept quiet in times like these."

"I was expecting this," Luka sighed, running a hand through his hair before turning to Aydiin. "Someone must have recognized me."

"Did you have some sort of interaction with them, sir?" Davi asked.

"You could say that," Luka responded with a smile, pointing to the massive bruise around his eye. "How many men do we have on hand?"

"Only about three hundred, sir," the colonel responded. "I had to send the majority of our men out west—Lord Augustine is making a play for Stonebrook."

"Can't say I blame you," Luka said, looking around and exhaling slowly. "Bring all the civilians inside the keep and make sure to keep plenty of scouts on patrol."

"Of course, sir," Davi said with a bow.

"Thank you, and please bring me all the maps of the area you have—we've got some planning to do," Luka replied with a salute before motioning for Aydiin and the others to follow him as he set off toward the keep.

Aydiin caught up to Luka as they entered the large stone building. The young aristocrat was shaking and running a hand through his hair. The bruise around his left eye looked bothersome, although Luka wasn't complaining about it. Aydiin worried about the amount of stress going through the man's body.

"I have a feeling there's something you haven't told me," Luka said without slowing.

"Trust me when I say that we never intended to get you in trouble," Aydiin started out.

"Oh, I expected plenty of trouble," Luka shot back with a laugh. "We are trying to overthrow a maniacal king and restore the Republic, after all."

"But you weren't expecting an immortal enemy who can somehow survive a hole to the head," Aydiin said, finishing the man's thought.

"Well, yes, there's that. However, I was referring to your little display—the one where I saw you not only manipulate fire but also water," Luka said. "I've got more questions than I can handle right now."

"I'll explain when we get to your study," Aydiin said. "I have a feeling that Alise and Cael have a lot of the same questions."

"Can you at least tell me what we're up against?" Luka asked.

"I only wish I knew," Aydiin said. "I've never seen anything like this before."

After a few minutes, they reached Luka's study—a fine room lined with bookshelves and oil paintings. The right side was dominated by a round card table while on the left side of the room, two sofas and an armchair huddled around a crackling fire. A steaming pot of tea complete with bowls of cream and sugar sat on a small end table near the sofas, ready for consumption.

"So, what are we talking about first—the ridiculous night we just had or the possibly worse day ahead of us?" Alise said as she threw herself onto the armchair.

Aydiin grabbed Byanca's hand, and they took a seat together on one of the sofas. Cael, still clutching his blanket, crammed in next to his sister. It was tight, but the contact was probably something they all needed right now.

"Let's start with what just happened," Luka said, pouring a cup of tea for himself. Aydiin turned to look at Byanca—he knew she hadn't told Luka much of anything about the Stones or his status as the Heir of Alarun. He knew it was his responsibility to let the truth be known.

"Well, I don't know what Byanca told you before we came," he started, "but you've thrown your lot in against some very powerful people."

"We've guessed that much," Luka said. "Otherwise, we wouldn't be preparing to fend off an attack in the next few hours."

"Okay," Aydiin continued, trying to collect his thoughts. "Tell me, what do you know about the Knights of the Raven?"

"You mean the Order? It's a myth," Cael piped up.

"I have a feeling that Aydiin is going to prove otherwise," Alise interjected, staring into the flames.

"They're real enough," Luka broke in, taking a sip of his tea and sitting down on the other sofa. "I've read their book—*Prophecies of the Return*. An old man gave it to me once on the train. My curiosity got the better of me, and I wish I could forget what I read."

"Luka's right," Aydiin said slowly. "The group is anything but a myth. They're powerful, probably more powerful than most governments. Worse, they're completely dedicated to freeing the Undergods from their prison. They call it 'The Return', and there isn't anything they wouldn't do to make it happen."

"Supposing this group is real, that doesn't really explain why they're in Genodra or why they were so happy to have you," Alise responded, turning to look Aydiin in the eye. "I heard some of them talking. That creepy officer was happier than a farmer at the Harvest Festival."

"Well, I'm still not sure how to explain this part," Aydiin sighed. "Basically, I'm the key to either destroying the Undergods for good or setting them free. The Order knows this and has been after me for quite some time now."

"Does this have anything to do with your extraordinary display of fire-dancing back there?" Luka asked. "You could have destroyed all of those men if it weren't for that...thing."

"It does, and it doesn't," Aydiin responded. "First, I don't have any idea what happened to my powers last night. Second, have you ever thought about the possibility of a Divinity Stone created by Alarun?"

"Alarun?" Luka said. "The Church teaches that the God of Gods didn't make a Stone because his power would have been too great for mortals to possess even a portion. I haven't ever given it much thought."

"The Church in Genodra is much kinder to Alarun than most," Aydiin said. "In Salatia, the priests preach that Alarun was too selfish to give up his divinity at the Final Battle. The truth is, he did make a Stone. Just one."

"And where is this Stone?" Luka asked, setting his tea down to look Aydiin straight in the eyes.

"It's in me," Aydiin responded.

"What does it do?" Alise asked, leaning forward in her chair.

"Well, for now, nothing," Aydiin responded.

"Have you tried properly?" Alise interrupted.

"It allows him to absorb Great Stones," Byanca answered.

"That's not how those are supposed to work," Alise said, leaning back into her chair. "If you're going to invent a story, at least come up with one that makes sense."

"The Stone of Alarun pretty much defies everything we know about the Divines," Aydiin said, squeezing Byanca's hand. He could tell from her posture that she was getting frustrated with Alise. "It allows me to use the powers of all the Gods. So far, I've found the Great Stones made by Katala and Surion."

"That's why you can command both water and fire simultaneously?" Luka asked. Aydiin nodded in response.

"Then maybe we're not really in trouble after all," Cael said, his voice still trembling. "What good are a few hundred soldiers against that kind of power?"

"You didn't see what happened," Alise answered. "Aydiin was using his powers like a Divine, reducing soldiers to nothing but ash when, well...I'm not sure exactly what happened."

"As I said, I don't know either," Aydiin responded, his posture deflating at the memory. "It was as if my powers were a river, and that man with his black stone dammed it up. I've never experienced that much pain before."

"So, they have something that can stop you from using a Divinity Stone?" Cael whistled. "Why didn't it affect me?"

"I'm not sure," Aydiin said. "Although I've been thinking about it the whole way back. My guess is it needs to focus on you, and since you came along later, you were still able to use your powers."

"All the old rules are breaking down," Luka said. "We'll need to think differently to survive."

"Sounds like we're in the presence of the most dangerous man in the world," Alise said, eyeing Aydiin up and down. Byanca noticed the look and gave Aydiin's hand a good squeeze.

"I guess so," Aydiin said. "I think the biggest danger is from the Order chasing me."

"And they're not going to stop until they're either all dead or they have you," Luka said, taking a sip of his tea.

"This is all my fault for bringing us back to Genodra," Byanca said, her voice trembling. "I'll understand if you want us to leave now. Maybe if they know we're gone, they won't attack the town."

"Are you kidding?" Alise said, rising from her chair. "How could you have possibly known we'd be faced with an immortal clown intent on killing you. Besides, life here is so boring—I haven't had this much fun in ages."

"I'm glad for your help," Byanca responded with a weak chuckle. "Luka, what about you? You shouldn't feel pressured into helping us if you don't want to."

"Well, I'm definitely not bored like Alise," Luka responded with a smile. "But I don't think I could live with myself, knowing what you've told me and not doing anything about it."

"And I may have been resistant to the idea of coming back," Aydiin began, a smile on his face as he looked into Byanca's eyes. "But it's obvious that there's something happening here that we need to stop. We may have come with nothing but the intention of restoring the Republic, but it seems that the world's fate may be decided along with Genodra's."

Byanca smiled and opened her mouth to respond when the sound of pounding footsteps reached Aydiin's ears.

"Cael Cavour!" an all-too-familiar voice shouted from the hallway, and the door burst open.

Elegant as ever, Lissandra Cavour strode into the room. She wore a blue silk dress that hugged her curves and high heels that cracked on the stone floor. Her red hair was perfectly curled and her normally creamy cheeks burned crimson to match it.

"You have some explaining to do, young man," she screamed, finger wagging in the air. As she began taking in the scene, her face fell, and her mouth dropped open.

"Hi, Mom," Byanca said with a small wave.

"Byanca—but how?" Lissandra said, placing her hands on her chest. Lissandra staggered over to the open sofa and collapsed onto the cushions.

"It's—um—good to see you, too," Byanca said.

"Where have you been?" Lissandra shouted, the color returning to her face.

"I really don't want to stop this happy little reunion," Luka said, rising to his feet. "But we have a hostile army marching this way."

Footsteps sounded as Colonel Davi entered, his arms full of rolled up maps. The man gave a look around the room, the confusion evident on his face.

"Excuse me, my lord," the man said, placing the rolls on the coffee table.

"Not a problem, Davi," Luka said, his eyes turning to Alise. "Sis, would you mind taking care of Madam Cavour?"

"Not at all," Alise said, rolling her eyes and rising to her feet. "It's not like I wanted to be part of a war council anyways."

"I'm not leaving until you tell me what's happening," Lissandra said, jumping to her feet. Any sign of her momentary weakness had dissipated.

"We may have run into an approaching army intent on killing us all," Luka said, rising to his feet and unrolling one of the maps. "You're welcome to stay, Lissandra, but you'll need to either add to the conversation or remain quiet."

"A war council can wait until I've properly berated Byanca for disappearing the way she did," Lissandra shouted, rising to her feet and placing hands to her hips before turning to her gaze to Cael. "And you, young man—don't think that you're going to escape punishment. I can't believe you would sneak off in the middle of the night."

"I'm sorry to do this, Lissandra, but we really don't have time right now," Alise said, grabbing the Cavour family matriarch by the arm and moving her toward the door. "If you want to be disruptive, you'll have plenty of time after the battle."

"I am the wife of the Doge, and I demand answers," Lissandra shouted, ripping her arm out of Alise's grasp.

"If you want that title to actually mean something again, then you'll need to leave," Byanca said, rising to her feet. "We're in more trouble than you could possibly understand, Mother."

"Fine, do this to your poor mother. I've only cried every night, wondering where you were," Lissandra said before straightening her dress and tucking a lock of hair behind her ear. "But I'll leave—I can tell when I'm not wanted by my ungrateful children."

"So glad you understand," Alise said, pushing Lissandra out of the room and closing the door.

"Has she always been like that or has the stress of recent months unhinged her?" Luka asked, moving over to the table with the maps.

"She's definitely gotten worse," Cael answered, not moving from his spot on the couch, even as Aydiin and Byanca arose to look at the maps brought in by Colonel Davi.

"How long do we have?" Aydiin asked, placing his hands on the table.

"I don't think they'll get here until tomorrow morning," Davi said, unrolling one of the maps. "From what our scouts have reported, the royalists are mostly on foot."

"Then if we're all in, let's not waste any more time," Aydiin said, grabbing Byanca's hand as she came to his side.

The map showed a detailed view of the castle and the surrounding town of Monterosso. A river curved in a large arc, surrounding the town on three sides.

"I don't remember seeing this river," Byanca said, pointing to the map.

"That's because it's at the bottom of a gorge," Davi responded. "It's almost impossible to see until you're right on top of it."

"So, we know which way the royalists have to come in," Byanca said. "Is there a bottle-neck we could take advantage of?"

"Not with the troops we have," Luka spoke up. "Maybe if we had enough time and a thousand of our own soldiers, we'd be able to stop them outside of town. As it is, I think stopping them at the fortress walls is going to be the best we could hope for."

"They only outnumber us by about three to one," Aydiin said. "That's really not terrible odds when we're dug in like this."

"The numbers are deceiving, sir," Davi spoke up, pulling out a report. "Our men are militia—until a few months ago, they hadn't even seen any real combat. The invaders are dressed in regular army uniforms, so we have to assume their training and experience far exceed that of our own forces."

"Plus, our men are armed with older muzzle-loaded rifles," Luka added. "From what I saw at their camp, we're going up against new bolt-actions. They can reload exponentially faster than we can."

"Are these walls built to withstand cannon fire?" Byanca asked.

"Not really." Luka shook his head. "Monterosso predates gunpowder, and we haven't exactly made any structural updates in the past hundred years."

"They won't have any cannons," Cael said, still sitting on the sofa. "I blew them up this morning."

"You're a good man," Luka said, a smile spreading across his face. "See? Disobeying your mother has resulted in a lot of good."

"Make sure to tell her that," Cael responded.

"They'll have to march at the walls," Aydiin said, turning his eyes back to the map. Unless they could somehow scale the cliffs, there was only one way up the hill.

"Cael, how would you feel about going out into danger one more time today?" Aydiin asked, and a smile lit up the boy's face. "I think your powers might come in handy before the day is out."

5

Barrick sat, glaring out from the shadows of yet another dirty tavern. For a moment, he almost missed his time spent at the *Maiden*. Well, he missed Lilah, a sentiment he'd spent the past week trying to push aside.

There were perhaps a dozen reasons he couldn't return, even for a brief moment, to the *Maiden*—not the least of which was the myriad of mundane tasks he'd been assigned. He pulled out his hipflask filled with fine brandy and, ignoring a dirty glare from a rather large man behind the bar, took a deep pull.

It shouldn't anger him that he was only performing menial tasks, but he had certainly been hoping for more opportunities to gain high-level information on the Order's plan. After a single meeting with a few other Knights, he'd been promised a "glorious role" in serving the Raven. Instead, he'd been given an endless series of boring and pointless tasks, mostly meetings with informants. While delivered to him by Tamden, they were supposedly from the figure who led the Order in Naerdon. The only thing that was clear to Barrick was that his patience was growing thin.

His thoughts were disrupted by a young man, face and clothing covered by a dark cloak, slipping into the bench facing Barrick. He sat in silence, his face remaining covered.

"The Return approaches," Barrick sighed, unable to even fake it anymore.

"The Elect await the Return," the young man replied, pulling down his hood.

Despite the lack of a uniform, the man's short hair, square jaw, and crooked nose set him apart immediately as a soldier. Men in that particular profession made for some of the most interesting informants, offering minor state secrets rather than just gossip.

"What do you have for me, my child?" Barrick asked without removing his hood. It would never do for an informant to see the identity of his contact within the Order.

"It's Crown-Prince Philip," the man whispered. "He took a wild bore's tusk to the stomach this afternoon while out hunting."

"I'm assuming by the tremor in your voice that he isn't long for this world," Barrick responded, doing his best to disguise his voice.

"Doctors don't expect him to last the night," the young soldier responded.

"Pity," Barrick sighed. "He wasn't a half-bad human being."

"May I ask a question, sir?" the man said, wincing as if he expected to be reprimanded.

"You may," Barrick responded.

"There are rumors that a newcomer is in the city, and that he survived the destruction in Maradon," the soldier said, the question obvious in his tone of voice.

"Rumors are generally not to be trusted," Barrick said.

This was precisely the reason he had tried so hard to infiltrate the Order in Albona as Mr. William Jones. He'd created the perfect backstory, had even memorized minute details about the man's life. He should haven't underestimated the Order's organizational structure. Now, everyone knew his real name—something that left Barrick in a precarious position.

Yes, his heritage lent him a certain amount of prestige—for the time being, at least. It meant he didn't have to sneak in, and now he was in the rather enviable position of giving commands rather than just taking them. However, Barrick also knew it was just a matter of time before these people found out that he was not only just a Squire but that he was the one responsible for the destruction of the Order in Maradon.

"My deepest apologies, sir," the man said, bowing his head. "I'll leave you now if you so desire."

"It was a bloodbath," Barrick said, his voice cracking. "One moment, we were on the brink of victory. The next, I was watching my brethren fall to the hands of nomads and sheepherders. Is that what you wanted to hear?"

"I'm sorry, sir," the man replied, his eyes focused on the table.

"In the future, don't ask questions to which you don't want the answer," Barrick responded. "It's only the information you've brought me tonight that has saved you from your own insolence."

"Yes, sir," the soldier stammered. "My deepest apologies."

"You may leave," Barrick spat, and the young soldier lifted his hood and sped out of the tavern without another word.

With yet another sigh, Barrick took out his flask and drained the contents. He began mentally counting the seconds until he could reasonably make his own exit. His brain had a hard time focusing, considering the news he'd just received.

Sliding out from the bench, Barrick slapped a coin on the table, more for its use than any beverage he'd taken from the tavern owner. Ignoring the stares emanating from both the barmaid and some of the patrons, Barrick slipped out of the tavern, hoping he would never have to remember its name.

He took a deep breath as he entered the night before remembering that the air was far from fresh. During the day, the city's smokestacks pumped soot into the sky, much of which made its final home on the city's buildings and inhabitants. The economic advantages the nation wielded certainly came at a price.

Walking through the streets of Naerd at night was certainly not for the faint of heart. Automobiles rushed in all directions, their headlights glaring, and horns were used at the slightest provocation. The sidewalks were littered with homeless individuals huddling around small fires, which only added to the smoke from the factories. Aydiin could cite statistics all he wanted about the nation's industrial revolution, but it was clear that the economic boom had not spread among all classes.

As he walked, Barrick forced his mind back to the immediate task at hand. He would, of course, need to report to Tamden, although this particular piece of news didn't seem ground-breaking. Yes, the Crown-Prince was popular, and the nation would likely enter into mourning for the next month or so. That didn't really mean much for the Order's plans.

Of course, I haven't the slightest clue as to what those are, Barrick thought, again resenting the little box into which he'd been placed. Tamden had passed on enough work to keep him busy, but nothing that was truly important. All the same, his bed called to him, and Barrick rushed toward Tamden's home in the wealthier section of the city.

"A few pence for the baby," a voice called out, and Barrick looked down to see an old woman holding a wad of rags. It was possible the trick worked on some, but Barrick had passed the woman practically every night as he returned to his rooms in Tamden's mansion.

"What do you know tonight?" Barrick asked, flipping her an entire Crown. Her fake baby didn't persuade him, but whoever this woman was, she had some of the best gossip in the city.

"Word is the Crown-Prince won't last through the night," the woman replied, biting the coin before stuffing it into a pocket.

"That's already old news," Barrick responded. "If you don't have anything else, I'll be taking—"

"There's been a string of robberies the past month," the woman shrieked, clutching at her pocket. "They've been taking everything from food to ammunition. They don't care much about value or protections. They just steal from everyone and everything."

"Everyone's been talking about that for a month," Barrick said, moving to take back his coin from the woman. He didn't really need it, but it wouldn't set a good precedent if word spread through the underground that he paid well for useless information.

"That's not the juicy part," the woman said, shaking her finger. "The latest is that they've stolen an entire armory's worth of supplies straight from the palace."

"What am I supposed to do with that?" Barrick scoffed. "I'm not interested in criminals."

"I'm sorry, m'lord, but that's all I have," the woman cried out, placing her arms over her head.

"I guess it'll be enough for now. But next time, don't ask me for coin unless you've got something of interest."

Barrick turned away from the beggar and continued toward the Tamden home. The news was actually rather interesting, considering that it wasn't on the lips of every drunk in the tavern. The only way the incident hadn't become common knowledge yet would be if the monarchy were exerting a lot of effort to keep it quiet.

As he approached his temporary home, his eyes couldn't help but take in the view. The mansion's granite walls extended three stories tall and hundreds of spans wide. Within, there were enough bed-rooms, kitchens, and libraries to house dozens, if not hundreds, of families. Yet, it was all for Boris Tamden, his wife, and three teenage children.

And, of course, members of the Order.

Lurching through the wrought-iron gate surrounding the manor, Barrick snuck through the hedge-maze that dominated the south-east corner of the grounds. He'd heard Tamden question the guards and servants, wanting to be informed of Barrick's movements. It brought him no small amount of pleasure to keep giving the man heartburn about it.

Slipping through a small side door, Barrick found himself in one of the smaller kitchens. Its staff had already turned in for the night, the ovens cooling down from the day's usage. He padded along, his soft leather shoes practically silent on the stone floor, hoping that no one had been awake to see him enter.

Removing his hood, Barrick entered one of the main hallways of the mansion. A polished marble floor was partially covered by a thick carpet of deep indigo running down the center. The mahogany walls were decorated with priceless oil paintings and marble statues. It gave Barrick the impression of living in a museum.

The building was so massive, Barrick was yet to make the acquain-tance of Tamden's family. His poor wife and children likely had no idea their beloved husband and father was part of a group they both feared and scorned as a myth. Of course, Barrick had also gone most of his life without knowing his very own father had risen through the ranks of the Order to become the Grand Master.

He strode through the hallways and climbed several staircases to arrive at Tamden's private study. It was almost midnight, and the past few days had taught him that the Finance Minister would be alone, drinking a glass of wine before bed. Barrick approached the door and lifted his hand to the knob.

Voices whispered on the other side of the door. Not only was Tamden accompanied by someone, they were having a conversation important enough that they felt the need to speak quietly. He placed his ear to the door, but the thick hardwood wasn't meant to carry sound.

Barrick padded along the carpeted hallway to the next door over, peeking in to find Tamden's unofficial bedroom. While still elegantly furnished, it contained only a single bed large enough for one person. The idea was that it could serve the wealthy aristocrat when he had a late night in his study and didn't want to disturb his wife by retiring to their shared quarters in the early morning hours. From the look of it, Tamden used the room almost exclusively.

The bed was unmade, and clothing was strewn around the floor. A desk sat crammed into the corner, a mixture of papers and dirty plates covering every bit of surface space. Both windows were wide open in an attempt to entice an evening breeze to cool down the room.

Barrick dashed toward the window and poked his head out. Looking to his right, he smiled to see one of the study's windows ajar, the indistinguishable sound of conversation emanating from within. Redirecting his gaze down, his smile grew even wider to see a ledge just wide enough for a nimble young man such as himself.

Inching out onto the ledge, Barrick began crawling toward the open window, all the while hoping that nobody was watching from below. He could hear Tamden's voice, still muffled, as he drew closer. Although he couldn't hear the words, he could pick up a hint of fear in the man's voice.

"Yes, I'm sure," an unfamiliar voice hissed. "No amount of planning can make up for this opportunity. It has to be tonight."

"I only have a few dozen men on hand, including Mr. Fortescue," Tamden said, spitting the last part, and Barrick couldn't help but smile at their shared enmity.

"If you want to be king by the end of the night, you'll get rid of that insolent child," the second voice replied, a smile evident in the words. "Just make it look like an accident."

Barrick's mouth dropped open at the words. He'd heard members of the Order—most often, his father—casually order murders before, but it was disturbing to hear his own name included. Turning to focus his gaze on Tamden's bedroom, Barrick lurched from his position on the ledge.

Poking his head out into the hallway, Barrick let out a deep breath as he found it empty. Focusing on the end of the hall, he lurched. Winded as if he'd run the distance, he focused on another spot further down the hall, reached into the powers within him, and found himself on the other side.

Ignoring the ache appearing in his side, he continued down the hallway to the rooms that had been set apart for him at a brisk walk. Opening the door, he found the quarters dark, and he immediately stopped in case the "accident" had already been arranged.

Inching over to the wall, Barrick flipped on a switch, and yellow light inundated the room. His eyes did a quick scan to see everything as he'd left it—his bed untouched, a wash basin still filled with water, and his bag sitting at the foot of his bed.

Grabbing the green sack that he'd used to hold all of his personal belongings since leaving Maradon, Barrick untied the drawstring keeping everything inside and dumped the contents onto the bed. Clothing, matches, half-empty bottles of rum all fell onto the mattress.

Barrick reached to the very bottom of the sack and ripped away a false bottom. His hands grasped a roll of bank notes, which he stuffed into his pocket. As he reached back into the bag, his hands began to tremble at the second item he'd stowed away.

His fingers found the incorporeal piece of cloth that he wished he could never see again. Withdrawing the shadowy article of clothing from the bag, Barrick's mind reflected on the last time he'd worn it. Disappearing into the night had made him stronger, nearly invincible as he assisted his father in taking out a group of Salatian rebels who had stood in his way.

Holding in a shiver that wanted—more than anything—to run up and down his spine, Barrick donned the jacket. It was time to once again embrace the darkness in order to stop it.

6

Barrick stood motionless in the shadows, less than a span from a rifle-armed guard making his nighty patrol. The black jacket clung to him, molding its intangible fabric around his arms and chest. Despite the heat that still hung over the city, Barrick felt a chill that ran down to his bones.

As the guard moved past, Barrick darted into the light, knowing that for a moment he was visible before melting back into the shadows as footsteps approached. Another guard appeared around the corner, his eyes focused directly on Barrick's position. After a moment, those eyes moved on, and Barrick let out a sigh as he began scanning the surrounding area. He still didn't like the blasted jacket, but he had to admit it was useful.

From his new position in the palace's gardens, Barrick could see the entire rear of the massive main building. The little time he'd spent with Tamden told him that the Minister of Finance was the type to enter through the back door, no matter the advantages he held. Infiltrating the heavily guarded palace of one of the world's most powerful monarchs certainly seemed like a situation in which Tamden would not hold the advantage.

King Frederick was growing old and—if rumors were to be believed—senile. However, based on the number of guards out on patrol tonight, he'd chosen a well-qualified individual to run palace security.

He smiled at the thought of one day running security for Aydiin and Byanca. The job must be incredibly boring, but that might be a nice change of pace. Or maybe not.

Barrick's smile faded as he noticed a flicker near a lamp posted to the palace wall. He had seen that flicker before. In fact, he had been the cause of it many times. He apparently wasn't the only one with a shadow jacket.

"Stone-blasted fool," Barrick muttered as he ran through the darkness, careful to avoid the pools of light from the lanterns scattered throughout the gardens.

He should have guessed that the Raven would have given tools and weapons to his servants across the globe. His pace slowed as he imagined the possibility of other weapons gifted to these men by the Undergods. Worse, he didn't know how many shadow-clad warriors were in the group ahead of him or if there were more groups behind him.

You could still run away, a voice whispered in his head.

Barrick shook off the fear that gripped him and picked up his pace. It would be better to die than to abandon Naerdon to a puppet king whose strings were pulled by the Raven. If he were to die tonight, he would make sure to take as many members of the Order with him as possible.

Barrick slipped past another patrol, purposefully tripping a soldier. The man fell to the ground with a thud, his rifle spilling onto the ground.

"Hey, watch it!" the guard shouted at one of his companions.

"I didn't do anything!" his fellow soldier retorted.

"You did, too. I wouldn't just fall down like that. I'm not an idiot!"

"Stop it—you're both idiots," an officer shouted. "You were pushed, but not by Private Coombs. There's a Creep here, or I'm a stone-blind fool. Coombs, go get the message out to the other patrols. We need to get as much light out here as possible."

Barrick smiled and slipped past the thoroughly panicked guards through one of the palace's entrances. Unfortunately, he had no way of warning the guards about the potential of more shadow-clad assassins, but those men knew plenty about finding a Creep.

The trouble with a Creep's invisibility was that it usually left a hazy outline where the light bent around the body. Depending on the individual's skill, the outline could be almost imperceptible. Almost.

A sharp eye could still spot a Creep, especially with enough light. While the shadow jackets didn't leave any sort of outline, the increased light would help level the battlefield. Of course, that also meant they were more likely to see Barrick, so getting back out of the palace could prove problematic. It was a risk he would just have to take.

He ran through the halls, trying not to think too much about the value of even a single painting that graced the walls. He was, after all, saving the king's life. It wouldn't be unreasonable to help himself to one little painting.

Shaking himself from the thought, he headed toward the king's bedchamber, hoping the assassins didn't get there first. As he ran, the complete dearth of soldiers began to gnaw at him.

The muffled sound of battle hit Barrick's ears just before he turned a corner to see a dozen guards fighting—and dying—against nothing. Without squinting, Barrick could feel the shadows moving among the soldiers, cutting them down without a fight.

His eyes cast about the darkness, searching for—he'd found it. Dashing to the wall, Barrick flipped on a switch, and the entire hall-way filled with the soft light of incandescent bulbs. Silence filled the hall as the remaining soldiers shielded their eyes from the sudden intrusion. At their sides stood a dozen men in black coats, their mouths agape and blades held to their sides.

One face didn't display confusion. Rather, those dark eyes locked with Barrick's. Within, he saw only recognition and hatred.

"Well, what are you doing here, Sanborn?" Barrick drawled, finally recognizing the voice he'd heard in Tamden's study.

"I could ask you the very same question," the man said, pulling both an obsidian blade and steel rapier from the chest of a fallen soldier and moving toward Barrick.

Barrick thought back to the night at sea he'd gotten Sanborn so drunk that the man had passed out. He'd taken advantage of the situation to discover that the man was indeed carrying a message on behalf of the Order. Barrick had never dreamt that the message would be bound for his very own father.

"Well, that's not exactly fair, is it?" Barrick asked, pulling out his revolver. "Seeing as how I asked you first."

"You lying traitor," Sanborn growled, his slow advance continuing.

A chill ran down Barrick's spine at the sight of the shadow blade. Forged in the Underworld—practically pulsing with dark power—the blades created wounds that could never heal. He'd even used one to kill his own father, slicing through the protections he'd been given by the Undergods.

Barrick squeezed the trigger on his revolver. Sanborn dodged, but another shadow-clad figure fell with a scream as the bullet took him in the chest. As if the sound had awoken the guards from their shock, the professionally trained soldiers lunged toward the assassins.

Screams sounded as four assassins were skewered and dropped to the ground. The sound of battle resumed, although Barrick's eyes were fixed completely on the approaching Sanborn and his blade.

"Shouldn't you be in the Beyond with Arathorm?" Barrick asked, bending down to grab the saber of a fallen guard. "I'm sure he'd love the company."

"I knew you couldn't be trusted," Sanborn growled as he took his first thrust at Barrick's chest.

"Well, if you knew that, why didn't you say somethin'?" Barrick asked, parrying the blow. He stepped forward, taking a swipe at the man's legs. Steel made contact with flesh, and blood began to trickle down Sanborn's calf.

"It's your fault that Arathorm's dead," Sanborn continued, ignoring the wound and lunging at Barrick. "I don't know what you did, but I know the disaster in Maradon was your fault."

"That's a bad thing?" Barrick shot back, slamming his blade into Sanborn's and shoving him away. "I think most people could argue that the world is a better place without my father in it."

"Don't you dare call him that," Sanborn shouted, launching himself blade first toward Barrick.

Rolling out of the way, Barrick struck another quick blow on Sanborn's back. The man howled in pain as he turned around.

"Well, he did impregnate the woman who gave birth to me. What should I call him?"

"I'll kill you," Sanborn raged, his face growing red as he again launched himself at Barrick, both blades held high above his head.

With both hands on the hilt, Barrick lifted the rapier to catch Sanborn's blades in mid-air. He could feel the man's breath as he struggled to push back on what he had likely considered to be an inferior opponent.

"You're absolutely right. It really is my fault he's dead," Barrick smiled, shoving Sanborn backward. "All it took was one of those shadow blades. He turned to dust and everything. Let me tell you—it was the most satisfying experience of my life."

With a scream, Sanborn lunged at Barrick. Steel hit steel, followed by shadow. Heedless of Barrick's ability to run him through at any moment, Sanborn began raining blow after blow on his opponent. Barrick began backing away, giving ground as each impact rang through his bones.

Sanborn jabbed with his sword, and Barrick dodged to his left, but this time, the rabid attacker was ready. Time slowed as the shadowy blade slipped from the man's hand, flying through the air. Barrick rolled to his right, but the blade caught on the tip of his jacket, nicking his skin and drawing a single drop of blood.

Turning back to Sanborn, Barrick thrust his rapier into the man's chest. A smile spread across Sanborn's face.

"I'll see you soon," Sanborn whispered as Barrick withdrew the blade. The man fell to the ground, the life draining from his eyes.

Footsteps sounded in the hall, and Barrick turned to see a dozen soldiers rushing down the hallway. Dropping his weapon, Barrick placed his hands on his head. Rough hands grabbed him by the arms, and he didn't struggle as iron manacles were placed on his wrists.

7

Dawn brought neither hope nor sunlight to Monterosso. Even as the sun rose, thick clouds covered the sky, threatening to bring down a deluge on the castle. Of course, all those within the ancient fortress knew that rain was the least of their worries.

Aydiin pulled the collar of his thick jacket up against the winds threatening to knock him from his vigil. From atop the central keep, he focused his gaze on the southern horizon—on the village and its surrounding plain and, of course, the forest beyond. It was only a matter of time before a living nightmare would shed the protection of the trees and rear its ugly head in the light of day.

"Enjoying the view?" Byanca asked, snaking an arm around his waist as she moved by his side. She gave him a squeeze, and Aydiin brought an arm around her shoulders, enveloping his wife and reveling in the warmth of her body.

"I take it you couldn't sleep either," Aydiin said, not bothering to answer her question. She knew exactly what he was doing up here.

"My night wasn't terrible—considering the circumstances. It's just hard to sleep in and miss what could very well be my last sunrise."

"We've made it out of worse scrapes than this," Aydiin said, giving his wife a squeeze.

"I still feel bad that we're here on my account. We could be in Margella, trying to steal the Great Stone of Okuta."

"I know that's what I wanted to do, but that plan was filled with just as much danger. Besides, we thought I was powerful enough to take on anything. There was no way of knowing the Undergods would create an immortal enemy."

"And now we've mixed up an entire village in our struggle," Byanca sighed.

"They were going to get mixed up no matter what," Aydiin said, and he felt Byanca give him another squeeze. "This is the fate of the world we're fighting over, after all."

"Look at them down there," Byanca said, gesturing her head toward the soldiers training on the castle grounds below despite the early hour. "They're not actually soldiers. Unless there's a miracle, we're going to be looking at a slaughter."

A group of men and women marched in formation, a sloppy affair as many had never even held a rifle until a few months ago. Of course, most of the farmers in the group would have spent ample time hunting in the forests, but that didn't necessarily translate to battlefield prowess. The vast majority that had been left at Monterosso were residents of the village who not had relied on firearms to help put food on the table.

Some of the soldiers were dressed in the green jackets and white trousers of the republican militia. Those marched a little smarter and knew how to wield the weapons clenched in their hands, even if they weren't professional soldiers. The vast majority, however, wore a random assortment of clothing from their former lives. Farmers with simple, home-spun shirts marched next to merchants wearing fine yet dirty silks. Several clerks with simple white shirts and brown trousers filled out the ranks, giving the whole group a sense of chaos and disorganization.

"At least we have you on our side," Byanca said, rising up to give Aydiin a kiss on the cheek. "That evens the odds a bit."

"Assuming I can use my powers before that...thing shows up. It's not the enemy soldiers I'm worried about. It's that immortal colonel with his black stone."

"Luckily for us, we've been able to leave a few surprises," a voice sounded from behind, and Aydiin turned to see Cael approaching, followed closely by Luka.

"Does Mother know you're up here?" Byanca asked.

"Of course not," Cael said with a laugh, moving toward the battlements to take in the view. "She's too busy barricading the door to her rooms. Maybe we shouldn't tell her when this is all over—that way we might get a few hours of peace before she comes out."

"Monterosso's never been taken by force," Luka said, obviously trying to move on from the subject of Lissandra. "I'll not see the ancestral home of my family fall easily."

The man was dressed in the green jacket and white trousers of the militia. With a saber in hand and two pistols strapped to his belt, the young aristocrat looked the part of a general—even if he had simply inherited the rank rather than earned it on the battlefield.

"I'm inclined to believe you," Aydiin said as Luka approached, and they all turned back to admire the engineering wonders of the fortress.

As he'd noticed at first glance, the fortress was protected by sheer cliffs on three sides, with the only access to the castle consisting of a single road. Yet under further inspection, Aydiin had noticed that the cliffs had been made smooth by workmen. There were no handholds, no conceivable way that an enemy could scale the rock.

The single road switched back and forth several times on its journey to the castle gates, leaving any invading army within rifle range for the entire climb. Completely barren, the road offered no natural cover to hide behind as Monterosso's defenders rained death on any approaching soldiers.

Once reaching the top, an outer wall would need to be either surmounted or toppled before reaching the keep. Built of massive granite blocks, Aydiin knew that without heavy artillery, toppling the structure would be an impossibility. Even an enemy Stone-weaver would be able to do little against such a structure—unless, of course, he also held the Great Stone of Okuta to magnify his powers.

"Let's hope we can keep that tradition of impregnability alive," Byanca said.

"Those soldiers won't know what hit 'em," Cael responded. "Aydiin's a genius."

"Let's hope it's enough," Aydiin said. "Tricks are great, but they don't necessarily make up for such a disparity in manpower."

The beating of several snare drums reached Aydiin's ears, the sound distant as it carried from the forest and across the plains before reaching the town. Lifting a spyglass to his eye, he looked at the source of the drums.

Aydiin's hands began sweating as a column of grey-clad soldiers came into view. Easily visible through the spyglass, the front row marched in unison like the professional soldiers they were. Their boots hit the hard-packed dirt in time with the beating drums, the sound carrying on the wind toward the castle. A shiver ran down Aydiin's spine, adding to the sweat forming in his palms and on his forehead.

"We'll know soon enough," Byanca said as shouts sounded from their soldiers below.

Men and women scrambled, their formations barely deserving the name, as the castle's defenders rushed to the walls. The three hundred or so soldiers left in Monterosso barely seemed enough to man the massive fortifications, and Aydiin didn't like the size of gaps forming in between troops.

Again lifting the spyglass, Aydiin's gaze returned to the grey-clad invaders marching toward the village. His mind wandered, trying to not think about the vindictive colonel and his black stone. With every beat of the drum, the sun rose higher in the sky behind the clouds and the river of grey grew closer.

The column slowed as it reached the first buildings of Monterosso. The town had been evacuated, the residents now huddling within the hall of the keep below Aydiin's feet. Yet that didn't mean the buildings were empty, and these highly trained soldiers knew that.

"What are they doing?" Byanca asked as the regiment began splitting up into three columns. One began marching down the village's main boulevard while the other two took smaller streets toward the fortress.

"They're expecting an ambush," Luka replied. "They want to keep three independent groups so that if one gets in trouble, the others can go around and attack from behind."

"Joke's on them, I guess," Aydiin said. "They must think we have enough soldiers to do anything but try and hold the walls."

"You and Cael weren't the only ones to cook up a little surprise," Luka said with a smile. "Keep your focus on the main avenue. It should be happening right about...now."

Aydiin lifted his spyglass just as a massive volley rang out from one of the windows lining the wide street. The entire front row of grey uniforms fell to the ground amidst shouts from the soldiers still on their feet. An officer pointed toward the cloud of smoke coming out from the window, and a dozen soldiers rushed into the building.

As the column continued, a second blast from another window reached his ears, and several more soldiers fell. This was accompanied by even more frantic shouting, inaudible to Aydiin's ears, as another squad broke off from the column to storm the building.

"They sure are going to be baffled to find a dozen old muskets connected to a platform," Luka said as the wind kicked up.

"Luka, that's genius," Aydiin said. "How many more do you have?"

"Couldn't really spare any more muskets," Luka said, running a hand through his hair. "Still, I'm sure it will make those boys look at every window with healthy suspicion until they're through the village. If they're shaky before even getting to the hill, maybe they'll break and run instead of climbing up under all that gunfire."

As Aydiin looked on through his field glasses, the soldiers in the main column did more than just look. At every building, a dozen soldiers peeled off the main group to search as the remaining soldiers marched on. The going was slow but thorough.

The two side columns barely even slowed their pace as they marched through the side streets. Within minutes, they reached the edge of town and began forming into ranks as the middle column devolved into nothing more than dozens of small groups. From below, Aydiin heard a sharp whistle and the column began marching up the road.

"Looks like your plan took care of nearly a third of the army," Cael said. "Are they really going to just march up like that? Seems kind of suicidal to me."

"Professional soldiers do as they're told," Luka said. "And from what we saw of their commander, he doesn't hold human life in high regard."

The first volley from the wall's defenders exploded, covering the fortifications in a haze of gunpowder. Through his spyglass, Aydiin could see dozens of grey uniforms fall to the ground. The rest, however, began a quick march up the hill.

"Should I do it?" Cael asked, his face turning toward Aydiin.

"Hold on a bit," Aydiin whispered. "Let's not get too hasty."

The group watched as the column snaked up the switchbacks, uniforms falling to the ground with each salvo from the castle's defenders. Far too many were making their way up, and Aydiin's chest began to tighten as the column continued its climb.

"How about now?" Cael asked, his voice squeaking.

"Now," Aydiin said, and Cael lifted his hands.

Aydiin knew that if the boy's upper arms were bare, he'd be able to see the brown Markings of Power identifying his brother-in-law as a Stone-weaver. A look of concentration overtook that freckled face, and his hands began to shake.

"I'm too far," Cael said through gritted teeth.

"Just focus," Aydiin said. "Block us out and just think about the dirt and stone."

Cael's brow furrowed, and a cloud of dust sprang up from the road, accompanied by screams as the young man opened a gaping hole in the middle of the grey column. The soldiers already past the trap turned in dismay while those on the other side began moving to the edges of the chasm. Another volley of rifle fire slammed into the column, and more men fell to the ground with screams.

"I like that—simple yet eloquent," Luka said, patting Cael on the back.

"It was Aydiin's idea," Cael responded, wiping the sweat that had beaded on his forehead. "We just created a hole and then covered it up with a thin layer of packed dirt. Easy enough to break, even at this distance."

"How deep is it?" Luka asked.

"Only a few spans," Cael responded with another shrug.

"Then what's to stop them from just climbing back out?" Byanca asked.

"You don't need to fall very far when there's a bed of razor-sharp stone waiting to do you in," Aydiin said. "That part was Cael's idea."

"What a terrible way to die," Byanca said, her face growing pale.

"It's either us or them," Luka grunted. "We don't have to like it, but I'd rather make it through this day alive."

The hole began closing up, dirt moving without hands to fill the gap left in the road. Aydiin moved his spyglass to see a soldier directing the dirt and stone with his hands, sealing his fallen comrades below ground.

"Stones, they've got some tricks of their own," Luka said, pulling out his own spyglass.

"You're surprised?" Aydiin asked.

"A little bit, yes," Luka said. "Stone-weavers aren't exactly common in Genodra. Still, it was a good trick. Those men won't easily trust the ground beneath their feet until they reach the walls."

The grey snake continued its way up the hill, shedding plenty of its skin on the path. Grey uniforms dotted the road, and Aydiin tried to not focus on any individual corpse as he surveyed the battle. Unfortunately, the bulk of the beast reached the hilltop, leaving only the wall and its poorly-trained defenders.

A tremor—faint but close—overtook the castle as the ground rose up near the outer fortifications. Aydiin redirected his focus toward the front rows of grey-clad soldiers to see stone walls rising up from the ground. With shouts from officers, the soldiers began taking cover behind the impromptu fortifications.

"Why aren't they just storming the walls?" Aydiin asked, pressing his stomach against the battlements as he leaned forward.

"I have no idea," Luka said, doing the same. "Even with cover, they're at a disadvantage when it comes to a shootout. Their best bet is to just climb the walls."

"I'm not quite so sure," Aydiin said as a rumbling from town caught his attention. Raising his spyglass away from the battle, his eyes caught hold of a dust cloud at the far end of town.

Three large trucks appeared out of the forest, jostling and bouncing on the dirt road as they barreled toward Monterosso. With steel frames painted green and canvas canopies over beds large enough to transport a dozen soldiers, the trucks sped toward the fortress with a speed Aydiin had not thought possible. The trucks reached the village, slowing down as they approached the now-cleared main avenue.

"The middle column's job wasn't to march through town," Aydiin gulped. "It was to clear a path."

"What do I do?" Cael asked, turning to Aydiin. "This wasn't part of the plan."

"I know," Aydiin said without pulling his eyes away from the trucks as he thought about the additional traps they hadn't yet sprung.

The trucks reached the end of town, slowing as they started up the switchbacks leading to the castle. Behind them, a cheer went up from the soldiers of the middle column, and a second wave of grey began its way up the path in the vehicles' wake.

"Now, do it now," Aydiin said, and Cael lifted his hands.

Nothing happened.

"Cael, he said to do it now," Luka barked.

"Luka, not helping," Byanca said, placing her hand on Cael's shoulder. The boy was shaking.

"You can do it," Aydiin said. "Just empty your mind and focus."

On the road below, Aydiin felt, rather than heard, the shifting of stone. A cloud of dust rose up as the ground again opened its jaws, and the last of the three trucks slammed into the hole. The sound of steel crashing into stone erupted as the front two trucks continued up the hill.

An explosion shook the ground, followed by a fireball rising a hundred spans into the air from the fallen truck. A wave of heat slammed into Aydiin, and he struggled to remain on his feet. Heedless of the explosion at their rear, the two remaining trucks whined as their engines brought them closer to the fortress.

"Looks like they don't need artillery," Luka said. "Any chance you've got another trap ready?"

"Just one," Aydiin said, moving over to place his hand on Cael's shoulder. "Cael, do you remember where we placed it?"

"Of course," the young man said with a nod.

"Okay, focus and make sure that we get that first truck. The explosion just might take care of the one behind it."

The boy again nodded, and Aydiin turned his gaze toward the convoy barreling toward them. An explosion that massive would rip through the gates, leaving them wide open. The keep was solidly built, but it was meant to be a last line of defense.

"We've got another problem," Luka said, his spyglass lifted. "Take a look at the driver of that first truck."

Aydiin lifted his spyglass to see a long, pale face topped with even paler hair. Dark eyes were focused as the immortal colonel led his vehicle up the switchbacks. With a gulp, Aydiin lowered his spyglass as the trucks wound around the penultimate switchback, approaching the last trap Cael had put into place.

Cael raised his hands, and even without looking, Aydiin could tell the boy's muscles were tense. An eternity passed as the trucks' engines whined. Aydiin's eyes widened as the lead truck approached the trap.

"I can't," Cael gasped, sweat beading at his forehead in concentration.

"If one of those trucks hits the wall," Luka began, his voice trembling, "this battle will be over, and we'll all be—"

"Not helping, Luka," Byanca snapped again, and Luka shut his mouth.

The ground shifted on the final trap. The lead truck's front tires cleared the hole while the back tires fell, and the entire vehicle shuddered. Aydiin held his breath as the monstrosity began slipping backward, into the hole created to trap it.

The second truck, its brakes squealing, careened headlong into the trap. Steel crashed into the stone spikes below, and a massive explosion rocked the entire hillside. As the fireball erupted into the sky, the lead truck's back wheels were rocketed out of its skid, and all four tires regained the final stretch of road.

"Sound the retreat," Luka shouted, his eyes locked on the truck now barreling toward the gate. "Get those soldiers off the wall."

Aydiin was sure nobody heard their commander's shout, but the soldiers below knew what they faced. The castle's defenders began scrambling off the wall, running toward the keep. Aydiin's muscles tensed as the truck approached, its engine roaring.

Men and stone flew into the air as it slammed into the wall, the explosives within detonating into a massive fireball. A cloud of dust rose into the air, obscuring Aydiin's view. For a moment, he let himself believe that the ancient fortifications had held.

As the dust cleared, his heart fell at the sight of a gaping hole in the wall. Before the dust settled, he could see grey uniforms flooding in through the breach. He didn't even need his spyglass to see that the fight was over.

"Well, what do we do now?" Cael asked. Nobody responded.

Aydiin flinched as steel collided with the stone battlement to his right. He poked his head over to see soldiers rushing in through the destroyed gate, some holding gas-powered grappling hooks. Two more men discharged their weapons at the top of the keep, and two more ropes connected the battlements to the ground below. The men began staking their end of the ropes into the ground, creating taut lines, allowing soldiers to attack the final redoubt from above and below.

"Somebody cut that," Luka shouted, and Cael pulled a knife out from his belt.

"Wait," Aydiin said, nudging Cael away from the rope. Grabbing his rifle, Aydiin placed it over the line. It would be a rough ride, but he should be able to use the rope to see him safely to the ground below.

"Aydiin, you can't go down there," Byanca said, grabbing him by the shoulder.

"How do you kill a snake?" Aydiin said, looking into her eyes.

"By cutting off its head," she whispered, tears forming in her eyes.

Aydiin grabbed the back of Byanca's head and pressed his lips to hers. Before she could protest further, he grabbed onto his rifle and leapt into the fight below.

8

As Aydiin hurtled toward the ground, wind rushing through his hair, it occurred to him that this may not have been the best idea. Under normal circumstances, sliding from the top of a fortress down a rope could be considered fun. Today was anything but normal.

Lifting his feet as gravity brought him closer to the soldiers already using the rope to assault the keep, Aydiin launched a kick at the first man's head. The man fell to the ground below with a shout. His legs straight from the kick, Aydiin careened into the second soldier, and they both fell to the ground in a heap.

Rising from the ground, Aydiin looked up to see hundreds of grey-clad soldiers forming into lines, even as the keep's defenders made holes in their ranks. Without a doubt, Aydiin knew this had been a foolish idea.

The few defenders who had made it off the wall before the explosion had retreated to the keep. As his eyes surveyed the battlegrounds between the wall and the inner fortress, Aydiin had the sudden realization that he was alone in a sea of grey.

"Company—ready," an officer shouted, and hundreds of rifles were raised in his direction.

Aydiin reached for the well of energy within him. The power of both Surion and Katala sat within his grasp, and he began stoking them. Drawing them into his body, he felt the raging inferno of Surion mixing with the cooling tranquility of Katala.

"Company—aim," the same officer shouted.

Aydiin lifted his hands and unleashed a torrent of molten flames into the sea of grey. The fire threatened to engulf Aydiin, and he unleashed a portion of Katala's powers, creating a barrier of cool water around his body. For what felt like an eternity, the two forces battled, threatening to tear Aydiin apart.

As if a cork were being forced into a flowing bottle of wine, Aydiin felt the flow of both powers grow weak. With no outlet, the powers began to attack their host, the pain growing intense as he wrestled with the divine energy forced to remain inside of him. This time, Aydiin knew to stop before the pain took him completely.

Gasping, Aydiin opened his eyes. Where only moments ago had stood an entire army ready to assault the keep, his eyes saw only empty ground covered in smoldering ash. No corpses or anything recognizable as once human remained. His eyes found their way toward the pile of rubble that had once been the gate to see a solitary figure standing atop the wreckage.

The immortal officer stood tall, that same grin on his face. While his clothing was little more than charcoal, his skin showed no signs of the massive explosion that had destroyed the outer fortifications.

"I'm going to be in trouble for this," he said, gesturing to the burning remains of his army. "Two-thirds of a regiment—gone in the blink of an eye. Quality soldiers aren't replaced overnight."

The officer jumped off the rubble and began approaching Aydiin. Unable to use his powers, he stood, awaiting his fate. He kept his gaze focused on the villain, not wanting to think about the hundreds of lives he'd just wiped out.

"You don't remember me, do you?" the immortal colonel asked as he approached. "This face hasn't changed much in the millennium since you last saw it."

Aydiin stood silently as the man came within a few spans. He had no solid memories of this man. Yet somehow, that face and voice were familiar.

"Think through those memories you stole," the officer said. "I'd be terribly upset if you couldn't remember me before the Great Lord takes your life."

"Well then, you'll just have to stop him from killing me," Aydiin responded with a smile, unwilling to show fear to this...beast.

"I like a man who laughs in the face of death," the officer said, narrowing his gaze.

The sound of an automobile approaching from the keep made Aydiin's ears perk up. A small red car sped out—one of those pieces of art that had been visible in the streets of Palmas before the chaos—from the other side of the keep. Behind the wheel sat Cael, his jaw clenched in concentration.

The officer's eyes widened as the car slammed into his body, launching the man into the air before he hit the ground a few spans away. With a nod from Cael, Aydiin jumped into the car. With a whoop, Cael sped through the rubble of the broken fortifications and down the road.

"I've got an idea," Cael shouted over the wind.

"I was assuming so," Aydiin shouted back.

Looking in the rear-view mirror, Aydiin saw the officer rise to his feet. Without a moment of hesitation, the man sped after them on foot.

"What is he doing?" Cael asked, also keeping an eye on their pursuer through one of the mirrors.

"I'm not sure," Aydiin said as the officer picked up speed. With giant bounds, the man began to gain on the small automobile. Aydiin heard the engine's tone change as Cael shifted gears and pressed harder on the accelerator.

Soldiers marching up the hill to reinforce their comrades jumped out of the way as the car slammed into others. With the insane officer gaining on them, Cael didn't slow the vehicle as it barreled into grey uniforms.

Reaching the bottom of the hill, Cael swung the steering wheel. The car veered to the left down a side street rather than going straight through the village's main boulevard. The noise of the engine and wind began to roar in Aydiin's ears as the vehicle picked up speed.

Behind them, the officer leapt onto the road, his bounding leaps more than enough to keep up with the car. Aydiin looked at Cael, the young man's face scrunched up in concentration. As they neared the edge of town, Aydiin thought back to the maps he'd seen of Monterosso.

"Cael, we're going to hit the ravine," Aydiin shouted over the wind and roar of the engine.

"I know," Cael said, a smile spreading across his face.

Cael summoned a stone bridge, and the car hesitated as it slammed into the uneven ground. It rumbled, and as they reached the other side of the ravine, the young man slammed on the breaks. With a squeal, the car spun to face the pursuing officer. As their pursuer began his journey across the gorge, Aydiin could see a look of confusion enter the man's face.

With a smile and flick of his wrist, Cael disintegrated the bridge into dust. The officer's countenance showed nothing but anger as he fell hundreds of spans into the raging river below.

9

Barrick awoke to complete darkness, letting out a groan as memories from the night before flooded into his brain. Rubbing his wrists where the iron manacles had chafed the night before, he sat up on the stone floor that had served as his bed. The darkness remained as he opened his eyes, his mind straining to make sense of his surroundings.

Moving to his knees, Barrick fumbled around until his hands made contact with an almost intangible lump. Picking up the jacket he'd apparently used as a pillow, Barrick slipped his arms into the sleeves. The room around him came into focus, a soft twilight filling his vision.

The cell was about what he would expect for a man accused of attempted regicide. No more than a few spans in any direction, it was barely large enough for him to lie down. The ceiling was only high enough for him to crouch, and not a single piece of furniture was present to offer comfort.

Barrick found his way to the rough wooden door that served as the only exit—or entrance—to his cell. It was thick, and the hinges were of a heavy steel. There was a small slot near the bottom where the guards had slipped in a bowl filled with some sort of gruel. From the smell alone, Barrick knew it would be days before he was hungry enough to force it down.

The cell was permeated by the moist smell of subterranean air. The smell, along with the absence of even a barred window, told him that he was underground—just how deep, he couldn't be sure. To his knowledge, there was only one prison in the city that held prisoners in such dungeons—the Carcern.

The Carcern was reserved for only the worst criminals—murderers and traitors, mostly. Of course, there were rumors the king had placed a fair number of journalists and outspoken nobility into some of the forsaken cells. For most people, this situation would be a death sentence.

Luckily, I'm not most people, Barrick thought, a smile making its way onto his face despite his hunger and exhaustion.

Crawling on hands and knees toward the door, he placed an ear against the wood. He strained for any indication of human life in the hall—footsteps, breathing, muffled conversation. Holding his breath, all he could hear was the rhythmic pounding of his pulse. If someone were outside the door, they were either asleep or going to great lengths to remain quiet.

Steeling himself for the wave of nausea, Barrick lurched through the door and into the hallway. His stomach roiled in protest, and he bent over as the few remaining contents were ejected onto the stone floor. Wiping his mouth on the shadowy sleeve, Barrick straightened up and took stock of his new surroundings.

The hallway was bathed in the same darkness as his cell, only visible to Barrick through the powers of his jacket. He smiled at the thought of patrolling guardsmen wandering the hallways in vain after the oil in their lamps burned out. Without the soft, life-preserving light of a lantern, these corridors would be impossible to navigate.

For the moment, the darkness was his ally. As long as he could keep to the shadows, any guards he encountered would be able to neither see nor hear him. Of course, just because his eyes could pierce the darkness didn't mean he knew how to escape the underground prison.

From what he knew of the Carcern, it had been carved out of a pre-existing complex of caverns in the hills surrounding Naerd. This hallway was merely part of a warren of narrow corridors meant to confuse any prisoner who managed to escape his cell. Looking to his left, Barrick could make out an almost imperceptible incline to the floor.

"Well, I might as well be moving up instead of down," he whispered, his voice shattering the silence that enveloped the corridor.

As he walked, he wondered what was happening above ground. He'd managed to save the king—he hoped—while simultaneously taking out a dozen shadow-clad members of the Order. Yet, he still had no idea if word of his involvement had somehow reached the remaining members of the incredibly vindictive organization. There would be a lot of work to do once he reached the top if he even wanted to survive, let alone destroy the Order.

Voices reached his ears as another hallway met up with his. Poking his head around the corner, Barrick could see the orange light of a lantern approaching. Pulling back, he waited for the guards to approach.

"You should probably just try to forget about her," one of the voices whispered.

"How can I forget about the love of my life?" another voice shot back.

"The real love of your life won't leave you in the middle of the night," the first voice responded.

Two guards, each carrying a lantern in one hand and a rifle in the other, entered Barrick's line of sight. The man complaining about his love was tall and thin, with a long nose protruding from his face. His companion was of a more average height, his non-remarkable face and stature making him difficult to pick out in a crowd. They both wore the standard mustard brown coats of the city's police along with simple round caps.

"I just don't know how I'm ever going to find another one like her," the taller of the two said.

"Let's go get a drink—my treat," his friend replied. "Our shift will be over by the time we finish this route. After that, we'll drown your sorrows in the strongest mead we can find."

Barrick hung back far enough that he could keep an eye on the two. Based on the mind-numbing conversation, the guards were near the end of their circuit. Even if they weren't, they had to lead him to the surface eventually. Focusing his mind on other tasks to block out the cuckold's self-loathing, Barrick began plotting his next steps.

He briefly considered returning to Tamden's estate but quickly decided against it. If even a single assassin had escaped death, his cover would be blown with the Order. Any further attempt to infiltrate the organization would just be too dangerous.

That meant it was time to find Aydiin. True, he hadn't really succeeded in uncovering any real information about the Order, but that seemed rather impossible at this point. Besides, Aydiin was probably going daft with nobody to keep him company except that wife of his. Poor bloke.

As the guards turned a corner, Barrick could see a spot of daylight up ahead, and he let out a sigh. Even the Carcern couldn't hold him, equipped with the power of both a Divine and the Undergods. Still, he didn't know what obstacles he would face at the prison's exit.

With freedom and daylight only a few hundred spans away, a door with a sign above it caught Barrick's eye. Peeking through a small, barred window on the door, he was greeted by the sight of shelves fully stocked with everything needed to run a prison. There were cans of food, uniforms, even weapons—things he would likely need as he made his way back to Aydiin and Byanca.

Taking in a deep breath, Barrick lurched through the door and into the storage room. Looking around, he grabbed a standard-issue canvas knapsack and began stuffing it with provisions. He wasn't exactly sure what he'd need, so he just grabbed everything. As he reached for a box of matches, a noise on the other side of the shelves brought him to a stop.

"No, not that one," a voice whispered. "Get that big wheel of cheese."

"But this one is so much tastier," a second voice shot back. "Your palate is so unrefined."

"What do you know about cheese?" the first voice said.

Barrick crept around the shelf, relying on his shadow jacket to keep him hidden. Poking his head to see around the shelf, his eyes caught the strangest sight he'd ever seen.

Two children were jamming wheels of cheese into large burlap sacks. A small lantern at their feet gave off just enough light for them to see but not enough to give any indication of the thieves' presence to someone outside the storage room. Guessing by the way those sacks bulged, they were much too heavy for children to carry.

Although short, both spoke with rich, baritone voices. One had long, dark hair and a muscular build. The other sported close-cropped blond hair and a much thinner frame.

"Oh, look at this wine," the blond thief cooed, ignoring the other's jab at his lack of knowledge. "The Protector will love this."

"I've never seen him drink wine," the dark-haired child hissed.

"That's because you never bring him any," the blond turned and stuck out his tongue, revealing a bearded face.

Barrick crept closer, his footsteps especially silent when compared to their bickering. He needed to get a better look at them, his curiosity unwilling to let him just leave. Their size, their mannerisms, and their conversation told him they were far from home.

He drew closer, unsure of what his actual plan was. Lifting his foot for another step, it caught on something littering the ground, and he fell forward with a yelp. His hand grabbed onto the closest child's burlap sack, and Barrick saw a wide-eyed face turn toward him.

The world around him shifted, and his stomach began screaming in protest. The edges of his vision grew blurry, his eyes filling with shifting images of places he'd never been. Fields of green crops, mountains blanketed in trees, ocean waves stretching in every direction flashed before his eyes as his stomach demanded that it end quickly.

A blast of dry, hot air assaulted his face, and his eyes slammed shut in protest. The smell of running water hit his nose, and the sound of muffled conversation reached his ears. Shaking his head, Barrick opened his eyes.

He stood on the edge of a green river flowing lazily through red sandstone at the bottom of a deep canyon. More than a hundred spans across, the flowing water had spent millennia cutting its way through the stone, creating the magnificent view around him. Blinking again as his sight adjusted from the darkness of the Carcern to the broad daylight, Barrick's mouth dropped open as he took in the view.

Ancient buildings, carved from the sandstone cliffs, towered above both banks of the river. Many contained ornate statues carved out of the cliffside, integrating perfectly into the architecture. Everything was immaculately maintained, not a single building showing any sign of wear. Staircases and ladders crisscrossed the buildings, forming a network of passageways that honeycombed the cliffs.

Child-like figures streamed through the passageways. Women carried cloth-wrapped bundles atop their heads and children on their backs. Men carried large bags tied to sticks, which rested on their shoulders as they transported their loads.

At the banks of the river, groups of women sat doing laundry as children splashed in the water. The women were tall as most children he knew, yet their bodies were fully developed, even if most were little more than skin and bones. The children were also tinier, and he could see more ribs poking out than he would have liked.

"What did you do?" a voice hissed at his side, and Barrick looked down to see both of the thieves standing at his feet. Both men took turns glaring at each other before rounding on Barrick.

"It wasn't me; it was you," the blond thief shouted.

"Get him out of here or we'll both be dead," the dark-haired man barked, pushing his companion toward Barrick.

Without so much as addressing their guest, one of the thieves grabbed Barrick by the legs. His head immediately began to spin as the entire canyon disappeared in a blur. Bile rose up from his stomach, and Barrick forced himself to keep it down. Panting, he collapsed onto dry grass.

"What just happened?" Barrick asked, looking up at the bearded child just as a tiny foot slammed into his ribs.

"Don't try that again," the small thief shouted, pointing a finger in Barrick's face. "It was rude, bordering on heretical."

"I have no idea what I did," Barrick panted, trying not to throw up again.

"Neither do I," the man said, shaking his head. "Just don't do it again."

As the words left his mouth, the thief disappeared into thin air. Barrick rose to his feet, a smile creeping onto his face as thoughts formed in his head.

Those men were Lurchers. The power of travel he'd possessed for nearly a decade had never allowed him to move more than a hundred spans at a time. He'd never even heard of the ability to bring someone else along for the ride.

He knew that there was only one explanation for what he'd just experienced. For the first time since foiling the Order's assassination plot the night before, Barrick no longer questioned his next moves. There was a mystery to be solved.

Now, the only question was how to solve it.

10

B arrick fidgeted in the dilapidated armchair facing the small bedroom's empty fireplace. The quarters reminded him of Aydiin's—the walls were lined with bookshelves, leaving only enough room for a small bed, a washbasin, and a reading chair. Based on the shelves' contents, the room's occupant had a deep love for the social sciences.

Fighting the desire for a good wash, fresh clothing, and a strong drink, Barrick forced himself to remain seated. Of course, the unbandaged nick on his arm was bothering him worse than anything—that couldn't be ignored for much longer. He'd seen what a shadow blade was capable of doing.

The clock sitting on the mantle told him the wait was almost over. Some people were creatures of habit, their patterns refusing to change. Even after all these years, Barrick had a strong suspicion that the room's occupant would be retiring shortly.

The dull hum of crickets drifted in through the open window, mixing with the heat to remind him that summer was in full swing. Staring at the fireplace, he wondered what it would be like to feel cold again. Footsteps in the hallway outside pulled him from those thoughts, and he straightened his posture as the doorknob began turning.

A bespectacled woman in her early thirties sighed deeply as she opened the door before flinging a leather satchel onto the floor. Even in the darkness, Barrick could picture her face as she ran a hand through her hair. The young woman lifted a hand to the light switch but stopped before flipping it on.

"I knew it had to be you," she said before flipping the switch and flooding the room with the warm glow of incandescent bulbs. "Everyone at dinner couldn't stop talking about the young man who escaped the Carcern."

"So, word's already gotten out, has it?" Barrick drawled, remaining in his seat. "I was thinking they wouldn't want that bit o' news leaking to the street."

"Oh, nothing official has been said," the woman replied, taking a seat on her bed and removing her shoes. "I notice you're not denying it."

"No point in denyin' it to yeh," Barrick said, rising to his feet and offering his hand to the woman. "It's good to see yeh again, Amelie."

"I wish I could say the same," Amelie said, sliding her shoes underneath the bed and ignoring his outstretched hand. "It's not enough that you escaped from prison, but now you have to incriminate me too?"

"Nobody even saw me escape," Barrick drawled, returning to the armchair. "Can't imagine they woulda followed me here. Besides, I figured it's about time I dropped in on my favorite cousin."

"We're *second* cousins," Amelie replied, sticking out her tongue. "Just because we used to go on holiday together at the beach doesn't mean I won't report you. I'm not exactly a fan of the king, but I absolutely detest anarchists."

"Yeh know I'm no assassin, lass. If yeh really thought that, you wouldn't be chatting with me right now."

"I *think* you're no assassin," she said. "But I could be wrong. You did just escape from Naerdon's most infamous prison, after all. You must have done something."

"Right or wrong depends on who yer talkin' to," Barrick said. "Those assassins I killed probably thought it was wrong of me to stop them from regicide, but I have a feeling that most everyone else would say I did right."

"You?" Amelie gasped, and her eyebrows shot up. "You expect me to believe that you—of all people—risked your life for the king?"

"Oh, I've changed a lot since yeh last saw me," Barrick said with a wink. "I'm a right old outstanding citizen now. I shake hands and kiss babies, the whole lot."

"Okay, Mr. Citizen," Amelie said, "enlighten me then. Why would you be willing to risk your life to stop the king from being assassinated?"

"Well, despite my apathy toward the aging gentleman, I have a strong dislike for the people who were trying to kill him," Barrick said before lowering his voice and furrowing his brow. "You might even call it enmity. Tell me, Amelie, have you ever heard of the Knights of the Raven?"

"The Order?" Amelie asked, raising an eyebrow. "Are you really trying to convince me that a mythical group of devil worshippers is responsible for all this?"

"I know it sounds ridiculous," Barrick said. "They've been trying for hundreds of years to make everyone think they don't exist. It's probably the biggest success they've had—if yeh don't exist, no one worries about protectin' themselves from yeh."

"Barrick," Amelie said, moving to lie down on her bed. "Why are you really here? I've had a long day, and I don't have the energy to put up with a grown man telling me fairy tales."

"That's fine; don't believe me—you're the one who was askin'," Barrick said, lifting his hands in surrender. "There actually is another reason I came to yeh."

"I'm not going to hide you forever," she said, placing a hand to her forehead. "Life at the Institute is hectic enough without trying to harbor a fugitive."

"I'm actually here for yer knowledge—and the wealth of resources at your disposal," Barrick said, rising up from his chair to look at her bookshelf. "Even as a child, all you cared about was history and geography."

"Interests that are apparently of little use," she replied, sitting up from her bed. "The Royal Institute of Technology is the only place I can find employment, and there are even people here who think my passions are pointless."

"In all your studies, what have yeh learned about Gorteo?" Barrick asked, his eyes refusing to focus on any individual book.

"Gorteo? Hermit kingdom in the southern hemisphere. Shares a border with Genodra and Pilsa," Amelie said, moving to stand next to Barrick at the bookshelf.

"I'm not asking about basic facts that everyone knows," Barrick said, turning to face his cousin. "I want to know details—has anyone ever described the country? How do the people live?"

"Well, a group of explorers in the second century got lost while hiking in the Pharone Mountains," Amelie said. "They actually were the ones who discovered that there were even people living in that vast desert."

"Wait, so for the first hundred years after the Final Battle, people didn't even know Gorteo existed?" Barrick asked, his eyes bulging.

"They've cut off pretty much all contact with the outside world," Amelie said, moving toward the bookcase. "Sometimes, they'll send a diplomat to Genodra or Salatia for certain negotiations, but our knowledge of the country is pretty much based on the occasional prisoner who manages to escape."

"What do people say about the country?" Barrick asked, fixing his eyes on Amelie's.

"I can't remember exactly," she replied, turning back to the book-shelf. "Obviously, it's a desert—lots of sand, red rock, and the like."

"Did they describe the citizens as shorter than average?" Barrick asked. "Maybe the size of children?"

"Yes, they have, actually," Amelie said, pulling a book off the shelf. "You can read all about it in here."

"I don't have time for that," Barrick shook his head. "So, it's a desert. Has anybody said anything about a city carved into sandstone cliffs?"

"Not that I can think of, but I really only scanned through the book—I tend to focus my studies on countries we can actually visit."

"I was hoping you were going to say that," Barrick said, unable to control the smile spreading across his face. "What would yeh say if I wanted ter go there?"

"That you're insane," Amelie scoffed, turning away and moving to sit on her bed. "The Gorteon navy is constantly patrolling their shores. Merchant ships who get too close are taken, and it's rare that anyone gets out alive."

"Come on, think of the adventure," Barrick said, wanting to smack himself as he realized he'd heard those words before coming from Aydiin's mouth. "Aren't yeh bored of reading books all day, cooped up in the Institute?"

"Not at all," Amelie said, lying back down on her bed. "I actually find my profession to be very fulfilling. I can't risk everything I've acheived by trying to visit the world's most backward country."

"Amelie, when I was escaping the Carcern, I came across two very small thieves stealing from a supply room," Barrick said, unsure how to phrase his words.

"Are you really trying to tell me that two Gorteons were stealing from the Carcern?" Amelie scoffed.

"That's not even the craziest part," Barrick said, trying to keep his voice steady. "I accidentally grabbed one of 'em, and the next thing I knew, we weren't in the Carcern anymore."

"Where were you?" Amelie said, rising up from the bed to stare at him in the eyes.

"In a canyon with a river flowing through it," Barrick responded, his gaze refusing to break away from his cousin's. "Carved out of the red rock were hundreds of buildings. I saw very short women doing laundry and scrawny children playing in the water."

"And then?" Amelie asked, her eyes wide.

"One of the thieves grabbed me, and I was suddenly on the hills outside the city. I need to know what happened. I need to know how a Gorteon Lurcher was able to take me to the other side of the world and back again."

"You should probably just let it go," Amelie said, looking away from his gaze. "Getting into Gorteo is practically a death sentence. Just don't tell anyone else about what you saw—they'll think you're crazy."

"I have to get into Gorteo," Barrick said. "I have a hunch that it could be the most important thing I'll ever do."

"Well, if it's the only way to be rid of you, I guess I can help. I have some friends who have been working on some pretty interesting devices that might be just what you're looking for."

"I still hear hesitance in yer voice," Barrick said.

"You'll need funding. There's an engineer at the Institute who has quite the passion for nautical travel, but he won't come cheap."

"Money shouldn't be a problem," Barrick said, thinking about the hollow tree on the north side of Cumberland Park that held his bag. While he'd taken the shadow jacket with him to foil the Order's plan, he'd decided that hiding his wad of bank notes was prudent. At this moment, he was very glad he'd done so.

"Oh, you're always so confident," Amelie said.

"Of course I am. After all, I am Barrick Fortescue."

11

Seb opened his eyes as the grey light of dawn streamed in through the bars of a high window, illuminating the cell that had served as his home for far too long. His chest lightened at the sight, alleviating the fear that gripped him each night that—for one reason or another—he would not see the sunrise in the morning. Weak and cold as it was, the light meant another day of life—another day to fight and survive.

It doesn't really make a difference. The thought came to his mind unbeckoned as his eyes scanned the cavernous prison cell. While large enough to hold a dozen men with ease, the cell contained nothing but a pile of straw for a bed and a wooden bucket for waste disposal. Even with the light giving some amount of comfort, the stone room felt just as cold and wet as it had during the night.

Joints groaning in protest, Seb lifted himself into a sitting position, his back resting on the rough stone wall. While the uneven edges dug into his skin, Seb knew he didn't have the strength to remain sitting up without the help. That reality made him shudder, the movement not brought on by the cold.

With a deep breath, Seb drew the cold winter air into his lungs. The vile fluids that collected nightly caught in his throat, and his body instinctively reacted. Seb's entire core tensed and spasmed as the muscles exerted themselves in an attempt to expel the phlegm.

The taste of warm blood filled his mouth, and Seb grabbed his waste bucket. Spitting out the foul-tasting liquid, he wiped the remnants from his lips before another fit of coughing took over. With fewer fluids to object, the spasms grew harsher, leaving his throat burning as the coughing subsided.

His morning ritual now observed, a wave of shivers overtook his body, and his skin prickled in the crisp air. His arms trembled as he placed the waste bucket back to the ground before fumbling for his only protection against the cold—a soiled, paper-thin blanket he'd found in a corner of his cell.

"I don't like the sound of that cough," a voice said at his side. Seb jumped at the sound, his head slamming against the wall. As the stars cleared from his vision, a broad, freckled face topped with matted red hair came into focus.

"Joon, my boy," Seb croaked, his voice sounding unfamiliar in his own ears after weeks of disuse.

"Sorry to scare you, old man," Joon said with a smile. His diminutive frame, red hair, and freckles gave him the appearance of a small child, yet Seb had seen the man wield a knife with skill and precision. Joon was no youngling.

"You're alive," Seb replied, his brain now spinning. Without thinking, Seb let a smile spread across his face, and he winced as the skin cracked and opened in response.

"Of course, I am," Joon said. He extended his hand to help the old soldier to his feet. "Just because you don't know how to dodge bullets doesn't mean I'm so clumsy."

Seb thought back to the last time he'd seen the young Gorteon. With a dozen agents of the Order in hot pursuit, Seb had fallen off Askari's back, a bullet lodged into his shoulder. While his fevered mind had sometimes drifted to his friend's fate, he'd never let himself hope that the young man had actually survived.

"I'm filled with questions right now," Seb croaked as he took his friend's hand. Small yet strong fingers wrapped around his own, and Seb let the childish Gorteon lift him to his feet. His shoulder howled in protest, the hole created from the bullet struggling to heal properly.

"Well, luckily for you, I'm filled with answers."

"For now, I'll settle with asking what you're doing here."

"Rescuing you, of course. What else would I be doing here?"

"Alright, then onto the next question—where in the world have you been?" Seb exclaimed, ignoring the protests screaming from his muscles as he remained on his feet.

"The sewers, taking care of my kin," Joon replied, his face growing serious. "You have to understand—I thought you were dead, and my people need me."

"Can't say I blame you. I can't imagine these are easy times for anyone, let alone a group of Gorteon refugees."

"Things are bad out there, not just for us but for everyone. We've been making plans to get out of town," Joon said, wrapping his arms around Seb's waist to help him walk. "But then last night, I got word that you're alive and locked up. Came as fast as I could—we need to get you out of here."

"That's an astute observation. I won't last much longer with this cough."

"No, it's not that. It's—"

Heavy footsteps sounded in the corridor outside his cell, the sound reverberating on the bare stone. Joon's eyes grew wide as the footsteps stopped—directly outside Seb's door. The jangle of keys became audible, and the heavy locking mechanisms groaned as someone on the outside began opening the barrier.

Without any prodding, Joon dove straight for the pile of dirty straw. With heart pounding, Seb tossed his blanket over his small friend and fell to the floor, using the lumpy pile as a pillow while the cell's door creaked open.

"Stand back," a strong voice called out, and the barrel of a rifle became visible.

"I'm just a weak old man," Seb called out, his shaky voice adding credibility to the words. "I can barely even stand, let alone attack you."

The door opened wider, and a grey-clad soldier entered the room, his heavy boots pounding on the stone floor. Dark hair sat atop pale skin—the standard combination of southern Genodra. Light blue eyes made contact with Seb's own before scanning the rest of the cell.

"It seems safe enough, sir," the soldier said before opening the door even wider.

Lighter footsteps sounded as a second man entered the room. Unlike the simple clothing of the soldier, this man's chest was heavily decorated with various medals. Matching silver epaulettes hung on his shoulders, and a bicorn hat adorned the top of his head.

"Well, well, look what we have here—Sebastian Montague, First Champion of Margella," the second man said, striding into the cell's interior. "I must admit that I'm quite honored. It's not every day I get to meet one of the world's most-wanted men."

Seb had no need to ask the name of the pompous officer. That hat and splendid grey uniform were not part of the Genodran standard issue. Even outside the Republic, everyone knew of the decorated military career—and pompous style—belonging to Field Marshal Armando Diaz.

The man who stood before him had made a name for himself during the nation's revolution. His reputation had only increased after decades protecting the southern border from the anarchy of Pilsa. While it had been years since he'd faced a major threat, the tales of his bravery—likely with a fair dose of hyperbole—had made their way across the globe.

Most recently, Field Marshal Diaz was responsible for the rebellion that had upended Palmas. Worse yet, Seb had good reasons to believe this man either belonged to—or was being controlled by—the Order. Either way, he would need to tread carefully.

"I think you have me mistaken for someone else," Seb replied before his body sent him into another round of coughing. "I'm just a poor old man caught in the middle of all this chaos."

"You can give up the charade, Montague," Diaz replied, his eyes scanning the cell with a certain amount of disgust evident on his countenance. "I knew it was you the moment I first saw your unconscious face—nothing in this world could convince me otherwise."

"If I could just—"

"We met once. Do you remember?" Diaz asked, moving into a crouched position to bring his face closer to Seb's. "I'm sure you don't. It was years ago—just before that dreadful civil war of yours broke out."

Seb didn't respond. He instead focused on meeting the Field Marshal's gaze. There was a fire in those eyes that made Seb repress a deep shudder. Behind the fire was something else—something he couldn't quite identify.

"I was just a young boy, so pleased to be accompanying my father on official government business to the famed city of Madras," Diaz continued, his face growing closer to Seb's. "I couldn't even close my eyes for fear of missing the smallest detail."

"The queen was, of course, beautiful—beyond words, really," Diaz said, his eyes drawing upward as he spoke as if he were trying to re-live the moment. "I remember her hair was of pure gold. Those eyes were a magnificent azure—deep enough a man could get lost in them. Her voice was strong like the wind. Even as a young boy, I could appreciate that beauty."

Seb didn't respond. His muscles began trembling at the words. The mere mention of Queen Isbyl made his entire frame quake, and this moment was no time to show weakness.

"And at her side stood a man—strong, proud, and silent," the words left Diaz's mouth slowly, and his eyes darted back from the ceiling, making contact with Seb's own. "You."

Seb's muscles could no longer support him, and the old man fell backward onto the blanket covering Joon. His head crashed into his young friend, and the small Gorteon let out a stifled yelp. Diaz's eyes widened, and his expression grew dark.

Seeing the look on his captor's face, Seb forced out a cough to cover the sound. The motion irritated the fluid in his lungs, and another—very real—coughing fit took over his body. Diaz rose to his feet as Seb shifted to his hands and knees. Diaz stood in silence as every muscle in Seb's core spasmed, forcing the fluid out of his lungs. The man made no move toward the blanket covering Joon, but Seb wasn't able to see his face amid the coughing.

"If only I had known then that this is how it would end for the great Sebastian Montague," Diaz began, looking in disgust at the pool of blood and vomit. "You were like a Divine to my childish eyes. Yet now you have fallen, just like your queen—and just like the man you now foolishly worship as a god."

"I'm sorry to disappoint," Seb grunted, rolling onto his back, narrowly avoiding the fluid that had only moments ago filled his lungs and stomach. "Now that you've had your moment to gloat, please just leave an old man to die in peace."

"I'm afraid this little visit isn't just about my ego," Diaz replied, a smile spreading on his lips. "It's about money. The price on your head is so large I'm surprised you haven't spent your entire life fending off bounty hunters."

"I've killed my fair share of young hotheads dreaming of riches and glory," Seb replied, the sentence sounding almost comical in his hears—strong words from a weak voice. "If you're planning on sending my head on a pike to Silvino, you'd better do it quickly before I waste away to nothing."

"Unfortunately, Emperor Silvino wants you alive," Diaz said before snapping his fingers.

At the signal, four soldiers entered the cell from the hallway—two carrying chains while the others trained rifles directly at Seb's chest. Dressed in the standard grey, their faces betrayed no sign of emotion or sentiment.

"As gratifying as it sounds to leave the Lion of the Segre in here to die of cold and pneumonia, I could certainly use the fortune promised from His Imperial Majesty," Diaz said as one of the soldiers knelt down near Seb and placed his hands on the old man's chest. "I do have an entire nation that needs re-conquering."

The soldier closed his eyes, and Seb felt a rush of warmth enter his chest. His lungs grew stronger, the infection within drying out and dying. He breathed in deeply, allowing his lungs to fill with the cold, wet air of his cell. It was the first time he'd been able to do so without repercussion in weeks. His own powers of a Healer had been idle for all this time as they could only be used on others.

Before Seb could let the breath out, firm hands gripped his arms, lifting him to his feet. Seb groaned in protest along with his stiff joints—apparently, the Healer had only focused on his pneumonia and bullet wound. The man's goal was to help Seb survive the voyage to Margella. His comfort was not really of any importance. The soldiers carrying the chains secured them to his wrists and ankles, ensuring that any attempt to flee would result in Seb falling to the ground in a tangle of iron.

Seb couldn't bring himself to respond as the tip of a bayonet pressed into his back, forcing him forward. Seb did his best to ignore the lump hiding under his blanket as his feet shuffled out of the room. Poor Joon was about to take his place in this prison cell, and Seb could only hope that his young friend would be able to find his way out as easily as he had found a way in.

The soldiers—accompanied by a smiling Diaz—led Seb out onto the street. Never having spent much time in Palmas, Seb had no idea where they were. Yet even if he had spent his entire life in the city, he may not have recognized the sight before him.

Across the street stood the empty shells of what had once been a row of three-story apartment buildings. The plain brick—never beautiful or ornate— was now blackened by ash and soot from the fire that had raged through the city. While still standing, it was obvious that none of these buildings were fit for human habitation.

Windows that had once contained glass to protect the buildings' inhabitants now stood open, revealing the burnt-out interiors. Fatally weakened by the blaze, these buildings looked ready to topple over at the slightest breeze. The front wall of one building had already done so, its remains piled onto the sidewalk below. Looking to his right and then to his left, Seb could see dozens of such piles below broken buildings.

Joon wasn't lying about times being tough, Seb thought. The burnt-out buildings and rubble weren't the worst of it. Dozens of pedestrians walked along the road, coats turned up against the cold, hurrying toward some destination or another. The occasional automobile even sped by, wheels rattling on the broken road.

There was a despondency in the way these people walked. Eyes downcast, shoulders hunched—they were protecting themselves from far more than just the cold. The buildings could be repaired, the streets cleaned up and repaved. These people, however, may never truly recover.

The soldiers forced him toward the road as a black motorcar pulled up, its engine rumbling. The black steel frame rattled—this was no luxury vehicle fit for the Field Marshal. This was merely the most efficient way to transport a prisoner from point A to point B.

As if echoing Seb's thoughts, Field Marshal Diaz gave the car a disgusted look but opened the front passenger door and climbed in. Still without strength, Seb let his guards drag him into the vehicle, smashing his head as they stuffed him into the back seat. One of the grey-clad soldiers sat beside him, revolver drawn.

"Do you really think you need that?" Seb croaked at his captor. "You're sitting next to an old man who hasn't eaten a proper meal in months. I could barely walk the few hundred spans from my cell to the street—what makes you think you have anything to fear from me?"

The young soldier didn't respond, but he did lower the revolver to his lap. The barrel was still pointed at Seb, and the hammer remained ready to fire, but the man's face softened. It was almost imperceptible, but Seb could tell that his words had made at least a small change.

"Constant vigilance, Corporal," Diaz said from the front seat without turning around. "This 'feeble old man' has eluded the Margellan secret police for nearly two decades. I wouldn't trust this little act of his."

Seb chose to ignore the man's words, and he turned his attention to the window as the automobile sped through the streets of Palmas. The sights that greeted him did little to help the heaviness that was settling in on his chest.

Dirty and emaciated refugees crowded the sidewalks, huddling around open fires for warmth. Men and women with gaunt faces stared into the flames, their eyes telling of horrors they'd experienced over the past months—horrors that until so recently had been unthinkable in one of the world's most stable and prosperous nations. Even from the automobile, Seb could feel their hunger, their cold.

"How does it feel to see your handiwork close up?" Seb grunted.

"This is the price we must pay for progress," Diaz replied without an ounce of remorse in his voice. "I'm providing bread and fuel for these people—more than I need to really. Genodran winters aren't exactly known for their brutality."

Spoken like a man who has spent the winter inside a real building complete with fireplace and hot meals, Seb thought. It didn't matter how mild a winter was, being caught out in the open could mean death.

Yet it was more than just the weather that was making the people despondent. Cold was something that could be handled. Even an abnormal winter wouldn't produce this kind of depression. This was from a lack of hope, a lack of faith that a better life awaited come spring.

As they approached the harbor, Seb saw a single steamship dominating the docks. The large smokestacks belched clouds of pure black as coal burned deep within the ship's bowels in a massive furnace. Two giant paddle wheels—one on each side—stood ready to guide the ship out of the harbor and across the ocean.

The ship's deck bristled with cannon, and dozens of gun ports lower down hinted at even more weapons below. This was no merchant vessel with enough weaponry to defend itself from the odd pirate. No, this was a battleship, meant to project raw power on the open seas.

A breeze lifted a banner attached to the ship's flagpole. Seb's heart fell as he saw the red cloth, and his stomach retched as the image of two golden hammers crossing over a crown met his eyes.

"How did you lot track down a Margellan naval ship?" Seb croaked, not sure if he wanted to know the answer.

"Once I told Emperor Silvino that the First Champion was rotting away in one of my dungeons, he was rather anxious to see you returned home," Diaz said, turning around to smile at Seb. "No expense is going to be spared in seeing you returned safely."

"I'm glad to know I'm such a priority," Seb replied, meeting Diaz's gaze.

"Oh, you don't even know the half of it," Diaz chuckled, turning back around in his seat.

As the car drew closer, Seb squinted his eyes to better see the name emblazoned on the hull—*Glorious Revolution*. He'd heard talk of the ship. It was said to be the fastest, most powerful in existence, although both Albona and Naerdon were working on their own monstrosities to match it.

The automobile stopped just short of the pier, and Seb was pulled from his stupor. Soldiers opened his door, and rough hands yet again grasped his arms as the guards yanked him from the car. The young corporal who had sat next to him during the drive again lifted his revolver as Seb's feet made contact with solid ground.

"Glad to see he's still alive," a cold voice shouted from the gangplank leading onto the deck. Two men—one dressed in the dark blue of the Margellan navy, the other in the bright vermillion of the Imperial Guards—descended onto the dock, accompanied by a squad of heavily armed marines.

The man in blue was thin yet lithe, the mark of a seasoned sailor who'd spent his life at sea working hard and eating nothing but rancid bacon and hardtack. On his shoulders sat the epaulettes of an admiral along with medals marking him as a veteran of several wars. That face showed little emotion as steely eyes made contact with Seb's own.

The second man—one of the largest Seb had ever seen—descended with a furrowed brow. Easily a head taller and several years' worth of good meals wider than Seb, the man looked solid as a mountain. Yet there was apprehension in that bearded face—an oddity in the elite ranks that protected Margella's usurper. As he drew closer, Seb could see the decorations on his pristine uniform designating him as a general.

"As we agreed, here is your prisoner," Diaz spoke up, joining the group from the automobile. "I must say it's been a pleasure doing business with the famed Admiral Ferdinand."

Seb's ears perked up at the name—one of Silvino's earliest supporters. He'd never had much contact with the man, but he had a reputation for fierce loyalty to his sovereign. The look of pure disgust on the Admiral's face told Seb he would have no friendship with his captor.

"You're a lucky man, Diaz," Ferdinand responded, his voice colder than ice. "It's not every day you find yourself in possession of a criminal worth a large fortune."

Seb switched his gaze to the obese general. There was something familiar about him. He looked about ten years Seb's junior with dark brown eyes and even darker hair. The thick beard covering scarred cheeks had flecks of grey and red mingled in with the brown. Yet most striking of all was the look of surprise on his face.

"Harlin?" Seb croaked, the realization flooding into him like a tidal wave. He felt his blood run cold—before it began to boil.

"That's, er...*General* Harlin," the man stammered.

"I'm glad to see the old man still remembers you," Ferdinand said.

"I didn't expect to ever see you again, sir," Harlin replied, looking at the ground. Apparently, old habits were hard to break.

"Stones, you look terrible," Seb growled.

"Watch how you address a servant of His Imperial Majesty," Ferdinand barked, the cold smile refusing to leave his eyes.

"You don't look any better yourself," Harlin replied, apparently finding his voice. "You're nothing but skin and bones."

"I'd rather waste away to nothing than grow fat off my treason," Seb growled, feeling the anger welling up inside him. That face—that voice—it was like reliving the memories that had haunted him for two decades.

"That's what happens when you choose the winning side," Harlin said. "If you hadn't been so stubborn, you'd still outrank me."

"As much fun as this little reunion is to watch, you really should be going," Diaz interjected, his nose turned up in disgust. "I have my gold, and you have your prisoner."

"I can't believe this moment is finally here," Ferdinand said, approaching Seb. "It's been decades since I've seen the 'Lion of the Segre'—I want to make sure we have some fun before the Emperor kills him."

The admiral began a slow walk around Seb, examining his rags, matted hair, and loose-hanging skin.

"After twenty long years, you'll finally be joining your precious queen," Ferdinand said before spitting in Seb's face.

With hands and ankles shackled, Seb let the liquid roll down his cheek. The rage continued boiling in his chest, contained only by the manacles and the rifles held by his guards.

Let it go, he thought, focusing on controlling the rage.

"I look forward to seeing you beg for your life—just like *she* did," Ferdinand whispered, bringing his face within a few fingers from Seb's own.

The words made his blood boil, and Seb lost focus. His fists began trembling. The sound of his heartbeat in his head began to throb.

"Didn't you know? She begged for mercy and death by the end," Ferdinand whispered so only Seb could hear. "It was a request I was glad to fulfill."

The volcano within erupted.

With a yell, Seb slammed his head into the admiral's. Stars appeared in Seb's vision, blurring the image of his opponent falling backward off the dock and into the harbor. A satisfying splash met Seb's ears, accompanied by shouts and the feeling of hands grabbing him by the arms. Seb felt the butt of a rifle smash into the back of his head, the pain blurring his vision even further.

"Get him below decks," Harlin yelled. "But don't hurt him too much. Our heads will roll if we rob the Emperor the pleasure of killing the First Champion with his own hands."

12

Sitting on the wooden floor of his new cell, Seb grabbed the last remaining morsel of rye bread, wiping it around the now-empty bowl of stew. By normal standards, the bread was dry and the stew greasy. Yet after weeks of starvation rations, the simple meal was a veritable feast.

Seb popped the moistened bread into his mouth and set the wooden bowl and spoon on the ground. With a heavy sigh, he leaned against the rough wooden wall to let his stomach relish in the satisfaction.

In his mind, he knew that this was still a prison. Yet the contrast between the Divine-forsaken dungeons in Palmas and the gentle swaying of the *Glorious Revolution* was tangible. Pine walls had replaced the hewn stone to which he'd grown accustomed. The air was still cold and moist, but now it was mixed with the salty tang of the ocean.

His eyes drifted to the small cot sitting in the corner of the room. After months of sleeping on the ground, his joints ached at the thought of a good night's rest. Tomorrow, he would let himself feel like a prisoner again. Tomorrow, he would start thinking of how to escape. But today, he just wanted to revel in the fact that he would be going to sleep with a full stomach and empty lungs.

"How's your head?" Joon's voice came from under the cot, and Seb jumped as the small Gorteon crawled out into the cell.

"Joon," Seb exclaimed. "You can't keep scaring me like that. I'm an old man—you could give me a heart attack."

"You're not as feeble as you claim," Joon said with a laugh. "I've never seen someone attack so viciously with his own head."

"That was a mistake. I just couldn't help myself."

"That imbecile got what he deserved—he looked rather silly trying to appear tough," Joon replied, pulling out an apple from his sleeve and taking a massive bite. "So, do you want to tell me why you get so riled up when people talk about the queen?"

"Only if you tell me how you got in here," Seb replied with a smile.

"The only thing that matters is that I'm here. Your secrets sound much more entertaining. Why do people call you the 'Lion of the Segre'?"

"That's a title I haven't heard for a long time," Seb said. "If I tell you, will you tell me how you snuck into my cell in the middle of the world's most powerful battleship?"

"Depends on how good your story is. I've got a ten-crown secret, and I expect a story of equal value."

"I expect you already knew I was a member of the Queen's Guard," Seb said, rubbing his head absent-mindedly.

"Everyone knew that," Joon said through a mouth full of apple. "Nobody runs around the world with a thick Margellan accent and sad eyes unless they're an exile."

"What I haven't told you is that I wasn't just a guard—I was the First Champion."

"So, you were in charge of the guards?"

"A little more than that. I was the personal bodyguard to the queen and in charge of the entire Margellan military, second-in-command only to Her Majesty. For most members of the Queen's Guard, a return to Margella would mean a quick execution. For me—well, I'm not quite sure. I just know it will be anything but quick, and it most definitely won't be painless."

"And how did you become the 'Lion of the Segre'?" Joon asked, his eyes wide.

"The Segre is an ancient fortress, the ancestral home of the Margellan queens," Seb said. "During the civil war, it was our military headquarters. Ten times, Silvino's forces tried to take it—ten times, we pushed them back. More than once, I fought hand-to-hand with the Usurper. After the third attempt, people began to say that I fought like a lion, and the name slowly began to stick."

"You fought personally against Silvino? Isn't he the world's most powerful Stone-weaver?" Joon asked. "Am I thinking of the right guy?"

"You are. Without the Great Stone of Okuta, the war would have never even started."

"And you'd still be head honcho in Margella," Joon interjected with a smile. "And you wouldn't even know who I am—so something good came of it all."

"Yes, I suppose it did," Seb responded, giving his friend a smile that didn't reach his eyes.

"Wait, if Silvino never took the Segre, how did you lose the war?"

"It was Harlin," Seb growled. "He was nothing but a fresh-faced young officer—noble blooded and all that. Wasn't cut out for army life, but he inherited an officer commission anyway. There were children who could fight better than him."

Joon coughed, and Seb stopped his rant.

"Anyway, I left the Segre to steal the Great Stone of Okuta from Silvino," Seb said, remembering the all-night ride on horseback. "When I reached Silvino's camp, it was empty. I returned to the Segre the next day to see the imperial flag flying over the fortress."

"How do you know it was Harlin who betrayed you?" Joon asked.

"The man's a national hero for his role in the 'great victory,'" Seb growled. "He's the bloody commander of the Imperial Guard—a nice, comfy position that doesn't require much of him. From what I've heard, he's been living the good life in Silvino City."

"He sure looks like he's been living it up. I saw what he eats for dinner—it could feed my whole family for a week."

Seb chuckled, and a silence settled over the cell.

"I'm a Lurcher," Joon whispered. "That's how I got into your cell back in Palmas. That's how I'm here now."

"Can't believe I didn't already put the pieces together."

"You're not the first to be fooled," Joon replied.

"And the 'ability,'" Seb prodded, referring to the man's powers of tracking, which he had used to help Byanca follow Aydiin across the Genodran countryside. "Can you explain that?"

"I've already sullied my honor just by telling you I'm a Lurcher. Discussing the Ability is more than I'm willing to do," Joon said while shaking his head. "I want to help you, but you just have to be okay with not understanding everything I do."

"I can manage that. After all, it is better than dying a horribly painful death at the hands of my greatest enemy."

"Now we just have to figure out the best time to escape," Joon said. "I'm assuming they'll have to stop in at some port—Margella is an awfully long way away."

Seb opened his mouth to respond when the sound of metal locks turning stopped him. Joon's eyes widened as the door began to open, and—before Seb could react—the diminutive man disappeared into thin air. With barely a noise on well-oiled hinges, the door opened to reveal the bearded face of General Harlin.

"You're looking much better," Harlin said, nodding to Seb's empty bowl. "I guess to a starving man, this slop must taste like something fit for the Divines."

Seb didn't respond, trying to weigh the pros and cons of leaping on his unwanted visitor. He began mentally calculating the distance between him and Harlin, wondering if he had enough strength to reach the traitor—and how long it would take to rip out that fat throat.

"All things considered, I am glad to see you," Harlin stammered, bringing the rest of his body into the cell and closing the door behind him. "Although I'm sure you can't say the same—I certainly don't blame you."

Seb continued staring straight ahead, refusing to make eye contact with the man who had cost him everything. He had no idea what brought the traitor here tonight, but he would not give him the satisfaction of the slightest interaction.

"I didn't think I'd ever see you again," Harlin said. "I thought you were living on some island like a king, or maybe that you'd died somewhere nice and quiet. I certainly didn't expect to be in this position."

Again, Seb sat in silence, trying to make his face unreadable.

"What I really want to say is...well, I'm sorry," Harlin blew the words out. "You most certainly don't have to forgive me, but I was just a kid. I was offered all the money and glory in the world—all to let some saboteurs into the fortress in the dead of night."

"Even children understand honor," Seb croaked, unable to keep the words in.

"You're right, my age is no excuse," Harlin replied. "And I know my apology is twenty years too late—but I think that you being captured may be the best thing to ever happen to Margella since the end of the civil war."

"I'm glad you think my death will be good for the country," Seb growled.

"That's not what I meant," Harlin said, moving to sit on the floor across from Seb's cot. "I meant your return—things aren't exactly going well for the regime. There are whispers from more than a few that it's time for a change. The Lion of the Segre could turn those whispers into open rebellion."

"I don't know what you're doing, but it won't work," Seb grunted.

"Believe it or not, your name still holds a significant amount of weight—almost more than when you last set foot in Margella," Harlin said. "You're practically a legend—who else has fought off an entire regiment single-handedly?"

"If you're referring to the Battle of Hidden Pass, I had several dozen other fine soldiers," Seb replied, looking at Harling for the first time. "And I recall the 'regiment' to be only a few hundred imperial militiamen."

"Exactly," Harlin said, a smile coming across his face. "You know that, and I know that. But the people—they think you're practically a Divine."

"And Silvino hasn't squashed that perception by now?"

"He's gone to great lengths. The harder he tries, the stronger your legend grows."

"Why are you telling me this?" Seb asked, staring Harlin in the eyes. The man seemed eager, hopeful even. There wasn't deceit or anger in his face.

"As I said—things aren't exactly going well. There's famine in the south, and bread prices are through the roof. Majestic buildings of stone may be impressive, but they don't put food on the table. The economy's in complete shambles, and we're on the brink of war with Albona. More than a small group thinks it's time for the Emperor to go."

"And if I were to replace him, I'd be no better. It was by Okuta's decree that Margella be governed by a queen—something that so many seemed to have forgotten."

"Theology is beyond me," Harlin said with a smile. "All I'm saying is that you should strongly consider not just giving up—there are people in the city eagerly awaiting your return."

"Tell me, what would our good friend Admiral Ferdinand say if he heard you speaking this way?" Seb asked, the words coming out slowly.

"That man is an imperialist to the very end," Harlin replied. "But right now, he's in bed recovering from your little...exchange—could be days before he's ready to do anything."

Seb didn't respond. His own head was beginning to spin. Part of the spinning was from his attack on Ferdinand. Most of it came from this inane conversation.

"Please, just think about what I've said. I know you have every reason to not trust me, but I know you're what Margella needs. Give me the word, and I'll make sure your head never sees the chopping block once we reach Margella."

"I guess there's not much for me to lose," Seb growled. "I'm already marked for death. I'll...consider it."

"Glad to hear it," Harlin said before clapping his hands and rising to his feet. "I won't be able to visit you too often—even the common soldiers and sailors might notice. I'll make sure you get some extra rations, though. Do your best to regain some strength during the voyage."

With that, Harlin opened the cell door and disappeared. Seb fell back onto his bed, vision swimming. He closed his eyes, but the sensation remained.

"You can't possibly be considering that giant buffoon's offer," Joon said, again at Seb's side. "I don't care what he wants you to do in Margella—Aydiin and Byanca need our help. I'll have you off this ship long before you even need him."

"I have to admit, it's tempting," Seb said, letting out a deep breath. "The idea of crushing Silvino's head under my foot has sustained me for years."

"Just in time for the Undergods to come back and destroy the world," Joon said. "If I have to abandon my people to help Aydiin, I think you need to as well."

"Yeah, I know you're right," Seb said. "I can't let my thirst for vengeance overcome my real duty. Still, it hurts my soul to turn down such an opportunity..."

"I know how hard this must be for you, I really do," Joon said, placing his hand on Seb's. "Maybe you can go back and kill Silvino once this business with the Undergods is over. Seems kind of anti-climactic though."

"I have a hunch freeing Margella from Silvino would be more satisfying than even destroying the Undergods," Seb responded. "That man took everything from me. While the Raven would do the same, it wouldn't feel so personal."

"I know a thing or two about being a refugee, even though our circumstances are different. You really can't let your mind get too fixated on the thought of revenge. Even if the fate of the world weren't in the balance, it would just be damaging to your soul."

The man's words rang true, even if Seb didn't want to admit it. He felt the seconds tick by before responding.

"So, what's your plan to get out of here?"

"Not much of a plan," Joon said with a shrug. "I'll get the keys, and we'll walk out of here once the ship stops somewhere."

"Simple is good. Complicated plans have too many things that can go wrong."

"You should take Harlin's advice on one matter," Joon said, producing another apple from his sleeve and handing it to Seb. "I can practically see your bones poking through the skin. Even in Gorteo, you'd be considered malnourished."

"Maybe if I'm starved much longer, I'll be able to slip through walls without being a Lurcher."

"Let's not test that plan. Just leave the sneaking around to me," Joon said. "In no time, we'll be out of here helping Miss Byanca."

"Assuming we can even find them," Seb grunted, taking a bite of the apple. "Aydiin could be anywhere—he is looking for Great Stones, after all."

"We'll cross that bridge when we come to it," Joon said. "For now, just get some sleep. Divines know we could both use it."

13

Byanca's legs wobbled as the smell of unwashed bodies mixed with burning refuse assaulted her nose. Behind her, she could tell without looking that both Aydiin and Cael each held a cloth over their faces. As they followed Luka and Alise through one of the narrower alleyways of Palmas, the sight—and smell—of displaced humanity was everywhere.

Crammed into every nook and cranny, those unable to find real shelter had made camps where they could. The narrow alleyways already blocked the wind better than the wide boulevards, and it only required a few scraps of wood or tin to create an impromptu roof.

The few glimpses she'd had of the larger streets weren't promising either. With checkpoints spread throughout the city and random patrols, only the alleyways were safe for someone trying to come and go in secret. That was certainly different from how she'd felt only months ago.

Ahead, a group dressed in rags huddled around a burning trash can. From what her nose could pick up, wood and coal made up a minority of the flame's fuel. She'd lost track of how many such groups they'd passed since entering the city. In their week-long journey through the mud and rain, she'd seen even more desperate citizens trekking toward the capital, hoping to find the very basics for human survival.

As they approached the group, a figure broke off from the refugees. With a hooded face and pronounced limp, the figure approached without the slightest hint of fear, and Luka held up his hand to signal a halt.

"Grindel, at your service," a raspy voice whispered in the cold air, his breath creating a cloud laced with liquor. "What can I do you for on this lovely night?"

"I hear you're a man who can get things," Luka whispered.

"Depends on what you be needin'," the man replied. "A nice bottle of wine, a hot meal, some...companionship, if you know what I mean."

"We need passports to enter the city," Luka snapped, obviously not wanting to hear what the old man meant.

"Why would you be wantin' those?" the old man said with a wink. "You're already in the city."

"We need to get past the internal checkpoints," Luka sighed, his patience obviously running low. "Why else would anybody need them?"

"Well, it's your lucky night," the old man said, pulling a bundle of papers out from his coat. "I've recently had the good fortune of obtaining some."

Byanca didn't want to think about how this man had come upon the necessary papers needed to navigate through the city, nor did she want to know what he meant by companionship. She wanted nothing more than to be off the streets and in the relative safety of the Marzio home. Of course, getting there meant passing through a government checkpoint.

"I'll give you a hundred Albonan crowns for five of them," Luka said, moving to pull the necessary banknotes from his pocket. Genodran currency—just like everything else these days—was worthless on the streets. Before the chaos, that amount would be enough to feed the man for the remainder of his days.

"I can't be letting these go for less than two hundred," the man said, sliding the passports back into his coat.

"One hundred and fifty, then," Luka sighed, pulling out additional bank notes. "If you'll be wanting more, then I'll just take my business elsewhere."

"No need, no need," the man wheezed, pulling out the documents and handing them to Luka. "I know a good deal when I see one. Be careful out there tonight, my friends. A storm's comin'."

Stuffing the notes into his coat, the old man shuffled back to his fire. Byanca held in a shiver at his words, and she felt no small amount of relief as Luka led them through another side street and onto Republican Avenue.

It was hard to believe that only a few months had passed since she'd sped down this thoroughfare in her father's favorite automobile, evading agents of the Order. In the dim moonlight, she couldn't see any remnants of that day. There were no tire marks, no sign of wrecked motorized bicycles, nothing. Only the sight of miserable soldiers and refugees filled the street.

She could see Luka's posture stiffen as they reached the checkpoint. There was no good way around it to reach the Marzio home, the only place they might reasonably be safe in the city. Now was the moment they would find out if that old man was good to his word.

"Passports, please," a man called out as they approached.

Four soldiers stood outside a small building. Sandbags piled about two spans high blocked off the street, the only access controlled by a mechanical arm. Byanca found herself holding in a breath as they neared the soldiers.

"Gladly, my good man," Luka said with a smile, pulling the set of five documents from his coat. The soldier looked at each passport in the lantern light, lifting his eyes to scrutinize each of their faces in turn.

There was something familiar about the man. He was young, maybe only a year or two her senior. From somewhere, she recognized that face. As his eyes made contact with hers, they widened. Apparently, she had met this man at some point. A rush of adrenaline coursed through her veins, and she readied herself to run.

"Everything looks to be in order," the soldier said with a nod, and his eyes returned to their normal state. Byanca held in a sigh of relief as the mechanical arm flew upward, and Luka led them through.

Despite the relief coursing through her veins, Byanca couldn't shake off the feeling that the soldier had recognized her. As the group continued through the streets toward the Marzio home, Byanca couldn't help but wonder what it meant. Was the young man a republican who wanted nothing more than the destruction of Bertrand's monarchy? Perhaps he was simply a hormonal male whose gaze had found a pretty face.

As Byanca's thoughts were focused on the soldier and the task ahead of them, the group entered a wide street lined with what had recently been palatial estates. As Byanca looked around, she saw gardens either overgrown with weeds or filled with charred remnants of bushes and trees. Some of the homes themselves were little more than charred husks, while others had merely been looted for the valuable goods inside. Not a single home stood completely untouched, however.

"Home, sweet home," Luka said as they approached a stately red-brick mansion. Luckily, the Marzio family's home had been spared from the flames, and only the overgrown weeds and broken windows spoke of the recent chaos.

"I like it better this way," Alise said with a smile before pushing the wrought iron gate open, allowing the others to enter.

Luka led the group into the entrance hall, which Byanca remembered as one of the finest she'd ever seen. Now, empty walls showed the theft of priceless works of art, and shattered glass covered the floor. Down the hall, a door leading to the family's library hung on broken hinges. Byanca felt her shoulders sag at the sight.

"We'll have this place back to its former glory in no time," Luka said. "I've always wanted to have a say in how the place looked. With Mother gone, I'll finally have the chance."

"Where are your parents, Luka?" Byanca asked, afraid to hear the answer.

"They were on holiday in Lusita, fortunately," Luka responded, his eyes still surveying the scene. "I received a letter from them a few weeks ago. They'll just stay there until things settle down on the home front."

"We'll need to hire some staff to get this taken care of," Alise said, shrugging at where to start. "Luckily, there are literally thousands of people outside who would love a job."

"You know we can't do that," Luka chided his sister with a smile as the group headed toward the home's library. "We can't let it be known that we're here. The house isn't in great shape, but it's at least out of the elements. That will have to be enough for now."

The group shuffled into the once-immaculate library that Byanca remembered as a safe-haven during balls held at the Marzio residence. The room had been filled with bookshelves and tasteful oil paintings with plenty of comfortable chairs. Now, however, the windows were shattered, the sofas were crushed, and books sat strewn across the floor along with broken glass.

"It's so hard to see the city like this," Byanca said as her eyes drank in the scene.

"We'll make it right," Luka replied as he moved over to the library's wet bar. The bottles of liquor were gone, either stolen or smashed. The young man began whistling as he found a glass and blew the dust out of it. Bending down, he popped back up with a dusty bottle of wine.

"Luka always liked to hide the good stuff," Alise explained as she moved over to join her brother.

"I think we all deserve a drink," Luka said, finding other glasses that had survived the looting. "Even you, Cael. You're a man now, in my book."

"Now that we're finally here, we need to figure out our next move," Aydiin said, accepting a glass from Luka.

"Ideally, we need to figure out all of our moves," Alise said. "Don't they have chess in Salatia? Thinking only one move ahead ends up in a check-mate far too quickly."

"We need to gather enough information so that we can figure out our next five moves," Byanca broke in. "Trying to make plans with almost no data is foolish, at best."

"Luka, do you still have any contacts within the city?" Aydiin asked.

"I'll have to ask around in the morning," Luka said, downing the last of his wine. "My main concern is that the only nobility left in the city are those loyal to the new regime."

"While you're at it, we should start probing to find out how strong republican sentiment is here," Byanca responded, thinking of the soldier at the checkpoint who had obviously recognized her. He'd said nothing, yet she didn't know what exactly motivated his silence.

"I thought getting into the city was going to be difficult," Alise said, plopping down onto one of the least-dilapidated armchairs. "But this is starting to sound impossible."

"On top of everything else, we have to keep our presence a secret," Byanca added. "If Bertrand knows we're here, I don't think he'll hesitate to kill us. Even you, Luka. I'd be surprised if news of your forces taking out an entire regiment hasn't reached his ears by now."

"Do you really think so?" Luka asked. "His anger at me, I can understand. You, however, have always had a special place in his heart. I was rather hoping we'd be able to take advantage of those feelings."

"Luka, just because you've always wanted to marry for love doesn't mean that others feel the same way," Byanca responded. "Trust me—Bertrand's only feelings for me were greed and a lust for power. Now that I can't satisfy either of those base desires, he's much more likely to have me executed than anything else."

"I think you're all forgetting something," Cael broke in, his glass of wine sitting untouched in his hand. "We keep talking about Bertrand as if he's some supernatural being. Why can't Aydiin and I just run to his palace right now and end this?"

"It's not that simple," Byanca replied, shaking her head. "If you just kill Bertrand, it will create a power vacuum."

"Quite right," Aydiin said, placing his hand on Cael's shoulder. "I appreciate your enthusiasm, but Bertrand's premature death could actually be terrible for the city. Shaky as it is, that boy's hold on power is the only thing keeping Palmas from ripping itself apart. I think the worst possible scenario would be Bertrand's death before we have a solid plan ready to go."

A knock sounded on the front door, and Byanca's entire body went cold. Luka's eye went wide, as did Cael's. She looked over to see Aydiin's mouth hanging open. The only person who seemed unaffected was Alise—her eyes were closed, and her breathing pattern said she'd already fallen asleep, curled up in a broken and dirty armchair.

The knock sounded again.

"Who could know we're here?" Luka asked.

"Nobody," Aydiin said. "I thought we were very careful on our way in."

"Well, Luka, you're the man of the house," Byanca said. "You'd best answer the door."

Luka's face was white, and his footsteps cracked on the wood floor as he left the room. Byanca listened to the sound of the front door opening, although no words reached her ears. After a moment, the door closed, and she could hear Luka's footsteps echoing on the walls as he entered the library...alone.

"That was a royal courier," Luka said, his face even whiter than before. Within his hands, he clutched a small envelope. He handed Byanca the paper, and she turned it over in her hands.

It was addressed to her.

Byanca's fingers trembled as she opened the letter. Her eyes had a hard time focusing in the dim lantern light.

My Dearest Byanca,

I was so pleased to hear of your return to Palmas—our country needs your strong and reassuring presence during such uncertain times. There will be a

ball at my humble residence tomorrow evening, to which, you are cordially invited. Bring that Salatian brute if you so desire.
  With Love,

King Bertrand of Genodra
Byanca paled and her head began to spin.
"Well, so much for secrecy," she sighed.

14

"Why are we doing this again?" Aydiin asked Byanca as their limousine rumbled through the streets of Palmas. "We can't even be sure this thing is taking us to the ball. We might be headed to our death."

"How is that different than every other day?" Byanca asked, raising her brow as she turned to look him in the eyes. "Aydiin, we've discussed this. Everything's out on the table now—if Bertrand wanted us killed, he could have already done so."

Aydiin didn't respond. He'd spent the entire morning fighting against their attendance, to no avail. Both Luka and Byanca thought their presence at King Bertrand's ball was, if not essential, at least a good idea. The argument that it would be good to show both Bertrand and the city's remaining aristocracy that they weren't afraid. With Cael and Alise abstaining, Aydiin had been outvoted. Sometimes, he wasn't sure he liked democracy.

Despite his frustration, Aydiin couldn't help but admire his wife. For the first time in months, her hair was professionally done up, and she wore a fine black dress. He scooted closer, placing his arm around her. She smelled of soap and a light perfume, and he had to stop himself from going further.

"I'm sorry," he whispered. "I'm just nervous."

"Would you be less nervous if we weren't headed to a ball?" Byanca asked, a smile coming across her face.

"You know how I feel about dancing. Maybe Bertrand knows too, and he's planning on sweeping you off your feet on the dance floor tonight."

"You, my dear husband, are a fabulous dancer," Byanca said, snuggling into his chest as the vehicle began to slow. "Don't think of tonight as our final battle with Bertrand. It's more of an opening skirmish."

Aydiin hoped she was right. It was certainly true that Bertrand could have easily sent a group of soldiers with guns instead of a courier with an invitation. If this were a trap, it was certainly an unnecessary one.

The limo came to a stop, and Aydiin was pleased to see that their driver had actually taken them to their stated destination. Byanca lifted her head from his chest, and they both peered out the window.

The Alfonzo mansion—Bertrand hadn't moved into the Doge's Palace for obvious political reasons—was well maintained. In fact, there was little evidence of the turbulence that had engulfed the city. If one were to only see the mansion and its immaculate grounds, it would be easy to forget the thousands of people camping in the streets with little to eat.

The crowd walking into the ballroom was significantly smaller than the one Aydiin had seen months ago. From what Luka's contacts had told them, a solid majority of the city's nobility hadn't yet returned. However, the fact that there were still several hundred people congregating tonight in spite of all the troubles spoke volumes about Genodran high society.

Aydiin's father never held balls—occasionally, he would throw a small feast, but they were rather subdued affairs. Genodrans, on the other hand, loved their parties. Providing the nobility with their customary form of entertainment was certainly a cunning move on Bertrand's part.

Their driver exited the vehicle and opened the door. Aydiin stumbled out of his seat and took Byanca's hand as she made a much more graceful exit. He offered his arm, which she took with a smile, and the young couple began crossing the lawn to the mansion's entrance.

As they drew closer, Aydiin tried to focus on the path forward and not on the stares of those also entering the ball. He focused on the sound of music emanating from within and not on the whispers behind cupped hands. This night would most certainly not resemble their previous ball.

As they entered the Alfonzo mansion's great hall, Aydiin's ears began to pick up the dull hum of conversation mixed with the sound of a small string orchestra. His eyes caught the sight of a dozen small clumps of aristocrats standing around, drinks in hand as they enjoyed their conversations. He didn't know which would be worse—dying from an assassin or from the terribly dull verbal exchanges.

Aydiin spotted Bertrand at the opposite side of the hall, surrounded by a small crowd. He had the same blond hair, slicked straight back with enough oil to keep a lamp burning for an entire evening. His face still looked like it belonged to a teenager, although there was a weariness that hadn't been present before.

The crowd surrounding him consisted of nothing but sycophantic nobility. A woman hung on each arm. Both wore dresses that showed more than enough skin as they shot glares sharp as daggers at the other. A man with dark brown hair, also slicked back to imitate his king, lit a cigar and placed it in the monarch's mouth.

"I suddenly remembered why I never wanted to become Sultan," Aydiin whispered, gesturing to the far end of the room as Byanca led him into the party.

"That's supposedly why we did away with the monarchy in the first place," Byanca whispered back.

They approached the nearest group of couples, about ten older lords and ladies with glasses of champagne clutched in their hands. Without exception, they looked to be a few decades older than Aydiin and Byanca, which was probably for the best. Most of the younger guests were currently attending to Bertrand.

"Madam Byanca," a white-haired gentleman said with a bow. "I can't fully express how good it is to see you."

"Thank you, Lord Renault," Byanca replied with a curtsy. "It is a pleasure being back in Palmas."

"I haven't yet been able to express my condolences," a woman—presumably Lady Renault from her gown and jewelry—said. "I can only imagine how difficult this must be for your mother."

Aydiin's eyes widened at the words but quickly regained control. It was only logical that everyone would assume Marcino's absence to mean his death. Nobody would believe that he had been kidnapped by a mythical secret society.

"Thank you, Cora," Byanca replied. "My family is dealing with the pain as best we can. For now, the best thing I can do is lose myself in service to my country."

"May I inquire as to what has brought you back to Palmas?" Lord Renault asked. Aydiin could hear the tension in his voice.

"To help, of course," Byanca responded. "There is so much suffering here. I won't let it be said that House Cavour sat idly by during our darkest hour."

"Yes, it is a shame," Lady Renault—Cora, as Byanca had called her—said, shaking her head. "I know King Bertrand is doing his best to help the masses. We'll just have to do what we can and hope for the best come spring."

Others nodded, and the conversation moved to more benign topics. Of course, Aydiin could guess the real question they were dying to ask: how are you going to overthrow this prepubescent excuse for a ruler? Of course, he wouldn't know how to answer even if they did have the courage to ask.

Instead, Aydiin forced himself to feign interest in Lord Renault's discussion over the lack of good tobacco. After an eternity of nodding his head and agreeing, the music began to change. Aydiin looked around to see dinner being brought to the tables by a horde of servants.

"Madam Byanca," a white tuxedo-clad servant droned. "Please, allow me to accompany you and Prince Aydiin to your table."

Without another word, Byanca took Aydiin's arm and the two followed the man across the room to a small table, separated from the others. There were place settings for three, but Aydiin didn't see anyone else approaching.

"With whom are we dining tonight?" Byanca asked as the servant helped her into the chair.

"Tonight, we will be serving a delectable chicken breast with a red sauce on a bed of noodles," the servant said, ignoring Byanca's question as a young woman brought three steaming plates.

"Bertrand obviously doesn't want us mixing, does he?" Aydiin said as the servants left.

"Of course not," Byanca responded. "I wouldn't expect anything less. I am interested in who will be joining us, though."

"Maybe it's just to keep us guessing," Aydiin said, poking at the chicken and spreading around the pasta. He wanted to make it look as if he'd eaten some of the food without actually running the risk of consuming the poison he suspected to be within. Memories of men falling dead at his father's dinner table were still too fresh in his mind.

Byanca grabbed her fork and took a delicate bite of pasta, showing she was not afraid to eat. Aydiin didn't know what to say as the low hum of conversation grew quieter, the food occupying a majority of the mouths in the room.

"Prince Aydiin, this is for you," another white-clad servant droned, leaving a note on Aydiin's table. Without a word, he disappeared, and Aydiin unrolled the small piece of paper.

Don't be afraid to eat. I promise I won't poison you—that would spoil all the fun.

Aydiin's eyes shot up toward Bertrand's table. The young king said something, and his crowd of admirers burst into laughter. There was no indication that he'd even noticed Aydiin's presence, let alone been observant enough to send a note.

"I don't like this," Aydiin said, skewering a piece of chicken on his fork and shoving it into his mouth.

"Neither do I," Byanca said. "The food's not even good."

"We're doing the best with what we have," a booming voice sounded from behind, and Aydiin jumped as an aging gentleman dressed in grey took a seat across the table.

The man's face was dark from years spent in the sun, and his jet-black hair was covered by a bicorn hat. His grey jacket was no simple tuxedo—it was a military uniform. With the gold braid on his shoulders and a chest covered in medals, Aydiin had little difficulty guessing the identity of their dinner companion.

"It's an honor, Field Marshal," Aydiin said with a nod. It was hard to believe that the cause of Genodra's current problems had just sat down across from him at dinner.

"Oh no, the honor is all mine," Diaz replied, grabbing a fork and digging into the pasta. "I've been looking forward to meeting you for quite some time."

For a moment, Diaz ignored the couple as he stuffed chicken and pasta into his mouth. Aydiin couldn't tell if the man really was oblivious, or if this were some sort of game. Either way, he wanted to be gone from the Field Marshal's presence sooner rather than later.

"I really must thank you for your service to Genodra," Byanca said, her voice betraying the discomfort she felt. "Your reputation precedes you."

"As does yours," Diaz replied, his mouth full of pasta. "I count myself lucky to have secured a spot at your table this evening. Our young king is too generous."

"Yes, his hospitality is impressive," Byanca said. "The cost of such an evening must be tremendous considering the enormous amount of suffering in the city."

"Oh, I almost forgot," Diaz said, taking a sip of his wine and ignoring Byanca's less-than-subtle criticism. "I'm supposed to tell you that your presence is requested by the illustrious King Bertrand in his private study."

Aydiin's eyes shot toward the head table to see two surly young women sitting alone, the object of their attention conspicuously absent. The other young men and woman surrounding the king had abandoned the table and were presumably now spread throughout the party.

"Well, I'm currently eating dinner with my husband and Genodra's finest military commander," Byanca replied. "He'll have to wait."

"He thought you might say this," Diaz said, a smile spreading across his face. "And I must tell you that this would be a most unwise course of action. His Majesty does not wish you any harm, but he will not tolerate disobedience."

"I most certainly wouldn't want to do anything...unwise," Byanca said, lowering her brow.

"Excellent," Diaz said, waving a servant over to the table. "Edward here will make sure you arrive safely for your appointment."

Aydiin rose to his feet along with his wife and set down his napkin. He wasn't about to let Byanca face this alone.

"Ah, Prince Aydiin," Diaz said, motioning for Aydiin to sit down. "I thought it was clear that Bertrand wishes to see Madam Byanca alone."

"Of course," Aydiin muttered, heart beginning to pound as he returned to his seat. Byanca raised her brow as she turned away from the table. His eyes followed Byanca as she crossed the room and disappeared into a small alcove. For what felt like an eternity, Aydiin sat in silence, wondering what would become of the woman he loved as the sound of Diaz's chewing filled his ears.

"I really can't express the pleasure of finally meeting you in person," Diaz finally said, interrupting Aydiin's vigil.

"The pleasure is all mine," Aydiin lied, turning back to face the Field Marshal. "I've been told you're responsible for the peace that Palmas currently enjoys."

"Well, I can't be given all the credit," Diaz laughed, stuffing a roll into his mouth. "The twenty thousand men I have camped south of the city sure help. Say, you should come for a visit sometime. I'd love to have a foreign military leader inspect my troops. They need something to shake up their boredom."

"I can assure you, I'm no military leader," Aydiin said, shaking his head.

"But your title is Prince-General, is it not?"

"I led one campaign against a band of brigands, yes. That doesn't make me a military leader."

"Oh, I appreciate an honest and self-deprecating man," Diaz laughed, and a few small chunks of bread flew from his mouth. "Still, you absolutely must inspect our camp. His Majesty is planning a trip for tomorrow afternoon. I'll let his steward know you will be joining him."

"Oh no, I really must decline," Aydiin said.

"You know, Aydiin," Diaz began, swallowing the food in his mouth as his face grew serious. "I've been wanting to thank you. My predecessor was so stuck in his ways. Your genius in removing him from the picture was really quite astounding."

Aydiin's blood ran cold at the veiled words. Was he referring to Marcino as the leader of Genodra? Or was Diaz confessing that he was now the Grand Master of the Order?

"Oh, you don't have to worry about your safety," Diaz said, a smile returning to his face at Aydiin's silence. "My worldview is almost the polar opposite of the late Mr. Fortescue's, and I have little desire to see any harm come to you. You're much more useful as a pet than a corpse."

"I'd rather be neither," Aydiin whispered.

"Well, I'm afraid that's quite impossible," Diaz said with a chuckle before taking another bite of his roll. "In time, you'll find that being under my guidance isn't so bad. However, I can't speak for a mutual friend of ours. I believe you two met near the village of Monterosso."

"What do you want with me?" Aydiin asked, lowering his voice and leaning in.

"Why, you're going to help me rule the world, of course," Diaz said. "You might have to face some punishment first—Skraa certainly has a bone to pick with you."

Skraa? So, the immortal officer had a name. It was somehow familiar, just like the mans' face. He still couldn't figure out how he knew the man, but he had the feeling it had something to do with the memories that didn't belong to him.

"Do you know what you're dealing with here?" Aydiin asked. "I blew a hole in that man's head, and he survived it."

"Oh, I know very well what I've gotten myself into," Diaz replied, waving his hand. "You are the one who has no idea what you are about to face. I must say that I'm rather excited to see what you come up with next."

Aydiin tried not to let out a sigh. Before he could answer, something crashed into a table across the hall. A woman let out a high-pitched wail. She was joined by others, and pandemonium broke out.

Byanca let out a slow breath as the aging servant led her up a narrow spiral staircase. Keeping her eyes peeled for some sort of surprise, she began focusing on the conversation ahead. She would never admit it to Aydiin, but she was rather excited for the verbal skirmish.

"His Majesty is most anxious to see you," the white-haired butler said as they reached the top of the stairs and walked out into a wide hallway filled with marble sculptures. At the far end sat the door to Bertrand's study—a place she had the misfortune of already knowing too well. Far too many evenings had been spent there while Bertrand and his friends smoked pipes and discussed bad literature.

Without knocking, the butler opened the door, and Byanca saw the oily-haired tyrant sitting at his desk. For a moment, Bertrand didn't seem to notice their presence, and he sat hunched over, staring at a paper.

A grey-clad army officer sat in one of the room's overstuffed arm-chairs, a pipe in one hand and a glass of wine in the other. There was a nervous expression on his weathered face, and his wispy grey hair certainly seemed as if it had seen better days.

The servant let out a small cough, and Bertrand jumped in his chair. He turned around, a scowl on his face. As his eyes met Byanca's, it was replaced by a smile.

"Ah, Byanca," Bertrand said, rising to his feet and giving the woman a bow. "Thank you for gracing my humble home with your presence."

"Your Majesty is too kind," Byanca responded with a curtsy. "I must thank you for your hospitality this evening."

Byanca forced the words out as she looked around the room. While the study was largely the same as she remembered—bookshelves lined one of the walls, two armchairs huddled around a fireplace, and a few grotesque animal heads hung on the wall—there were a few stark differences.

Where Bertrand's desk had once stood empty, a sign that he didn't have any real work to do, a stack of papers stood nearly a span tall. Perhaps the young king was actually taking his duties seriously, after all. However, most striking of all was the absence of an entire wall.

The far wall was now open to the ballroom below—only a wooden banister separated the two spaces. She'd never thought about the study's location in relation to the ballroom, but apparently, Bertrand had. The intimate study was now more of a private balcony.

"I like what you've done with the place," Byanca said, gesturing to the open wall.

"Oh yes, it gives the whole room a sense of freedom," Bertrand said.

Byanca didn't mention that it also made her feel more secure, know-ing if she let out a scream, Aydiin would hear her in the hall below. She hoped it wouldn't come to that.

"Thank you, Alonzo," Bertrand said, dismissing the aging servant.

"Let me introduce you to Colonel Russo, of the Twelfth Regiment," Bertrand said, gesturing to the man sitting in the chair. "He was just leaving, weren't you, Colonel?"

"It's a pleasure," the old man said with a nod to Byanca. He turned his eyes back to Bertrand, remaining seated.

"The Colonel has just been telling me how the entirety of his regiment was wiped out during an expedition into the north," Bertrand sighed. "These are difficult times, and we can't afford such losses."

"The blame rests with that...man," Russo huffed, taking a sip of his wine.

"I'll talk with the Field Marshal about him," Bertrand said, moving over to the chair and lifting the old colonel to his feet. "I promise."

"This is a matter of national security," the old soldier huffed, his eyes growing wide as Bertrand pushed him toward the door. "I cannot see how a meeting with your mistress can be of more importance."

"I already said it will be taken care of," Bertrand said, grunting as he pushed the old man toward the door.

"Alright, there is no need for further physical force," the officer said, pushing his king off him and straightening his uniform. "I wish you a good night, Your Majesty. I will be by in the morning."

With that, Colonel Russo opened the door and—with a glare at Byanca—exited the study. Byanca watched the man leave, upset at not only being mistaken for Bertrand's mistress but also at being left alone with the man. She opened her mouth to also beat a quick exit.

"That was—"

"Oh, how I've missed you," Bertrand cut her off, rushing to sweep Byanca up in an embrace. She stood motionless, the man's arms wrapped around her chest and oily hair pushing against her cheek.

"Wait, what?" Byanca stammered, pushing the blond mass of hair away from her face.

"It's been so hard, not knowing where you were," Bertrand said, lifting his face to stare into her eyes. "I didn't know if you were even alive. It's been dreadful."

"Why—how—"

"You can only imagine my relief when I heard that not only were you alive and well, but that you'd returned to the city."

"When—"

"Of course, I've been worried about what this meant for our future," he said, moving out of his embrace and pulling away to look at her. "But when my spies awoke me last night with the most joyous news, that's when I knew."

"Knew what?" Byanca finally managed to say.

"That you returned for me," Bertrand said, tears coming to his eyes. "That you really do love me."

"You think I returned for *you*?" Byanca gasped, pushing his hands away from her.

"Of course," Bertrand smiled, placing a hand to his forehead and moving over to one of the chairs. "Byanca, you have no idea what I've been through for you."

"Based on those two young ladies dangling on your arm tonight, I think I might have some idea," Byanca said, remaining on her feet.

"Oh, they're just for show," Bertrand said, waving his hand. "They were a 'gift' from the Field Marshal to keep me...compliant."

"Compliant?" Byanca asked.

"Diaz thinks he can control me," Bertrand said, pounding his head against the back of the soft chair. "He wants me to be his little puppet, just because he controls that blasted army."

"Men with guns can be quite persuasive," Byanca said, moving to sit down in the chair opposite Bertrand. Perhaps she had just found an ally—an insane one, but an ally, nonetheless.

"Yes, yes they can," Bertrand said, looking up at her with a smile. "But now that you're here, we can cut my strings. With you by my side, we'll be able to truly rule Genodra."

"Well, I'm already marr—"

"It's okay, my love," he said, leaning forward in his chair. "You don't have to be afraid of that Salatian barbarian down there anymore. I'll protect you from him."

"Protect me?" she asked, unsure of where this was going.

"I was so distraught when your father arranged that blasted marriage," Bertrand said as he leapt to his feet and ran to the fireplace. With a quiet wail, he placed his head against the mantle.

For a moment, he stood, hiding his face in his arm. Byanca looked around the room, unsure of how to respond. With a gasp, Bertrand lifted his head, a smile on his face.

"But your father is no longer the Doge," he said, leaving the mantle and walking back over to Byanca. "We can finally follow our hearts!"

"Follow our hearts?" Byanca said, her eyebrow raised.

"Yes, and I don't see why we have to spend any time apart," Bertrand continued, grabbing Byanca by the hands and lifting her up. "We were already practically engaged, so no one will think it strange that we marry soon. You're going to love being my queen."

"First, I'm already married," Byanca said, ripping her hands from his grasp and forcing the words out before he could interrupt her. "Second, we were never 'practically engaged,' and third, I love my husband very much."

Bertrand's face fell.

"Surely, you don't mean that," he stammered. "What we have is special. A love this strong only comes along once every thousand years!"

"I don't know what's gotten into you, but we never loved each other," Byanca responded, inching toward the door. "Now, if you want help in taking care of Diaz, I'm willing to talk. However, let's leave behind this nonsense of me being your queen."

"You can't be serious, my love," Bertrand said, his face falling even further.

"I am," Byanca responded. "Now, if you'll excuse me, I'll be leaving now so you can take a moment to compose yourself."

Byanca moved toward the door, her hands beginning to shake. She still had no idea what had happened, and she wanted more than anything to speak with Aydiin.

"You are not excused from the presence of your king," Bertrand said, interrupting her flight and pulling a rather large and ornate knife from the desk. "I wanted you to be my queen willingly, but if that's not an option..."

Byanca turned as Bertrand lunged, his arms grabbing her by the waist and his weight bringing them both to the ground. Her head hit the wood floor with a thud, and her vision began to swim. Bertrand crawled up her body, bringing his face close her own.

"We could have done so much together," he hissed, bringing the knife up. "Why would you throw that away?"

Byanca rammed her forehead into his nose, and Bertrand dropped the knife as blood spurted into his hands. With a shove, Byanca rolled out from underneath the tyrant and scrambled toward the door.

A sticky hand grabbed her by the ankle, and she fell back to the ground. With her free foot, she launched a kick at Bertrand's head, and he let go with a howl of pain. She ran to the door and twisted the handle.

It was locked from the outside.

As she stared at the locked door, Bertrand lunged for her again. With a twist, she caught his wrist as the steel pressed into her chest. With a growl, Bertrand pushed her to the side, and she caught herself on the banister separating the office from the ballroom below.

The young tyrant slammed his body into hers, bringing the knife up. Byanca grunted as her back slammed into the hardwood of the banister, and she brought her hands up, again catching Bertrand's wrist before he could connect steel to skin. She willed her throat to scream, to do anything useful. Only a small gurgling noise resulted.

As they struggled, her eyes locked onto Bertrand's. Those orbs displayed only madness—madness and a determination to see her blood shed.

"You were supposed to save me," he whispered as he pushed the knife closer to her throat. "You were supposed to free me from this darkness."

Bertrand's superior strength was slowly pushing the knife closer to her throat. The steel made contact with her skin, and she could tell that it would soon draw blood. Tears sprang to her eyes at the thought of her life ending this way. Then an idea appeared in her mind's eye.

Byanca let herself fall backward, using the banister as a fulcrum. Her leg went into Bertrand's crotch, lifting him skyward as her body rotated in a backward arc. With the bulk of his strength pushing forward, Bertrand flew off the balcony.

As she completed the backward motion, Byanca's hands caught hold of the banister. Behind, she heard Bertrand plummet toward the party below.

15

A combination of footsteps and sunlight awoke Byanca from her uneasy sleep, and she lifted herself up onto her elbow. Squinting against the light streaming in through the barred window, she winced as her aching muscles groaned. She could have slept more comfortably on frozen dirt.

"I shouldn't really be surprised," she muttered.

She had, after all, spent the night in a jail cell.

As consciousness took hold of her brain, the events from the previous night came flooding back. She could almost feel the rush of fear and adrenaline, could smell Bertrand's hot, moist breath on her cheek. A shiver overcame her entire body as she remembered the look of pure madness in the late king's eyes.

She'd allowed an entire squadron of police officers to escort her out of Bertrand's mansion—running away hadn't even occurred to her at the time—ignoring the shouts from the confused aristocrats and furious protests from Aydiin. She hadn't said a word as the police stuffed her into the back of a vehicle and checked her into jail.

Well, this certainly isn't ideal, she thought. She had been alone with the king when he fell from the balcony. While she hadn't exactly pushed him, it was because of her that Bertrand was dead. Of course, it had been in self-defense, but she wasn't sure if that argument would save her.

She brushed off the thoughts and let her eyes take in her surroundings. Her cell was made entirely of iron bars—no privacy was given. Luckily, she seemed to be the only occupant at the moment. The police were probably too busy or scared to actually make many arrests these days.

The footsteps that had awoken her drew nearer, mixed with muffled conversation. One of the voices lifted her heart.

"Aydiin," she called out, her voice much hoarser than she had expected. The footsteps picked up, and the face of her beloved prince appeared from around a corner.

"Well, there's our little troublemaker," Aydiin said, flanked on either side by a set of police officers. Despite his laugh, there was concern in those beautiful eyes. Yet just the sight of her husband launched a wave of relief that flooded through her entire being.

"We'll be right outside," one of the officers said to Aydiin, lifting an eyebrow as he spoke. The man's message was clear: you have privacy, but don't try anything stupid. "Just holler when you're done."

"Yes, sir," Aydiin said, nodding his head. As the footsteps faded away, Byanca rose to her feet and rushed toward the bars. Aydiin pressed his head against the iron and slipped his arm through the gaps. With tears in her eyes, Byanca grabbed the man's hand and pressed it to her face.

"What happened last night?" he asked.

"Well, remember how I said Bertrand only wanted to marry me for wealth and prestige? I turned out to be...not exactly correct."

"Is that how you admit to being wrong?" Aydiin asked, a smile spreading across his face. Byanca only smiled in response.

"Well, of course you were," Aydiin said. "How could anyone not want to marry you?"

"How was I supposed to know?" Byanca almost shouted, her voice raw. "When I told him that I didn't want to be his queen, he came at me with a knife and, well...I sort of knocked him off the balcony."

"I guessed that much, seeing as how his body came crashing down onto some poor woman's table. I'm just glad to know you didn't do it on purpose."

"Aydiin, it was on purpose. I had no choice. The man was trying to kill me."

"Right, I meant that I'm glad it wasn't done in cold blood. I knew you weren't capable of that."

"What are people saying?" Byanca asked, and her eyes widened. "Genodra hasn't had a king for a while, but I'm fairly sure that regicide is punishable by death."

"There are definitely those who want to see you hanged," Aydiin said, his eyes darting toward the window. "But there are even more who want to see you leave this cell before the sun's fully risen."

"Which side is going to win?"

"Well, right now, there are thousands of people outside this prison demanding your release. I'm not sure if you know this, but you're a very popular public figure."

"I'm safe," Byanca sighed. "Well, for the time being, at least."

"That's a pretty good bet. The city's mostly calm, but if word leaked of your execution, there would be riots."

"How long before Diaz just does it anyway?" Byanca asked.

"The Field Marshal has actually been rather magnanimous through all of this," Aydiin said. "He's been fighting almost as much as I have for your release. He's even withdrawn all of his men to their winter quarters outside the city—surprising for someone who practically confessed to me that he's now in charge of the Order."

"He what?" Byanca yelped, her eyes growing wide.

"We had the most interesting conversation after you left. Instead of trying to kill us, he simply wants to turn us into puppets. Something tells me that his withdrawal from the city is part of some grand strategy."

"If he's gone, who's in charge of Palmas?" Byanca asked.

"Actually, Lord Renault and several others have taken control of the city's garrison and reinstated the Republic. They've formed some sort of interim government, and elections for the Senate are to be held next week."

"That's fantastic," Byanca shrieked. "Why didn't you lead off with that?"

"I just wanted to make you sweat a little bit," Aydiin said. "Also, I've been sent on their behalf. Byanca, you've been selected to be the 'interim president' of Genodra."

Byanca's mouth dropped open at the words.

"What does that even mean?" she stammered.

"I haven't the slightest idea," Aydiin said with a laugh before summoning a thin stream of water from the air and slamming it into the lock. "They just sent me to get you out of here. Unfortunately, the officers at this particular jail haven't declared their loyalty to the interim government yet, so we'll just need to...make them see reason."

As he finished, Byanca could hear something within the cell's lock snap, and the door swung open.

"Do you mean by forcing them to decide between letting me go and facing that mob out there?" Byanca asked, breathing a sigh of relief as she left the cell.

"Exactly, Madam President," Aydiin said with a smile.

"Hopefully that title won't last," Byanca said. "When will the new Doge be elected?"

"About two weeks after the senatorial elections," Aydiin said. "That's how it works, right? The Senate votes for the Doge? Representative government is messy."

"You're right...on both counts," Byanca said as her mind began to spin. "We need to get going—I don't have much time to gather support."

"Byanca," Aydiin said, grabbing her by the shoulders as she tried to run off. "Don't go down that path. We came here to restore the Republic, which we've done. I know we still need to deal with Skraa and Diaz, but I have a feeling I'm not powerful enough yet to do that. Once the new government is set up, I was thinking we would slip away."

"I can't abandon my country at a time like this," Byanca said, throwing Aydiin's hands off her shoulders. "We'll find a way to defeat Diaz and Skraa—we can't just run away from them forever."

"I know that," Aydiin said, folding his arms and leaning against the cell's bars. "However, if you're elected Doge, I'm afraid your strings would be rather short. We need to be able to disappear for a while, get out of the public eye while we figure out exactly how to defeat the Order."

"That will be difficult to do if we leave Diaz ruling the country," Byanca said, moving again toward the hallway. "He'd have almost unlimited resources to hunt us down. There's too much to do and too little time."

"I agree that we need to save the Republic from Diaz, but I need you to promise me something," Aydiin said, again grabbing Byanca by the shoulders. His big, beautiful brown eyes stared into hers. "Promise me that you won't try to become the Doge. Find someone else that will be able to do the job. There's so much more at stake here than just Genodra, and I need you by my side."

Byanca's mouth dropped open at the request, and she couldn't stop staring at her husband. How could he not see that this was her home? How could he not see that her duty was to her people? She couldn't just leave them to be governed by just anybody at such a critical time.

"I guess I'm not looking at the whole picture," Byanca said, the realization hitting home as the words left her mouth.

"I care about Genodra, too," Aydiin said. "But staying here any longer than we have to could result in the end of the world."

"You're right," she said, wiping a tear that had come to her eye. "I've gotten a little too caught up in the love of my nation."

"It's okay," Aydiin said, a soft smile brightening his countenance. "That's not necessarily a bad thing, but right now, we need to focus on finding the other Great Stones. If we don't, then the world doesn't stand a chance, and suddenly it won't matter who the Doge is."

"Oh, I'm so sorry," she said as tears began flowing from her eyes, and she pressed her face into Aydiin's chest.

"Don't be sorry," Aydiin said, embracing her. "Just promise me that we can go underground and start searching for the other Great Stones when you get this situation settled."

"Yes, the moment a new Doge is elected, we can be on our way—assuming we can wriggle free of the Field Marshal's grasp."

"Thank you," Aydiin said, lifting her face to look into his eyes. "I know how much Genodra means to you. As for Diaz, I'll figure out something."

"I know this has been hard for you," she responded, wiping tears from her eyes and regaining her composure. She couldn't afford to be emotional for too long.

"Guards," she called out for the two officers who were waiting in the hallway. They came in, eyebrows raised and eyes wide at the sight of their prisoner standing outside the open cell. "Please bring me my things. I have a government to lead, and I can't afford to waste any more time in here."

Without waiting for a response from the officers, Byanca grabbed Aydiin's hand and strode out into the hall. For a moment, she heard only silence behind her.

"Well, what are you waiting for?" she snapped at the guards, without looking back. "Let's get going."

For a long moment, she strode down the hall with confidence she didn't really possess. At any moment, she could feel a bullet in her back or at least hear the pounding of footsteps before she was tackled to the ground. After a moment, she did hear their footsteps pick up, but they were the slow, methodical steps of two men walking despite their confusion.

As she reached the jail's exit, Aydiin rushed to hold the door open for her. With a kiss on the cheek, Byanca stepped out into the fresh morning air. The sun was already warm, doing its best to usher in spring. A cold breeze did its best to fight back, showing that winter was nowhere near ready to relinquish its grip on the land.

A cheer erupted as she emerged onto the steps leading down to the street, and she squinted in the bright sunlight. Aydiin had told her of a large crowd gathered outside, but the sight that met her eyes was far beyond her imagination.

Packed with refugees in tattered rags and factory workers in grime-covered smocks, the street was essentially closed to all traffic. The crowd extended beyond her sight into other nearby streets and alleys. Many held rough wooden signs saying "Free Byanca" or "Long Live the Republic" in rough charcoal or paint. A smile crept onto her face at the near-deafening cheers from the crowd. She lifted her hand to wave, and the cheers grew into a roar.

"You made the right choice," Byanca said to the pair of guards now standing at her side. Aydiin grabbed her hand and led her down the steps to a waiting car. He opened a door for her, and she climbed in.

Looks like I'm not going to find myself at the end of a rope, she thought, continuing to wave at the crowd through the car window. *At least, not today.*

The car took off, and she settled into the comfortable leather seat. With a deep sigh, she let her head fall back. Without a doubt, she was going to need a long nap when this was all over.

"Wow sis, you look terrible," a voice said from the driver seat, and Byanca lifted her head to see Cael. The young man was dressed in the uniform of a chauffeur, complete with black coat and top hat.

"What are you doing?" she asked, the words coming out like an obese gentleman sitting on an accordion.

"Aydiin still doesn't know how to drive," Cael said with a shrug, and the Salatian prince gave her a sheepish grin. "So, until further notice, I'm the family chauffeur."

"Alright then," she said, settling back into her seat. "Just don't kill anybody, okay?"

She closed her eyes and allowed her thoughts to wander, content to just bask in the low rumble of the engine. As the car jostled its way through the streets, she could almost fall asleep. Almost.

A thought popped into her mind, and her eyes shot open.

"Cael," she called out to her brother. "Let's make a quick stop at the Palace. There's something I want to see."

"The Council of Ministers is waiting for you," Aydiin said, sitting up and turning to face her.

"The what?" she asked, turning to look her husband in the face.

"It's what Lord Renault and the others are calling themselves. They're meant to advise the president. Something tells me they're looking to retain some sort of power even after the Senate is put back into place."

"They can wait," Byanca said, the energy returning to her bones. "I think I just realized why the Order took my father."

"Because he's Genodra's head of state?" Aydiin asked.

"That would explain an assassination, but not why they would go to such great lengths to kidnap him," Byanca replied. "The only reason they would take him somewhere would be to *interrogate* him."

"What kind of secrets would Dad have for the Order?" Cael asked from the driver seat.

"What does the Order care about more than anything?" Byanca responded.

"Destroying the world," Cael said.

"Finding the Great Stones," Aydiin replied at the same time, his voice just slightly louder than her brother's.

"That's exactly right," Byanca said, placing her hand on Aydiin's leg. "I think there's a very good chance that my father had a Great Stone in his possession."

"Well, if he did, what are the chances the Order now has it?" Aydiin asked, grabbing her hand and squeezing it.

"Probably higher than I'd like to admit," Byanca said. "But my father's tough—he might not have given in. It could be hidden somewhere in the palace."

"Well, now's the time to find out," Cael said as the car began to slow. "Wow, this place looks worse than usual."

Byanca looked out the window to see the palace. It certainly did look worse than the last time she'd seen it when it had been somewhat of an island in the middle of the chaos. Now, it bore the signs of ransacking, along with almost every other mansion in the city. Windows were broken, doors hung open, and the grounds were overgrown with weeds.

"I'll just wait with the car," Cael said, turning around to smile at his sister.

"Don't you want to come in?" Byanca asked.

"And leave our only remaining vehicle for some opportunistic thief?" Cael asked. "If somebody tries anything funny, I've got a few surprises for them."

For Cael, it must be a shock to see his home in such a state. For Byanca, it was even harder to return with the memories of her father's abduction still fresh in her mind. However, she knew there was no choice.

Aydiin leapt out of the car and offered his hand, and she descended to the sidewalk. Taking a breath, Byanca led them through the open gate, across the palace grounds, and through the massive oak doors covering the main entrance.

Byanca steeled herself as the doors opened to reveal bare marble walls, the priceless art that had adorned them conspicuously absent. The massive chandelier that had acted as the centerpiece of the entryway was gone, and only a few scraps of wood remained of the furniture.

Without the velvet carpets in the hallways, their footsteps echoed loudly on the stone. Byanca winced at the sound of each footstep as they ventured further in. A chill wind blew through the hallways, and she clung tighter to Aydiin's arm.

"This was my home," Byanca said, the words coming out slowly. "So many memories were here, and yet it feels so foreign."

"Maybe we should do this tomorrow," Aydiin said, and he began turning around. "You've had a rough night, and this can't be easy for you."

"No, I'm fine," Byanca said, yanking her husband back around. "If my father really did have a Great Stone, you're going to need it sooner rather than later."

"How likely is it that he had one?" Aydiin asked, pulling her closer. "I mean, it's not exactly the kind of thing people keep private, is it?"

"My father was—is—a secretive man. If he had a Great Stone, he might have wanted it for any number of reasons beyond political ones."

"Assuming you're correct, that means it's probably not here," Aydiin said. "The Order has certainly had enough time to question him. Even if a Great Stone were here at some point, the Order would have probably already come back for it."

"That's assuming my father cracked," Byanca said as they continued through the palace. "He's much tougher than he looks. He once spent three months in a Pilsan warlord's dungeons."

"I'm not questioning his strength, Byanca," Aydiin said. "But we're up against a shadowy group that's had a thousand years to prepare for this. I think they may have means available to extract information that aren't available to a Pilsan tyrant."

"Okay, maybe you're right," Byanca said, her patience wearing thin. "But we at least need to look. My father told me how to enter his safe room. If we don't find anything, then we don't find anything, and I'll shut up about it."

"I never want you to shut up," Aydiin said with a wink. "But I do think we have other things to be concerned with."

"One thing at a time, please," Byanca responded.

"Exactly," Aydiin said. "Who do you think should be the next Doge? The election for the Senate is in a week, so we should already be thinking about who needs our help to elect the best Doge possible."

"Right," Byanca responded. "Did I mention my request to handle only one thing at a time?"

"And then there's still the question of Field Marshal Diaz and his army," Aydiin continued. "What happens if he decides to run for Doge? What happens if he wins? Worse, what happens if he loses?"

"Aydiin," Byanca barked. "One—thing—at—a—time."

"Sorry," Aydiin said, his cheeks turning red. "Great Stone. Right now. Got it."

"Thank you," she said, patting his arm and moving up to give him a kiss on the cheek. "I didn't mean to snap. It's just that I know we need to think of all these things. They're just longer-term projects. This is something we can cross off the list in about an hour or so."

As the words left her mouth, the couple reached one of the private staircases near the back of the house. It was the same that led to Marcino's study, and Byanca wondered if Ven's decaying corpse still sat upstairs. Luckily, she didn't need to climb all the way to the top and risk seeing it.

"Now, I believe it was right about here," Byanca said, stopping on the third step to place a finger on her chin. She began chewing her lip before grabbing one of the balusters with both hands. With a quick yank, the wood came free from the handrail above and began sinking into the staircase.

The soft clanking of gears filled Byanca's ears, and she peaked over the handrail to see an opening appear in the wall below. With a smile, Byanca leapt from the stairs.

"I've seen my share of safe rooms," Aydiin chuckled, rubbing his hair, "but this one was clever. You may be onto something."

"Thank you," she beamed up at him and offered her arm.

Footsteps echoed on the hard marble floor as the couple strode into the dark hallway, which held its own set of stairs that ran parallel to the public set. They emerged into a windowless study, its walls lined with shelves holding weapons, food storage, and—of course—books.

"You take the desk," Byanca said to Aydiin, pointing to a table littered with papers that dominated the far corner of the room. "I'll look through the bookshelves. We're bound to find *something* of interest."

"It doesn't look like anyone's been in here for a while," Aydiin said as he shuffled through papers.

Byanca only grunted in agreement, her attention focusing on the bookshelves. He was right, though. The room smelled of stale tobacco smoke, and dust covered both the floor and bookshelves. If anyone had discovered this room, they had done a good job of not disturbing anything.

"I've never been allowed in any of my father's safe rooms," Aydiin said. "I know he has them, but he's certainly never taken any interest in sharing them with me. Maybe that's because I'm the one he wants to hide from."

Byanca let out a chuckle but kept searching through her father's books. The contents were all dusty—not just the dust of a few months, but the kind that collected over years. She read over the book spines—they were mostly practical things discussing farming techniques, blacksmithing, wilderness survival. Her father had apparently been preparing himself for the collapse of society.

"I don't see anything," Aydiin sighed. "Any luck on your end?"

Byanca didn't answer as a book called out to her—*The Song of Alarun*. It was jammed in among a set of treatises on the economic development of Naerdon. If it belonged in this library at all, it should be with the other works of fiction.

As she lifted herself onto her toes to get a closer look, she could see a line in the dust. It had obviously been pulled off the shelf more recently than the others.

With her heart pounding in her ears, Byanca grabbed the book and pulled. Her ears expected to pick up the sound of a mechanism, and she looked around the study for any sign of another secret passage.

She was met with silence.

"What are you doing?" Aydiin asked, walking over to join his wife.

"I thought there might have been something to this book," Byanca responded, looking down at the cover. "I thought that taking it off the shelf might lead to another secret passage or something. Silly, I know."

"Not silly at all," Aydiin said, grabbing her hand. "We'll keep looking for a bit longer. At the very least, we could find something useful."

With a sigh, Byanca strode over to her father's messy desk and tossed the book onto it. The cover fell open and a loose page spilled out onto the desk. Furrowing her brow, Byanca bent down to pick it up.

"What did you find?" Aydiin asked.

"I'm not sure," Byanca responded, rotating the paper to get a better look.

The page contained what looked to be a rough, hand-drawn map. It depicted a valley surrounded by mountains on all sides with a river running through the middle. Near the center of the map was a hand-drawn star with the word *Aldeia* scribbled next to it.

"I think it's a map," Byanca said. "I can't figure out where it leads, though."

"Byanca, I think you were right," Aydiin said, moving over to eye the map. "I don't know if it's a Great Stone, but your father was obviously intent on hiding something."

"Well, I'm glad this wasn't a waste of time, after all," Byanca said, folding the map and stuffing it into her pocket. "Now, we have a republic to defend."

16

Byanca resisted the urge to pick at her nails as Lord Stefanson finished his report on the city's food stores. She knew the subject matter was important, but the absolutely ancient aristocrat, with his stringy white hair and bushy mustache, was far from charismatic. He could be delivering an account of a tremendous battle, and Byanca would still have a hard time staying awake.

Despite that, she did understand the basics of what the man was saying, and it wasn't great. With the influx of refugees, the food stores brought by the army would run out before the autumn harvest. However, with Diaz's forces camped outside the city limits, the crippling food shortages were only a portion of her worries.

"Thank you, Lord Stefanson," Byanca stammered as she realized the Minister of Agriculture had finished his report. "The city is already in your debt for the measures you've taken to increase the grain supplies. However, I believe that any further action should be overseen by those elected to the Senate."

Byanca looked around at the Council of Ministers, the group of aristocrats who had proclaimed themselves the legitimate government of Genodra after Bertrand's death. There were seven in total, including herself, and all were scions of wealthy and powerful families.

Even after spending the past week in meetings, Byanca still couldn't comprehend how she had been selected as the president of this little interim government. Worse, she had an even harder time trying to figure out how to survive the rocky waters that accompanied a crisis of this magnitude.

"I agree with Madam President," Lord Renault said, his white hair perfectly combed to the side. "Our focus should be on the immediate needs of our citizens and handing power over to our successors with all possible haste."

"Thank you for your support," Byanca responded, ignoring the fact that Lord Renault was himself one of those "successors," having secured his own election to the Senate.

"With that being said, I say we discuss the state of our armed forces," Lady Margarite piped up, her voice surprisingly strong, considering that it emanated from a shriveled body covered in wrinkles. "As commander-in-chief, what does Lady Byanca think of our chances against any conflict with that army camped outside the city?"

"The Field Marshal has officially pledged his support to the Republic," Byanca said, trying to keep her voice steady. "However, none of us can be sure what that actually means. He is, after all, the reason we're all in this mess in the first place."

"It's obvious that the man is planning on making himself Doge," Lord Chavron said, his heavy jowls bouncing as the words came out. "What happens if he wins the election?"

"Worse, what happens if he loses?" Margarite said. "There's little stopping him from just taking the city no matter what the Senate has to say about it."

"That's not entirely true," Byanca said.

"Oh, are you referring to the rabble occupying the city's forts right now?" Margarite scoffed.

"I have the utmost faith in General Marzio's abilities," Byanca replied. Almost as soon as she'd been named president, she had appointed Luka as commander of the city's garrison. Her young friend had taken up the appointment with a zeal that seemed to stem from more than just a sense of self-preservation.

"Already, we've had nearly ten thousand volunteers sign up," Byanca continued. "Given enough time, we'll not only be able to defend the city, but I have faith we'll be able to deal with the Field Marshal."

"Unfortunately, time is not on our side," Lord Chavron said, his jowls continuing to bounce up and down as he spoke. "Those men in the militia just march around in their green coats to impress young ladies. They've never seen a fight—what do you think will happen the moment they catch their first whiff of grapeshot?"

"I'm not saying they're as professional or well-trained as the boys in grey camped outside the city," Byanca said. "But they're better than nothing."

"You mentioned ten thousand new recruits," Lord Renault said, his voice cutting through the tension. "How many actual soldiers do we have? Not just men and women with zeal, but soldiers who know how to fire a weapon."

"So far, we've mustered three thousand militia soldiers who have at least some training," Byanca began, seeing the look of disappointment on each of her colleagues' faces.

"That won't even make Diaz blink," Chavron barked, a single fleck of spittle flying from his mouth.

"Diaz had already begun converting the city's factories to a war-time economy months ago," Byanca said. "And now they're churning out hundreds of rifles per day—rifles that we now control. Just imagine what we can assemble in the two weeks remaining until the election of the Doge."

"We need more than weapons to form a real army," Renault whispered, stroking a waxed mustache. "Two weeks isn't enough time to turn shopkeepers and refugees into soldiers."

"True, but that doesn't change the fact that we hold the ring of forts around the city," Byanca said, looking around the room. "That army isn't equipped for a siege, and storming those forts will come at a great cost."

"All of your arguments are under the assumption that we have another two weeks until the election for Doge," Lord Renault broke in. "The nomination process is tomorrow. If no one else runs, then Diaz will be automatically elected by the Senate. I can't think of anyone foolish enough to run against the Field Marshal."

"It's funny you should say that," Byanca said, directing a smile at the aging aristocrat. "I was rather hoping you would."

"Oh, I think that ship has sailed," Renault replied. "Even if Diaz weren't hanging over our heads like a shroud, I'm much too old for that level of responsibility. We need someone young and full of energy—someone like you."

"At a moment like this, I rather think we need an experienced hand guiding the Republic," Byanca said, smiling at the nods from around the table. "You have more than enough experience in both military and civilian affairs. There isn't a soul in the city who wouldn't find you to be a far superior choice to the Field Marshal."

"I'm glad to have such a strong vote of confidence," Lord Renault said, taking a sip of his tea and ignoring the nodding from the other members of the Council. "However, I don't think that's the issue at this time."

"Lord Renault, I've put a lot of thought into this, and it is my firm belief that you are Genodra's only hope," Byanca said, letting the words sink in around the room.

"When your father was elected, we had the luxury of deciding between several good men," Renault sighed, setting down his cup of tea. "But these are different days—darker days. We don't have the luxury of voting our conscience. We vote for whoever holds the biggest knife at our throats."

"Diaz is nothing but a bully and a tyrant," Byanca said, rising to her feet. "Isn't that what the Revolution was all about? Showing men like Diaz that they don't control the destiny of Genodra?"

"Of course," Lord Renault replied before letting out a sigh. "But in those days, we also held a big knife. I'm afraid to say that this match is a little one-sided."

"Are the ideals of freedom and democracy for sunny days only?" Byanca asked, her eyes moving around the room to make contact with the other members of the Council.

"Now, I wouldn't say that," Renault sputtered. "I just don't want to destroy this city merely to prove a point. It's all fine and good to talk about ten thousand new recruits from the comfort of our meeting, but battle is a different thing entirely. Do you really think they can stand against the cream of the Genodran army?"

"I know that we control a complex series of fortifications," Byanca said. "I know that Diaz will have to sacrifice thousands of his men just to get past them before making it to the winding streets of the city proper. Even if he wins, he'll be so weakened that his new regime won't last long."

"You would sacrifice that much Genodran blood?" Lord Chavron shouted, his eyes bulging.

"Those men out there are willing to die for their freedom," Byanca shouted back. "Are you? What was the point of restoring the Republic if we're just going to give it away?"

"Madam Byanca, you're filled with youth and idealism," Renault said, lifting his hands in surrender. "Both are traits that I view with envy and admiration."

"I'm not the only one who feels passionately about this," Byanca said. "Our new recruits may lack training, but they fight for their homes. They fight for their freedoms. Diaz's men fight because they are compelled."

"She's right," Margarite piped up. "In the Revolution, I saw bands of farmers hold their own against the king's soldiers."

"I'm not just asking—no, begging—you to run for Doge," Byanca said, shifting her gaze to Lord Renault. "Your country is asking this of you. You are the only one who can stand up to the charisma and military record of the Field Marshal."

"You are persuasive enough to get yourself elected," Renault sighed. "I'm sure this will be the end of me, but yes—I will do it."

"Well, Madam President," Lord Chavron spoke up, his jowls again bouncing with his words. "With your eloquent words, you have both saved the cause of freedom and doomed thousands of innocent lives to a horrible death. May the Divines have mercy on your soul."

Byanca hoped they would. If they failed, she would need more than just mercy.

17

Seb watched the sun set over Maradon—at least, the small part of the Salatian capital he could see from the tiny barred window in his cell. The sky was awash in an array of oranges and reds, mixed with a hint of purple indicating that darkness soon approached. He pushed his mind, focusing on the escape and not on what would come afterward.

Seb moved to wipe his moistened brow with an equally damp sleeve. The Salatian heat, even at sunset, was a wonderful sensation after the weeks spent shivering in his cell in Genodra. While the city of Palmas rarely saw freezing temperatures, it was nothing compared to the tropical heat that engulfed Maradon and the rest of Salatia year-round.

The sky began to darken, the purple turning to blue and dominating the oranges. The time had come. Seb sat ready for Joon to appear, keys in hand.

Iron ground on steel, and Seb looked over to see his door opening. The thick wood panel swung silently on its well-oiled hinges. Seb didn't look up from his window-side vigil.

"I'm really not in the mood, Harlin," Seb grunted, knowing that it wasn't quite late enough for Joon to be entering the cell. The general's company had been rather pleasant over the past days, but his presence at this moment could ruin everything.

"You always did seem to have a talent for winding up in a prison cell," said a deep, melodic voice that definitely did not belong to his old comrade. Heart pounding, Seb turned to see a tall, dark-skinned man standing at the door.

"What do you want, Rashad?" Seb asked. "Using your powers to once again show up where you're not wanted?"

"Alarun gave me these abilities to use in His service," Rashad said, stepping further into the room. Seb was struck at the gleam on the man's head, and he suddenly became conscious of the weeks' worth of growth on his own scalp. "I'm here to stop you from wasting a golden opportunity."

Seb wanted to tell the man to keep his voice down, but he knew it wasn't necessary. He could yell at the top of his lungs, and nobody would hear them. Rashad's powers had always seemed strange to him, but he knew that much at least.

"I'm about to escape this ship, avoiding a painful death at the hands of a despot," Seb replied. "That seems like a pretty golden opportunity to me."

"Yes, but what will you do after escaping?" Rashad asked. "You are a man of great faith and ability. Do you really want to do nothing to serve Alarun?"

"I want nothing more than to serve," Seb replied. "I plan on finding Aydiin and helping him in any way possible."

"What if I told you that the best way to serve the Sun God was by staying on this ship?" Rashad asked.

"I would say you've been talking to Harlin too much," Seb replied. "The moment I set foot on Margellan soil, my life is forfeit. Emperor Silvino will throw me into the darkest cell imaginable until my inevitable execution."

"There are many ways to return to Margella," Rashad said, a smile widening on his face. "You know your allies—both in the city and aboard this ship—are feeling bold and desperate."

"As I've been told," Seb replied. "Are you sure you haven't been talking with Harlin?"

"He's a smart man with a good heart," Rashad said, approaching Seb and placing a hand on the old man's shoulder. "Together, you'll figure something out."

"You still haven't explained what this golden opportunity is," Seb replied, rising to his feet and brushing the man's hand off him.

"I thought at least one of the reasons was obvious," Rashad said, his smile undiminished. "I think it's about time the Great Stone of Okuta found its way out of the Imperial Throne Room and back to its rightful place. Wouldn't you agree?"

"That sounds more like a suicide mission than a golden opportunity," Seb said slowly. "Rashad, I haven't seen my home in decades. What you're asking of me is impossible."

"You spent that time not only estranged from your home but also your faith," Rashad replied. "And yet you witnessed the Rise of the Forgotten Sun—an event that many within the ranks of the Disciples had begun to doubt. After all that, do you really think that *anything* is impossible?"

"I don't think your logic is sound," Seb replied. "Just because Aydiin found the Stone of Alarun doesn't mean I can suddenly waltz into the Imperial Palace."

"I'm not suggesting you 'waltz' anywhere," Rashad said. "I've never met anyone with the cunning and craftiness of Sebastian Montague. Please, I wouldn't be asking if I didn't know you were capable—and if it weren't absolutely essential."

Seb didn't respond for a moment. Rashad was telling him exactly what he wanted to hear—that pursuing his dream of destroying Silvino would actually be the best way to serve Aydiin. He just didn't like that doing so meant placing his trust in both Rashad and Harlin.

"You honestly believe this is what I should be doing?" Seb asked, letting out a deep breath.

"I wouldn't be here if I didn't," Rashad smiled.

"A return to Margella has dominated my dreams and nightmares for decades," Seb replied, trying to hold back some rebellious tears coming to his eyes. "Do I really have to stay on this ship, though? I'm sure there are plenty of others who can take me to Maradon."

"Time is running short," Rashad said. "The end is drawing near much too quickly. Besides, Harlin is here. That man is the difference between your return ending in death or victory."

"He's betrayed me once before," Seb growled.

"I have the utmost confidence in the both of you, especially with the help of your friend from Gorteo," Rashad said as he moved toward the door. "Oh, and one last thing."

Seb looked up, his eyes making contact with Rashad's. The man's dark orbs bored into his very soul. This man—no, this high priest—had near infinite wisdom. That gaze was enough to disarm even the most ardent of skeptics.

"More than the Stone awaits you in your homeland," Rashad finally said, the words coming out slowly. "Not only the fate of the world hinges on your success, but I believe you will also find your redemption."

Without another word, the man shut the cell door, and Seb could hear soft footsteps fade down the hallway.

Seb let out a deep sigh and fell back onto his cot. It had been decades since he'd seen Rashad, since he'd hailed that dark-skinned man as high priest. Yet even after all these years, he still felt an obligation to follow his counsel.

Going to Margella means death. Rashad was wise, and he knew more than he was disclosing. He wasn't, however, omnipotent. Seb would be walking on a knife's edge. A misstep in either direction would lead to his demise.

Perhaps that is the point.

The thought came to his mind, sending a shiver down his spine. Yet it made sense. A conviction swept through his entire being—it was time for his exile to end.

"Get up, we need to leave," Joon hissed, appearing at his side. Letting out a breath, Seb looked over at the man.

"Unfortunately, I think we need to stay," Seb responded, his voice low. The words sounded strange in his ears, as if they were being spoken by another man. In a way, they were.

"We can't do that," Joon said, his voice growing louder. "We need to find Byanca and Aydiin."

"There is another way—a better way—that we can help them," Seb grunted. "We need to steal the Great Stone of Okuta."

"That's..."

"I know it sounds crazy. I know it will likely result in our deaths. I also know it's what we need to do."

Joon stood for a moment in silence, Seb unable to tell what his thoughts were in the darkness. Then he saw a very perceptible nod.

"You're much more persuasive than I ever gave you credit for," Joon finally said. "Maybe Harlin's right—you would make a good ruler."

18

Sophie wiped the beads of sweat collecting on her forehead, a regular occurrence in the humid summers of Silvino City. Her eyes drifted toward the nearest window, its leaded glass distorting the view from the outside. Although nothing but a hazy blur through the thick window, she could almost feel the cool ocean breeze on her skin.

Drying her damp hand on the white apron she wore to protect the dark blue dress identifying her as a lower-class palace maid, she took another look at the display of silver plates, bowls, and utensils spread out in front of her. The silver covered nearly the entire surface of the massive table, a rough and unfinished monstrosity used only by servants. Nearly three-quarters of the precious metal glimmered in sunlight filtering in through the window; however, that meant the remaining quarter still needed to be polished. Trying to not think about the sun descending in the afternoon sky, Sophie picked up a tarnished plate and began rubbing with her exhausted fingers.

She had spent much of the morning daydreaming about eating a fine meal of venison and wild potatoes with the polished silver. The fantasy had also involved a lovely dress, dazzling jewelry, and a handsome gentleman to match. Of course, while she was lost in that other world, the hours had crept by, and she would be lucky to finish in time for a simple stew served in a wooden bowl.

Out on the palace grounds, the clock tower's chimes began their hourly announcement. Sophie's heart began to race, the deep sound reverberating on the rough stone floor and walls of the servants' section of the palace. Against her most fervent prayers, the chimes continued, and her fingers polished furiously. Yet she knew it was too late. By the last chime, there was little doubt she'd wasted her day.

Sophie kept polishing, despite the signal to the entire palace that the day's work was over. In the winter months, darkness would have already been several hours old. As it was the height of summer, the sun was just beginning its nightly descent. As the room began filling with vibrant orange and red light, footsteps sounded in the hallway, and Sophie lifted her head.

A diminutive woman, with hair whiter than a winter snow, appeared in the doorway. She wore a dark blue dress similar to Sophie's, marking her as a common servant. Yet while Sophie's apron was a dirty white, the woman's was the brightest of reds and freshly cleaned—the only outer markings of her rank as Mistress of the Kitchens.

The woman's face—weathered from years of hard work both in and out of the sun—was hard as stone. Sophie smiled to see the smallest of glimmers in those deep brown eyes, betraying the truth behind that rough exterior.

"What do you think you're doing?" the woman called out, a hint of amusement in her thick Albonan accent. "Didn't you hear the chimes? It's eight o' clock—you'd better hurry or you won't get any supper."

"But I haven't finished, Miss Margaret," Sophie replied, gesturing to the pile of silverware covering the table.

"That you haven't," Margaret frowned, placing her hands behind her back as she examined the silver. Silence gripped the room, broken only by the old woman's footsteps. She stopped and looked up at Sophie.

"I'm rather disappointed in you," Margaret said, her voice louder than it had been, but not exactly filled with anger. "You'll just have to spend the rest of your night washing pots with me in the kitchen."

Margaret spun on her heel and gestured for Sophie to follow. Heart falling, Sophie rushed to follow the surprisingly quick woman out the door and into the hallway.

A young soldier—dressed in the bright vermillion uniform of the Imperial Guard—stood at attention outside the room. Sophie knew she was being punished, but a guard? That seemed like a little much.

"This one hasn't quite learned her lesson," Margaret said to the soldier. "I'm taking her to do kitchen duty with me for the rest of the evening—maybe all night, if that's what it takes."

"Yes, ma'am," was the soldier's only reply. His face and voice betrayed little emotion beyond boredom.

Margaret grabbed Sophie's hand and began dragging her down the hallway. Still somewhat stupefied, Sophie had no choice but to follow. She'd been looking forward to evening all day—the cool breeze coming off the ocean, free time to spend wandering the grounds. Now, it would be spent washing dishes.

"I've had Lana set aside some stew and something special for you, dearie," Margaret whispered after turning a corner. "You've had a long day—I think if anyone deserves a good meal and a night off, it's you."

"Oh Maggie, you gave me such a fright," Sophie scolded the old woman. "I've been thinking I'd spend the entire night washing dishes."

"I had to say something to get you out of there," Maggie said. "When the clock struck eight, I knew you'd wasted your day—how was I supposed to know they'd put a guard in the hallway?"

"I didn't even know he was there."

"Was he handsome?" Maggie asked.

"Who? The guard? You got a better look at him than I did," Sophie said.

"No, not the guard," Maggie said as she nudged Sophie in the ribs with her elbow. "The man in your fantasy—the one who stopped you from getting all that silver polished."

"How could you possibly know about that?"

Sophie stopped dead in her tracks and stared at the woman.

"I raised you," Maggie said, grabbing Sophie's hand and continuing toward the kitchens. "I may be older than this palace, but I haven't lost my wits yet. When you don't get your chores done, it's almost always because of some imaginary gentleman."

"You don't know that I was imagining a man," Sophie chided. "I could have been thinking about adventures on the high sea or finding a buried treasure."

"Yes, you could have been," Maggie replied, the smile evident in her voice. "But you weren't."

The two turned another corner, and a wall of heat slammed into them. The sound of voices and banging pots reached Sophie's ears—the sounds of a bustling kitchen. After a few more steps, Maggie led them into an open doorway and into the kitchen.

Sophie looked around at the two-dozen serving girls washing pots in as many sinks along the far wall. Another dozen wooden tables dominated the center of the room, recently wiped down and cleaned after being covered in raw meat and vegetables used in tonight's supper. In the far corner, opposite the sinks, sat four large ovens whose heat made the entire room nearly unbearable.

"Miss Margaret," one of the girls at the sinks called out, "some of the stew burned, and I'm having trouble getting it out."

"Get a lemon and some vinegar," Maggie called back, a smile on her face. "It works every time."

Maggie, and the kitchen she so skillfully led, was responsible for serving meals to every servant in the palace complex—quite a feat considering it required the work of hundreds to keep it maintained and pristine. The meals made here were hearty, nutritious, and simple. Sophie had never even seen the kitchens used to cook food for the imperial household.

"Sophie m'dear, come here," a large woman called out from the other side of the kitchens. "I made sure to set some supper aside for you."

"Thank you, Lana," Sophie replied, reaching for the wooden bowl filled to the brim with meat and vegetables. "I thought today would never end."

"Well, that's your own fault for being caught out past curfew," Lana chided, a smile on her face. "You could have spent your day doing something useful instead of polishing silver nobody is ever going to use."

Sophie took a bite and smiled at the woman. Opposite in nearly every way to Maggie, Lana acted as the diminutive woman's second-in-command. While Maggie was short and wiry, Lana was taller than most men and twice as wide. Lana's laughter was as explosive as her rage, and both were well-known among the palace staff.

"I can't just stay inside on these summer evenings," Sophie replied, her words muffled by a mouthful of bread she was working to devour. "And the stars are just so beautiful, but you can't see them until right before lights-out. Sometimes I just lose track of time."

"Don't tell me you're going out again tonight," Maggie cut in, joining the small group.

"I've been stuck inside polishing silver all day—of course I'm going out," Sophie said in between spooning the savory supper into her mouth.

"And if you're not careful, you'll spend another day inside," Maggie chided.

"If you insist on going out, please make sure to be back before the guards catch you," Lana cut in. "I don't like seeing you get punished."

"And I don't like being the one to punish you," Maggie said.

"I don't do it on purpose," Sophie replied, shoveling the stew into her mouth. If her concept of time was anything to be relied on, she needed to hurry.

"Slow down, girl," Lana said. "You're going to choke."

"Sorry," Sophie said, shoving another chunk of bread into her mouth. "The sun's just setting so fast, and the gardens really are far too lovely to miss for even one night."

With the last of her bread, Sophie mopped up the remaining stew and stuck the doughy, savory goodness of the final bite into her mouth. Wiping her hands on her already filthy apron, she headed for the door that led out of the kitchens and into the gardens.

"Wait, I saved something special for you," Lana smiled, putting a finger to her lips.

"Just don't tell anyone," Maggie said. "We're not supposed to be giving you anything but bread and stew."

Lana produced a rather large lump surrounded by a dish towel. Sophie grabbed the package and unwrapped it to find three sweet rolls, a small jar of elderberry jam, and a knife. Her mouth began to salivate, despite protests from her stomach that she was already full.

"Oh, thank you," Sophie squealed and grabbed both women in a hug. There was little else in this world as delightful as one of Lana's sweet rolls smothered in jam. Rewrapping the little package, Sophie sped out of the kitchen and into the gardens.

Sophie's feet carried her along the stone pathways that led from the servants' quarters through the gardens that stretched on for leagues in all directions. The air was sticky on her skin, a fact not helped by the urgency she felt to reach her destination as quickly as possible. Beads of sweat again began forming on her forehead, a fact she did her best to ignore.

She turned to admire the palace proper in the setting sun. Unlike the servants' buildings, which were constructed out of a rough grey stone, the palace was an ornate array of marble. Half a dozen white spires topped with caps of various greens and reds rose among the clouds, a feat only made possible by the power of the Emperor. It looked almost on fire in the sunset. Sophie realized the sun was setting quickly, and she turned again to her destination.

Ahead, lush hedges rose from the ground almost ten spans into the air. Perfectly manicured by a small army of full-time gardeners, the vegetation created a maze that could occupy Sophie's attention for hours. Tonight, that's exactly what she intended to do, curfew or no curfew.

The hedges had an almost magical cooling effect on the air. Entering their shade seemed to be the only way to escape the summer heat besides jumping into one of the ponds that dotted the garden's landscape. Her feet carried her through the hedges—left, right, straight, left again, straight until it forced her into a right turn. She had long ago memorized the quickest path to what was quickly becoming her favorite spot in the world.

Arriving at a stone bench and a statue of some ancient figure in Margellan history, Sophie took a deep breath and wiped the sweat off her forehead. She took a seat on the cool stone bench and unwrapped her contraband dessert. After spreading at least half the jar of preserves onto a single roll, she took a bite and leaned back against the hedge.

Except for the chirping of crickets, silence enveloped her world. The silence meant that she wasn't too late. It meant that despite her long day, the best part of her life could be experienced for at least a little while.

It could also mean that she'd missed it. Or that it wouldn't happen tonight at all. It could mean a lot of things.

She took another bite, reveling in the cool air and the deep purple that now painted the sky above. Even if she were too late, she couldn't imagine a better way to pass a summer evening. From the other side of the hedge, footsteps sounded. Sophie's stomach flipped in excitement at the noise.

The soft strumming of a mandolin began to drift through the leaves, and Sophie had to stop herself from sighing in relief. The music was joined by a gentle yet masculine voice that far exceeded the beauty of the mandolin.

Oh, my sweet love,
How long have I waited,

To feel your sweet embrace.
Yet my longing has been sated
Now that I see your face.

The voice went silent for a moment, and the mandolin began to play a more upbeat tune. It was not accompanied by lyrics, a fact that deeply upset Sophie. She overwhelmingly preferred that magnificent voice to the mandolin's strings.

She took another bite, enjoying the mixture of the tart berries battling with the sugary bread. Her day had been filled with hard work in a stuffy room, but at this moment, life was absolutely perfect. She closed her eyes, cherishing the simple joy.

The voice started into another song, and a wide smile filled her entire countenance. She had no idea to whom the angelic voice belonged. It was he who dominated her daydreams, although she had never seen his face.

She admired his lack of fear, playing music in the gardens until well past curfew. Three times now in the past two weeks she'd been caught outside after everyone else was in bed. That meant three days of work starting before and ending after the rest of her fellow maids. Yet she couldn't bring herself to stop—the joy of this moment far outshone the dread of tomorrow's punishment.

The mandolin continued—sometimes accompanied by the voice, other times on its own—until stars began appearing in the sky. Sophie grabbed her second sweet roll and began spreading jam on it.

Her ears perked up at the sound of approaching footsteps . Pulling herself away from the hedge and onto her feet, Sophie strained her ears to pinpoint the new footsteps. Her stomach tightened, and she knew it wasn't from eating too quickly.

Whoever approached was on the other side of the hedge, growing closer to her beloved. Yet the mandolin did not cease its strumming, and the voice continued in its singing. It was as if Sophie were the only one who could hear the newcomer's approach.

A heavy thud sounded, and wood cracked as the mandolin fell to the ground. She could hear the sound of grunts accompanying more thuds, the sound of a man reacting to fists hitting flesh.

Sophie's eyes scanned her surroundings, her head spinning. The knife Lana had given her to spread the jam sat on the stone bench, illuminated by the moonlight, the dull blade covered in preserves.

Trembling, she grasped the handle, and Sophie took a deep breath before barreling through the thick bushes.

Thorns, branches, and leaves caught on her dress, ripping the wool. Some grabbed her skin, refusing to let this intruder pass through what should obviously be an impregnable wall. Yet she continued on, oblivious to the blood now trickling out of a dozen minor wounds.

Bursting out onto the other side, her eyes caught sight of three figures—two clothed in black and one sporting a grey suit coat. One of the black-clad men secured the soldier from behind while his companion rained blow after blow on the struggling captive.

Fist clenching the knife, Sophie screamed and leapt onto the nearest assailant. The dull blade glanced off the figure's torso, and the man fell to the ground with Sophie on top of him. She raised her knife again, hoping this time to strike a more direct blow.

The figure rose to his feet, brushing Sophie off as if she were a mere annoyance. Her meager weapon fell to the stone pathway, the steel clattering in the night. Sophie leapt to her feet and let out a scream.

It hung in the air, propelled by her fear and panic. Strong arms wrapped around her, and a meaty palm covered her mouth. With the echo of her scream ringing through the night air, her cries became muffled by her attacker.

Sophie tried to pull away from the man, but his grip grew tighter, pulling her into his chest. Without thinking, she planted her feet into the ground and instead of pulling away from the assailant, she pushed into him. A sickening thud met her ears as the top of her skull collided with the man's nose.

Her senses were immediately assaulted by the scent of warm blood, and she could feel the liquid streaming into her hair. The strong arms that surrounded her withdrew, accompanied by a moaning as her would-be assassin fell to the ground.

More footsteps came pounding down along the pathway, accompanied by shouts. Sophie looked up to see six vermillion-clad soldiers running toward them, rifles in hand. Footsteps sounded behind her, and she spun to see the two assailants sprinting off into the night.

Sophie collapsed to the ground, adrenaline rushing through her veins mixing with disbelief. Her muscles were completely exhausted, and she couldn't force herself to stand.

"Are you alright, Your Majesty?" a soldier called out. The words sent a jolt through Sophie's entire body, and her brain could barely comprehend them.

"I'm fine, thank you," said the all-too-familiar voice she'd been listening to for weeks. She heard footsteps approach her prostrate form. "Check on the girl."

Sophie opened her eyes to the most beautiful sight imaginable. A long face, with a sharp nose—two features she had never thought of as handsome but combined made for stunning beauty. A mess of shockingly dark hair sat atop that beautiful face, contrasting sharply with pale blue eyes. At least, she thought they were a pale blue—it was hard to tell in the moonlight.

"Are you alright?" the man asked. It was the voice. She couldn't believe that after so long, it was addressing her face to face.

"I—I think so," she finally stammered.

"I'm not quite sure how to thank you," the man said, offering his hand. Trembling for more than one reason, she grasped it. His grip was firm, yet gentle—just like his voice. With ease, he lifted Sophie to her feet.

"I was just passing by, and I couldn't help but overhear the scuffle," she lied. Telling him that she was eavesdropping on his nightly singing just wouldn't do.

"Well, I'm deeply in your debt," the man replied with a bow.

"As is the entire empire," one of the soldiers piped up, picking up a small circle of white gold from the ground and handing it to the man. Sophie's jaw dropped as her beloved musician placed the circlet on top of his head.

"I'm afraid we need to get you back to the palace before word of this spreads," one of the guards said, grabbing Sophie's beloved by the arm. "I'll have Santiago take the girl back to her quarters."

Without another word, Sophie felt strong hands grab her shoulders, shepherding her away. Unable to concentrate, she didn't protest. The act of walking in the cool night air helped her head to clear.

"Who was that?" she asked her escort, knowing the answer. She just needed to hear it for herself.

"I didn't think you'd need to ask," the soldier replied, a smile in his voice. "You're a lucky girl—it's not every day you have the privilege of saving the Crown-Prince."

THE IMPENDING NIGHT

Sophie didn't know how to respond. She had fallen in love—unwittingly—with Prince Tomas, heir to the throne of Margella.

19

Gamila peered through the window of her rumbling carriage, trying her best to block out the images that showed how precarious her position was. The streets—normally filled with pedestrians and horses—sat practically unused, the inhabitants of the city choosing to stay indoors whenever possible. The overall sobriety wasn't helped by the clouds rolling in from the sea, marking the beginning of monsoon season.

The carriage entered the main street of the Grand Bazaar, and the driver slowed in the mass of humanity. For a moment, it was a relief to see that life still moved forward in the city, that the people were still out making purchases. However, a longer look confirmed the depression that had settled in over Maradon.

More than half the stalls were empty, their keepers having either fled or gone into hiding. The shelves of those who remained were half empty, and what was on display was hardly worth purchasing in better times.

"I still don't see why you insist on these most depressing rides," Bayram mumbled, shifting in the bench opposite Gamila. "I already know the city is in a sorry state. You don't need to remind me of that fact every single day."

"It's good for us to get out of the palace," Gamila responded, leaning back into her seat. "That way, we don't lose our connection with the city."

"If I really wanted a connection to the city, I'd come out here with Askari once in a while," Bayram chuckled. "Still can't believe that kerton just showed back up in the stables one day."

"I can't believe you've started riding him," Gamila laughed. "You'd better be careful, or Father's going to forget that you're an invalid."

"That kerton's got a good soul," Bayram responded, again running a hand through his curly hair. "He seems to know I'm not nearly as capable as Aydiin, so he takes things slow. He sure beats riding in this carriage, rumbling our way through the most depressing scenes imaginable."

Gamila sighed at the words, and the two siblings drifted into silence. She knew her brother was right to complain, and to be honest, she didn't enjoy the daily carriage ride any more than he did. It would perhaps be enjoyable atop a kerton, but she wasn't so sure.

She hated the sight of her home entering a death spiral, hated the smell of burnt out buildings and the unwashed bodies of those now homeless. Despite the nausea that swept over her body at every new turn, she couldn't just hide in the palace. She had to come out into the city.

She had to find *him*.

"Wait, you're trying to catch a glimpse of your mystery man, aren't you?" Bayram said, sitting up in his bench.

"I have no idea what you're talking about," Gamila said, turning toward the window just in case her cheeks took the opportunity to blush.

"I can't believe it's taken me all these weeks to put that together," Bayram said, running a hand through his hair. "These dismal rides suddenly feel much more purposeful."

Gamila only sighed in response. She hadn't seen Rashad since he'd forced her back to the palace on the night of the riots. She hadn't heard a single word from him. The silence in her life was deafening.

"As I said—it's important for us to remember what our people are experiencing," Gamila finally said, turning to face her brother's smiling gaze. She was very much regretting her decision to tell her older brother anything about Rashad.

"Hey, I can't say that I blame you," Bayram said amid a fit of laughter. "If I had found a woman shrouded in that much mystery, I'd be turning the city upside down to find her."

"Maybe that's what I should be doing instead of hoping to just see him walking the streets," Gamila said, trying to meet her brother's gaze without blushing. "It's been months—he's probably not anywhere near Maradon."

"You should have brought me into your confidence earlier," Bayram said, shifting in his seat toward Gamila and placing a hand on her knee. "I'll put an ear to the ground and see what I can find. My spies are getting awfully bored with nothing but talk of rebellion filling their ears."

"It certainly sounds better than what I've been doing," she said as her eyes fell upon a young boy standing in the street, his clothing nothing but rags. She should be spending her time doing something much more constructive than looking for Rashad. "I always seem to forget that you have an entire network of eyes and ears. Now you add Askari to your retinue, and you could be in the running for most eligible bachelor in the city."

"It helps to be the moribund heir," Bayram said, his face scrunching up at the sight of the young boy outside the carriage. "Although, I do wish that I could do more than just sit in the palace and read cryptic reports. It's frustrating to see the world falling apart like this."

"There must be something that we can do," Gamila said, slamming back into her seat. "We can't be completely powerless."

"I think you're forgetting that I'm sickly and you're an underage princess," Bayram replied, removing his hand from her knee and flashing her a smile. "Can you imagine what Father would say if he knew we were hatching plots in our spare time? Something tells me that Father isn't exactly thrilled about these morning jaunts—imagine if he found out we were trying to save Salatia on our own."

"He probably doesn't even know about our carriage rides. Even if he does, I think he's a little preoccupied with more pressing matters."

"What? Like trying to hold the Sultanate together? That hardly seems more important than the comings and goings of his precious daughter."

"I haven't even seen Father in days," Gamila replied as the carriage approached the palace. "He's constantly meeting with his advisors."

Bayram didn't respond as the carriage rolled through the open gates and into the palace grounds. Here, life at least resembled something akin to normalcy, even if the edges were obviously fraying.

Across the courtyard, an aging gardener directed a small team of young boys in caring for the plants, ensuring that they weren't growing out of place. However, the large fountain that dominated the courtyard wasn't running, a reminder that fresh water was an increasingly valuable commodity.

The almost-normal scene was marred by a passing squadron of rifle-toting soldiers in the light blue of the regular army—a sign that trouble was brewing and could boil over at any moment. In days past, only the white-clad members of the Sultan's Guard would be seen in the palace. After the riots, her father had called in several regiments of regulars in a desperate attempt to protect the nation's ruling apparatus from the threat of extinction.

The collection of troops in and around Maradon led to rebellions and revolts throughout the entire country. The farms, plantations, and mines that created the commodities that kept the Salatian economy moving were no longer coming into Maradon, which made the situation even worse. Disaster seemed imminent.

She knew that the Stone of Surion's disappearance, which triggered these events, had something to do with Aydiin, but—again—her knowledge of events was hazy at best. She'd barely had a few minutes with Byanca before she and Rashad had rushed off, leaving Gamila in the dark.

As the carriage came to a halt, Bayram climbed out of the horse-drawn vehicle to the ground below. With yet another sigh, Gamila took her brother's outstretched hand. She did have to admit that it was nice to be back in the relative comfort and safety of the palace.

"Well, I'm ready for a tall glass of lemonade," Gamila said. "The day has already grown so hot, and those storm clouds aren't exactly helping."

"You might not get a chance any time soon," Bayram said, gesturing to a white-clad figure crossing the courtyard.

Jabari's signature blood-red cape streamed behind him, a feat only made possible in the still morning air by the immense speed created by his overly-eager gait. One look at the young man's face, and Gamila found herself wishing that she were back in the city.

"What business does our dear Princess Gamila have outside the gates?" Jabari called out, an attempt at a smile plastered across his face.

"Is it suddenly a crime to go out and visit our fair city?" she shot back.

"My sincerest of apologies if you mistook my concern for an accusation," Jabari jeered before bowing. "However, you didn't answer my question."

"As much as I would love to stay and chat, I'm feeling the effects of the weather," Gamila said, fanning herself. "I have the strongest of urges to retire to my rooms with a glass of lemonade."

"You look fine to me, dear sister," Jabari said, stepping closer before turning to Bayram. "And what of you, brother? Just thought you'd like to see the city a bit without that kerton?"

"The doctors tell me that staying in bed all day isn't ideal for my health," Bayram responded. "And I didn't particularly feel like risking my life on Askari, so I asked Gamila to accompany me on a little ride, and she was gracious enough to accept."

"These are dangerous times, and caution is the order of the day," Jabari said, a frown on his face. "You should have at least taken a contingent of guards on your little excursion. I would hate for something to happen to either of you."

Gamila didn't respond as she tried to meet the young man's gaze. There was something behind his words, beyond his nosiness. Perhaps it would be for the best to stop these little trips through the city, after all.

A commotion near the gate sounded, breaking the young man's undivided attention away from Gamila. With a smile, she looked to see what had brought her this tiny victory.

A young soldier dressed in the blues of the regular army burst through the gates atop a horse foaming at the mouth. Without a word, the man leapt from the saddle, tossing the reins to a wide-eyed boy. The soldier took off on foot through the courtyard, sweat pouring down his face, his clothing soaked.

"This isn't over," Jabari whispered, before taking off after the man who was obviously bringing some dire news.

Gamila stood, watching her younger brother move through the courtyard. Unwilling to dismiss decorum enough to run, the young man's rear end swaggered in his rush. With the cape trailing behind, he looked like the villain out of some long-forgotten story.

"Something tells me we should also be a part of this," Bayram said, offering his arm to escort Gamila.

"Do we have to?" Gamila asked as she took his arm. "I wasn't exactly lying about going to my rooms with a glass of lemonade. I could have sworn a shipment of ice made it from the mountains this morning."

"I'm sure that can be arranged, but for now, I think we should hear that soldier's message with our own ears," Bayram said, pulling his cane out from the carriage before leading her through the courtyard.

"Oh Bayram, I knew that—deep down—you cared about what happens around here," she chuckled, sending her elbow into his ribs. "You really will make a great ruler one day."

"Don't let Jabari hear you say that," Bayram whispered as the two siblings walked toward their father's throne room. "If he achieves his dream of taking Father's place, you'd best not be on record supporting someone else for the job."

"If Jabari becomes Sultan, I'll send myself into exile," Gamila said. "Maybe I'll take Aydiin's way out and marry some foreign nobility."

"With all the chaos, I'm starting to consider that myself," Bayram sighed. "And if this messenger has dire news, we may need to both board a ship before things grow much worse."

"Do you really think it's coming to that?" Gamila asked.

"It's quite possible," Bayram said. "I think the situation is worse than even Father realizes. He's been deaf for too many years, now, and unless he's willing to take drastic action, I don't see how he can survive without the Great Stone of Surion."

As the two penetrated deeper into the palace, the sight of blue-clad military couriers running in all directions became increasingly prevalent, mingling with the regular servants. Their small red hats—the most impractical part of their uniforms in Gamila's opinion—somehow stayed on their heads as they bobbed up and down at a run. Their hurried movements began tying knots in her stomach.

A young servant girl stood outside the throne room, ready to fetch whatever was required by those conferring inside. Gamila couldn't help but notice that the girl was a scrawny little thing, barely coming into her womanhood. How she had gotten stuck with such a duty, Gamila had no idea.

"Would you please go get me a tall glass of lemonade?" Gamila asked the young girl, whose eyes went wide.

"Of course, Princess," the young girl stammered before trotting away.

"What an odd young thing," Bayram said as the servant disappeared behind the corner. He turned to his sister and took a deep breath. "Well, shall we?"

As the large doors opened in near silence, Gamila found her father sitting on his throne in full regalia. His head was wrapped in a turban of pure violet, over which sat his crown of delicately crafted gold. A braided beard hung down onto his chest, contrasting with robes of dark red.

After nearly a week of not seeing the man, Gamila was struck by the exhaustion that lined his face. His eyes were drooping, and deep shadows were forming around the sockets. A grey pallor had overtaken his skin, a further indication of the man's lack of both sleep and proper nutrition.

At the Sultan's feet, three men—well, two men and Jabari—sat on silk pillows around a low table. The aging Captain-General Hamza of the Sultan's Guards sat in his perfectly pressed and decorated white uniform, his own grey beard outshining the Sultan's by far. At his side sat the much younger General Tartlan, commander of the city's garrison. Tartlan's blue uniform was ragged and dirty, a sure sign that he'd only recently returned from the city's unruly and dusty streets. Jabari sat with his back to her, his posture rigid in a studious silence. The messenger who had started this little adventure now stood before the group, catching his breath with a goblet of wine in hand.

Bayram led Gamila toward the corner of the room where she had a chair ready and waiting. Father often requested her presence to watch the reactions as he held court. He valued her ability to read people, and having a seat far from the center of attention allowed her to observe almost unnoticed, especially when she engaged in "womanly tasks" like silk embroidery.

"The rebels must be willing to negotiate," Hazma said, his voice strong and calm in a room where Gamila could cut the tension with a knife. "What's stopping us from sending an envoy to begin peace talks before the blood of thousands is shed in vain?"

"You think it in vain to protect our lands from those wretched dogs?" General Tartlan shouted back, despite the other soldier's calm demeanor. "This 'army' probably contains little more than women and old men. I say we march out and crush them."

"How do you suggest we do that?" Hazma shot back. "We barely have—"

"Gentlemen," Oosman said, clearing his throat. Tartlan closed his mouth, swallowing whatever response he was about to shout directly at the aging head of the Sultan's Guards. "I believe we need to take a moment to inform the Crown-Prince of our situation."

The men turned, noticing the entrance of Gamila and Bayram for the first time. She turned toward Bayram, expecting to see a look of shock on his face at being addressed in an official meeting. After all, he'd been practically shut out of the official decision-making process. However, her brother's face was unreadable.

Bayram dropped his sister's arm, and Gamila crept toward her chair. The collective attention of the room's inhabitants had turned to her brother, for a change, and she didn't want to be anywhere near that. Besides, she wanted to watch from the shadows.

"My Prince," General Tartlan began as the two senior military commanders rose to their feet and Gamila snuck to her chair. "We have just received a message from the interior—a rebel army has formed on the Plateau of Surion. Within the month, they'll be at the gates."

"I've been receiving news of various rebellions for weeks now," Bayram said, ignoring the look on Tartlan's face at that casual revelation. "Why are you choosing this moment to panic?"

"Well, the reports we've been receiving have looked like individual pockets of rebellious activity," Hazma cut in, rubbing a hand through his grey beard. "And along the coastal plain, that's true. However, this rebellion in the interior is turning out to be one massive, well-orchestrated undertaking."

"Our scouts have brought back a report of a camp numbering in the hundreds of thousands, flying the flags of all eight tribes of the interior," Tartlan said in an obvious attempt to take back control of the conversation from his colleague. "None of the other rebel armies we've been seeing represent a real threat, but this one is different."

"This is dire indeed," Bayram replied, stepping toward the table. "How many men do we have?"

"Now that Prince Bayram has been appraised of the situation," Oosman said, ignoring Bayram's question and gazing around the room. "What do my *generals* say?"

Silence overtook the room as both Hazma and Tartlan shot glares at each other. Bayram remained still, his face unreadable after Father's deliberate snub.

"Your lemonade, Princess," a whisper sounded at Gamila's side, and she looked over to see the young servant girl with a goblet. The sight of crushed ice in the tart beverage reminded her of the intense thirst gripping her throat.

"Thank you," she whispered back, taking the chilled chalice before returning her attention to the discussion at hand.

"Our walls are strong, and the rebels have no way of cutting off our supply from the sea," Tartlan finally said, his voice hoarse. "Let the fools break themselves as an ocean wave on the rocks."

"What if they have artillery?" Hazma shot back. "Our walls won't last an hour against a sustained barrage. We have to convince them to stand down. I'm sure this is nothing but a play for water and grazing rights."

The lemonade was beautifully tart, and despite the discussion of national importance, she found her thoughts drifting toward the beverage. In times of great unrest, she was glad to have something so simple as a cold drink. She looked over at Bayram, and she almost dropped her glass as the man opened his mouth.

"You severely misunderstand the tribes of the interior," Bayram said, stepping toward the center of the room as the bearded generals fell silent. "This may seem sudden to you, but grumblings of their discontent have been smoldering under the surface for decades. This rebellion is hardly a flash of gunpowder—it's several tons of dynamite. And after everything that has been done to them, I can't exactly say they're wrong for rebelling."

"How dare you," Jabari shouted, leaping to his feet. "Your presence is only suffered here—"

"Silence, Jabari," Oosman said, lifting his hand. The youngest prince turned red at the words but sat down, and Gamila could practically see steam rising from him. "Your elder brother has the right to weigh in on the situation, no matter his opinion. Please, Prince Bayram, continue."

Oh, this is getting good, Gamila thought as she took a long draft of lemonade. It made her heart soar to see Bayram speaking up, and it almost made her dance for joy to see Jabari put in his place.

"We like to tell ourselves that Oosman the Great *united* the tribes of Salatia," Bayram began, his trembling voice growing firm as the words left his mouth. "However, from what I hear out of the tribesmen, they feel more like he *subjugated* them with the Great Stone of Surion. Now that it's gone, I don't see any sort of serious rebellion petering out before Salatia has been turned upside down."

"If that's your analysis, what would you have me do?" Oosman replied.

"Turn Salatia upside down before they can," Bayram replied, a smile spreading across his countenance. Jabari's face grew red, and he again leapt to his feet.

"If you're implying the Sultan should abdicate—"

"Far from it," Bayram cut off his brother, the younger man's rage no match for his elder brother's calm. "There are several foreseeable scenarios that will end up with our esteemed Sultan not only keeping his head, but also his throne."

"Please continue, my son," Oosman said. "However, do so carefully—I will not tolerate any ideas filled with cowardice."

Bayram took another step forward before taking a deep breath. He had the look of a man who was finally going to say something that he'd been waiting years to let out.

"Make concrete plans to include everyone—including the tribes—in the governance of Salatia," Bayram said, the words pouring from his mouth. "Let's give the people a written constitution that turns the subjects of the Sultan into a cohesive nation of citizens. In short, we give them part of what they're asking for without the shedding of blood."

"This will be seen as nothing but an admission of weakness," Tartlan scoffed, folding his arms. "What will stop them from just marching on Maradon anyway?"

"Well, we are weak—there's no hiding that," Bayram said. "And while the majority of the nation isn't part of this rebellion, they're not exactly passionate about defending the Sultanate. However, if we give everyone a say in the government, we'll be creating something worth defending. We could diffuse the entire rebellion and stop numerous others with the stroke of a pen."

Gamila wanted to applaud her brother's words, but her head began to spin as the room erupted into chaos. Jabari and the two generals began shouting, her father's attempts to quiet them fruitless. Bayram shouted back—a sight she had never dreamt of seeing in her entire life. Yet as the noise grew louder, the more it began to dim in her ears. Her vision grew fuzzy, and her head felt as it would float away.

Placing the empty chalice on the floor, Gamila made her way toward the small side door separating the throne room from a back courtyard that eventually led to her apartments. She must have over-taxed herself this morning, and she was now paying the price.

The sunlight was nearly blinding as she breathed in the fresh air of the open courtyard, and she placed a hand to her forehead to provide shade. She forced her legs forward toward her apartments.

"Here, Princess, let me help you," a strong voice sounded in her ear, and she could feel strong hands grab under her arms and legs. Her head was spinning too much to protest as she felt her body being slung over a pair of wide shoulders.

A voice in her head said that something was wrong, and Gamila began to flail in an attempt to wrestle her way out of the strong grip. Yet she found her limbs too weak to do anything as consciousness slipped away.

20

B ayram stood, his feet glued to the floor, as he braced himself against the hurricane of stupidity that was attempting to topple him. Jabari and Tartlan both shouted accusations of treason while the Sultan and Hazma sat in silence. A quick glance at the corner of the room revealed Gamila's empty chair—the young woman must really have been serious about retiring to her rooms.

"The fact that you can suggest such treasonous ideas against the leader anointed by Surion himself is beyond reason," Jabari shouted, his words standing out while Tartlan was taking a breath.

"You seem to be forgetting that we're in this situation because of this belief that the Sultan has been chosen by Surion to lead the nation," Bayram responded, struggling to keep his voice level. "What if we do somehow manage to put down this tribal rebellion? What will happen when an even larger horde of angry peasants is at our doorstep? They're already in revolt—all they need is someone to unify them."

"Those ingrates don't understand how lucky they are to have such wise leadership," Jabari shot back. "Our loyal soldiers will cut down the tree of rebellion where it stands."

"Father, I know you have done what you believe to be best for everyone," Bayram said, ignoring his twit of a brother and turning to the Sultan. "However, you have to face facts—nearly everyone is upset with your rule. Now that you lack the Great Stone, they can finally express that dissatisfaction. You can make some major changes and sacrifice a portion of your power, or you can give a grand speech at your execution. The choice is yours."

"What kind of changes are you proposing?" Oosman replied, his exhausted gaze turning to Bayram.

"As I said before, we give the people a written, formal constitution that spells out the government's powers along with checks on that power. We set up an elected legislative assembly that has some real teeth to give everyone a voice. You need to see the people of Salatia as your partners in government instead of mere subjects of your royal whims."

"Imagine what we could accomplish," Bayram continued after his words were met with silence. "There is a tremendous amount of pent-up energy in Salatia. If we were to unleash it, there's no limit to what we could accomplish."

"You're asking a divinely appointed monarch to admit defeat and take power from the people instead of the gods," Oosman said, his voice trembling. "You're proposing that I give up my crown from above and replace it with a crown from the gutter. I will not and cannot let such a thing weigh down my head. I would rather die first."

"Father, don't be such a stubborn foo—"

An explosion shook the ground, and dust fell from the ceiling. Bayram steadied himself, and the generals leapt to their feet as another explosion sounded, this time further away. More dust fell from the ceiling, and Bayram could feel his sweaty skin clinging to the filth.

"We're under attack," General Tartlan cried out, unsheathing his long, curved sword. The two guards at the door readied their rifles and moved toward the Sultan.

Another explosion outside rocked the heavy doors, and Bayram looked over in time to see the ancient barriers fall to the ground, the vibration of the impact rattling his core. Dust hung in the air, and—for a moment—the world was still.

Gunshots rang out, and Bayram dove to the floor as one of the guards was hit in the shoulder. A scream filled Bayram's ears, but it was cut short as another round lodged into the fallen guard's body. The remaining soldier began firing into the dust without any sign of a target. More shots rang out from the doorway, and the guard fell to the ground.

Three men dressed in the colorful robes of the inner tribes leapt into the room, rifles at the ready. Jabari and the two generals moved closer to the Sultan, creating a small, protective ring around their sovereign. Bayram sidled toward the wall, hoping that the attackers were yet to notice his presence.

"We've come to put the usurper who calls himself Oosman the Third under arrest," one of the men said, lowering his rifle. "If you men stand down, I give my word that none of you will be harmed."

"How dare you," Oosman shouted, rising to his feet. "Even rebels should have more honor than to launch a sneak attack like this."

"You're in no position to lecture us about honor," the man shouted, spitting on the ground. "Now, stand down and come with us."

Bayram turned his head to see his father's reaction as the old man lifted his hands. Flames erupted from his fingertips, and the tribesmen screamed as they were engulfed. Bayram's mouth dropped open at the sight.

Charred bodies fell to the ground, unrecognizable after the inferno passed over them. A wave of nausea swept over Bayram as the stench of burnt flesh and clothing assaulted his senses. Still, he knew that this was not over and now was not the time to lose his breakfast.

"Those fools will have to do better than that," Oosman roared, ripping off his robe to expose the red Markings on his hands. "Follow me, men. We have a palace to defend."

With a cry, Jabari, Tartlan, and Hazma followed their sultan out the door, not bothering to wait for Bayram. For a moment, he stood there, unsure of how to respond in the empty silence of the throne room.

Another explosion rocked the room, although he could tell it was further away and targeted at another spot in the palace. Letting out a deep sigh, he knew that hiding just wouldn't do. If he were to have any say in coming events, he couldn't be seen as the prince who fled from the face of danger.

Bayram moved toward one of the fallen guards and picked up the man's rifle. Opening the soldier's satchel, Bayram found only a handful of bullets. He prayed to the Divines that they would be enough.

Rifle in hand, Bayram closed his eyes and focused on the well of power inside his chest that he had kept secret for nearly two decades. The world grew quiet and still, the chaos surrounding him becoming distant. For a moment, the gunfire and explosions throughout the palace grounds belonged to another world. Letting out a deep breath and opening his eyes, Bayram knew that unless someone were to be looking very closely for him, he would be all but invisible.

Bayram moved into the courtyard outside the throne room, eyes wide open to survey the carnage. Sections of walls had been blown to bits, the remnants scattered throughout the courtyard. Fires dotted the garden, the smoke rising into the air, casting a haze on the scene.

At the far end of the garden, Bayram spotted the Sultan, Jabari, and the generals with a dozen guards around them. Shouts rose up as they fought in hand-to-hand combat with a much larger group of rebel nomads.

Oosman grabbed one of the attackers—a large brute who resembled a troll—and summoned the power of Surion. The Sultan's hands displayed fiery Markings as the warrior screamed, his flesh melting and peeling away from his bones. The man's clothing caught flame, the smoke adding to the haze that had already engulfed the courtyard. Without any indication of joy or remorse, Oosman threw the charred corpse to the ground.

Bayram bent down to one knee and leveled the rifle, taking aim at a soldier wielding a large scimitar against Jabari. Letting out a slow breath, Bayram squeezed the trigger, and the rifle butt slammed into his shoulder as the tribesman fell to the ground.

Pulling back on the bolt action, Bayram expelled the spent casing and rammed another bullet into the chamber before again taking aim. His gaze found two men fighting against General Hazma, seconds away from overwhelming the old soldier. Letting out another breath, Bayram squeezed the trigger.

As the rebel warrior fell to the ground, something slammed into Bayram's back, and the prince fell onto his face. Turning to look up, he saw a man standing over him, surrounded by the familiar glow of another Creep only visible when calling on his own powers.

The Creep wore the colorful robes of a warrior from the inner tribes, which accentuated his large frame. His stature was unusual for one holding the powers of Vindred—such bulk was a waste when engaging in subterfuge. However, at this moment, the man's brawn was certainly an advantage.

"Who would have thought—the sickly Crown-Prince is actually a fighter," the man said, his voice just loud enough to carry over the din of battle.

Bayram lifted his rifle, but the Creep's foot slammed into his chest, and the weapon fell from his grip. Ribs popped as the foot again made contact, and Bayram let out a howl. Through watery eyes, he could see the attacker lift a knife above his head.

"You don't have to do this," Bayram said, his breathing worsening in the smoke and from exertion.

"Oh, I know," the man said. "That's why I'm going to enjoy it."

A snarl sounded from behind the attacker, and Bayram's mouth dropped open as a familiar set of teeth sank into the man's neck. The Creep's eyes grew wide as Askari flung him aside like a rag doll. The crunch of a body slamming into stone assaulted Bayram's ears, and he forced his gaze to avoid the undoubtedly gruesome sight.

"That's a good boy," Bayram shouted through the pain of what he hoped were only bruised ribs. Askari's eyes flashed a smile along with an expression that Bayram couldn't quite read, but there was certainly more than a hint of sarcasm.

He directed his gaze toward the fighting in time to see Jabari run the last remaining rebel soldier through with his scimitar. The battle—at least in this particular section of the palace—was over. Letting out a breath, Bayram let himself collapse back down to the ground.

Letting go of the power of Vindred, the world came back into focus. The roar of the fires that had been set by the explosions mixed with the cheers of victorious soldiers filled his ears. Smoke—both from rifle shot and fire—filled his nose. He could feel the sweat pouring down his face, and he couldn't tell if it was from the heat or exertion. At this moment, he didn't particularly care.

Another explosion shook the courtyard, and Bayram shot up to see a mushroom shaped set of flames fill the air. Coming from the southern portion of the palace, he could feel the heat on his skin, even from this distance. Conjuring up a mental map of the palace, his heart began racing faster as he realized exactly where flames were.

"Come on, boy," Bayram shouted, ignoring the pain in his ribs as he leapt onto Askari's bare back. Apparently sensing his distress, the kerton needed no prodding, and he leapt toward the explosion.

Moving into the next courtyard, Bayram noticed a small group of outnumbered rebels fighting against a contingent of guards and regular soldiers. He quickly dismissed the action and urged Askari onward. This particular fight would be over within a few minutes. There was little point in letting it deter him.

Bayram could feel the heat of the flames before he rounded the corner to see the inferno that had caught. The fire roared as it devoured everything in its path, and Askari skidded to a stop before being consumed. The kerton let out a groan as Bayram slid onto the ground, his brain unable to comprehend the sight before him.

The familiar arched doorway was now open, the heavy wooden door blown into the courtyard during the initial explosion. Inside were the charred remains of couches and silk pillows. Tapestries were nothing more than piles of ash, and the very stone itself was marred.

Bayram let out a howl as his eyes made contact with a charred form, the remnants of a white dress still discernible. The dark hair was gone, but he could still see it in his mind's eye.

"Gamila," he shouted, leaping toward the flames.

Askari's teeth caught him by the collar and flung him backward. His ribs popped again as he slammed into the marble floor, but he ignored the pain as he rose to his feet. Tears flowing from his eyes, he ran again toward the fire.

Askari leapt into his path, his green tail wrapping around Bayram's torso. Struggling against the strength of ten men, Bayram clawed at the scaly skin as he lunged toward the flames.

He had to see for himself. It couldn't be true.

Yet as the exhaustion and pain began to take over, he knew his eyes couldn't be lying to him.

Gamila was gone.

21

The cuts covering Sophie's arms burned, immersed in the hot soapy water used to wash the myriad of dishes required by Lana and her other cooks. Now completely puckered from the morning spent washing pots and pans, her already-sore hands were now begging for relief. Yet she knew it wouldn't come.

"It really is unfair," Maggie's voice sounded at her side, and—completely lost in her own thoughts of how unfair the situation was—Sophie jumped at the sound. A pot fell into the sink, splashing no small amount of hot water onto her dress.

"Well, someone's a bit jumpy today," the old woman said with soft laughter, apparently delighted that she'd been able to sneak up on the girl she'd raised since infancy. "It's not as if you had a rough night or anything."

"I don't understand—I saved the heir to the throne from assassins last night, and here I am being punished for being out past curfew," Sophie said, picking the pot back up and attacking the oatmeal that had dried to the metal with a stiff brush. "You'd think I would at least get a day's rest as a reward."

"We can't be expecting rewards for just doing our duty," Maggie said. "Anyone else in your situation would have been expected to risk life and limb to save a member of the imperial family. What you did was really nothing special."

"I think it was magnificently brave of the lass," Lana piped up, joining in on the conversation. The large woman held a mixing bowl under one arm while the other rapidly mixed a thick dough that was only a few minutes away from requiring kneading.

"Oh, you know I'm only teasing," Maggie said, giving her signature laugh, despite the fact that no one else understood the joke.

"There's more than enough truth in it though," Lana said. "I'm sure Prince Tomas is right grateful, but the Emperor can't go around bestowing massive rewards on people just for doing their duty."

"I never expected gold or anything," Sophie said. "But I certainly didn't expect the guards to write me another citation for staying out past curfew. My minor breaking of the rules resulted in quite a bit of good."

"I know, dearie," Maggie said, flashing her a warm smile. "That's why I'm letting you wash dishes—at least it's not as lonely as polishing silverware under an armed guard."

Sophie wasn't so sure, but she bit her tongue. Lana and Maggie were both on her side...for the most part. The two women were at least sympathetic, and it wouldn't do any good to argue.

"Besides, I think we'll look the other way if you need to head out early for some rest," Lana said. "After all, someone who—"

A hush settled over the entire kitchen, and Lana trailed off, her mouth hanging open as her eyes darted toward the door leading to the rest of the palace. Maggie's face had taken on a similar look, although the old woman's mouth didn't hang open. Yet the shocked expression on both faces made Sophie's stomach fall.

Sophie turned to see a man enter the stifling kitchens. His perfectly groomed mustache, close-trimmed hair, and dark brown coat marked him as one of the Emperor's personal retinue. This was no guard, no simple soldier, not even a high-ranking servant—the man now in their vicinity had personal and daily contact with the Emperor. Such a figure had likely never set foot in the lowly servant kitchens.

"I would very much like to speak with the maid called Sophie," the man said. His voice wasn't loud, but it rang throughout the room, the sound echoing on the stone walls. It was met with a silence, but several serving girls raised their hands, pointing directly at Sophie.

Sophie could feel the weight of the stares, the eyes of all her fellow servants boring into her. These twenty or so girls had grown up with her, had played with her in the gardens. Now they were looking at her as if she were a complete stranger.

"Allow me to introduce myself," the man said, striding over and giving Sophie a deep bow. "I am Reginald Montero—Steward of House Silvino."

"I'm Sophie, but you already seem to know that," she responded with a curtsy, tripping over her words.

"His Majesty requires your presence in the Throne Room," Reginald responded with a smile, "and I have the pleasure of accompanying you."

The silence in the room somehow deepened, as if her fellow serving girls had stopped breathing. Sophie wanted desperately to ask what the man meant, but she knew that doing so would be improper. If the Emperor requested your presence—an event completely unheard of in the servants' ranks—you did not question it for even a moment.

"May I have a minute to um..." Sophie began but didn't quite know how to end.

"Clean up?" Reginald finished for her. "I'm afraid not. I have been instructed to bring you immediately, and the slightest of delays would likely be met with displeasure from His Majesty."

"Yes, of course," Sophie said, grabbing a towel and drying her hands. "I wouldn't dream of keeping the Emperor waiting for me."

"I'm so glad you understand," Reginald replied with a smile, offering his arm to Sophie. She took it, and the two began walking through the kitchens. She didn't dare make eye contact with anyone. Instead, she kept her eyes on the doorway as Reginald smiled to the servant girls, giving them a series of small nods.

As they left the kitchens, and the oppressive heat provided by the ovens, a chill ran down Sophie's spine. Despite the warm summer heat settling over the palace like a wool blanket, she felt only cold.

"I can tell the Emperor is quite grateful for your actions last night," Reginald said, apparently sensing Sophie's anxiety. "I don't know exactly what he wants to say, but I can assure you there is nothing to fear."

"This has just been a rather unexpected turn of events," Sophie replied, searching for the right words. "I didn't wake up this morning thinking I would be meeting the Emperor—especially covered in kitchen grease."

"His Majesty is not one to judge a servant from a temporary appearance," Reginald said. "When I first met him as a young lieutenant, I was completely covered in mud and excrement after marching all night in the rain. I can assure you the Emperor looked nearly as disheveled. It is well known that you are being called into His Majesty's presence directly from performing service, and your appearance will be more than forgiven."

The sound of their footsteps changed as they left the rough stone floor of the servants' quarters. Rather than the dull thud to which Sophie was accustomed, her shoes began emitting a loud crack on the highly polished marble. She felt confident that her reflection would be easily visible were she to look down, but Reginald looked forward, and Sophie wanted to do the same.

"I've never been in this part of the palace before," Sophie said, strongly resisting the urge to look all around with her mouth open in awe. "It's hard to believe I've spent my entire life only a few hundred spans from such beauty."

"And here I am taking it all for granted," Reginald replied, allowing his eyes to wander from their path forward. "I do remember my early days, back when I was first adopted into the imperial household. I could hardly concentrate on my work being surrounded by such divine beauty."

They walked through what would likely be considered a rather simple hallway by palatial standards, but to Sophie, it was absolutely breathtaking. Besides the red marble floors, massive columns lined the walls, supporting the ceiling that stretched at least thirty spans into the air. Tapestries and oil paintings adorned the walls, a stark contrast to the sparse and narrow corridors of the servants' wings.

Sophie felt a chill run down her spine, and goosebumps rippled up and down her skin. It was as if a winter wind had swept through the palace, turning summer aside. She looked up at Reginald—the man seemed completely unaffected.

A woman turned the corner, dressed in a tailored red dress. Her shockingly black hair was pulled up into a tight bun, and a stern expression marred her otherwise beautiful face. She looked to be no more than forty, and while she wore the garb of an elite servant, she walked with the air of one who demanded respect from everyone.

"Well, well, what do we have here, Reginald?" the woman asked, and Sophie felt her escort's arm tighten on her own.

"Just doing the bidding of His Majesty," Reginald replied without slowing, the anxiety in his voice almost palpable.

"Is this the girl who saved Prince Tomas?"

The woman sniffed as her deep green eyes looked up and down Sophie's dirty clothing and loose bun.

"Very astute, Madam Esmerelda," Reginald responded as they passed her. His arm clenched her tighter still, and his pace quickened. "Sorry, but there's no time to chat—don't want to keep the Emperor waiting."

"Of course," Esmerelda chuckled, turning to watch them continue down the hall. "I look forward to seeing more of you, child."

The words hung in the hallway, and Sophie resisted the urge to look back. She hadn't realized her heart had begun beating faster, but it was almost coming out of her chest. Inhaling deeply, Sophie tried to calm herself.

"Who was that, sir?" she whispered. It seemed more than plausible that the woman could hear anything said anywhere.

"That's Madam Esmerelda," Reginald whispered back, apparently with the same fear. "She's the Mistress of the Linens, and she's well... you'll see."

"You can't leave me with nothing," Sophie gasped. "I felt something strange, even before she turned the corner."

"Just be careful around her," Reginald replied. "Be respectful and you'll be just fine."

"But I—"

Sophie stopped mid-sentence as the two emerged from the hallways into the palace's grand entrance hall. Rising nearly a hundred spans into the air, the domed ceiling was adorned by gold and oil paintings. Massive chandeliers dangled, their electric light dancing through the hundreds of crystals and illuminating the massive structure.

"This was created by the Emperor himself—with help from the Great Stone of Okuta, of course," Reginald said, smiling. "I will admit that it's one of the few things I never take for granted."

"It certainly makes one feel small," Sophie replied, her neck starting to complain from how much she was looking up.

At the end of the entrance hall, a twenty-span tall archway led to the throne room. The massive chamber dwarfed the beauty and size of the entrance hall. Sophie had seen it her entire life from the outside, but the beauty within was beyond her imagination.

Even from a distance, Sophie could see that a crowd was assembled within. The din of their chatter was just audible, and her stomach began to squirm at the thought of perfumed lords and ladies scrutinizing her. As she drew closer, the smell of so many competing perfumes from the assembled court began to assault her senses. Her stomach began to churn again, and this time it wasn't just from nerves.

At the far end of the room, three figures robed in a dazzling display of purple sat on golden thrones situated high above the crowd, accessible by granite steps. Above the thrones, embedded into the very stone of the palace, was the Great Stone of Okuta. It was a sight Sophie had wished to see her entire life, and she now found no time to revel in the beauty of something containing the very essence of a Divine. The three regal figures dominating the thrones demanded her attention.

Her eyes were immediately drawn to the largest throne, directly beneath the Great Stone. Emperor Silvino sat expressionless, with the bearing of a lifelong soldier. Although still trim, the Emperor's face showed signs of too much time spent in the sun as a youth mixed with the weight of responsibility in his old age. An ornate crown sat atop dark hair that was beginning to show signs of grey.

To his right sat a beautiful woman with dark, silky curls extending to her shoulders. Unlike her stoic husband, Empress Jilina radiated a warm smile, aimed directly at Sophie. Her dark brown eyes hinted at her humble roots, yet that simplicity somehow only added to her regal features. Wrinkles were forming around those eyes, although they appeared to be from a life spent smiling.

To the left sat Prince Tomas, and Sophie's stomach did another flip as his dark eyes made contact with her own. His features were even sharper in the light—his nose was still too long, his cheekbones sharp enough to cut a stone. There was evidence of the prior night's events—a bruise on his left eye, a deep cut on his lip that had required stitches. Yet somehow, it was the most beautiful sight she could possibly imagine.

A smile lit up the prince's countenance, and the young man winced, placing his hand to the stitches. A smile spread across her own lips at the sight, despite the increased churning in her stomach. She heard a few spurts of laughter from the crowd, and she suddenly remembered she was surrounded by aristocracy.

Approaching the thrones, Sophie dropped to her knees and placed her forehead on the ground. The marble was almost cold to the touch, despite the sunlight streaming in through the high windows. The room grew silent, the din of the nobility's conversation dying suddenly.

"Arise, my child," a strong voice sounded from the middle throne, and Sophie scrambled to her feet.

"I am told you are the one responsible for saving my son from certain death," the Emperor said, his voice echoing through the chamber. "For that, you have not only earned my gratitude but that of the entire empire."

The assembled crowd applauded, albeit quietly. Sophie had the suspicion that the assembled court didn't know any more than she did the purpose of this meeting. Yet so far, there didn't appear to be anything to fear.

"Step forward and tell the court your name," the Emperor continued, rising to his feet and motioning for Sophie to join him on the dais.

Sophie took a deep breath and did as asked. Her footsteps echoed in the silent hall, and her foot caught on one of the steps, causing her to stumble. Her cheeks immediately felt hot, even as she caught herself well short of falling. A few laughs sounded from the crowd, but Sophie ignored them as she continued her climb.

"I am called Sophie," she said upon arriving at the Emperor's side. She could feel the words catch in her throat and was sure the sound didn't carry past the Emperor's ears.

"I am forever in your debt, Sophie," the Emperor said, grasping her hand. "Let it be known that in the Empire, merit counts for more than birth. Sometimes, noble blood can reside in even the most common of my subjects—this young woman is proof of that."

The Emperor paused, and the assembled crowd responded with a small round of applause. Sophie tried not to focus on any single person within the crowd. She only focused on not letting her knees buckle.

"In gratitude for your services, I am officially raising you to the station of minor nobility," the Emperor said, waving the crowd to quiet itself. "You will be adopted into the imperial household, and you and your descendants will be given the honor of serving the imperial family."

Sophie's mouth dropped open, and tears sprang unbidden to her eyes. No longer would she spend her time cooking in the servants' kitchen. No more days would be spent polishing silverware for a rarely used dining room in the most remote corner of the palace.

"Thank you, Your Majesty," Sophie said, bowing yet again.

"Thank me by serving with all your heart," the Emperor whispered low enough that only she could hear, a smile spreading on his face.

"Please follow Madam Esmerelda to your new quarters," the Emperor continued, this time raising his voice for the assembled crowd to hear. Sophie looked up, her heart falling as she caught sight of the woman who had given her such a disdainful look in the hallways. "From this day forward, Esmerelda will be your mother, for all intents and purposes. She will see to your needs and ensure that you are properly instructed in your new duties."

A wide smile broke out on the woman's face—the type that didn't extend to the eyes. Sophie's stomach fell even further at both the words and the look on the woman's face. Perhaps life wasn't about to get better after all.

22

"Yes, Madam Esmerelda. Of course, Madam Esmerelda," Sophie whispered to herself as she folded linens, her mind refusing to move on from the verbal beating her new taskmaster had just delivered.

Her new sleeping quarters were absolutely stunning. Thick rugs covered hardwood floors while oil paintings graced the walls. A massive four-poster bed was hers and hers alone. She had never even dreamt of having her own bed, and now this entire room was hers to enjoy—that is, when she wasn't working or being berated by Madam Esmerelda.

"It sounds like someone hasn't exactly taken a shining to her new mentor," a voice sounded from behind, and Sophie jumped.

Prince Tomas stood in her doorway, that same smile gracing his face. Sophie had to stop herself from wincing as her eyes caught sight of the wounds covering his countenance. The young man didn't seem to mind, and he bounded into her room.

"Oh, I didn't realize—how long have you been standing there?" Sophie asked, the words sticking in her mouth.

"Long enough," Tomas chuckled. "And don't worry—I wouldn't dream of telling Esmerelda that you're less than happy with her treatment of you. She wouldn't really be surprised, though. From what I've heard, at least half the palace's staff would love to have a real shouting match with her."

"I—uh," Sophie stammered, absolutely unsure how to respond. The heir to the throne of Margella was in her room, gossiping with her as if they'd been friends for years.

"Oh, sorry," the Prince said, offering his hand. "I haven't ever properly introduced myself."

"I don't think the Crown-Prince needs any introduction," Sophie replied, giving him a small curtsy.

"Well then, I at least need to properly express my gratitude," Tomas said, bowing and kissing Sophie's hand. "If it weren't for your impeccable timing, I probably wouldn't have survived to see the sunrise."

"Right, yes—my...timing," Sophie said, her words trailing off before she realized where this conversation was going. "Prince Tomas, I'd love for you to stay and chat, but I have so much laundry to fold."

"Yes, I can see that," Tomas said, smiling as his eyes found the remaining three pillowcases that had not yet been folded. "However, I'm here on a very special assignment. My father would like to see you in his personal study, and he has asked me to accompany you. I'm assuming you don't know the way."

"That would be lovely," Sophie replied, unsure of how to avoid discussing exactly why she had been able to save the prince.

"Well then, let's not waste any time," Tomas smiled, offering her his arm. "Father is rather impatient and hates to be kept waiting."

Sophie took the young man's arm, her own trembling as she did so. For the second time in a day, she found herself being escorted through the palace by men far beyond her station.

"So, tell me young Sophie," Tomas said after a moment of walking in silence, his smile growing wider, "do you often wander through the hedge maze near sunset?"

"Not as often as I would like," Sophie answered. It wasn't exactly a lie—while she made her way there practically every night, she would love to spend even more time among the greenery. "Although I have spent enough time in there to know my way about. I enjoy the quiet and solitude that can really only be found there."

"As do I. In fact, I've been going there pretty much every night for months now to practice music."

"Oh, was that you playing the mandolin before the attack?" Sophie asked, trying to keep her voice steady. "I did hear a bit of music—before the beating began, that is."

"I've been playing music since I could talk," Tomas said. "Were you able to listen much before I was so rudely stopped? It's so rare that I get feedback from an audience."

"I really only caught the bit at the end," Sophie replied, the words catching in her throat.

"Oh, that's a pity," Tomas said, pausing for a moment before continuing. "Sophie, did you know that someone has been sitting on the other side of the hedge from me pretty much every night for weeks now?"

"I had no idea," Sophie lied, her blood running cold. "He must not have been there that night, otherwise I would have seen him."

"I've heard this person sigh quite audibly during my songs," Tomas said, the smile evident in his voice as Sophie refused to look up at him. "I have little reason to believe my admirer to be a man."

Sophie paused for a moment before responding, heat rising from her cheeks.

"How long have you known it was me?"

"Not until this exact moment, but I did strongly suspect it after you came running through those hedges," Tomas said, grabbing Sophie's hand. "Please don't feel embarrassed. To be honest, I've quite enjoyed having an audience. It's good to know that someone so lovely would think my music worth breaking curfew to hear."

"I really didn't mean any harm in it," Sophie said, stopping to face the prince. "I had no idea to whom that voice belonged. I've spent years wandering through those hedges, trying to escape...well, everything. I just happened upon you playing one night, and I couldn't resist coming back."

"Oh, don't worry," Tomas responded, patting her hand. "I'm glad it was you, and not someone following me for more nefarious reasons. We really should keep moving—I'm late for a nightcap with the Minister of Finance."

"You really do play quite well," Sophie said as the two continued walking. She barely had even registered where they were—somewhere behind the throne room, possibly. It was hard to tell. She hoped she would be able to find her way back.

"Tell that to my father when you see him. He keeps telling me that music is a waste of time—hence the nightly serenades in secret. He was most certainly not pleased to hear that I had put myself into danger just to play the mandolin."

"Who would expect assassins in the palace gardens?" Sophie asked. "I know it was certainly a surprise to me."

"They were most likely kidnappers and not assassins, but that doesn't change the fact that these are dangerous times. Several of our neighbors to the south are completely embroiled in revolution and civil war. Trouble is brewing on the western border with Albona—something about water rights. It's most certainly not a time to be filling my head with lighthearted things such as music."

"I must respectfully disagree," Sophie responded. "I think that in spite of these dark days, we should take time to find the beauty in life. Otherwise, what's the point?"

"Beautiful words of wisdom," Tomas said, stopping in front of a rather nondescript door. "And I would love to hear more of them, but unfortunately we've arrived."

Tomas knocked on the door, which was promptly answered by Reginald, the same man who had accompanied Sophie to the throne room that very morning. A smile was evident under his mustache, and his hair remained perfect, despite the late hour.

"Oh, come in Miss Sophie," Reginald smiled before turning to Tomas. "And thank you for bringing her. Please give the Minister my warmest regards, and don't let him bore you for too long with his budget reports."

"I'll be sure to surround my head in a cloud of inebriation before the discussion grows too serious," Tomas said before turning to Sophie. "I would like to see you tomorrow, if I may."

"Is that allowed?" Sophie asked, her cheeks beginning to burn. Tomas just gave her a smile and turned down the hallway without another word.

"It sure seems as if a certain young man has taken a shining to you," Reginald whispered, his eyes following Tomas down the hallway. "Come in, the Emperor doesn't have all night."

Sophie entered to find a rather plain study of traditional Margellan architecture and furnishing. A fireplace on the far wall sat empty, a flame completely unnecessary on such a hot summer night. Hardwood floors were accented by thick rugs similar to the ones in her own room. Overall, beyond the empty fireplace and the bookshelves laden with leather tomes, there weren't many differences between the study and her new quarters.

She still couldn't believe that this was her life now—only yesterday she had woken up in a bed she shared with two other girls. Now she was being called to a personal meeting with the Emperor. She didn't know if her mind would ever grow used to this.

"Ah, my dear Sophie," the Emperor called out, setting down a book on the small table next to his armchair. "I'm glad to see my son brought you directly here. I was rather worried you two would take the long way around."

"Please don't think that I would dream of entangling myself with Prince Tomas," Sophie said, giving a deep curtsy. "I have no intentions beyond serving Your Highness."

"I was only joking," the Emperor said before gesturing for her to take a seat. "And I would feel far more comfortable if you would sit down. Reginald, please pour Miss Sophie a glass of something to drink."

Still shaking, Sophie lowered herself into the armchair opposite the Emperor. Reginald poured some clear liquid from a bottle into a small cup and handed it to her.

"I promise my intentions tonight are not to leave you a nervous wreck. I just wanted to thank you in private for saving my son," Silvino said, grabbing a glass of wine from Reginald and taking a sip. "He's my only child and—just as importantly—he's heir to the throne. My own feelings of loss would be dwarfed by that of my subjects."

"I thank Okuta that I was able to be in the right place at the right time," Sophie replied.

"Yes, it seems you have quite the ability to be exactly where you're needed," the Emperor said, placing his wine cup down and leaning forward. "That's why I need to ask something very special of you."

"I am your humble servant, Your Majesty," Sophie bowed in her seat.

"I thank you for that loyalty," he said, his eyes looking her up and down. "Reginald, would you please excuse us for a moment?"

Sophie looked up at the steward. The man's eyes widened slightly, but he didn't betray any strong emotion at the request. Without a word, Reginald bowed and exited.

"Tomas is a foolhardy young man," the Emperor said after the sound of Reginald's footsteps faded outside the door. "He has no concept of his own mortality."

"I believe that is the case with most young men," Sophie responded, her heart pounding in her ears.

"That is an all-too-valid point," the Emperor said, sitting back in his chair and again grabbing his glass. "However, I believe there are certain events in a young man's life that tend to temper this sentiment."

"From our most recent conversation, it appears he has no desire to risk his life."

"He is shaken, and for the moment caution will be the order of the day. But tomorrow, who can say? With time, the memories will fade, and Tomas will lose his new-found vigilance. I can't afford for anything to happen to him."

"Of course, the entire nation would be devastated should harm befall the Crown-Prince. However, I'm unsure how such a lowly servant as myself could be of help."

"It has become rather apparent that my son is quite taken with you. He has spoken of little else in the past twenty-four hours."

"Your Majesty, I promise you that—"

"I want you to become his mistress. Of course, it would need to be discreet—an 'open secret,' if you will. Royalty across the entire world are entitled to dalliances with their servants. You are now a minor noble, so it will not be considered scandalous. It just needs to be kept quiet, and most importantly, I don't want any sort of illegitimate heir to become an issue."

"May I ask why Your Majesty desires this?" Sophie asked. First, she was raised to the nobility, and now she was going to be put in a rather intimate position with Prince Tomas. Her mind began to reel, and she forced herself to focus on this completely insane conversation with the most powerful man she'd ever met.

"I want you to keep a close eye on him—make sure he stays out of trouble," Silvino said, taking another sip of his wine.

"I would be more than happy to do so," Sophie replied, her voice little more than a squeak. "However, I am just a frail young girl and could hardly be expected to protect him from any real danger. We would have certainly perished had it not been for the guards coming so quickly."

"That may be true, but I have more on my mind that just his physical safety," the Emperor said. "I worry sometimes that Tomas gets dangerous ideas into his head. I want you to keep him on the straight and narrow—steer him away from any radical notions."

"I guess that sounds possible," Sophie said.

"And more than anything, I want you to keep an eye out for anything he does that's well...suspicious. I don't need regular updates or anything from you, but if you see anything regarding Tomas or any of his associates, you should let me know immediately."

Sophie finally understood. The Emperor wasn't looking for a daughter-in-law. He wasn't looking for someone to provide love, companionship, or even protection for the Crown-Prince. He wanted her to be a spy.

23

Thunder cracked overhead, the noise echoing in the now-empty Basilica of Surion. Throughout the day, thousands had filed through the massive structure to bid goodbye to one of the few royals that was actually loved and not feared. Now that the services were over, the priests would be coming to take the body down into the catacombs beneath the basilica.

"Goodbye, Gamila," Bayram whispered, placing his hand on the smooth wooden coffin sitting on a raised dais.

Another round of thunder rattled the building, and the sound of rain pouring from the sky met his ears. The array of flickering candles around the coffin served as the only source of illumination in the massive domed atrium. The darkness pressed in on Bayram, and he forced himself to his feet.

The bells began to toll high over-head, masking the sound of his footsteps on the marble floor as he trudged toward the open doorway. More thunder cracked, and a flash of lightning flooded in through the large doors separating the basilica's interior from the large plaza outside. Moving out into the open and holding back tears, Bayram spotted his carriage.

"I must insist that you join me," a voice called out from the carriage in front of his own, and Bayram looked up to see his father's face—gaunt and grey like he had never seen—poking out the window.

"And I must insist on riding alone," Bayram shouted over the rain without altering his course.

"Please," Oosman croaked, and Bayram stopped. "I don't have the strength to be alone right now."

The mixture of exhaustion and grief in the monarch's voice struck Bayram's raw heart, and he changed course with a heavy sigh. The coachman—looking rather miserable in his soaked raincoat—leapt from his seat and opened the door for the Crown-Prince. Bayram shook off the man as he attempted to help him climb into the vehicle.

"The service was lovely," Oosman sighed as Bayram took a seat. "But no one could ever properly pay tribute to Gamila."

"Funerals should be meant to celebrate the life of a loved one," Bayram replied, trying to keep his thoughts away from the past twenty-four hours. "Today, it's impossible to do anything but lament the loss."

"At least she gets a proper funeral," Oosman said, removing his crown and running a hand through his hair. "I fear that my own corpse will be fed to the dogs in a few weeks."

"I won't say you deserve it," Bayram said, shifting his gaze out the window and letting his father finish the thought in his head.

"How confident are you that this constitution of yours will work?" Oosman asked, and Bayram turned to face the Sultan.

"Not very," Bayram responded. "But I still think it's better than going out in a blaze of smoke and glory."

"If I were younger, I would say we could make a proper fight of it," Oosman said, removing a handkerchief from his sleeve and dabbing his eyes. "But now I'm old, and I can't see a way out of this damned situation."

"I wouldn't say you're old," Bayram said, unsure of how to respond. His father was yet to reach sixty—if the world weren't being turned upside down, he could easily expect another ten to twenty years on the throne.

"When we get back to the palace, assemble a team and write out the best possible document you can," Oosman said, his voice growing firmer. "I'm going to promulgate your little constitution."

Bayram's eyes grew wide, and he opened his mouth to respond. Nothing came out. It was as if a mountain had decided to pick up and move on its own accord.

"I don't know if this gambit is going to work, but I can't watch the rest of my family be slaughtered," Oosman said, his voice stumbling. "Burying my only daughter was harder than I could have possibly imagined, and I can't stand the thought of my sons facing a similar fate."

"You're making a wise decision," Bayram said, trying to find the right words for a moment such as this. "At least, it's the only decision I can see that doesn't necessarily end with mass slaughter."

"For everyone's sake, I hope you're right," Oosman said, and the two men slipped into silence.

The carriage rolled through town as Bayram's mind fluttered from one idea to the next, the excitement battling with his grief and exhaustion. He would need more than one cup of coffee—and potentially several shots of rum—for the late night ahead of him.

Entering the palace gate, the carriage rolled to a stop. Oosman returned the crown to his head and let out a deep breath.

"I'll have a draft to you by morning," Bayram said as the coachman opened the Sultan's door. "Then we can work out the finer points"

"Very well," Oosman said, his voice lacking even the slightest hint of emotion. "Just don't expect me to enjoy this process."

"I don't," Bayram said, scooting over toward the door. "I realize how difficult this must be for you."

"No, you don't," Oosman sighed, looking down at the ground, the rain beating down on him. "Oh, and one more thing..."

Bayram looked up at his father, the water soaking his hair and running down his face.

"After your new system goes into effect, I'm going to abdicate the throne in your favor. The Sultan is dead," Oosman sighed, bowing to Bayram. "Long live the Sultan."

24

Sunlight filled Gamila's vision as her brain regained consciousness. Lying on her back, she let her eyes remain shut against the brightness. Propping herself up onto an elbow, Gamila directed her gaze downward and pried open her right eye.

Instead of the blue and white linens of her bed, she was greeted by a thick rug of deep red. Shifting her focus, she was not greeted by the polished marble of her bedroom floor. Rather, her vision was filled with a coarse canvas. Raising her head and opening both eyes, she made out walls of the same material, glowing a brilliant white in the morning sun.

The floor was littered with silk pillows centered around a small table, upon which sat jug of water and wash basin. In the far corner sat a folding screen made of hand-woven bamboo. Behind that, she saw a heavy trunk with its top sitting open.

"Oh good, you're awake," a deep and familiar voice sounded from behind, and Gamila leapt to her feet. "I was beginning to wonder if you were having a bad reaction to the powder."

An apparition from her childhood stood in front of her. His dark skin and mustache contrasted with a pearly grin, still the same after all these years. The usual cigar hung lazily from his lips, the stench of the tobacco bringing back an array of memories to Gamila's mind.

"So, we've resorted to kidnapping now, have we, Uncle Agha?" Gamila said, placing a hand on her hips.

"Kidnapping is such an ugly word," Agha said, a mock frown spreading across his face. "I'd prefer to say that you've been sequestered—for your own safety, of course—until hostilities have ceased."

"Glad to know there's nothing wrong with me except for an inability to handle...whatever it was you had your thugs administer to me," Gamila said.

"There's no need to go into exactly how you got here, except that the rebel spies inside the palace were well-aware of your fondness for lemonade. When you're a man of my renown, the resources to kidna—sequester a single princess are easily obtained."

"Rebel spies? I should have known you were somehow part of that rebellion."

The initial shot of adrenalin was beginning to wear off, and Gamila could feel her head spin. Her legs protested the effort it took to stand, and they felt bruised in no less than a dozen places.

"I'm only a minor functionary, I assure you," Agha said, waving. "My particular set of skills does come in handy for such a campaign as this, however."

"Did they promise you revenge on my father if you lent a hand?" Gamila asked, thinking of the war he'd raged against the city of Oltu in the north.

"Oh, they promised me quite a bit more than that,"Agha said, moving over to help stabilize Gamila. "Now, be careful, my dear. Your body has been through a lot—you should try to stay off your feet for a few more hours."

"And I suppose that any thoughts of escaping are futile," Gamila scoffed, refusing the man's help and remaining on her feet.

"You're free to do as you choose," Agha laughed, backing away and lifting his hands in mock surrender. "However, you should really take advantage of your situation. It's not every day that a doting uncle goes to such lengths to save a niece."

"I hardly think that drugging me makes you a savior," Gamila scoffed, finally giving in and moving to sit on one of the silk pillows.

"What do you think happens to a royal family when their brutal regime is toppled?" Agha asked, his voice lowering as he took a seat of his own.

"Well, assuming that this tent is somewhere in the rebel's camp, you merely brought me to the very heart of those doing the toppling," Gamila said. "It's hard to imagine a more dangerous place for me at this point in time."

"You're quite right about our location, and you would normally have a point about being in further danger. However, Princess Gamila has the distinct advantage of already being dead."

Gamila didn't respond to her Uncle's words. She only raised her eyebrows, and the man sighed before continuing.

"Despite my objections, the rebel leaders sent in a group of their best men to assassinate my illustrious brother and his family. I made sure that some of my loyal men were sent along to make sure you were brought here instead of being sent to the grave. After my men kidnapped you, they packed your room with explosives."

"So, my father, he's..."

"Still in the land of the living," Agha said, and Gamila's heartbeat began to settle. "My colleagues seem to think that the Sultan is a weak old man. Reports from the few survivors who made it back to camp say that he fought with the ferocity of a kerton."

"And what's going to happen when the guards investigate my destroyed apartments and fail to find my body among the ruins?" Gamila asked.

"Oh, they'll find a body that could easily be yours—don't worry, the girl died a natural death," Agha said, noticing Gamila's angry stare. "There's no need to grow indignant with me."

"So, the idea is that nobody will be looking for a dead princess in the middle of the rebel camp?" Gamila asked, folding her arms. "May I ask why you went to such lengths to...'sequester' me?"

"Because," Agha began, pulling the cigar from his mouth, "you're my favorite."

"Right, you disappear from my life, wage war on my country, and then you tell me that I'm your favorite? That just doesn't add up."

"Sadly, a man in my position can't afford pure altruism," Agha sighed, his gaze narrowing as the cigar hung lazily in his hand. "Gammy, I need your help."

Gamila didn't respond. Instead, she raised an eyebrow and let her eyes bore into her uncle. Putting the cigar back in his mouth, Agha continued.

"By putting my lot in with these rebels, my position has grown somewhat tenuous. It's not that we're going to lose this little war—your father really doesn't stand a chance. It's just that my relationship to the current royal family has made me some enemies."

"And their enmity doesn't have anything to do with your life as a thief?" Gamila asked, a smile creeping onto her lips.

"Well, that too," Agha chuckled. "But there are many powerful figures within the camp who would prefer to see my head on the same pike as the Sultan's. Beyond my group of loyal thieves, I don't have anyone I can trust."

"So, you want me to be your...what? Representative? Spy? Confidant? I'm not really seeing how I come into the equation."

"You'll need to be a little bit of all those things—I need you to pose as my mistress," Agha said, shifting in his sitting position. "As a mysterious woman of some rank, you can be in a magnificent position to both discover information and influence those around you."

"You're sure I'd just be posing, right?" Gamila asked. "I believe that even you wouldn't stoop to incest."

"I'm not a vile beast," Agha said, rising to his feet and moving toward the folding screen and open chest. With his words hanging in the air, he pulled out a dress of fine, red silk that matched the pillows. In the other hand, he displayed a veil.

"A man in my position is entitled to a first-class concubine," Agha smiled. "And while I'd prefer to have a real one, I'd be blind to not see the possibilities this allows. Posing as my...romantic interest...will allow you the freedom to roam through the camp while being able to remain aloof."

"Beyond—er—gratitude for saving my life, what makes you think I'd go along with this?" Gamila asked.

"You have to understand that your father won't make it out of this situation alive. His public execution will be demanded by the tribal elders. However, if you were to cooperate, I'd be willing to stage Bayram's death as I did yours. After my position is secure, the two of you will be free to go wherever you please. You have my word."

The word of a thief and murderer, Gamila thought. She noticed that Jabari was not mentioned—a pity, but an understandable omission. The boy would prove a thorn in the side of the new government. She knew that his freedom couldn't be part of any deal. She would have to see if the young man's freedom could potentially be obtained. Jabari was an annoying twit, but he was still her brother.

"What kind of work would you like me to do?" Gamila asked, unable to hold back a sigh. It was apparent that if she wanted to survive, she would have to go along with her uncle's plan. At least, for a little while.

"Mostly the work of a socialite," Agha said. "Mingle with the other noble women, get a feeling for what is going on in camp. I need to stay ahead of any plots that would result in my death and cut them off before they grow into anything dangerous."

"Sounds terribly dull," Gamila said, a smile spreading across her face despite the pounding in her chest.

"Go get dressed," Agha said, tossing the dress at her and motioning toward the folding screen. "I have a rather important meeting, and I would like you to accompany me."

"What purpose would you have for me at a meeting?" Gamila asked, nevertheless grabbing the dress and moving behind the screen.

"It will be good for my rivals to see you with me," Agha said. "They need to become accustomed to your presence. Otherwise, you might look suspicious walking around the camp."

As her uncle spoke, Gamila slipped out of her dusty clothing and began donning the new red dress. She was rather surprised to see that it fit as if it had been custom-made for her. Then she realized that it probably had.

She was even more surprised to find that the dress was not overly revealing. In her mind, she had expected the silk garment to leave little to the imagination. However, she was nearly as well-covered as she normally was.

"So, today I'm pretty much a piece of eye candy," Gamila said, moving out from behind the bamboo.

"Your words, not mine," Agha responded as he moved toward the tent's exit.

Outside the tent sat a rather ornate litter crafted from hand-carved wood. Four muscle-bound men stood at each corner, ready to lift the vehicle onto their shoulders. Such manpower-intensive forms of transportation had long faded from use in Maradon, but Gamila reminded herself how little she knew of the inner tribes.

"Soon, I'll be riding through the streets of Maradon in a proper motorized vehicle," Agha said, taking Gamila's hand and helping her into the litter. "But for now, this incredibly antiquated transportation will have to do."

Gamila clung to one of the posts as the burly attendants lifted the litter onto their shoulders. The movement as they took off was surprisingly smooth, far less jostling than a carriage. As they moved through the camp, Gamila could see tents in all colors, shapes, and sizes. There was a certain order to their placement, creating streets and alleyways. However, there was certainly nothing uniform about the tents themselves.

"We've been camped at this oasis for weeks," Agha said, and Gamila turned to look at her uncle. "What once was a sleepy little village has practically turned into a city rivaling Maradon. We have bakeries, blacksmiths, tailors, taverns—anything you could ever want."

"Seems a bit excessive for an army, doesn't it?" Gamila asked, looking out onto a well-laid out street.

"This is so much more than just an army," Agha laughed. "And it's so much more than a rebellion—the inner tribes are migrating, taking the land and lives that should be theirs."

"And what about the people already on that land?" Gamila asked.

"Oh, I'm sure there will be some discomfort in the transition," Agha said, the words coming out slowly. "But there is enough for everyone."

Gamila didn't respond, and she turned back to her inspection of the camp. The more she looked around, it struck her how quiet the streets were. Not a soul was present beyond their litter-bearers and a small retinue of horsemen riding behind them.

"Wait, where are all the people?" Gamila asked, turning back to her uncle.

"I thought you would never ask," he replied, a smile spreading on his face. "You'll see in a moment."

Gamila opened her mouth to ask further, but the smile on Agha's face spoke of a secret in which he took great delight. Turning to face the orderly rows of tents, Gamila let out a sigh.

A cacophony of voices reached her ears, the distant roar of a mass of humanity. She perked up at the far-away din, trying to decipher the distance. It was muddled, difficult to tell anything of use from the sound. The litter crept forward, the noise growing louder, although her gaze was met by nothing beyond empty streets and multi-colored tents. She sat tall in her seat, craning her neck to see further. Yet it was useless.

After an eternity, the tents broke into open country, and the sound of a crowd reached new heights. They were well outside of the green landscape of the oasis, and there was little to greet her eyes beyond red rock and sand. Yet, she still could not see the source of the noise.

Ahead, she caught sight of eight aging figures standing at the edge of a cliff, their long grey beards drooping over colorful robes. The litter stopped, and the servants gently lowered their load to the ground.

"Come, Gammy—you'll want to see this," Agha said, climbing out of the finely-crafted litter and offering his hand to help her do the same.

"Something tells me this is more than just a meeting," Gamila said, accepting her uncle's hand and planting her feet firmly on the red soil.

"Lord Agha, you're late," the youngest looking of the men said as the entire group approached. "Is this historic occasion insufficient to require your punctuality?"

"My apologies, Master Yusef," Agha replied, a broad grin on his face as he slapped the man on his shoulder. "I just wanted to make sure that you had enough time to assemble everyone."

"Of course we did," Yusef scoffed, a snarl forming on his face. "We've been waiting for ages, and the people are getting restless."

"Trust me, this will be worth the wait," Agha said, turning to Gamila and offering his arm.

"Is this young thing the reason you're late?" Yusef asked, running his eyes over Gamila's figure. She was very glad to be wearing a veil at this moment, although she wished the dress covered up every bit of her skin.

"Oh, Yusef, you certainly have a way with people," Agha replied, seemingly unperturbed by the man's animosity. "And now you are the one holding up this procession. Let's get to it."

Agha led her toward the cliff's edge, and Yusef followed. Gamila could feel the man's gaze boring into the back of her head, and she wanted nothing more than to run away. However, she knew that for a variety of reasons, that would not be possible.

As they neared the edge, a valley opened up, and Gamila's eyes took in the mass of humanity in the shallow basin below. Like a small bowl carved out of red rock, the formation acted as a natural amphitheater—the perfect location to address such a crowd.

"Welcome, my friends," Agha shouted as they reached the cliff's edge, his words reverberating on the red rock. The buzz of conversation below went silent, and Gamila could feel the collective gaze of the crowd turning in her direction.

"I come before you this day with a humble heart," Agha continued, his voice growing stronger. "The very sight of you, however, fills me with joy—the joy of impending victory."

The crowd erupted into a cheer at the words, and Gamila let out a breath. She didn't know what Agha was doing, but he certainly wasn't playing some minor role in this rebellion. And if this crowd erupted into applause at the end of every sentence, she might be a grandmother by the time this speech ended.

"For too long, the usurper in Maradon has kept you oppressed," Agha began, and the noise below once again died down. "You've been forced to eke out an existence in one of the harshest regions known to man. The elites on the coast call you barbaric, uncivilized, and simple. However, we know that they are the ones who deserve these labels."

"The Sultanate—the institution that has been nothing but an oppressor for generations is on the brink of imploding under its own diseased and bloated weight. While the tyrants in Maradon have grown fat from our suffering, we have grown strong, forged in the fires of the desert. Now is the time to take what is rightfully ours."

The crowd erupted at this, and Agha lifted a fist into the air. Gamila turned to see the eight ancient figures approaching, and she moved away from her uncle. She still didn't know what was happening, and she had no desire to be part of it.

Yusef pulled a delicately crafted golden circlet from within his robes as the group of elders surrounded Agha in a semi-circle. Agha fell to one knee as Yusef lifted the gold above his head. The other seven men each placed a hand on circlet.

"Lord Agha," Yusef called out, his voice echoing on the red rock as the crowd again fell silent. "You have proven yourself worthy of our trust and admiration. You have proven yourself to be counted as a true friend of our people."

"As representatives of the eight tribes," Yusef continued, lowering the circlet onto Agha's head, "we anoint you Emperor of Salatia."

Agha rose to his feet and steadied his new crown as Gamila's mouth dropped open. The widest smile imaginable crept onto Agha's face as he stepped toward the cliff's edge.

"At this moment, the rule of tyrants is over," Agha cried, his voice growing hoarse. "The death of the Sultanate is at hand. Long live the Empire."

25

"What a beautiful evening," Aydiin said, letting the first warm air in weeks fill his lungs. The setting sun cast a deep orange glow on the world, and Aydiin was ready for the day to be over.

"I can see why you wanted to come up here," Cael said, also taking in a deep breath. "I can almost forget the stench of the city."

Leaning against the rough stone wall of Fort Savoy, Aydiin grabbed the young man by the shoulder and ruffled his auburn hair. With a chuckle, Cael pushed Aydiin away, and the two brothers returned to their vigil.

Only a few months ago, the vantage point atop the fort would have allowed for an unparalleled view of the city and its surrounding countryside. If he were on the other side of the fort today, the only sight to greet him would be the decaying husk of a city. As for right now, his eyes couldn't enjoy the rolling hills. They were distracted by the sight of Diaz's camp.

"I wish we could focus our time and resources on the city," Aydiin sighed.

"Hard to do that with Diaz hovering over our shoulder," Cael responded as footsteps approached.

"What did you think of Fort Savoy, General Aydiin?" Luka's voice called out as the young man approached, his beautifully tailored uniform looking worse for the wear after a week of uninterrupted use.

"Well, after three days of inspecting forts, I need a break," Aydiin said, pulling a face as he looked down at his own uniform. Out of the corner of his eye, he could see the epaulettes marking him as a general in the city's militia.

"Oh, don't tell me you're still upset about the promotion?" Luka asked, apparently noticing the look on Aydiin's face.

"I'm barely fit to be a common soldier, let alone lead anyone into battle," Aydiin said, straightening his posture.

"You're not the only one who feels that way," Luka replied. "How do you think I feel about being put in command of the entire city? Your command is almost ceremonial in comparison."

"I wouldn't call Aydiin's duty to oversee the central part of the city 'ceremonial,'" Cael cut in. "He's got to make sure we don't all die when the outer forts are overrun."

"Let's just hope it doesn't come to that," Aydiin said. "I still don't think leading a hundred men on a half-successful campaign against my uncle really qualifies me for the higher echelons of command."

"Byanca loves you," Cael said, patting Aydiin on the shoulder. "But she wouldn't have given you command if she didn't have absolute faith in your abilities."

"I'll second that thought," Luka said. "And you didn't really answer my question before—what do you think of Fort Savoy?"

Located on the southern end of the city, Fort Savoy was one of many that ringed Genodra's capital. From first glance, there was little to distinguish it from any of the others. However, with its position on the most prominent hill, the fort acted as the keystone of the complex defensive system surrounding Palmas. Its upkeep and defense were paramount to the survival of the revived republican government.

"It looks just like all the others to me," Cael said with a shrug. "The walls are still standing, and I see plenty of cannon lined up, ready to blow holes in anyone dumb enough to march up that hill."

"If this were a somewhat even fight, I wouldn't be so worried," Luka sighed, his gaze also veering toward the camp south of the city. "But those soldiers down there are hardened professionals. I grew up hearing stories about the daring fights of the First Army as they defended the country from Pilsan warlords."

"In contrast," Aydiin broke in, "most of our men have never fired a weapon in the heat of battle."

"It looks like the Battle of Monterosso, but on a much larger scale," Cael said.

"Except this time, I don't think Aydiin will be able to breathe enough fire to wipe out two thirds of the army," Luka said, turning to Aydiin. "Actually, that's not a bad idea. Think you could?"

"I might be able to come up with something," Aydiin said, pulling out his spyglass and directing it toward the menace that hovered over Palmas like a cloud.

At first glance, he could immediately see the professionalism evident in every aspect of the camp. Neat, straight rows of white tents extended in a large square surrounded by earthworks. There were mess and supply tents and even street signs. In many ways, it looked more civilized than Palmas.

Columns of grey-clad soldiers drilled in an open field at the camp's center, marching in perfect formation. Officers called out, and their men responded with alacrity and precision. After watching his own militia's attempt at training, it was an impressive and depressing sight.

"I can see those little wheels turning in your brain," Luka said. "What are you hoping to find?"

"I'm not sure," Aydiin said. "Some sort of weakness, maybe—something that could bring that army down a peg."

"Didn't you say that the Field Marshal invited you to inspect his camp some time?" Cael asked. "Why not today?"

"Diaz essentially confessed to being the Grand Master of the Order," Aydiin said. "Even though he's told me that he doesn't desire my death, I can't imagine that entering his camp would be in my best interest."

"We could wear disguises," Cael said with a smile. "You could wear a wig, and I could put on a fake mustache. It's foolproof."

"I'd give Askari to see that," Aydiin said, lowering his spyglass to look at his brother-in-law. "Probably not worth the risk, though."

"We've been trying to get spies into that camp for a week now," Luka replied. "None have returned. The best information I can get is based on far-off observations like this."

"I don't want to sound boastful, but I'm pretty good at getting in and out of tough spots," Cael said.

"I appreciate the initiative, but it's too dangerous," Luka said, rubbing Cael on the head.

"Yeah, I guess you're right," Cael responded as he fixed his hair. "Maybe someday—when the stakes aren't so high—we can sneak into something a little less dangerous. I've always wanted a mustache."

"That's a deal," Aydiin said, putting his spyglass away. "Now, come on. We need to get back home. I haven't changed out of this uniform in days. Luka, would you like to join us?"

"Wish I could, but I've just got too much work to do here. Crews are working around the clock shoring up the walls, and it just wouldn't look good for me to head back to my palatial manor while these men work out here in the cold."

"Well, thanks again for letting us take over your home," Cael said. "I feel like we've stolen it from you."

After Bertrand's death, Alise had decided to hire dozens of workers to restore the Marzio mansion to its former glory. Large enough to house the entire group quite comfortably, it had essentially become Aydiin and Byanca's first home together. It was certainly the longest they'd stayed in one spot for their entire marriage.

"Well, it's not like any of you are just sitting around reading books all day," Luka responded. "Even Alise has kept herself busy."

"Byanca's not exactly busy—she just sits in meetings all day," Cael said as the three began walking down the stairs. "And then she comes back late at night, grumpy at everyone and everything."

"I'd take inspecting forts and being outside all day over twenty minutes in one of those meetings," Aydiin said, the exhaustion threatening to overtake him as the group descended another set of stairs. "She crawls into bed every night absolutely exhausted. There's a lot on her shoulders."

"While you're pretty much on vacation," Cael cut in. "After three days spent inspecting forts and sleeping in your uniform, you must be second-guessing some of your life choices. Weren't you supposed to be saving the world or something?"

"Right now, I'm just focusing on Palmas," Aydiin said as they reached the bottom of the fort. "Once that's done, I'll be able to focus a little bit better on the rest of the world."

"Baby steps, Aydiin," Cael said as he climbed into the driver seat of the car they'd brought. "Going from Palmas to the whole world might be too big of a leap. Maybe you should just focus on not getting captured for a few months."

"Nah, I'll just count on you to save me," Aydiin said as he climbed into the passenger seat before turning to Luka. "Thank you again for everything you're doing. Make sure to get some sleep tonight."

"Don't worry about me," Luka said with a smile. "Let's just get through this, and then we'll all take a nice long vacation."

"Oh, I wouldn't mind seeing Alise in a bathing suit," Cael said, starting the engine and pressing on the accelerator with all the grace of an elephant before Luka could respond to the comment. The tires squealed as the automobile's engine roared, and Aydiin felt the force of the sudden movement slam him into his seat.

"Alise is a bit old for you, don't you think?" Aydiin asked as Cael directed the car through the winding streets that led up to Fort Savoy.

"Of course she is," Cael said with a wink. "Not to mention that she doesn't know how to have any real fun. I just wanted to see how Luka would react."

The road leading up to Fort Savoy wound down the hill toward the city, and Aydiin had to focus his gaze on the window to keep his lunch down. Yet Cael handled the curves with the skill of someone who had spent years driving. Somehow, Aydiin felt confident that the young man had started driving long before it was legal to do so.

In an obvious attempt to avoid the refugee-packed city center, Cael directed the automobile through the deserted streets of the outer city. Here, the wide avenues were either lined with derelict homes or fields of ash. It was much faster moving through the abandoned streets, but the sight made Aydiin feel more uncomfortable than the mass of starving refugees crammed into the center of the city.

"I still don't see why we couldn't move back home," Cael said, nodding to the Doge's Palace in the distance as the automobile entered the wealthier section of town.

"Well, besides the fact that it's not exactly habitable at the moment," Aydiin began, "there is the fact that there isn't yet a Doge. As far as the nation is concerned, your father is dead. We'd just have to move out again after the election."

"Yeah, alright. I just miss my real home. The Marzio's house just isn't the same."

"After this is all over, you can come with Byanca and me," Aydiin said. "I know that's not home, but it's at least something."

"Where do you think you'll go?" Cael asked.

"Probably Margella. We've got more Great Stones to find. The only other one we know about is part of the Imperial Palace."

"Wow, you really are taking this one step at a time."

"I don't even know where to begin finding the Lost Stones," Aydiin sighed. "They are *lost*, after all."

"Well, for now, you should at least get a good night's sleep," Cael said as he pulled the car through the gate of the Marzio home. "Maybe before you head off to bed, you should take a bath—you certainly smell like someone who hasn't been taking care of himself."

"That, my dear brother, is a most excellent idea," Aydiin said, a smile spreading across his face despite the exhaustion weaving its way through his bones.

The reality of their situation, which he'd been able to keep at bay, was now pressing on his soul. He didn't know what to do. He didn't know how to save the world. All he wanted was a bath and a decent night's sleep.

"It's obvious Alise is home alone," Cael said, pointing to the mansion as they drove in through the courtyard.

The renovated Marzio home was well-lit, despite the shortage of both electricity and lamp oil. While Alise certainly had shown herself more than capable of immense bravery, she also hated being home alone in the dark. With everyone else out, often until the early morning hours, Alise generally kept the lights on throughout the entirety of the house.

"We should probably at least pop in and say hello to the girl," Aydiin said. "She's probably bored out of her mind, sitting around all day sewing uniforms."

"Not a bad idea. I might even try to steal a goodnight kiss," Cael said, and Aydiin raised an eyebrow at the young man. "What? She may be too old for me and incredibly annoying, but you've got to admit that she's beautiful."

"I'll admit no such thing to the brother of my beloved wife," Aydiin responded, opening the vehicle's door and walking toward the house.

Cael didn't respond as he caught up, but Aydiin could tell the young man was smiling in the darkness. It was good to see Cael enjoying some of the perks of teenage life amidst this insanity. Of course, he was also participating in the kind of adventure many young men spent their lazy afternoons dreaming about, so he couldn't feel too sorry for the boy.

Cael led them through the hallways to Alise's bedroom and knocked on the door.

"Hey, it's Cael and Aydiin," he whispered through the door. "If you're asleep, give us one long snore, and we'll just leave you alone."

"A lady never snores," Alise's voice replied as she opened the door, the permanent scowl on her face fighting with a smile for dominance. "How can I help you, gentlemen?"

"Just wanted to pop in and say hello," Aydiin said. "I feel like it's been ages that we've just been living in your house rent-free."

"Oh, it's not free," Alise said, a smile spreading across her face. "We'll be sure to send you the bill when this is all over."

"Well, assuming we survive, I'll gladly pay it plus some sort of tip," Aydiin responded before letting out a chuckle.

"I am actually glad to see you two," Alise said. "Don't tell Luka, but it's pretty lonely here without anybody but the waiting staff. For some reason, they don't really like to stand around and chat with me."

"They're just busy trying to make enough money to feed their families," Cael said with a yawn.

"Look, you two should stay up for a while," Aydiin said, pushing Cael into the room. "I'm absolutely exhausted, and a good night's sleep is all I can think about at the moment."

"Oh, alright," Alise said, genuine disappointment evident in her voice. "Good night, Prince Aydiin."

Leaving Cael to take his chance for a goodnight kiss, Aydiin began shuffling toward the bedroom he shared with Byanca. Opening his door to find a darkened room—likely the only one in the house—Aydiin didn't bother turning on the light before unbuttoning his jacket. Looking to the bed, he wished Byanca didn't have to spend so much time in meetings. He could barely remember the last time they'd gone to sleep at the same time.

"It's nice to see that the Heir of Alarun does actually sleep on occasion," a cold voice sounded from the corner of the room, and all thoughts of sleep evaporated from Aydiin's mind.

A mess of nearly white hair sitting atop a long, pale face emerged from the shadows. Piercing black eyes caught Aydiin's gaze, boring into his soul. A grey officer's uniform, immaculately pressed, seemed to be almost part of the man rather than just a piece of clothing. Dangling from a golden chain around the man's neck, the familiar black stone sat against a strong chest, pulsing in the darkness.

"Don't be alarmed," the man said, lifting up his hands. "I don't mean you any harm...tonight, at least."

"Well, if you're here to chat," Aydiin said, picking up his green jacket and moving to flip on the lights, "we should properly introduce ourselves."

"I have a few names, but you may call me Skraa," the officer said with a bow, squinting as the lights came on. "And, of course, I already know all about the illustrious Aydiin—Prince General of Salatia and Heir of Alarun. Please, take a seat. There's no point in standing around like barbarians."

Aydiin moved toward a set of armchairs in front of the room's fireplace. Without a word, Skraa poured a set of drinks, handing one to Aydiin. He held it in his hand, unwilling to consume anything given to him by such a creature.

"May I ask what brings you to my home?" Aydiin asked as Skraa took his seat.

"Let's just call it a social call," Skraa said with a smile. "You've proven yourself to be a worthy adversary—one that deserves some attention before being destroyed."

"In some cultures, it's considered rude to discuss the destruction of your host," Aydiin replied.

"I can't think of a single culture where that kind of thing is actually considered polite. Yet you and I—we're above culture. We're above anything these humans have devised."

"I hate to shatter any delusions you may have, but I am human," Aydiin said.

"See, that's where you're wrong," Skraa said, leaning forward in his chair. "Those Stones you've stolen have done something to you. I'm sure you've felt it—memories that aren't your own, abilities to control and manipulate your surroundings beyond your wildest dreams. You're not quite human, not quite Divine. You're something else entirely."

"For someone who likes to hide in dark bedrooms, you sure seem to know a fair amount about what's happening," Aydiin said, placing his drink on the ground. "Mind telling me how you know so much?"

"Oh, that's not a question I need to answer. You just need to look a little harder and think back to your former lives. The answer is within you, somewhere."

"Look, I'm completely exhausted, and I don't have the time or energy for this," Aydiin said, sitting back against his chair and rubbing his temples. "If you don't want to kill me tonight, then please just leave me in peace."

"Ah, yes, you've been rather busy running around, preparing for the inevitable battle against that imbecile I'm forced to serve," Skraa said, remaining in his chair and taking a sip of his drink.

"Is that little revelation supposed to shock me?" Aydiin sighed, opening his eyes. "Diaz already strongly hinted that he's the new Grand Master of the Order. You'll have to try harder than that."

"But what if I told you that pathetic man has no intention of actually using his army against this city?" Skraa said, his smile growing wider.

"Right, Diaz marched an army all the way up from the south and doesn't plan on using it," Aydiin said, only just curious enough to not simply get out of his chair and leave the room.

"Outsiders tend to think of the Raven's servants as a monolithic, hive-minded group," Skraa said, settling back into the chair. "Yet among the faithful, there are vast differences of opinion. The old fool that you so fortunately killed was a firm believer in the Chaos Theory."

"Let me guess—that's the idea that the world needs to be thrown into chaos in order for the Undergods to return?" Aydiin asked, his eyebrow rising.

"Oh, you're a smart one. It was certainly fun to let them believe that for a time. However, the current leader of those pathetic fools subscribes to a theory that I personally find to be a little more fun."

"What's that?" Aydiin asked, growing tired of this conversation. "Does he want to give out free puppies and plant flowers?"

"It's not quite that altruistic. He wants to rule the world, bringing order to the chaos."

"So, Diaz has practically the opposite intentions as Arathorm did. Seems like quite the shift in policy."

"Oh, it really is rather annoying. This army was meant to destroy the city, but then you came along and cleared the way for Diaz to pursue his own agenda. Not that it really matters—once the Raven has returned, this world won't have long to enjoy the order secured by Diaz and his followers."

"Why tell me all this?" Aydiin asked, leaning forward again. "Are you really just that bored?"

"Look into your memories," Skraa said. "Delve into the other lives you've now lived, and you'll understand why."

"Please stop telling me to do that," Aydiin said, leaning back and again closing his eyes. This conversation was going nowhere, and he just wanted it to end.

His words were met by silence, and Aydiin opened his eyes.

The chair that had been so recently occupied by Skraa now sat empty. Aydiin turned his gaze around the room, only to find no sign that the man had ever been there. Yet his words hung in Aydiin's ears.

Look into your memories. Delve into the other lives you've now lived, and you'll understand why.

26

Barrick stood at the bow of the *Preston*, the sun beginning to set in the west, as his eyes caught their first glimpse of land. It was still hazy, but at the ship's ridiculous speed, he had no doubt they'd be arriving in Gorteo before long. He couldn't help but marvel as the small ship practically flew across the waves, taking him back across the same waters he'd traversed a few months ago on his way to Naerdon. Only this time, the journey had only taken half as long.

The cut on his arm—freshly bandaged and treated with ointment—reminded him of its presence. It brought his mind back to the night in Naerdon and his duel with Sanborn. His mind couldn't help but drift toward the future of the wound.

Looking out across the horizon, he forced his mind back to the task at hand. It didn't matter if he had a shadow-blade cut or not if he couldn't get into Gorteo. Hopefully, there would be enough time to deal with the wound later.

At his side, Amelie stood with her hands raised, breathing in the hot air of the equator and soaking in the oranges and reds of the sunset. Her dark hair—normally in a tight bun—was undone and billowing in the wind. The prudish little scholar he remembered had certainly come alive on the voyage, and Barrick had to admit that he liked this relaxed version of his cousin.

"You seem worried," Amelie said, breaking the silence.

"That's a surprise?" Barrick asked, tightening his grip on the metal bar as the wind rustled his hair. "I'm not sure how much I like the idea of trusting my life to a *prototype*."

"Oh, Barry, you should just relax and enjoy yourself," Amelie replied with a smile, using the name she'd called him as a child. "We're out here in the sunshine, the ocean spraying on our faces. People pay big money for this kind of experience."

"I did pay big money," Barrick responded, thinking about the massive roll of bank notes he'd used to charter both the *Preston* and its inventor. "And it's kind of hard to relax when I'm about to sneak into a country so repressive that people die trying to escape it."

"It's not too late to change the destination," she said. "We haven't even run into any Gorteon naval patrols yet. There's a good possibility that we could turn around without anybody knowing we even got this close."

"After everything I've been told, the silence is downright eerie," Barrick said, leaning against the steel railing. "Do you have any idea what that nutty professor is doin' below deck?"

"Oh, don't worry about him," Amelie said. "I've been working with Nathaniel for years, and I can say with certainty that he's an absolute genius."

"I think that's taking it a bit far," a voice sounded from behind, and Barrick turned to see a round, sunburnt face topped with thick, blonde hair. The man's hands were covered in grime, and he was wiping them off with an almost equally filthy rag.

Despite the youthfulness of his countenance, Barrick knew that Nathaniel was well into his thirties. Having spent the past decade as an engineer at the Institute, he was probably one of the most qualified individuals to help Barrick get past the Gorteon blockade. That also meant that his services didn't come cheap.

"I can't even begin to express how happy I am with the *Preston*," Nathaniel smiled, gesturing to the ship. "We'll be arriving off the shore in just a few minutes—that's almost half the time of a traditional vessel."

"The ship's a certifiable work of art," Barrick replied. "And what about yer secret device? Is it ready, Mr. Genius?"

"That's actually why I'm here," Nathaniel said, smiling at the jab. "My assistant is just going through the final inspection, and I believe it's time to give you a quick tutorial."

Barrick shouldered the revolver at his side and picked up the small bag that contained everything he'd be taking with him—a change of clothing, a few coins, and his jacket formed from pure shadow.

Holding back a deep sigh, he began following the professor across the deck.

"Is that really all I need? I was expectin' a few days of trainin', at least," Barrick said, following the man across the deck and toward the stairs leading down into the hull. "Yeh haven't let me even poke me head below deck since we started this trip. It's given my stomach more nausea than the waves."

"I'm sorry to be so secretive, but I promise that the machine is user-friendly as possible," Nathaniel said. "If your little test-run goes well, I'm hoping to sell this to every government, gentleman explorer, and seaside resort in the world."

"And what if it doesn't go well?" Barrick asked as they descended the stairs.

"Well, let's hope you're a strong swimmer."

Nathaniel let out a laugh at his own wit, and Barrick didn't reciprocate the gesture as his eyes struggled to adjust in the low light below deck. The smell of grease and recently welded steel assaulted his nose, and he fought the urge to breathe through his mouth. As his eyes adjusted, he could see why Nathaniel had felt the need to be so secretive.

"Barrick, I'm pleased to present my latest invention—the *submersible*," Nathaniel said, spreading his hands out.

"It's great," Barrick droned, unsure exactly what he was seeing.

Suspended by a small crane, a ten-span steel cylinder with a propeller protruding from the back greeted Barrick's eyes. The front was dominated by reinforced glass, and he could see a single chair within surrounded by an array of controls. The entire structure made absolutely no sense as his brain struggled to determine the steel cylinder's purpose. A young man stood atop a ladder leaning against the monstrosity, a clipboard in hand as he went over the inspection checklist.

"Everything looks ready," the young man said, a smile spreading across his face as the group entered. He looked to be no more than fifteen or sixteen, although his messy brown hair and freckle-smattered cheeks made it hard to tell for sure.

"Thank you, Carl," Nathaniel said, moving to take the checklist from his assistant. "Did you find anything?"

"Nothing, sir," Carl responded. "She'll glide beautifully through the waves."

"I have to admit that I'm quite jealous," Amelie interjected, her voice trembling. "Nathaniel's been talking about this for months."

"Well, you're welcome to come along," Barrick said, unsure how to respond to her envy.

"I would strongly advise against that," Nathaniel replied, pushing his clipboard back to Carl. "This prototype only has enough power to comfortably accommodate a single passenger, I'm afraid. The later models I'm envisioning will be able to ferry dozens—or even hundreds—under the waves."

"Wait, I'm goin' *underneath* the water?" Barrick shouted, eyes bulging. "I gotta say—I'm quickly fallin' outta love with this idea."

"Oh, don't be silly," Amelie laughed. "Why did you think it's called a *submersible*? What did you think it would do?"

"I wasn't quite sure, lass," Barrick drawled, turning to face his cousin. "Yeh just told me it would help get past the Gorteon ships. That was good enough for me."

"I assure you that it's quite safe," Nathaniel said, turning toward the cylinder. "There's a series of pumps that bring water in and out of special tanks, allowing you to control your depth. The Gorteon naval ships won't be able to do anything because they won't even be able to see you."

"How close can you get me ter the shore before I hafter get in this thing?" Barrick asked.

"Oh, I think we'll be able to get you within about fifteen minutes of the Gorteon coastline," Nathaniel responded, and Barrick could feel his stomach settle back down.

"I'll bet you were wishing it could be hours and hours," Amelie said, grabbing Barrick around the waist and giving him a squeeze.

"Someday, that could be true," Nathaniel said. "But for today, he might have about an hour if he's lucky."

"What happens after an hour?" Barrick asked, eyebrow raised.

"Well, first, you'll run out of fresh oxygen," Nathaniel said, chewing on his tongue in thought. "Then, the power will run out, leaving you in darkness. So, unless you want to asphyxiate in the dark, I'd suggest you avoid too much joyriding."

"Yer not exactly fillin' me with confidence," Barrick said. "Why can't we just sail past the ships? The *Preston* is bound ter be faster than anything the Gorteons have."

"The *Preston* would hit the sand long before reaching shore," Nathaniel said as he shook his head. "And besides, I thought the whole point of this was to get into Gorteo without dying. The *Preston* is certainly quick, but they'd take us the moment we reached the beach."

"I'm sure you'd like to avoid a Gorteon prison," Amelie said. "I have to imagine it's the exact opposite of a luxurious vacation in the Capos Islands—assuming they don't just kill you outright."

"Yeah, let's just focus on getting you to shore undetected," Nathaniel said, patting Barrick on the shoulder. "I'd sure hate to..."

The words died on the professor's lips as the *Preston* lurched, the hum of its engines growing silent. Overhead, the electric lights began to flicker, the already weak light growing dimmer.

"I should go check with the captain," Nathaniel said, moving toward the staircase.

"I can do it," Carl said, leaping down from the ladder and running toward the stairs. A deep moan rang throughout the hull as the young man neared the deck. The ship rocked, and flames shot down from above deck, engulfing the steps. With a thud covered by the explosion's shockwave, Carl fell to the ground.

His skin was charred, his clothing smoldering.

Gripping his bag in one hand, Barrick rushed over to the fallen boy. Carl's chest failed to rise and fall, and his lifeless face was charred and broken. Looking back toward the stairs, Barrick's mouth dropped open as a young child leapt onto the floor only a few spans away.

Dressed in a simple brown tunic, the Gorteon sported a sword in one hand and what looked to be a rudimentary grenade in the other. A smoldering piece of rope stuck out of an iron ball, the flame quickly approaching the explosives packed within. The light reflected off the small man's pale face and brown hair, revealing a deep smile. That smile widened as the Gorteon charged toward Barrick.

Pulling a revolver off his hip, Barrick cocked the hammer and discharged a round into his attacker's chest. All semblances of life fled the small man's face as he fell to the ground, followed by both the sword and iron grenade. Barrick leapt onto the ball, grasping it in his shaking hands, and tossed it across the hull. With a clang, the metal ball landed somewhere—the explosion from such a crude grenade should be fairly weak.

Nathaniel and Amelie both sat with eyes and jaws wide open at the sight of two dead men at their feet. Barrick found himself wishing he were less familiar with the sights and smells of death.

"We need to get out of here," Barrick shouted, and his companions shook themselves at the words. "Nathaniel, is there—"

Barrick fell flat on his face as the Gorteon grenade exploded with completely unexpected force a dozen spans away. His face hit the wooden floor, and he could already feel a bruise forming on his forehead. His ears began to ring, mixing with the groans of the ship and water springing into the hull.

Flipping onto his back, a massive hole greeted his sight. The ocean was taking advantage of the breach, and water was gushing into the ship. The steel and wood of the *Preston* began groaning under the weight, and the lights gave out.

"Get into the *submersible*," Barrick shouted, scrambling to his feet as his eyes struggled in the darkness.

Nathaniel rushed ahead, grabbing Amelie by the hand, rushing the woman toward the steel cylinder. Shaken from her stupor, Amelie rushed ahead of him, climbing the ladder and leaping into the steel tube. Barrick began climbing the ladder as Nathaniel rushed to the top, swinging his feet through the hatch.

"The *submersible* can't handle all three of us," Nathaniel shouted.

"Neither can the ship," Barrick responded, shoving the professor through the opening.

Jumping through the hatch as water continued to pour in through the gaping hole in the bottom of the ship, Barrick slammed the opening shut before climbing down into the main compartment. His head pounded, his muscles ached.

Only a few spans in either direction, the space within the *submersible* really was less than adequate for the three of them. Nathaniel had already taken his seat in the pilot's chair while Amelie stood behind, grasping the leather seat with white knuckles. Barrick settled in behind her, gripping the ladder that led to the hatch above.

"Can we squeeze through the hole?" Barrick panted, his gaze returning to the reinforced glass at the front.

"We don't have any choice," Nathaniel replied, flipping a few switches. Lights within the compartment began to flicker on, accompanied by the hum of an engine. The front window was nearly covered by the intruding water as another explosion rocked the *Preston*.

Nathaniel pulled down on a lever, and Barrick's ears were met by the sound of the crane above letting go of the steel tube. He tightened his grip as the *submersible* began drifting in the water, its only tie to the ship now severed. The small craft began to vibrate, the propeller in back kicking into gear.

"Hold onto something," Nathaniel hollered, pushing forward on a lever near the control stick.

The sub lurched forward, and Barrick tightened his grip on the ladder as momentum pushed him backward. The side of the ship drew closer, the sub pushing against the water gushing through the hole. The screech of steel on wood filled Barrick's ears as the *submersible* squeezed through the opening and out into the open sea.

"Okay, what in the Underworld just happened?" Amelie asked. "We were on deck only a few minutes ago, and I didn't see another ship."

"Maybe the *Preston* isn't as fast as we thought," Barrick panted. "Or maybe, the Gorteons aren't as simple as we all believe."

"Are you suggesting they have a ship that simply came out of nowhere?" Amelie scoffed.

"I hate to put a stopper on this most enlightening conversation," Nathaniel said, pulling down a tube and peering into it. "But we should probably be judicious with our oxygen supply."

"How long do we have?" Amelie asked, gripping the chair tighter.

"Well, one person would have about an hour," Nathaniel sighed. "With the three of us, we've got about twenty minutes...assuming we don't waste it all fighting."

"Gotcha," Barrick said. "Silence. Shallow breathes."

"Exactly," Nathaniel said, focusing on the controls. "Just relax and meditate a bit."

Taking the professor's advice, Barrick slid down the wall of the submersible, resting his back against the cold steel, and focused on his breathing. A little voice in his head told him he should be planning his next steps. Yet a much louder voice told him that he wouldn't survive to see Gorteo, so it didn't exactly matter what he planned.

"I'm sorry that I got you lot mixed up with this," Barrick said without looking up at Amelie and Nathaniel.

"Can't imagine a better way to go," Nathaniel replied, checking a few switches. "Things were getting a bit boring at the Institute."

"All the same, I'm sorry," Barrick sighed.

Well, at least it's over, he thought. No more sneaking around, no more meeting shadowy informants in dingy taverns. He didn't even have to worry anymore about the end of the world. For him, it was already over.

Grabbing his satchel, Barrick pulled out the shadow jacket. Rising to his feet, he slipped it on and braced himself as his eyes adjusted to the darkness within the *submersible*. Looking out the front window, he could tell the seabed was growing closer.

"Can yeh see where yer goin', mate?" Barrick asked.

"Not exactly," Nathaniel said. "If we had more time, I could take things slow. As it stands, I'm just heading full steam toward the coast."

"Well, yeh might want ter be careful," Barrick said, moving toward the front and placing his hand against the glass. "That sand is getting close."

"How can you—"

"Pull up," Barrick shouted as a sandbar appeared in his view, only a few dozen spans ahead.

"What do you—"

Barrick cut off Nathaniel, lunging toward the control stick to bring them closer to the surface.

"Get off me," the professor shouted, pushing Barrick away. "You're going to get us killed."

"Yeh don't get it," Barrick shouted back, rushing to the sub's controls, pushing Nathaniel away. "The sand—"

Amelie's scream reverberated through Barrick's ears as the *submersible* slammed into the seabed at full speed, the force launching the steel cylinder into the air above the waves. Barrick lost his grip on the control stick, slamming into the back wall. Despite the fuzziness crowding around his head, his eyes caught a glimpse of the outside. Less than a hundred spans away, he saw a beach filled with beautiful sand.

It was also crawling with armed Gorteons.

The submersible crashed back into the water, slamming Barrick against the front window. As the propeller touched the waves, it launched them forward like a rock skipping across a pond.

"We need to turn," Barrick grunted, lifting himself to his feet. "That beach ahead is full of soldiers."

"Impossible," Nathaniel grunted. "It's too dark to see us—nobody could possibly know we're coming."

Barrick grabbed onto the wall as the submersible crashed into dry sand, the steel body screeching as it came to a stop. For a moment, there was silence as the engine died.

Footsteps pounded on the metal above them, accompanied by voices. The words were indistinguishable through the steel exterior, but Barrick didn't have to hear perfectly to understand what was happening. Judging from the wide-eyed glares from Nathaniel and Amelie, they didn't either.

An explosion ripped the hatch open, illuminating the interior of the submersible in an orange light. As it died down, a lantern-wielding figure jumped down the ladder, rendering Barrick's shadow jacket useless, and he made eye contact with the diminutive attacker. Barrick simply held up his hands in surrender as the child-like figure brought a club down on his head.

27

Barrick's eyes fluttered open to a darkness broken only by the flickering of torches. His tongue felt like leather, and his head pounded as if he'd consumed rat poison. Letting out a soft groan, he lifted his head.

"Careful there," Amelie's voice sounded, and he felt a soft hand against his forehead. "You had a rough night."

"I've been out all night?" Barrick gasped, pushing himself into a sitting position despite his cousin's resistance. "From a hit to the head?"

"They used some sort of drug to keep us out," Nathaniel cut in, the professor's shadowy form moving toward him. "You had a particularly bad reaction to it. I would suggest waiting a while before moving too much."

"Well, if you were a doctor and not an engineer, I'd be inclined ter take that advice," Barrick responded with a forced laugh, trying to take in his surroundings.

The group was in a small room, three-fourths of which was carved out of a dark stone. The far wall consisted of iron bars, completely covered in rust, that led to the rest of the prison. Running around the perimeter of the room, a low bench carved from the wall held bedrolls and blankets. It was good to see they had at least a single piece of furniture.

"I need to stop waking up in prison," he said, rubbing his head and rising to his feet. "Otherwise, this is going to become a habit."

"They call it 'the pit,'" a trembling voice said from the shadows. "And you won't be able to make it a habit because there is no escape."

Barrick jumped as a stooped skeleton of a man hobbled out of the cell's corner. Tattered remnants of clothing hung on the man's sickly frame, which was little more than skin and bones. Thin wisps of white hair clung to a waxy scalp, threatening to fall as the man moved.

"Barrick, this is Silas," Amelie said, gesturing to the man. "He's the unfortunate soul sharing our cell."

"I'd say it's a pleasure to make your acquaintance, but that would be a lie," Silas wheezed as Barrick moved toward the iron bars. With a sigh, he grabbed onto the rusted metal and directed his gaze toward the outside. "The Pit" was an all-too descriptive term for their location.

A look directly ahead revealed a massive, circular chamber lined with iron-barred cells. Like the rifling of a gun barrel, a pathway carved from the walls spiraled downward into the darkness. The pit's open center extended downward for an eternity, like the maw of an Undergod.

"How long have you been here, Silas?" Barrick asked, his gaze focused on their prison.

"Hard to say in this place," the man replied, his voice weak. "Probably been years."

"If you don't mind me saying," Barrick began, trying to pick his words carefully. "Your physique is rather lean. Do they ever feed you?"

"Guards bring in slop about once a week," Silas said. "I'm so used to the hunger now that I can't even remember the taste of real food. Most of the other prisoners down here are Gorteons—they don't believe me when I tell them about three meals in a day."

"Great. A dreaded prison for political foes to die a slow, agonizing death," Barrick responded, looking down to see his captors had not removed his shadow coat. "And you say escape is impossible?"

"Well, I guess nothing is impossible," Silas replied, moving to join Barrick. "I've just never seen it happen. From what I've heard the other prisoners say, nobody has ever escaped."

"I'm assuming you're one of those unfortunate souls whose ship drifted into Gorteon waters," Barrick said.

"I am indeed," Silas responded, nodding his head. "We were loaded up with Salatian tobacco, heading for Palmas. A storm blew us off course, and when the sun finally came out, we were under attack by those blasted Gorteons. They took a few of us prisoner—I haven't seen anyone else in ages."

"I'm sorry to hear that," Barrick responded. "And if you'll excuse me, I have some exploring to do."

Taking a breath, Barrick lurched onto the other side of the bars, his feet planting firmly onto the path. The usual shiver rolled down his spine, and a wave of nausea rose and dissipated. Turning around to face his fellow prisoners, a smile spread onto Barrick's lips.

"This explains too much," Amelie said, moving toward the bars.

"Can you get us out of here?" Nathaniel asked, his eyes wide.

"Lurching doesn't work that way," Barrick said, shaking his head. "I can't take anybody with me. Besides, we need to see what we're up against before making a legitimate escape. I'll head up above ground and see what I can find out. With luck, we'll be eating some real food before the day's out."

Howls of fear sounded from the cells around him, which were followed by an eerie silence as Barrick slipped back into the darkness, his shadow jacket hiding him from view. His feet were silent as he made his way up the stone ramp, worn smooth by what must have been thousands of footprints over the years.

His eyes piercing the darkness ahead, Barrick made out a trap door where the ramp ended at the ceiling of the Pit. The moaning of rusted hinges reached his ears, and Barrick pressed himself against the wall. The door swung open, and the young Albonan checked his surroundings to make sure he was sufficiently covered in shadow.

Two small men entered the Pit, dragging an unconscious figure between them. The closest guard came within inches of Barrick, and he pushed himself further against the wall. As their footsteps continued down the ramp, Barrick snuck again toward the trap door. Ignoring the pain in his stomach, he lurched to the other side.

Barrick found himself in a small hallway carved from red rock. The stone walls, while relatively smooth, were far from polished, and they lacked any sort of decoration. A single torch hung on the wall, filling the corridor with smoke and flickering light.

Following the corridor, Barrick made his way to a set of crude, short steps leading up to a wooden door. Taking three at a time, Barrick steeled himself before lurching through the barrier. Blinking in the white moonlight, he found himself in the most unexpected of settings.

Gone were the rough walls carved from red rock, replaced by polished white and grey marble. The smoke-spewing torches were replaced by bronze lanterns hanging from ornate hooks. Thick rugs blanketed the marble floor while colorful tapestries adorned the walls.

An open hallway, supported by columns and archways, surrounded a courtyard filled with greenery and fountains. The smell of vegetation and the trickling of running water filled his senses. Taking in a deep breath, Barrick picked up another, even more welcome, scent.

Bread was baking somewhere nearby, the smell causing a riot in his stomach. Sticking to the shadows forming in the twilight and following his nose, Barrick made his way toward the tantalizing aroma. His feet led him out of the courtyard and through a wide interior corridor that led to an almost identical garden. As he emerged, the sound of footsteps forced him to crouch in the shadows.

One of the tallest men that Barrick had ever seen came around the corner, followed by an entourage of seven men, heavily armed and armored. While the others fit all descriptions he'd ever heard of Gorteons—short and thin, with an array of skin and hair colors—the man leading the procession stuck out like an eagle among sparrows.

Long, thick hair of pure silver shone in the lantern light, resting on the man's broad shoulders. He wore a simple tunic of deep blue, which was open at the top, revealing powerful muscles on his chest. The man almost glided more than walked, his lithe frame making the movement appear effortless.

"Make sure to double the foraging parties," the man said, and one of the shorter Gorteons scribbled down some notes on a pad of paper. "I want them working around the clock."

"Yes, Lord Protector," the scribe said, his scribbling growing furious. "It will be done."

"I know it will be," the man replied, a smile on his face, as the group moved past Barrick.

Barrick's heart pounded in his ears as the group passed his hiding spot, although not one member of the entourage came near him. More words were said, but Barrick couldn't process them—that man was the Lord Protector, the ruler of Gorteo. He wasn't being held prisoner in just any old dungeon, he was being held directly underneath the heart of the hermit kingdom.

Plans began forming in his mind as he picked himself up. The smell of baking bread again assaulted his nose, slamming the breaks on long-term planning. For now, he needed to put some food in his stomach.

The smell led him through another hallway, which ended at a small, open doorway. Barrick poked his head inside to find a rather large kitchen—the far wall held counters and sinks for the preparation of food while the wall to his right was dominated by two large ovens. A table in the middle of the room held a basket of steaming loaves, the smell filling his brain with promises of a full belly.

A dozen small Gorteons lay curled up in the corner, their clothing and skin covered in sweat and soot. He didn't know how they could sleep next to the sweltering heat of the ovens, but he reminded himself that he'd have to figure out a way to do so in the Pit. People adapted, simple as that.

Moving into the completely dark kitchen, Barrick let out a sigh. For a moment, at least, he would be able to relax in the completely dark room. Nobody would be able to hear him. Nobody would be able to see him. For all intents and purposes, he wasn't even here.

Ignoring—for the moment—the loaves of bread on the table, Barrick walked toward the pantry on the far wall. Moving into the small room, he began taking stock of the foodstuffs on the shelf. His eyes scanned the half-bare shelves for something better than bread.

A few bottles of fine, Pilsan wine sat next to an entire case of cheap moonshine. Three bags of wheat bearing the seal of the Albonan army were piled in a corner, and cans of pineapple, peaches, and pears took up one of the shelves.

Everything in here has been stolen, Barrick thought. Apparently, the two men he'd come across in the Carcern were more of the rule than the exception. If he had any doubts before, they were now evaporated—the Protector of Gorteo had the Great Stone of Hermnes. All Barrick had to do was find it.

Grabbing one of the wine bottles, Barrick slipped back into the kitchen and grabbed the basket of bread. Stopping to take one last look at the slumbering forms on the floor, Barrick moved back through the hallway and into the courtyard.

Barrick's mouth began salivating at the smell of the bread, and his stomach demanded that he not withhold the sustenance for another moment. Finding a nice shadow to hide him, Barrick sat down to enjoy a loaf for himself. The loaves were simple—little more than yeast, rye, and water. However, with hunger gnawing at his stomach, they tasted better than even the finest baked goods he'd ever consumed.

With the hunger taking a step back, Barrick wandered into the courtyard. Lit by dozens of lanterns, Barrick could see a perfectly manicured lawn, broken up by white stone pathways. The courtyard was dominated by three fountains of solid gold—one at each end and one in the middle. Each held statues that looked to be twice the height of an average man—or four times the height of a Gorteon. Precious gems lined the edge of the fountains, glittering in the low light of the moon and lanterns.

Drawing closer to the middle fountain, Barrick recognized a figure much like the impossibly tall and muscled man he'd narrowly avoided just a few minutes ago. Standing majestically amid the water, the only difference between the statue and the man was a crown adorning the golden figure's head. At the center of the crown, a yellow stone shone, independently of the low ambient light.

The stone was too small to be the Great Stone that Barrick was searching for. It was a similar one that had given Barrick his powers so many years ago. Divinity Stones created by Hermnes, the Messenger of the Gods, were the rarest in the world, sought after by the wealthy and elite. To have one adorning a statue showed either great wealth or unbelievable stupidity. Unfortunately, Barrick had usually seen the two go hand-in-hand.

Footsteps sounded on the opposite side of the courtyard, and Barrick dove into a nearby shadow. Feeling the shadow jacket do its work, Barrick looked out to catch a glimpse of whoever had disturbed his inspection of the statue. His jaw dropped as his eyes took in the most beautiful sight imaginable.

She was dressed in a thin white robe, which flowed like water as she glided into the courtyard. If she weren't alone, the woman would tower over her fellow Gorteons, although she was much shorter than the Lord Protector. Her frame also lacked the impossibly muscular features, instead resembling a willow tree.

Raven hair framed her long, dark face, which was adorned by ruby lips and a sharp nose. Her eyes—a fierce blue—expressed a deep sorrow, which seemed to surround her like an aura.

The woman moved toward the fountain, her eyes making contact with his own, despite the shadow jacket, and Barrick's heart leapt into his throat. Her gaze quickly moved on, and she began humming a somber tune while taking a seat on the fountain's edge. The melody filled the courtyard as she let her fingers glide through the cool water.

His heartbeat slowing down, Barrick realized his mouth had been hanging open since the woman had entered. Closing it, he settled into the shadows, unsure of how to move forward. He couldn't move for fear that she'd see him. He also didn't feel comfortable staying.

The night dragged on, Barrick both loving and hating his de-facto captivity in the isolated shadow. The woman seemed content to spend her entire evening in the garden, humming and occasionally singing. There was a simple joy to it—there was also a great deal of sorrow in everything she did.

A clock chimed in the distance, marking the beginning of the fourth watch. With a deep sigh, the woman rose to her feet, straightened her dress, and glided out of the courtyard. He couldn't really describe her gait in any other word.

Breathing his own sigh of relief, Barrick crept through the palace, keeping to the shadows until he reached the entrance to the Pit. Lurching through the trapdoor, his mind and heart were still spinning as he lurched through the bars of his cell, ignoring the wave of nausea that washed over him.

"Any luck?" Amelie's voice sounded, interrupting his thoughts.

"What do you mean?" Barrick responded, looking up at his cousin, Nathaniel, and Silas. All three looked at him expectantly.

"Have you figured out how we can all escape?" Amelie asked. "It's only been a day, and I'm already going crazy in this cell."

"No, not yet," Barrick said, shaking his head, trying to stop the smile from creeping onto his face.

"Did you at least find any food?" Silas croaked.

"Oh yeah, I did," Barrick responded, pulling out the bread loaves and wine he'd taken from the kitchen.

"Well, what were you doing?" Nathaniel asked. "I may not have my watch anymore, but I assume it didn't take that long to find a few loaves of bread."

"I was able to confirm the very strong suspicion that brought me here," Barrick said, a smile creeping onto his face.

"That suspicion has also, unfortunately, brought Amelie and me here," Nathaniel replied, his frown growing deeper.

"Sorry 'bout that," Barrick said, unable to wipe the smile off his face. "But there's a good reason we're here."

"I'd love to hear it," Nathaniel replied, his words biting in the moist air.

"Well, I'm not sure exactly what's happening in Gorteo, but all the food I could find in the kitchens came from around the world—wheat from Albona, fruit preserves from Gendora, even that bottle of wine is from Pilsa."

"But Gorteo doesn't trade with anybody," Amelie said, her words laden with confusion.

"Exactly," Barrick said. "When I was escaping from the Carcern, I ran into two small men stealing from the armory there. When they saw me, they lurched...taking me with them."

"You said earlier that you couldn't do that," Nathaniel said, his brow furrowing.

"I can't," Barrick said, lifting his hands and shaking his head. "From what I've heard, no normal Lurcher has ever been able to transport another living thing."

"So, these aren't normal Lurchers," Amelie cut in, her hand on her chin.

"The only explanation I can think of is that the Lord Protector of Gorteo has the Great Stone of Hermnes," Barrick said, the words tumbling from his mouth. "If we can find it, I'll be able to get all of us away from here."

"You risked all our lives on nothing but a hunch for a lost Stone?" Nathaniel asked. "I respect that."

"This isn't just for the glory of a Great Stone," Barrick replied. "I can explain when we're not so tired, but the fate of the world is at stake here, mates."

"Well, then—I guess you'll just have to find that Stone," Amelie replied, grabbing a piece of bread off Barrick's lap and taking a bite. "Shouldn't be that hard, right?"

"Nah, piece of cake," Barrick said before turning to Silas. "Oh, and Silas, have you ever heard any of the other prisoners mention Gorteons who aren't short? You know, someone who is of a normal height?"

"Nothing comes to mind," Silas replied, his mouth full of bread. "Oh, except for the Lord Protector."

Barrick let out a sigh. He was going to need to find a different source of information if he was going to find out anything useful about that woman.

"Oh, yeah," Silas said as he took another bite of bread. "I've also heard them talk about a woman more beautiful than a goddess."

That was a good way to describe her—a goddess. Her flawless beauty and grace were certainly fit for a Divine.

"Any idea who she is?" Barrick asked, a smile creeping onto his face.

"Oh, I know that look," Silas chuckled, swallowing his mouthful of bread. "You really are a magnet for trouble. You, my good man, have just become smitten with the Lord Protector's sister."

28

Aydiin filled his lungs with the unusually warm air of early spring as he escorted Byanca through the street packed with civilians. Ahead, he could see the tip of the Senate Chambers, a grey dome topped with the golden statue of a winged goddess. Looking back at the crowd, he began to doubt their ability to make it on time.

"I can't believe how many people have turned out for this," Byanca said, clinging to his arm and fiddling with a handkerchief as Aydiin muscled his way through the crowd of overly-anxious citizens. With the streets jammed, they'd been forced to abandon their vehicle three blocks ago.

"I can," Aydiin responded, looking around at the assembled crowd. "It's not every day the Republic chooses its leader for life."

"But this isn't even the election," Byanca said. "This is just the nomination. These people aren't even allowed inside to watch."

"True, but their fates may very well be decided today," Aydiin said. "It's no secret that the Field Marshal is going to put his name forward. What if no one else decides to run? This could be over very quickly."

"I've taken care of that," Byanca said, patting his hand. "Lord Renault is going to throw his hat in the ring. Then we have two weeks to convince as many Senators as we can to not vote for Diaz."

"Can't remember the last time any of us got a good night's sleep," Aydiin said. "It sounds like another two weeks of late nights."

"We'll make it through," Byanca said. "We always do."

They walked in silence through the crowd until they reached the outer gates of the Chambers. Guards stood every few spans, surrounding the wrought iron fence and gates. Aydiin wondered how many people had already been caught trying to get in as his eyes caught sight of the building itself.

The front entrance consisted of a large, triangular pediment supported by six massive pillars. Behind the entrance, a magnificent dome capped the large chamber that held the Senate. Wings jutted out from either side of the building, holding offices and smaller chambers for committee meetings.

"I'm here to watch the proceedings," Byanca said to the guard standing in front of the gate.

"Yes, Madam President," the guard said with a salute before opening the gate.

Byanca led Aydiin past the soldiers and through the plaza. The grounds within the gates had been cleaned up, although Aydiin could see evidence of damage done during the riots. Most glaring was the dearth of flora, although a few sprouts of green were coming up in the flower beds. Maybe—just maybe—life could return to the garden and to the city as a whole.

The couple reached the stairs, and Aydiin forced himself to think about the meeting ahead. Without warning, Byanca stopped and turned to face the crowd. With her free hand, she waved to those assembled, and Aydiin could tell a smile had spread across her face.

A cheer erupted from the crowd. Aydiin joined in the waving, and he was pleased to see that the cheering didn't stop as he did so. However, he knew that the love of the people on the other side of that fence was directed toward his wife.

"Well, let's do this," Byanca said, stopping her wave and turning back around.

"I know it hurts to just watch this process from the outside," Aydiin said, grabbing her hand and heading up the stairs.

"It's not that," Byanca said, her voice cracking. "To be honest, this time as interim president has been an eye-opener to me. I really have no desire to be the Doge."

"Then what's wrong?" Aydiin asked.

"This nation needs a strong ruler," she sighed. "I always thought it could be me, but I've realized that I don't have what it takes. Even if we didn't have more important tasks at hand, I'm not the ruler Genodra needs or deserves. It's a hard truth to discover."

"You've steered your country through some of its darkest days," Aydiin said. "You're exactly the kind of leader that Genodra needs."

She grabbed his hand and gave it a squeeze as the Chamber's clock tower began chiming, and the couple finished climbing the steps into the building.

Aydiin marveled at the granite walls and columns of the building's foyer, but Byanca led him to a small staircase before he could take the time to properly take everything in. Their steps cracked on the stone floor, and Aydiin tried to bring his mind to more pressing matters.

Byanca led them to a balcony filled with benches occupied by prominent citizens of Palmas. He could smell the various perfumes and colognes mixing, fighting with each other for dominance. It was a vastly different sensation than the packed street they had just fought their way through.

Below, the newly elected members of the Senate were taking their seats. The room was dominated by two sets of benches facing each other. From what Byanca had explained to him, like-minded senators generally sat together.

Aydiin didn't know enough about the current senators to know if their seating arrangements actually meant anything. However, he quickly counted—ten on one side, and fifteen on the other. At the far end of the chamber, Lord Renault stood atop a dais, staring at notes he'd placed on a podium.

"Senators, Lords and Ladies, I would like to welcome you to this most solemn occasion," Lord Renault said before stopping to clear this throat. "Our nation has lost a great man in Doge Marcino. In life, he carried the torch of freedom with vigor. In death, we will honor his memory by continuing on the great work to which he dedicated his life."

"We thank Lord Bertrand for his stewardship of the country in these difficult times," Lord Renault continued, "and we mourn his passing."

"That's an interesting spin to put on things," Aydiin whispered to Byanca, and she nudged his ribs in response. However, he could see a smile on her face, and that was enough for him.

"Today, we are ready to nominate a new Doge," Lord Renault continued. "As stated in our constitution, anyone may come forward. With the support of at least three members of the Senate, that person will be considered for the office of Doge."

As soon as the words left his mouth, Field Marshal Diaz strode into the hall, his grey military uniform perfectly pressed and his medals polished. His boots cracked on the marble floor, and every eye in the building turned to him.

"I put my name forward and ask for consideration from the Senate," he said, his strong voice reverberating throughout the chamber as he strode toward the dais.

"My service to this great nation is unparalleled," Diaz continued, his voice booming. "For two decades, I've led the First Army in defending our borders from the anarchy of Pilsa. I've sent men to their deaths to stop despotic warlords from pillaging our lands and stealing away our citizens. I've held countless diplomatic negotiations, successfully diffusing tense situations without bloodshed. I've built and disbanded camps larger than many of our cities. There is no one else here that can match my ability to see to the well-being of Genodra."

"Thank you, Field Marshal," Lord Renault said with a nod, but Diaz continued.

"For too long, the revolution has languished under the shaky hands of weak-willed men," Diaz said, his voice turning to a growl. "The flame of liberty has been allowed to grow weak while politicians pander to the elite under the guise of economic reform. What Genodra needs now—what the world needs now—is someone with the strength to bring the fire of revolution to all mankind. I will not be afraid to take on the tyrants that oppress our neighbors."

"Together, we can make a difference. Together, we can be true to our forefathers. Believe me when I say Genodra cannot afford another weak leader," Diaz said, his voice growing quiet. "We are strong. We are fierce. We are Genodran."

As his words faded, the silence was broken by a raucous applause emanating from a group of grey-clad officers sitting in the mezzanine, across the hall from where Aydiin sat. Diaz stood alone on the Chamber floor, a smile across his face.

"We thank the Field Marshal for his years of service and devotion to the cause of liberty," Lord Renault said from behind the podium. "Senators, are there any among you who will nominate Field Marshal Diaz for the highest office in the Republic?"

A young man in a three-piece suit rose to his feet. Aydiin recognized him from Bertrand's ball as one of the young king's sycophants. Apparently, he'd been doing alright for himself since the death of his monarch.

"I nominate the Field Marshal," he said. "He has my utmost confidence, and I urge my fellow senators to join me."

The words were met with another round of applause from the officers sitting on the mezzanine, which was joined by polite clapping from others. As the noise died down, a tall woman with dark brown hair and a green silk dress arose.

"I also support Field Marshal Diaz. His years of leadership and devotion to the Republic make him an excellent candidate."

The room grew silent as the woman took her seat. Aydiin held his breath, waiting for a third senator to rise and speak up for Diaz. The seconds passed, his heart pounding in his ears.

"I support the Field Marshal," Lord Renault said, not moving from his spot behind the podium. "It is my profound belief that he has the unique skills necessary to guide our nation through such a tumultuous time."

Aydiin's mouth dropped open, and he turned to look at Byanca. Her mouth was also agape, and her skin had lost a few shades of color. That Lord Renault—the very man who had promised he would not let the Field Marshal run unopposed—would nominate Diaz must have shaken his wife to the core.

"Now, who else would like to be considered?" Lord Renault's voice rang out, ignoring the silence caused by his words.

Lord Renault looked around the room, his face as unreadable as a statue's. Aydiin didn't know why the old man had decided to support Diaz instead of running himself. Maybe he had been bribed. Maybe he had been threatened. Or maybe, he was just tired and didn't think this was a battle worth fighting.

"Well, if no one desires to step forward, then the Senate will declare Field Marshal Diaz to be our new—"

"I submit my name to the Senate for approval," Byanca shouted and rose to her feet.

Aydiin couldn't help but smile.

29

The sun was just beginning to peek over the horizon—little more than a sliver of grey—as Sophie let out a yawn that she thought would never end. Reginald let out a soft chuckle as she did so, sitting on the opposite side of the rumbling motorcar. Sophie tried to shoot him a scathing look, but she couldn't close her mouth long enough.

Reginald had been at her door early that morning—the middle of the night, really—to rouse her from sleep. She'd been told nothing and given only a few minutes to ready herself. Even after an hour on the road, she had been unable to wring even the smallest of hints from her escort.

"I would have thought a young girl accustomed to baking bread at dawn would be used to this early morning hour," Reginald said before letting out his own yawn.

"It's not that it's too early," Sophie said, stifling a second yawn. "I'm just not used to staying up so late. It's so strange not having anyone tell me when it's time for bed."

"You'll find the rules for the imperial family's personal servants much more relaxed than you're used to," Reginald replied. "Of course, you'll also find your duties to be more exacting."

"Like being taken outside of the city for no apparent reason?"

"Or being asked to ingratiate yourself with a certain young prince," Reginald responded. "For reasons that may not be known to you."

"So, you know?" Sophie asked, sitting straighter up in her seat.

Sophie still didn't know how she felt about her assignment with the young prince. On the one hand, she had been plucked from a life of servitude and obscurity. Only a short time ago, this would have been a dream.

Yet, she was finding that Tomas was better than those dreams. He was the perfect gentleman—he had barely even touched her in the days they had spent together. He definitely hadn't tried to spend a night with her yet.

"The Emperor took me into his confidences after speaking with you concerning the matter," Reginald said, shifting his gaze toward the window. "He thought that having me in the room when giving you the assignment would cause a certain amount of discomfort."

"It's hard to imagine such an assignment being any less comfortable. I presume you also know that the Emperor wants me to spy," Sophie said. It was not a question.

"Yes, although I don't honestly expect you to discover anything. The Emperor doesn't have any concrete suspicions, and Tomas really is a proper young man. It's just not unheard of for an heir to expedite the timing of his inheritance, and the Emperor doesn't want to take any chances."

"Now that you're opening up to me, how about we talk about where we're going?" Sophie asked, leaning forward in her seat.

"I never promised the Emperor that I wouldn't discuss your assignment—in fact, I was given strict instructions to oversee you. However, I have given Prince Tomas my word that not a hint of this little expedition will leave my lips."

"Well, I'm glad to know you're at least a trustworthy confidant. I'll need to remember that next time a secret requires a keeper."

"I'd prefer if you didn't. I just meant to tell you that I'm capable of keeping secrets—not that I enjoy it."

The man's words ushered in a silence, broken only by the roar of the engine and rumbling of tires on a dirt road. Sophie's curiosity didn't die, but she took the moment to rest her head against the window as the automobile careened through the open countryside.

So much had changed in such a short time, it was still difficult to comprehend. Her hands were still rather rough from a lifetime of hard work, but the creams she'd been given were softening them more than she had thought possible. The only official work she had to do was maintain a few linen closets supplied with fresh towels and sheets. Even Madam Esmerelda—the Mistress of the Linens—had been forced to back off.

All of this was, of course, because of Prince Tomas. She'd seen him nearly every day since being raised to the position of minor nobility. He was the perfect gentleman—everything and more that Sophie had spent her life dreaming of. She just found herself wishing that all of this could be more than just a somewhat-secret relationship convoluted by espionage.

"Let me see...you promised not to divulge any details of the expedition," Sophie began, turning back to Reginald and bringing her fingers to her chin. "I can probably get around that."

"I don't think that's how it works," Reginald said, but Sophie cut him off.

"We're leaving the city, so Tomas is trying to be discrete," she said. "Which also explains the early departure. So, this isn't going to be some innocent encounter."

Reginald only stared with a straight face, his countenance refusing to betray even a single emotion. The man brought his two fingers up to his lips and made a motion to lock them shut before throwing an imaginary key out the window.

"If you're trying to convince me to consider someone else as a future confidant, you're not doing a very good job," Sophie said. "I just want to know what he's got planned—is that so bad?"

At that moment, the automobile stopped, and Reginald motioned for her to look outside. Sophie scrambled to the window and poked her head through the opening.

They were at the seashore, on a cliff far above the waves crashing on the rocks below. It was difficult to see much else in the early dawn, but there was no sign of Tomas. There was also no sign of anything besides barren countryside.

"So glad you could make it," sounded a voice behind her, on the opposite side of the motorcar. Sophie yelped and pulled her head back into the vehicle to see Tomas peering through the other window. "Can't say I mind the view, but we really should get going if we don't want to miss it."

"Miss what?" Sophie asked.

"You really didn't tell her," Tomas said, smiling at the steward. "I'm glad someone in Margella can keep a secret."

Tomas opened the carriage door and held out his hand for Sophie to take. She could tell her cheeks were flaming as she did so, and she stepped out onto the dirt road. Then she turned back to Reginald.

"Aren't you coming with us?" she asked.

"You two are adults and don't need a chaperone," Reginald smiled with a wink before closing the door. The motorcar's engine grew louder and the vehicle lurched forward, kicking up a cloud of dust as it departed.

"Well, he was certainly in a hurry," Tomas laughed, his voice muffled by the collar of his jacket, which he was using to block out the dust.

"Reginald sure thinks he's funny," Sophie said, turning to face Tomas.

"Let's not waste any time talking about my father's steward," Tomas said, grabbing Sophie's hand and heading toward the cliffs. "We don't have much time."

"What is so important?" she asked, her feet moving quickly to keep up with the young prince.

"That would spoil the surprise," Tomas said as the two reached the cliff. As she approached the edge, Sophie spotted a narrow trail winding down the stony face to the beach below. Tomas wasted no time in pulling her toward the trail.

"Are you afraid of heights, Sophie?" Tomas asked, gripping her hand a little tighter and slowing his feet on the narrow piece of walkable landscape.

"It's not really the height that scares me," Sophie replied, placing one hand on the cliff wall to steady herself as they descended. "It's more the edge, and then falling off it that scares me."

"Yet more words of wisdom," Tomas said. "I can't wait to hear more."

"Here are a few more—tell the woman holding your hand exactly what the plan is."

"I already said that would spoil the surprise, and that would destroy all the fun."

"Couldn't we just spend the afternoon sipping tea at a cottage somewhere, enjoying the sea breeze?"

"I promise that you'll forget all about any such boringness after you see what I have in store."

"If we make it down this trail," Sophie said.

"We don't have to make it all the way down," Tomas said, stopping at a point where the trail leveled out for a moment. "Because the beach isn't our destination."

Tomas lifted his hand, placing it on the stone cliff. The prince closed his eyes, and a faint glow emanated from underneath his shirt. The stone began to shift, with rocks moving out of the way to reveal a door. Sophie shouldn't be surprised—every member of the imperial family was a Stone-weaver.

"Come on," Tomas said with a smile, holding out his hand for Sophie to take. "This is what I wanted to show you."

Sophie followed the prince through the recently crafted door, her legs rather unsteady. The opening led to a tunnel, lit only by the light streaming in through the entrance. Yet it was enough to see, and Sophie grasped the prince's hand tight as he led her along.

The sound of rushing water met her ears, and a light appeared ahead as the couple turned a corner. Tomas turned to her and smiled before putting a finger to his lips. Sophie only grinned in return and kept her legs moving to keep up. The corridor opened up into a massive chamber, its walls stretching dozens of spans into the air. Her eyes lifted upward, searching for the source of the light until they found it.

At the top of the chamber, the sunrise streamed in through a massive window of stained glass. The light bounced off the various colors, giving the room a spectacular display.

At the far end of the room, water cascaded a dozen spans from some distant spring. Plants grew along the banks of the stream, the large window at the top apparently allowing in enough light for the greenery to thrive.

"I've spent the past few years wanting a place to call my own," Tomas whispered, squeezing Sophie's hand. "There really isn't any privacy at the palace."

"Until this week, I didn't even have my own bed," Sophie responded. "The only time I ever had alone was in the gardens."

"I may have a large section of the palace to call my own, but my days are filled with ambassadors, ministers, and sycophants. So, I created this little refuge."

"It's absolutely wonderful," Sophie replied, stepping further into the cave. "Come on, I want you to show me all of it."

JON MONSON

"I can't think of anything I would rather do," Tomas said with a smile before gesturing to the waterfall. "I found this underground river, diverted it here, and gave it a place to cascade."

"I feel like it was definitely worth the effort," Sophie laughed.

"It really wasn't that hard," Tomas said. "I've been weaving stone for so long, it feels like second nature. See the window where light comes in?"

Sophie only nodded, hoping he would explain that exquisite piece of art.

"It looks like glass, but it's not. I just weaved the stone to be ultra-thin yet strong. That took infinitely more work than diverting the stream—finding the right balance took ages."

"Well I'm glad you persisted," Sophie replied. "It adds so much beauty to what could easily be a gloomy cavern."

"And I've taken the liberty of preparing breakfast," Tomas said, and Sophie noticed a small table set up ahead. A small basket—presumably filled with food—sat on top.

"You must not have slept last night," Sophie said. "I was up before dawn, and you've had time to prepare all this."

"Some people are worth staying up all night for," Tomas said, helping Sophie into her chair and lifting bread, butter, and ham out of the basket.

"Tomas, I have something to confess," she said.

"Is it that my father asked you to become my mistress?"

"How could you have known that?"

"My father is predictable as both an emperor and a father. He thinks the solution to strange behavior from any of his close associates is to find them a beautiful mistress."

"Well, as long as you're okay with that, I'm more than happy to oblige," Sophie replied, though the words immediately ate at her.

"And while we're confessing, I have my own to make."

Sophie just raised an eyebrow and motioned for Tomas to continue.

"I have no intention of making you my mistress," Tomas said, his smile growing wider. "In fact, I was rather hoping that we could start a formal courtship."

"You mean, bring this out in the open?" Sophie asked, placing a hand to her chest.

"Ever since the first time I heard you sigh on the other side of those hedges, I've known you were someone worth risking everything for," Tomas said, reaching a hand across the table to grab Sophie's. "The more you came back, the more I realized this was a woman worth sharing my life with—someone willing to shirk society's norms and rules for even a moment of happiness. I'm not saying that we will definitely wed, but I'd like to have our relationship move out of the shadows and toward matrimony."

"But I'm only a servant," Sophie replied, giving his hand a squeeze. "Aren't there rules about this sort of thing?"

"My father was born the son of a pig farmer. If he hadn't joined the army and been in the right place at the right time, I would be herding swine right now instead of eating breakfast in a cave I created with the powers of Okuta. Besides, my father raised you to the nobility—it will be a minor scandal, at best."

"But I—"

"I wouldn't dream of forcing you to marry me," Tomas said, his face falling with the words. "If you don't desire it, please just say the word."

"I would like nothing more than to spend my time being courted by you," Sophie said as she let a smile spread across her face. "You just have to remember that this is a lot for me to take in. It's not been very long since I was a kitchen maid being punished for wandering the palace grounds past curfew."

"I realize it must be—oh, look at the time," Tomas interrupted himself, looking up at the sunlight streaming in through the window. "I have something else I want to show you."

She took his hand, and he led her up a small trail near the waterfall. It took them to the top of the chamber where a large crystal sat on a ledge, the water cascading around it. As they reached the top of the trail, a beam of light hit the crystal, refracted, and cast the entire spectrum of light throughout the cavern.

"This is by far the best sunrise I've ever seen," Sophie sighed, leaning into the man who could someday be her husband.

"I would be a fool not to agree," Tomas said, looking down and cupping Sophie's chin with his thumb and forefinger.

With every color on the spectrum filling the air, Sophie closed her eyes as their lips touched. For a moment, nothing else mattered.

30

The sun was already well into its daily trek across the sky by the time Bayram pulled on Askari's reins, bringing the powerful lizard-like creature to a halt. Aydiin had always talked about the kerton's fiery temperament; however, Bayram was finding the lizard to be rather gentle. Perhaps he could tell that the Crown-Prince wasn't completely healthy and acted accordingly.

At his side, General Tartlan rode on a shadowy stallion, his blue uniform nearly blending in with the steed. The gruff, bearded soldier held Salatia's banner—the kerton and the flame—in one hand, the canvas flapping in a soft breeze. The man had been quiet during the ride, his posture stiff. Bayram had the sense that Tartlan would much rather be leading his men into glorious battle rather than on a milquetoast mission of diplomacy.

The day's heat—mixed with the humidity of the monsoon season—left Bayram drenched in sweat. Even Askari was panting as they stopped, and Bayram knew the creature had survived the Soulless Desert with Aydiin. It was a good thing the rebel army was only a day from Maradon; otherwise, he would be forced to amputate his stiff legs by the end of this. As he stopped atop a hill, the view made him forget—if only for a moment—the weariness that had settled in.

Tents of various colors and sizes stretched out in all directions, covering the floor of the shallow valley below. An orderly grid system had been put into effect with wide streets. All this from an army that General Tartlan had more than once dismissed as nothing but shepherds and women.

Reports from the scouts had said the rebel army numbered in the hundreds of thousands, including women and children. Bayram had been preparing himself for such a number of people on the move, but the sight that filled his eyes was beyond anything he could have imagined.

"On the march, this camp must extend for leagues," Bayram whispered, more to himself than to anyone around him.

"We should take advantage of that," Tartlan responded, apparently within earshot. "Spread out like that, they would make quite the target."

"With what men do you propose doing that?" Bayram responded, turning to the commander of Maradon's garrison. "We have barely twenty thousand soldiers who all know their chances of surviving into next week don't look good. What do you think a thousand men would do if you were to send them outside Maradon?"

"Don't talk like that," Tartlan snarled, shaking his head. "If you show any weakness at these talks, I'll kill you myself."

"Threats are such a pedestrian way of dealing with life," Bayram said.

"Wait, something's wrong," Tartlan growled, his horse pawing the ground. Bayram pulled on Askari's reins, bringing the kerton back to the disgruntled commander. "The air is still, even the wind is quiet."

"Shouldn't we have run into their sentries by now?" Bayram asked, turning back to survey the two dozen soldiers who had accompanied them. Below, Askari took in a deep breath, his nostrils flaring. The kerton began shifting his feet, the sharp claws digging into the ground.

"If this is the kind of military discipline we're up against, we should just turn back now and launch a direct assault," Tartlan spat. "What kind of army doesn't have guards?"

"Maybe they're overconfident," Bayram said, although he doubted that to be the case.

"Maybe they're a bunch of inbred nomads who don't know how to run an army," Tartlan responded.

"Maybe you lot are just blind," a voice sounded at Bayram's side, and the young prince nearly fell out of his saddle.

Sitting to his right on top of a pure black horse, Uncle Agha also stared down at the army's camp. He wore a set of pristinely white robes, complete with a lowered shemagh. A cigar hung lazily in the corner of his mouth.

"Lord Agha, I'm glad to see you still know how to make an entrance," Bayram said, trying to remain calm despite the adrenaline that his body had injected into his veins.

"You look tired, my dear Bayram," Agha chuckled, turning his gaze toward the Crown-Prince. "You should really try to get some sleep."

His spy network had once reported rumors that Agha was a Creep, and he was inclined to believe them. However, those blessed by Vindred, Goddess of Thieves, usually had an imperfect invisibility. Especially in the setting sun, he should have been able to spot the man's faint outline. He'd made a habit of looking for Creeps since becoming one himself.

More importantly, Agha should have still made noise as he walked. The man's ability to so completely sneak up on him like that was disconcerting.

"I can't believe my brother would be desperate enough to send his own heir," Agha continued, turning his gaze back to the camp and the valley below.

"Lord Agha, I have come as an official envoy from Sultan Oosman the Third," Bayram said, trying to keep his voice from shaking. "Before more innocent blood is shed, I seek permission to enter your camp and discuss the cessation of hostilities."

"Ah Bayram, I see that your father has underestimated his 'sickly' oldest son. And I'd be happy to let you and General Tartlan enter, provided you leave your guards here."

"As long as we have your word of honor that we will be returned unharmed," Bayram replied, knowing that even if he could bring his guards along, they would be able to do very little.

"You have it," Agha replied with a nod. "Although, I should let you know that the title of 'lord' is no longer appropriate."

"My apologies," Bayram responded. "May I inquire as to the status of your title? I hardly think 'uncle' is appropriate under the circumstances."

"The title is only a few days old, so I'll forgive your ignorance. I'm officially the Emperor of Salatia," Agha said, a smile on his face as he kicked his horse in the ribs. "So, you may simply call me 'Emperor' or 'Your Imperial Majesty.'"

Trying to not let his eyes widen in shock, Bayram followed his uncle down the trail leading into the rebel camp. Agha's words hung in the air, and he knew that the smile was yet to fade from his uncle's face, even though the man's back was to him. Behind him, Bayram knew that General Tartlan must be fighting with his own emotions that likely ranged from apoplexy to boiling rage.

As they reached the camp, Agha led them through the rows of tents, and Bayram took mental note of the various banners belonging to the tribes. There was certainly no small amount of segregation, no matter how unified the tribes were portrayed in the ceaseless rumors. Those rumors were starting to sound like little more than rebel propaganda.

Despite Agha's grandiose title, the man received very little deference as the trio rode through the streets. A few servants stopped to give small bows, a mark of respect no different than those generally offered to any noble person of rank. Soldiers and officers moving in the opposite direction barely acknowledged him at all.

Does he notice it too? Bayram thought. Agha had always been an informal man, the polar opposite of his father. Perhaps he simply didn't care for such things.

Agha led them to a massive tent near the center of the camp. The exterior looked new, although it was showing the dirt from being in use for several weeks. Bayram stopped Askari and dismounted near the tent. A servant opened the flap, allowing Agha, Bayram, and Tartlan to enter.

Bayram entered the tent to find a rather comfortable dwelling. Several silk pillows surrounded a low table. A canvas wall sectioned off a corner of the tent, likely for Agha's private quarters. With a nod, his uncle motioned for the young man to sit on one of the pillows at the table.

"I can't even tell you how good it is to see you," Agha said, pulling the stopper out of a wine bottle and pouring the ruby liquid into two small cups.

"I wish I could say the same," Bayram said, accepting one of the cups. Agha took the other for himself, and—without a glance at the empty-handed Tartlan—took a seat.

Bayram sniffed the wine, his nose trying to decipher the usual poisons. It certainly smelled like normal wine, and he was rather thirsty after riding Askari through the desert.

Well, you are in the middle of the rebel camp, he reminded himself. If Agha wanted to kill him, he didn't have to resort to poison. There was no lack of tribesmen who would gladly fill his corpse with bullets.

"Despite its fall from grace, Pilsa still makes a fine wine," Agha said, taking a sip from his cup. "You just need the right contacts. Some warlords control vast areas filled with the world's finest vineyards. They're always looking for ways to raise gold to fund their little wars."

Bayram stared at the contents of his glass—some of the most expensive he'd ever consumed—being held by a simple, wooden cup. Still, the beverage tasted as it should, the simplicity of its container notwithstanding.

"I understand your love of fine wine," Tartlan said, his gruff voice interrupting the contemplation of both men. "But if you want Salatia to avoid the fate of Pilsa, I would suggest starting our peace talks before the world descends into madness."

"Quite right," Bayram said, looking up from his glass. Now wasn't the time to give in to exhaustion. "General Tartlan speaks the truth—we should find a way to settle our differences before significant blood is spilt. The very future of our nation—not to mention thousands of innocent lives—could be at stake."

The tent flap opened behind Bayram, and he forced himself to maintain focus on his uncle. If the newcomer meant him harm, he couldn't really do much about it. Agha's eyes widened—if only slightly—as soft footsteps entered the room.

"Thank you, my dear," Agha said, handing his half-consumed glass of wine to a young woman who entered Bayram's line of sight.

She wore a fine dress of deep red silk, a veil shrouding her face. The clothing simultaneously accentuated her curves while covering more than enough skin to not be considered scandalous. With nothing more than a nod, she took Agha's glass and moved into a corner of the tent.

"Let me ask you a question," Bayram began, placing his wooden cup on the table. "What is your goal here? Is this rebellion about what is best for Salatia, or do you just want revenge on your brother?"

"I don't see why those two are mutually exclusive," Agha replied, his gaze narrowing. "Oosman has been nothing but a parasite since the moment he took the throne. Removing him from power will be a momentous day in the history of our nation."

"Even if it comes at the price of twenty thousand dead and the destruction of the nation's largest city?" Bayram asked, the words spilling from his mouth.

Agha opened his own mouth to respond, but the tent flap again opened, admitting another uninvited guest.

"Why wasn't the Council invited to this meeting?" a voice sounded from the tent's entrance.

This time, Bayram turned to look at the newcomer. The man wore a short beard of nearly pure black, although flecks of grey were beginning to show through. He had the look of a man accustomed to deference, despite his lack of years.

"Prince Bayram, please meet Yusef, one of the tribal elders," Agha said without rising to his feet. Of course, the Emperor rose for no man.

"It is a pleasure to make your acquaintance, Yusef," Bayram said, grabbing the man's hand.

"Unfortunately, I'm unable to return that sentiment," Yusef replied, withdrawing his hand from Bayram's grasp. "Your presence here only serves to pollute the purity of our cause."

"That's enough, Yusef," Agha snapped, although Yusef's smile only grew at the words. "Do you have a purpose in interrupting?"

"To ensure the safety of His Majesty, of course," Yusef replied, but Bayram knew the real reason. There was little trust between Emperor Agha and his supposed subjects. They weren't about to allow him a private meeting where he could sell out their interests.

"Well, then, please sit," Agha said, gesturing to one of the many pillows. "And remember that this discussion does not concern you—please refrain from any further attacks on our guest. You are allowed to remain only because I will it. The moment your presence becomes odious, you will be dismissed."

"As you wish, Your Majesty," Yusef replied without a bow, the last words coming out with a large dose of hatred.

"Now, Bayram, if you're concerned about casualties, I'll gladly accept your surrender," Agha said, trying to bring the conversation back on track. "However, I do not hesitate to do what is necessary for the future of Salatia, even if that means innocent citizens will have to suffer for the sins of your father."

"I understand that you want what's best for our nation. In fact, I believe we all do. That's why I'm here to offer a compromise," Bayram said, removing his satchel and pulling out a sheath of papers. "One that would allow Oosman to keep both his head and his throne. It would, however, solve many of the issues that have been plaguing our fair nation since our illustrious ancestor, Oosman the Great."

"The abolition of the Sultanate in favor of the Empire will solve those problems, I assure you," Yusef cut in, the words accompanied by a sniff.

"It has long been my opinion that we are overdue for a formal, written constitution," Bayram said, handing the stack of papers to his uncle and ignoring the impudent tribal leader. "I've actually been working on this for quite some time. Thanks to you, my ideas are finally allowed out of the shadows."

"I wasn't aware you specialized in this type of scholarship," Agha said, his eyes scanning the front page of the document.

"I've always chosen to be much more discrete in my revolutionary leanings than Aydiin," Bayram said. "However, the time has come to lead Salatia into the modern world, and neither the old system nor your proposed imperial system are prepared to do so."

"Checks and balances, separation of powers, elected bodies," Agha said, his eyes leaving the document and meeting Bayram's. "It looks like somebody really has been delving into political theory. However, Salatia isn't some laboratory—this is the real world, and we have real problems to solve."

As his uncle spoke, Bayram's gaze wandered to the young woman sitting behind Agha. Her eyes were wide, although the rest of her face was covered by a veil. Yet there was certainly something to her, young as she was. Apparently, his uncle didn't have the same reservations as Bayram about significant age gaps when it came to relationships.

"That's exactly why we need to make these changes," Bayram said, leaning forward and taking his mind and gaze away from the young woman. "When we start treating the people as partners in government rather than subjects to be ruled, I think we'll be able to not only catch up to the rest of the world, but we could outpace the other nations still entangled by despots."

"So, what exactly would my role be in this new government?" Agha asked, and Bayram could tell the man was at least interested.

"My father would retain the title and office of Sultan, albeit with a significant check on his powers," Bayram said, trying to rush past the part that would be disagreeable to both Agha and Yusef. "You would come in as First Consul, a new office to be created. You would work with an elected legislature—including representatives from the tribes—to govern all of the nation's internal affairs."

"This is a mockery," Yusef shouted, his face growing red. "You can't be ser—"

"Yusef, that's enough," Agha shouted. "I've already warned you that your position in this meeting is tenuous. At this point, I'm going to ask you to leave."

"I have already seen all I need," Yusef snarled, rising to his feet. "When the Council hears the ideas that you're entertaining..."

The man didn't finish his sentence as he stormed from the tent. For a moment, Bayram and Agha stared at each other, eyebrows raised.

"I believe that man is unstable," Bayram said, his voice breaking the silence.

"Those are the most dangerous types of opponents," Agha replied, and the man returned to perusing the document that Bayram had given him.

"Unhinged as he is, Yusef does have a point. This proposal falls far short of our stated goals," Agha said, setting the papers down on the table. "I could get deposed before even reaching Maradon if I take this deal."

"Be that as it may," Bayram began, wanting his next words to have the intended effect. "This constitution, which is only a rough draft, is being sent out to every town, village, and plantation in all Salatia. Within a week, the people, including the commoners in your camp, will be very aware of their new-found voice in the nation. You can either be a part of this new regime, or you can fight against it. The choice is yours."

"You're asking me to give up practically everything when I can just take it," Agha said. "Do you think me a simpleton?"

"Quite the opposite, actually," Bayram said, leaning back from his forward position. "You're obviously smart enough to know that your vast horde outnumbers the small, professional army of the Sultan."

"Exactly—we'll overrun Maradon in a matter of hours," Agha said, a smile growing on his face.

"However, you're also smart enough to know that the fortunes of war are uncertain," Bayram said, struggling to keep the words coming at a slow, pronounced pace.

"Your 'soldiers' are nothing but barbarians," Tartlan cut in, but Bayram lifted his hand to silence the man.

"Tartlan misspeaks," Bayram said, forcing the anger down. "However, your men are volunteers used to a life of fighting in the desert. How do you think they'll do in the tight, winding streets of Maradon?"

"Bah, you can't scare me with the threat of urban warfare," Agha said, waving his hand and launching a scathing glare at Tartlan.

"Our soldiers are hardened professionals, and they know their very way of life is at stake, along with their new freedoms," Bayram said, shrugging. "And let's suppose you do take Maradon. What happens to your army when the food starts running low? Worse, what happens when your volunteers start deserting so they can provide for their families?"

"We've made plans for that, I assure you—plans that need not be shared with my enemies," Agha replied, again waving his hands as if to dismiss the argument. However, from his tone, Bayram knew he had struck a nerve.

"Even if you do manage to keep this group together," Bayram again began, "you'll be trying to subjugate the majority of Salatia. If the common people were simply trading one tyrant for another, you might be able to get away with it. Yet, now they can taste freedom. I can't be sure how they'll react when that freedom is snatched from their grasp by a bunch of disgruntled nomads from the interior."

"Let's suppose that I were to be persuaded by your arguments," Agha said, again picking up the copy of the constitution and flipping through it. "I can almost guarantee you that this arrangement will not be acceptable when absolute victory is at hand. The tribal elders would never allow it."

"Where do you get your power? From eight old men? Or from the citizens of Salatia?" Bayram asked, rising to his feet with the question hanging in the air. "I will be returning to my camp, and I will not be returning to see you before heading back to Maradon at first light. This offer stands until the first shots are fired at the city. After that, you'll be forced to subjugate Salatia instead of governing it."

Bayram's eyes again found the young woman in red. Her eyes were even wider this time, a hint of desperation in those beautiful orbs. For a moment, he wanted to help her with whatever was vexing her. However, he'd said his final words to Agha, and staying would only ruin them. Flashing a quick and—hopefully—sympathetic smile, Bayram bowed and exited the tent.

"Let's get you some meat and a good night sleep," Bayram said to Askari, leaping onto the kerton's back. The lizard purred, either in greeting or the expectation of a meal and sleep. Bayram would probably never understand the creature the same way Aydiin did.

"Sounds like a good idea to me," Tartlan replied, apparently unaware that Bayram had been speaking to Askari.

"When we return to camp, I'd like your thoughts on that little exchange," Bayram said, looking around the array of rebel tents. Now was not the time for such a discussion.

"As you wish, my Prince," Tartlan said, the words dripping in sarcasm.

Riding out through the camp, Bayram's mind returned to the young woman in the tent. The look in her eyes had practically been a plea for help, and he was sorry to be powerless. However, he—

"Gamila," he whispered, pulling on Askari's reins.

"What's wrong, sir?" Tartlan asked, his head spinning to see what had startled Bayram.

"Nothing," Bayram lied, the word sticking in his throat. "We should really get back to camp. We can discuss the meeting in the morning—I'm feeling a bit ill, and I need some rest."

Bayram kicked himself for not recognizing his sister, even if the majority of her face was covered by a veil. There were a million questions running through his mind, but he knew one thing for certain—there would be no sleep tonight. There was a rescue to be planned and then carried out before the sun rose. The exhaustion fled from his bones at the very thought.

31

Gamila walked through the half-deserted streets of camp as the moon made its way across the night sky, trying to keep her mind away from the meeting with Bayram. She still didn't know if her brother had recognized her. Worse, she didn't know if she would ever see him again.

As she walked, the soldiers and citizens avoided her gaze, the deep red dress and veil marking her as someone above their station. That distinction had made the gathering of information nearly impossible, despite Agha's predictions. People tended to guard their words when the mistress of their emperor was near—that is, unless there was sufficient alcohol present.

Her stomach gurgled, and Gamila struggled to let loose a silent belch—the unfortunate side effect of her post-peace negotiations dinner. The pulled goat meat she'd just consumed had been heavily spiced, likely as a measure to cover up its age. The watered-down swill that counted as wine certainly hadn't helped. The desire for a solid meal and a nice dessert was almost too strong to handle.

The smell of bread and dried figs roasting on open flames drifted to her nose, and she reminded herself that she'd been lucky to have any meat for dinner. The common citizens were down to nothing but bread, dried fruit, and lentils. Still, after eating near-rancid goat meat, that didn't sound half bad.

The burp also brought a burning sensation in her throat, a reminder of the strong, home-brewed *raki* that had accompanied the dinner. She'd tried her best to consume only a little, but she was not accustomed to such strong drink. The small glass she'd nursed throughout the evening had certainly inflicted plenty of damage.

Her head began to spin as she reached her tent, and she was already dreaming of lying down on her bedroll. Bending over to remove her sandals, she sensed a motion in the darkness. Reaching deep within her, she summoned the powers of Surion and created a small flame in the palm of her hand.

"No need to summon divine wrath on me," Agha's voice chuckled in the darkness.

"You really shouldn't scare me like that," Gamila sighed, moving toward the lamp she kept on the ground near her bed and lighting it. Her allotment of oil was nearly gone, and she turned the brass dial to the lowest setting, allowing only a weak illumination in the tent. "How did you sneak up on me like that?"

"The world's most successful thief has his secrets," Agha said, a smile evident on his face, even in the shadows. "Now, tell me—how was your dining experience with the most powerful women in Salatia?"

"The wives of the tribal elders are some of the most boring women you'll ever meet," Gamila said. "That is, until you get a few glasses of *raki* into them."

"So, it was a productive use of your time, then?" Agha asked, leaning forward.

"If they remember their words from tonight, I fear some of them may want to cut out their tongues in the morning. It's been difficult to get anyone to even speak with me—my position as an imperial concubine doesn't have all the advantages you would expect."

"Yes, I should have realized that everyone would watch their words around you," Agha sighed. "But what did you learn tonight?"

"Well, their respect for you is practically non-existent," Gamila said, rubbing her eyes. "One of them openly referred to you as a puppet, and that she would love to make you dance. Some of them do rather fancy you, but not in the way you'd hope for as their leader."

"That rather confirms what I've been experiencing with the Council," Agha said. "The part about me being a puppet, that is. I went to all this work in uniting the tribes, and now those old men think they can just push me around. I just left a meeting where the Council practically ignored me. I believe it's only their centuries-old enmities for each other that stops them from ditching me altogether."

"So, you went to a lot of effort to bring me here, and all I've been able to do is confirm what you already knew."

"Well, now I know that I have a decent chance with some of the elders' wives," Agha said. "So, it's not all for naught."

"What do you think will happen when we get to Maradon?" Gamila asked. "We've already reached the coastal plain. The city is, what, one or two days away?"

"Less than a day on horseback, but probably three at the rate we're going," Agha replied. "A group this size moves slower than molasses. I don't think taking the city will prove difficult, but it's what will happen in the aftermath that worries me."

The two sat in silence, Agha's stooped posture discernible even in the low light. Despite the anger still simmering inside, Gamila was beginning to feel a certain amount of pity for her uncle.

"Why did you put yourself in this situation?" Gamila asked. "You could have retired to some tropical island and lived like a king with all the loot you've stolen."

"Such a retirement loses its appeal when I already spent my youth living that way. When I was your age, I wanted nothing more than to see the world and experience the finest wine and women it had to offer. My energy and appetite for life were boundless—the thought of ruling Salatia rarely crossed my mind, despite my father's constant efforts."

Gamila opened her mouth to respond but had no words to say. She'd never thought about Agha's age. Was he perhaps the first-born and rightful heir?

"When our father died, I was climbing Mount Mungumbo in Lusita," Agha continued. "It took weeks for word of his death to reach me, and when I returned home to take my throne, I found that my brother had already taken it and proclaimed himself Oosman the Third."

"If you hadn't prepared yourself, maybe that was for the best," Gamila said, cringing as the words left her mouth.

"You're probably right," Agha said. "And that's what has haunted me for decades. I've watched Oosman slowly strangle Salatia with his stubbornness as our neighbors pass us by in nearly every sense. If only I'd been a more responsible youth, none of this would be happening."

"If you let this army loose on the streets of Maradon, I'm not quite sure that's going to help things," Gamila said. "The loss of human lives certainly won't fling Salatia forward on the world stage."

"If you have a way to stop that from happening, I would love to hear it," Agha said.

"Well, I do have an idea," Gamila began, the words coming out slowly. "However, I have a feeling you won't like it."

"Oh Gammy, please don't suggest taking the pathetic deal that Bayram offered," Agha said, his head lifting to look Gamila in the eyes. "If I did that, the elders would simply depose me and move on Maradon anyway."

"That's exactly my point," Gamila said. "Your control over this situation is practically non-existent. If you use this army to take control of Salatia, it will cement your position as an impotent puppet. What you need to do is take control of Maradon without the use of your puppet masters. If you want what's best for Salatia, you need to take Bayram's deal."

"You can't actually be serious," Agha scoffed. "Even if I'm not immediately overthrown, I would be giving up everything the tribes are fighting for."

"It might be a betrayal to the tribal elders, but it would actually be giving the vast majority of your followers everything they want and more. And if you played your cards right, you would have more power as First Consul than as Emperor. You would be limited by the constitution and the people instead of controlled like a puppet by the elders."

"If I take Maradon by force, there's still a chance that I could cut my strings eventually. In time, I could become a true emperor."

"Your army is large, but you have to remember that the inner tribes only represent a small part of Salatia. The towns and cities on the coastal plain would see you more as a conqueror than anything else. You'll spend your short reign stamping out rebellions before facing your own execution."

"Oh Gammy, you certainly have become persuasive," Agha chuckled, pulling out a cigar and examining it. "As a thief, I'm not exactly accustomed to...traditional forms of government."

"Well, we have some time before reaching the city," Gamila said, shooting a disdainful look at the cigar. "Maybe you should read some political theory. If you are to play a part in governing our nation, leaving the ways of your bandit past behind you would be for the benefit of everyone involved."

"I'll have to think about this for a time," Agha said, rising from his seat and moving to light the cigar on the low-burning lantern.

"Be sure you think hard," Gamila sighed. "If you truly care about Salatia, you won't exchange one tyrant for another."

"I should have known it would be a bad idea to bring you here," Agha said, a smile spreading on his face as he began puffing, spreading the stench into Gamila's living space. "You're too smart for your own good, Gammy. I guess you always have been."

"I was hoping you'd see reason."

"I'll still need to think about it," Agha replied. "But I can't fight you on your logic. Yes, it's possible that I could find other ways to consolidate my power after a battle, but it would be difficult, at best."

For the first time in weeks, Gamila let a smile spread over her face. She could save Salatia. She could save her uncle. She could even save her father.

Bayram bent low behind a boulder as his eyes made contact with the polychromatic rebel camp. His feet were already tired from making the nocturnal trip without Askari, but he knew the kerton would have been too much trouble on a mission like this.

As he reached the perimeter, his eyes caught sight of a robed soldier standing watch. The man's eyes and ears would be on high alert for any indications of an intruder, and if Bayram weren't careful, he could spark an incident that would not only result in his own death, but the destruction of any potential peace deal.

Pulling on the well of energy deep within him, Bayram could feel himself become somehow less tangible. Even after nearly two decades of use, he still didn't understand the abilities granted by Vindred, the Goddess of Thieves. Even other Creeps he'd met had felt the same way.

The common perception was that Creeps became invisible, which was not exactly incorrect. However, there was much more to it than that. It was as if he partially left this world. No matter how much he thought about the matter, he decided that he could never truly describe it, even if just to himself.

The night grew brighter as he stoked the powers within his chest as if his eyes had turned into those of a cat. His ears began picking up the noise of the nearby guard's breathing, and his skin became instantly more aware of the dry night air.

Moving quietly as possible—he'd learned from experience that his abilities did nothing to muffle the sound of his footsteps—Bayram crept past the guard. Shrouded by the night, he made his way deeper into the rebel camp. With the power of Vindred now roaring within him, Bayram crept through the motley array of tents. Sticking to the shadows whenever possible, he began studying the nocturnal activities of his uncle's army.

He passed a tent filled with the warm light of burning lanterns. Within, he could hear boisterous laughter emanating from a dozen women. For a moment, he thought about poking his head in to see what he was missing, but he reminded himself of his true task this night.

His feet led him to the tent where he had met with his uncle only a few hours ago. Darkness hung over the entire structure, including the walled-off section that Bayram guessed was for Agha's personal quarters. The rebel emperor was nowhere to be seen.

The tent next to Agha's also had an interior light shining through its canvas walls, and his hyper-sensitive hearing picked up on hushed voices within. Looking around for any hidden guards, Bayram sidled over to the tent.

"If you have a way to stop that from happening, I would love to hear it," Agha's voice sounded through the canvas walls.

"Well, I do have an idea," a feminine voice began, the words coming out slowly. "However, I have a feeling you won't like it."

"Oh Gammy, please don't suggest taking the pathetic deal that Bayram offered," Agha scoffed, his emotion coming through even without being visible. "If I did that, the elders would simply depose me and move on Maradon anyway."

"That's exactly my point," Gamila's voice said. "Your control over this situation is practically non-existent. If you use this army to take control of Salatia, it will cement your position as an impotent puppet.

What you need to do is take control of Maradon without the use of your puppet masters. If you want what's best for Salatia, you need to take Bayram's deal."

The voice within was most definitely Gamila's, and it had never sounded so sweet. A million questions were swirling around in Bayram's head, and he didn't know where to begin. However, one stuck out above all others.

Did Gamila need to be saved?

The conversation certainly didn't sound like one between prisoner and warden. In fact, she was actually pushing Agha to accept the constitution. Worse yet, she sounded safe—safer than she would likely be in Maradon.

Bayram closed his eyes, clearing his brain as he rethought the rescue plan he'd concocted. Taking in a deep breath, he tried to push out all thought beyond the present. For a moment, the only thing in his head was the beating of his pulse.

There was also something else—a pulsing that washed over him like gentle waves lapping at the beach. It was soft, indiscernible if he hadn't stopped to think. Opening his eyes, Bayram tried to determine the source of the strange sensation. It hit him again, this time with less force. But it was enough, and with a smile beginning to form, Bayram returned to Agha's tent.

Bayram slipped into the canvas structure—his divinely enhanced vision cutting through the darkness—and looked around as he sensed yet another wave coming from the walled-off section. Moving silently along the canvas floor, he crept through the slit in the wall.

Pulling on the power of Vindred to enhance his night vision further, Bayram took in what looked to be an ordinary bed chamber—well, ordinary for a puppet emperor in a nomadic camp. A small, portable bed sat in the corner next to a tiny writing desk. Another wave washed over Bayram, and his eyes shot to a miniature chest sitting at the foot of the bed.

Opening the chest, Bayram's gaze was met by a nearly empty piece of furniture. Two robes of white sat neatly folded on the bottom, along with a pair of boots. Beyond that, the chest held nothing.

"Stones," he cursed. He must be losing his mind. Another pulse emanated from the chest, this one stronger than any of the others.

Feeling along the bottom of the chest, he could tell there was an uneven seam, and he wedged his fingers into the wood before pulling upward. There was a soft click, and the bottom of the chest lifted.

Letting out the tiniest guffaw, Bayram removed the false bottom to reveal a small compartment. Within, his eyes could just make out a tiny box of polished ivory. Hands trembling, Bayram lifted the container from the chest and opened it.

He was greeted by a stone of deep green, almost dark enough to be black. About the size of his palm, it pulsed with a warm glow, despite the color of the stone itself. There was a certain power contained within that he didn't comprehend.

Placing his hand to the stone, he felt the well of power within him roar to life. As if the divinity within him had been sleeping and he was experiencing it for the first time, Bayram felt the energy surge through his entire body.

The night grew bright as midday, and his ears picked up an array of whispered conversations. Yet, somehow, he was able to discern each one in turn. None were of interest, and he focused his mind on pushing them out. Closing the box, Bayram replaced the false bottom and neatly placed the robes and boots in their original spots.

The air of mystery around his uncle's unbelievable career as a thief was beginning to unravel within Bayram's mind. The greatest bandit in the history of the world had received a fair dose of divine help. With a smile, Bayram realized that very power would now be the man's undoing.

32

I barely even recognize it," Seb whispered as he stared out the small, barred window. The *Glorious Revolution* had brought him across the world and was now ready to deposit him on his native soil. As the massive ship steamed through the harbor of Silvino City, Seb's eyes refused to shut as they caught the first glimpse of his now unfamiliar home.

"Twenty years is a long time," Joon responded, his diminutive frame standing at Seb's side.

"More than just time has changed Margella," Seb replied, gesturing to the massive towers reaching into the heavens, barely visible in the cold light of dawn. "Before the war, this city was much like any other. With the Stone of Okuta, Silvino has completely changed everything."

A cool breeze—the first signal of a dying summer in the northern hemisphere—filtered in through the iron bars, caressing Seb's face. The wind carried with it the smell of home. While many things had obviously changed during his time in exile, there was something about the scent that calmed the weight in his chest.

"Please tell me I'm not crazy for doing this," Seb whispered, unable to take his eyes off the city. "We've sailed across the world, potentially thousands of leagues away from Aydiin and Byanca, all because an apparition from my past told me to."

"I don't think you're crazy," Joon said, apparently ignoring the last part. Seb hadn't told the Gorteon about Rashad. He didn't want to remember his conversation with the high priest, and he certainly didn't want to tell another living soul about it. "Even if you are, it's too late to do anything about it now."

"Well, that's certainly comforting," Seb chuckled without turning from his vigil. "How do you feel about the odds of all this actually working?"

"Well, from what I've heard and seen from the crew, I think Harlin's right about loyalty to the regime evaporating," Joon began. "First of all, pretty much everyone on the ship hates Admiral Ferdinand with a passion."

"Glad to see I'm not the only one," Seb grunted.

"Far from it," Joon responded, his smile fading. "Beatings are a daily occurrence, usually from the Admiral's own hand. He even threw a cabin boy overboard last week for sleeping in."

"Why didn't you tell me that before?" Seb asked.

"It was a tough thing to see, let alone talk about," Joon sighed. "And it never really came up. Honestly, there's a tension on board the ship that could be cut with a knife."

"I'd rather use that knife to slice through Ferdinand's throat," Seb growled, thinking of the man's depravity.

"You wouldn't be alone in that sentiment," Joon said. "It really seems like the crew is on the verge of mutiny—it's a good thing for him that the voyage is practically over."

"And what have you heard people say about their emperor?" Seb asked, turning to face Joon.

"Well, loyalty there is pretty thin, too," Joon replied. "Most men onboard were pressed into service after committing a crime or falling short on a loan payment, so they're not exactly ardent patriots. And it really does seem like the situation all over Margella is growing dire."

"But these men have been gone for almost a year," Seb said, trying to not let his hopes rise too much. "That's a long time in politics."

"Do you think people would go from rebels to loyalists in that time?" Joon asked. "That seems like a stretch."

"Not likely, but we have to strike when the iron's hot—even a severe grievance can become nothing but a mild annoyance with enough time. It doesn't matter what Silvino has done in the past; if things aren't too bad right now, there won't be many willing to sacrifice their lives for change."

"And do you think Harlin can stop that silly emperor from killing you the moment you step off the boat?" Joon asked, his face serious despite his attempt at humor.

"Harlin said the plan is for a public execution on the twentieth anniversary of Silvino's coronation. That's not for another month, so we should have enough time to get me out of prison."

"I sure hope he's right," Joon said, and the two men settled into a silence broken only by the ship's engines.

"Can I ask one more question of the First Champion?" Joon asked, the words coming out slowly.

"Not if you put it that way," Seb grunted.

"Do you think you'll find your redemption here?"

Seb's heart skipped a beat at the words, and he turned from his window-side vigil to face his small friend.

"You've been talking in your sleep," Joon said, shifting his gaze to the floor. "It's not my fault the best place to sleep on this ship is underneath your cot."

"What have I been saying?" Seb asked.

"Last night, you kept repeating 'redemption,'" Joon said, returning his gaze to meet Seb's eyes. "You said it with such intensity that I almost woke you up."

"Must have just been a nightmare," Seb grunted, turning back to the window.

More than anything else from his conversation with Rashad, those words bore into him. He'd never thought about the need for redemption—he had fought bravely in defense of his homeland, and he had few regrets. In fact, there was only one thing that came to mind.

Footsteps sounded outside his door, and Seb felt Joon disappear. Even without looking, he knew the space next to him was now empty. The Gorteon was almost too deft at disappearing at a moment's notice. The familiar sound of iron grinding on wood met his ears, and Seb focused on ignoring the intruder.

"Sir, you'll need to come with me," an unfamiliar voice coughed, and Seb turned to see two young soldiers in the dark blue of the Imperial Marines standing at his door.

"I'd be happy to, but I'm a little tied up at the moment," Seb smiled, lifting his manacled wrists in the air.

"I'm really sorry to do this, sir," the soldier said, pulling a ring of keys from his pocket. He reached for Seb's wrists and unlocked the old man.

Each soldier grabbed an arm and led the First Champion out of the cell. Seb didn't resist—for the moment, his curiosity was stronger than his survival instinct. Besides, resistance would be counter-productive at this point.

Where is everyone? Seb thought as the soldiers led him through the bowels of the ship. These hallways and cabins should be teeming with life, shouted commands filling the air. This morning, only the sound of their footsteps mixing with the ship's engines met Seb's ears.

The trio reached the stairs leading to the ship's deck. Too narrow for all three men to ascend at once, one of his guards stepped back. Seb could feel the man's gaze on his rear—there didn't seem to be any anger in the soldier, only sorrow. As his head rose above deck, the vision that met his eyes explained his escorts' sobriety.

The entire crew of the *Glorious Revolution* was assembled on deck, their ranks packed tight to accommodate the hundreds of individuals needed to manage such a vessel. There were engineers, dirty from the filth and soot of the engine room standing next to officers in blue uniforms. Common sailors in their blue and white striped shirts stood silently, posture straight at full attention. Mixed in with the sailors were both vermillion-clad imperial guards and the blue uniforms of the marines.

Not a soul made a sound.

In the middle of the deck, a raised dais two spans high had been constructed. It held a table where a single man sat, his blue uniform freshly pressed and laundered. The smile alone set Admiral Ferdinand apart from the somber inhabitants of the ship.

Seb walked along the pathway that had remained clear between the stairs and Ferdinand—the only space of open deck on the entire ship. Above, a seagull called out, breaking the silence as Seb locked eyes with the aging admiral. He walked slowly toward the man, unwilling to show any amount of weakness or confusion.

"You are, no doubt, wondering what you are doing here," Ferdinand called out as Seb approached, his voice loud enough for all those assembled to hear.

Seb didn't respond. He set his jaw and stared back at the man.

"You have already been found guilty for treason—that is an un-deniable fact. For this crime, the Emperor will have the pleasure of ending your life," Ferdinand continued, apparently undisturbed by

Seb's silence. "However, there is another—more recent—crime for which you need to pay a price."

Ferdinand paused to let the words sink in, although they didn't have the effect he'd apparently intended. Not a word was uttered in the crowd, and Seb didn't let a single emotion show on his face. After a moment of silence, Ferdinand cleared his throat.

"You have assaulted a servant of His Imperial Majesty, and while you will soon face execution for treason, this separate crime cannot be allowed to escape its own punishment," Ferdinand shouted. "By the power invested in me by the Emperor and the Divines, I sentence you to torture in the cold embrace of a terran snake."

An involuntary shudder ran down Seb's spine, although he maintained his gaze on the admiral's face. Two men emerged from the ranks, large bags tossed over their shoulders. The burlap sacks were thrown to the ground, and rich, black dirt spilled onto the wooden deck.

"As the ship's ranking Stone-weaver, I have the immense pleasure of fulfilling this punishment," Ferdinand shouted, a smile spreading across his entire face.

The Admiral lifted his hands, and the dirt began to coalesce. Particles that had been flung spans away from the bags zoomed back at the Stone-weaver's command. Within a few seconds, the dirt had formed into a long tube—a tube that began slithering toward Seb like a serpent.

Seb refused to acknowledge the soil moving toward him, refused to exhibit the fear that made his heart pound like a drum. He focused on Ferdinand, letting his hatred for the man overpower his fear.

The dirt, cold as a winter's morning, made contact with his ankle, and Seb unwillingly flinched. His legs were forced together, the snake tightening its grip as it climbed up Seb's body. Within seconds, the pain set in.

A terran snake wasn't made from just any dirt. The dark soil was mixed with glass and crushed scorpion peppers. As the snake wrapped around Seb's body, he could feel the crushed glass open up a thousand tiny wounds. He stifled a scream as the ground pepper made contact with the open flesh.

"Just utter a few words, and I can make this stop," Ferdinand said, stepping down from the dais and approaching his prisoner. The snake now completely enveloped Seb, the shards of glass ripping through both clothing and flesh. "Simply denounce your queen and hail the Emperor as the rightful ruler of Margella—simple as that."

Seb gritted his teeth against the pain, his jaw almost spasming under the pressure. He knew the man spoke nothing but lies. Were he to give in, Seb would be met with only disgrace.

"No?" Ferdinand laughed, bringing his face close to Seb's own. "Not so combative today, are you?"

Seb spat in the Stone-weaver's face, and the admiral's complexion grew red as the liquid dribbled down his forehead. Ferdinand wiped the spit from his face and flicked his wrist casually.

Seb's stomach did flips as he shot thirty spans into the air. The snake's grip grew tighter on his body, the fire on his skin growing into an inferno, as the crew of the *Glorious Revolution* diminished in size below him. For a moment, he hung in the air, the wind rushing through his ears as his eyes took in the sight of the ship and city below.

His stomach again reeled as Ferdinand commanded the snake to fall. The air roared in his ears, the tangy scent of the ocean filling his nose. Seb shut his eyes as the deck drew closer. Cushioned by the dirt that trapped his body, Seb crashed onto the wooden deck. Adding to the fire was a new pain in his left arm—he was certain that at least one bone was now broken.

"I can make what remains of your life pure suffering," Ferdinand whispered, crouching down next to the fallen First Champion. "You have the power to make it all go away."

The snake lifted Seb upright, a span into the air—just high enough for him to be seen by the entire crew. For the first time since coming on deck, he allowed himself to look into the faces of those assembled.

Not a single face expressed amusement. He saw no satisfaction at the sight of an old enemy brought low. There was, however, a fierce hatred in the eyes of many—that hatred was not directed at the First Champion. Ferdinand apparently wasn't paying attention to the mood of his subordinates.

"I will die a thousand deaths before submitting to men like you," Seb shouted, the words sounding strange in his ears.

He again fell to the deck, his face slamming into the wood. Blood filled his mouth, and he could tell that his teeth had done a number on the soft flesh. Parting his lips, he let the liquid pour onto the ground.

"I'll give you one last chance," Ferdinand shouted as the snake again gripped Seb tightly, lifting him to his feet.

Seb forced his eyes to focus on his tormentor, despite the blackness creeping in on the edges of his vision. His tongue worked in his mouth, the muscle trying to soothe the already lacerated flesh.

"That's enough, Ferdinand," Harlin's voice sounded, and Seb looked over to see his old enemy-turned-ally standing out from the crowd. The large man, dressed in his vermillion uniform of the Imperial Guard, stood with his arms crossed, and his eyes dared the admiral to defy him.

"This traitor needs to suffer," Ferdinand spat. "Perhaps you would like to share in his pain?"

"You wouldn't dare," Harlin growled, climbing the dais and bringing himself closer to Seb's torturer.

"I don't care about your authority on land—as long as you're on this ship, you answer to me," Ferdinand replied, turning away from the terran snake to face the general.

"Look around," Harlin said, spreading his arms and gesturing to the soldiers and sailors on deck. "Nobody else is reveling in the pain inflicted on this old man. In fact, I think we've had enough of your despotism."

At the words, a wave of murmurs swept through the men, and Ferdinand seemed to realize for the first time that his control of the *Glorious Revolution* may be slipping. The lithe old sailor narrowed his gaze and turned to a group of nearby marines.

"Take General Harlin to the brig for insubordination," Ferdinand growled, and the blue-clad marines moved toward the large man.

"My men won't allow that," Harlin growled, and several of the vermillion-clad guardsmen began moving to his side.

"My marines outnumber your pathetic contingent," Ferdinand laughed, again gesturing for his men to take the obese general.

"Wait," Seb called out, despite the blood in his mouth, and every eye turned toward him. "Don't follow the orders of this tyrannical traitor."

"Silence," Ferdinand snapped, and he flicked his wrist. The dirt surrounding Seb began to squeeze around him. The old soldier began to shake under the pressure.

"Can't you see this man has no regard for anyone other than himself?" Seb shouted despite the mounting pressure on his entire body. "I know what evils he has done to you. This man—and the emperor he serves—have brought you nothing but deprivation and slavery. All of you who still wish to breathe free air, arise and take command of your lives and liberty."

A heavy silence hung over the deck. Ferdinand stood, glaring at the First Champion. The marines charged with taking Harlin below deck looked unsure of themselves. In the midst of the crowd, Seb saw his small Gorteon friend appear. With a smile on his face, Joon opened his mouth to shout.

"Love live the First Champion!"

The Gorteon's words slammed through the silence, and—as if a dam had burst—a cheer arose from the sailors on board. The sailors rushed Admiral Ferdinand, and Seb could feel the dirt around him loosen its grasp as the man's focus turned toward his surroundings.

One of the sailors brandished a club and slammed it onto the grizzled admiral's head. The dirt holding Seb fell to the ground, along with the First Champion. The wounds all over his body continued to sting, but the sight of his old enemy falling to the deck unconscious dulled the pain.

"It appears all my scheming has been for naught," Harlin said, approaching Seb through the crowd of sailors as a group of his guardsmen dragged the unconscious admiral below deck. "You didn't need me, after all."

"Taking the *Glorious Revolution* isn't the same as toppling the entire empire," Seb replied. "We're lucky that Ferdinand was such a harsh commander. We need to get this ship somewhere safe, somewhere that we can meet up with your contacts in the underground."

"Strike the colors and get this ship out of the harbor," Harlin barked to the sailors. "If you want to survive the next few hours, get back to work."

Sophie sat reclined in her room's armchair, aching feet resting on a plush ottoman. For the first time in months, a flame crackled in the fireplace, its warmth pushing back the cool autumn air invading through the open window. The smell of changing leaves made its way in, mixing with the aroma of smoldering cherry wood, an almost intoxicating mixture.

Her thoughts drifted to yet another early morning hike with Prince Tomas. There was little the man enjoyed more than exploring the foothills surrounding the city, identifying birds and insects. She couldn't really see the fun in some of it, but the hours spent talking with the man were well worth blisters and sore muscles.

Had it really only been a few weeks since that night in the gardens? It felt like yesterday, but Sophie already felt that this was the only life she had ever known. It was hard to remember days spent working in the kitchens instead of exploring wooded hillsides.

A knock at the door pulled Sophie from her musings, and she rose to her feet and straightened out her disheveled dress.

"Come in," she called out. The door opened slightly, revealing the long face of Tomas. A smile graced that face, lighting his eyes.

"I'm sorry to disturb you," he said, opening the door wider. He hadn't yet changed from his dusty brown trousers, and his shirt showed where he'd perspired during their trek. "I just wanted to tell you again how much I enjoyed our morning."

"It was absolutely enchanting," she said, walking over and giving her prince a quick peck on the cheek. A thin veneer of salt clung to her lips, another sign he'd come without taking time to bathe. She found the taste not wholly unpleasant. "Did you want to come in?"

"Oh, I really shouldn't," Tomas chuckled, entering the room and closing the door behind him. "The palace gossips would have a field day if they knew I was visiting Miss Sophie in her own rooms."

"We really shouldn't," Sophie began before Tomas' smile cut her off.

"Sophie, there's something I've been wanting to tell you," Tomas began, the smile fading from his lips.

A second knock on the door stopped Tomas just as he opened his mouth, and the young man's eyes widened. Without waiting for a response, the door opened to reveal the smiling countenance of Reginald.

"Ah, I knew looking here first was a good idea," the steward laughed. "Tomas, your father requires your presence down at the harbor."

"The harbor?" Tomas asked, his eyebrows raised. "Why would he need me there?"

"I'm not entirely sure," Reginald responded with a shrug. "A motor carriage is being prepared as we speak, and His Majesty wants you inside it."

"In this state?" Tomas asked, gesturing to his filthy clothing. "If this is some formal affair, he'll be furious if I show up looking like this."

"Your father knows you were out this morning, and he told me to not let your clothing impede you in any way," Reginald smiled. "He also said that Miss Sophie is to accompany you."

With the look of confusion still evident on his face, Tomas offered his arm, and Sophie took it. Reginald smiled and without another word began leading the young couple through the palace.

The vehicle was ready for them as they exited through one of the side-exits—her relationship with Tomas was an open secret, but still officially a secret, nonetheless. Her prince still hadn't summoned up the courage to tell his father that Sophie was more than just a mistress. Only a few servants were around to see her lovingly attached to the heir, and they knew better than to spread the rumor any further than was desirable. With a bow, Reginal opened the motor carriage door, and Tomas helped her enter.

"My father must have quite the surprise up his sleeve," Tomas said, his brow furrowing as the carriage rumbled through the city streets. "That's not always a good thing."

"I'm sure whatever it is will be fine," Sophie said, looking up to see the expression on her prince's face. "What? Are you concerned?"

"You may not have noticed, but my father isn't exactly the loving protector of the people the propaganda machine depicts him as being," Tomas said, his face growing earnest.

"I don't like where this is going," Sophie responded. The words were bordering on treason—and she had no desire to report anything to Emperor Silvino the next time he questioned her.

"I'm sorry, but if I can't speak my mind with you—"

"No, please," Sophie interjected. "I want you to say anything on your mind—you can trust me."

"I know the newspapers will tell you that everything is going smoothly—production is up, the Imperial Administration has everything under control, blah blah blah," Tomas' words grew louder until he stopped himself. Taking a breath, he began again.

"The truth is that Margella is in trouble," he continued. "There's record drought in the south, and there just isn't enough grain. The people aren't stupid—they know that when the baker runs out of bread every morning that something is wrong. After too long of that, it doesn't matter what the *Imperial Gazette* tells you."

"What does this have to do with your father meeting us down by the harbor?" Sophie asked.

"Father's been looking for something to boost his popularity for months," Tomas said. "He's been alluding to something big these past few weeks—more than once, he's tried to get me to ask him what it is. The secret's been eating at him."

"And now you'll finally get to know what it is," Sophie said.

"That man and his secrets—he loves them more than anything else," Tomas sighed, and Sophie's stomach squirmed. What if her prince knew that she was part of one of those secrets?

"Are you hurt that he's kept you out of this one?"

"Not at all," Tomas replied, lifting his head. "My father isn't a great ruler—in fact, the only things he's good at are intrigue and war. I'm afraid this has something to do with the latter."

"With a famine, do you really think the Emperor would seek out war?"

"There's really no better way to boost public opinion than a quick war. It's a gamble—if it goes on too long or goes poorly, he could lose his throne. But from what I hear, the grumbling in the streets is that he doesn't have much to lose."

"Would people really rise up? He's our Emperor after all—it just feels wrong."

"Genodra's done just fine without a hereditary monarchy," Tomas laughed. "Who knows? I might be out of a job pretty soon."

"How serious are you right now?" Sophie asked as the carriage rolled to a stop.

"Being Emperor sounds terrible," Tomas responded. "Maybe Okuta was right about Margella needing a queen."

Before she could respond, the coachman opened the door for the young couple, and Sophie could hear the usual sounds associated with a port. The scent of salt water was stronger, along with the stench of fish and hard work.

Tomas leapt from the vehicle and offered Sophie his hand, and she descended. Standing atop one of the docks, she caught sight of the Emperor, surrounded by a small entourage of officers. The man looked jubilant, his smiling countenance barely able to contain the emotions struggling to burst out into the open.

"Come here, my son," Silvino shouted, opening his arms to embrace Tomas, "and witness our nation's greatest triumph since the Revolution."

Sophie followed her prince onto the dock, and Tomas returned his father's embrace, albeit with an observable dose of hesitance.

"Are we waiting for a ship with enough grain to feed the entire nation?" Tomas asked.

"The food shortages will seem insignificant soon enough," Silvino replied, apparently deciding to not punish his son's sarcasm. "Do you see the battleship entering the harbor?"

"Is that the *Glorious Revolution*?" Tomas asked, taking a spyglass from one of the officers and holding it up to look at the ship. "I have been wondering where our most powerful naval vessel has been."

"Wonder no more, my boy," the Emperor responded, pounding Tomas on the back. "I sent it on a mission to fetch a very infamous fugitive."

"Are you saying that you've apprehended Norwin the Fang?" Tomas asked. "He's supposed to be hiding out somewhere in Pilsa."

"No, you're thinking too small," Silvino replied, shaking his head. "I wouldn't send such a vessel to catch a simple bandit. Who is Margella's worst enemy?"

"The Undergods?" Tomas asked, turning to Sophie with a smile.

"Your Highness, are you talking about the traitor, Sebastian Montague?" Sophie piped up, wanting nothing more than to keep Tomas from irritating his father too much.

"That's my girl," Silvino replied with a wink before turning back to Tomas. "She's much too smart for you, even if you are a prince."

"So, you've finally caught him, eh?" Tomas asked, patting his father on the shoulder. "Less than a league away sits the Lion of the Segre, the First Champion, the one man who you could never seem to defeat."

"He was defeated long ago," the Emperor snapped. "Now, he's going to face a painful and humiliating death for his crimes."

"Your Majesty, look," Reginald said, handing his spyglass to Silvino. Sophie grabbed one from Tomas and placed it to her eye.

The imperial flag was being lowered, and the behemoth of a ship began to turn away from the dock. Sophie directed her spyglass to the ship's deck and saw a mass of soldiers and sailors moving in all directions. Standing against the railing, she saw a large man in a vermillion uniform and an emaciated old gentleman.

"There's something about that old man," Sophie whispered, more to herself than to anyone else.

"What's the traitor doing above deck?" Silvino shouted. Apparently, Sophie wasn't the only one to notice the old man.

As if the two men could feel Silvino's stare burning into them, the emaciated prisoner raised a spyglass directly at them. For what felt like an eternity, Sophie stared through the glass at this man who appeared to be staring back. Then, the aging soldier lowered the spyglass and smiled. Lifting his arm, he gave a big wave as the monstrous battleship completed its turn.

"Order all ships to pursue the traitors," Silvino shouted, motioning to his officers.

"Your Majesty, there isn't a breath of wind today, and there aren't any of our other steamships in the harbor," one of the officers responded, his voice trembling.

"I didn't ask for your excuses," the Emperor replied, turning away from the docks and heading toward his own motor carriage. "You will track them down, and I will kill Sebastian Montague with my own hands."

33

Aydiin sat on the cold marble floor staring into what he was quickly coming to call the "blood circle" as the sun continued its trek across the sky. The quiet solitude of the abandoned Doge's Palace soothed his aching soul, which was beginning to buckle under the weight of too many questions and expectations. As his gaze remained fixed on the circle painted onto the floor of the Grand Hall with human blood, his mind began reaching back to the day it was created.

It felt like a lifetime ago, although the calendar told him it had been only a few months. That day, the air had been crisp, the scent of autumn mixing with a burning city. Today, there was a hint of spring in the air. The sun was shining brightly through the dirty windows, and he could smell weeds beginning to grow in the unkempt garden.

This large hall, meant for hosting lavish parties, was the first place he had met his father-in-law. It was also the last place he had seen the man. He hoped it wouldn't be the final time.

The images from that moment still haunted him—the look of pain in that poor man's face as he dragged his severed stump of a hand across the floor, the look of relief as he was told he would receive eternal life, and Aydiin's own shock as that wicked sword severed the man's head from his body. He closed his eyes, and he could still picture the entire scene as if it had been burned into his memory.

Footsteps sounded behind him, stiletto heels cracking on the once-pristine marble floor. Without looking, Aydiin knew who it was. No one else walked quite the way she did.

"So, what are you hoping to find?" Byanca asked, her voice penetrating the silence.

"I'm not really sure," Aydiin said, rising to his feet, a smile spreading across his face.

Byanca wore a fashionable green chiffon dress, the sheer fabric bunched up in ruffles. Her hair was done up in an array of intricate braids, the various hues of auburn and strawberry blonde snaking back and forth. Her face was accentuated by a subtle blush and her lips were a soft pink.

"Really? Because you seemed completely lost in thought," she smiled, grabbing his hand and giving it a solid squeeze.

"I just feel like there's something to be learned here," Aydiin said, gesturing to the Blood Circle.

"This is the fourth time you've been here since we arrived," Byanca said. "What have you learned?"

"Nothing concrete," he said, blowing out a long breath. Byanca nodded her head for him to continue. "Well, it just doesn't make sense. I'm positive the hooded figure who led the Order here was Barrick's father."

"Right," Byanca responded. "The golden fringe on his purple robes marked him as the Grand Master. Not to mention that you recognized his voice."

"Exactly," Aydiin replied. "So, if this circle took Marcino and his captors back to Maradon, we should have found him during our search of the Order's headquarters there."

"True, but they had more than enough time to move him somewhere else," Byanca said. "Can you get to your point? I have tea with Lady Silva and a dinner with Lord North that I need to prepare for."

"I think...I think that your father was taken to the Underworld," Aydiin said, unsure of himself as the words escaped his mouth.

"That's...ridiculous," Byanca responded. "How would that even be possible?"

"Well, look at the pattern here on the floor," Aydiin stood up, and began walking around the circle. "It's around the same size as the altar in the Silent Chapel in Maradon. That altar acted as a gateway for the Undergods to potentially escape their imprisonment."

"Wait, you're suggesting that people can enter the Underworld," Byanca said, the words leaving her mouth slowly.

"It's just a hypothesis," Aydiin said. "Based on nothing but conjecture. However, it just feels right, somehow."

"Well, I've heard you say crazier things," Byanca responded, "but it is terrifying to think there is a way in and out of the Undergods' prison."

"I agree," Aydiin said. "If we want to rescue your father, we may need to find a way in ourselves."

"I don't want to think about that right now," Byanca said with a shiver. "I wasn't just trying to escape our conversation when I said I need to get ready for tea with Lady Silva. Will you be joining me for dinner with the Norths?"

"Of course. I can't just abandon you to those jackals—they'll tear you apart."

"I'd like to think that I'm more than capable of dealing with Lord and Lady North," Byanca said. "You're the one I'm worried about. However, I would very much enjoy your company—these particular jackals can be quite dry."

"I'll meet you at the Marzios' at seven, sharp," Aydiin said, running his fingers through his mess of curly hair. "And don't worry, I'll try to look presentable."

Byanca stepped closer and also ran her fingers through his hair. Without warning, she grabbed a handful of his curls and pulled his head toward hers into a long, slow kiss. Aydiin kissed her back, and the world's problems suddenly felt very far away.

Byanca pulled away after a moment, her cheeks flushed.

"I wish we could have time for a normal relationship," she said. "One that wasn't interrupted by power struggles and plots to destroy the world."

"I don't think we'd know what to do with ourselves," Aydiin laughed. "In fact, I'm pretty sure we'd get bored."

She smiled and put her head on his chest. He put his arms around her and nuzzled his face into her perfect hair.

"Uh, am I interrupting something?" Cael's voice sounded from the hallway.

"Yes, yes you are," Aydiin said without looking up

"I really do need to get going," Byanca said, her face still buried in Aydiin's chest.

"Yeah, I can just talk to you later," Cael said after a moment. "You two are obviously in kind of a weird place right now."

"No, it's fine," Aydiin said, lifting his face out Byanca's hair. His mouth fell open as his eyes found Cael.

The young man was completely decked out in the grey uniform of a Genodran regular soldier. The epaulettes on his shoulders marked him as a lieutenant, and the medals on his chest indicated that he'd been on several campaigns. He even sported a thick, red mustache.

"Cael, what have you been up to?" Byanca said, pulling her face away from her husband's chest.

"Look, I just really need to speak with Aydiin," Cael said, ripping the hair from his face. "In hindsight, I probably should have changed first, but I wasn't expecting to see both of you here."

"That doesn't change the fact that you're walking around in an official army uniform," Byanca said, pulling away from the embrace. "I think you have some explaining to do."

"I sure do," Cael said. "Just not to you. Aydiin, can we speak in private, please?"

"Until the election, I'm still president of the interim government," Byanca said. "If you have any sort of vital information, I need to know about it."

"It's kind of private," Cael said, rubbing the back of his neck. "You know—guy stuff."

"Right," Byanca said, the word coming out long and slow. Aydiin could tell by the look on her face that she wasn't buying it, but that she also didn't care that much. "Well, if you really insist on keeping me in the dark, that's fine. I am now officially late for tea with Lady Silva."

Byanca turned and gave Aydiin a quick peck on the cheek before making her exit. Her heels cracked on the floor, and Aydiin just smiled at Cael as the sound faded.

"How'd you know to find me here?" Aydiin asked.

"Well, you weren't at the Marzios," Cael shrugged. "This is pretty much the only other place you'd be."

"Am I really that predictable?" Aydiin responded, Cael opened his mouth to answer. "Wait, don't answer that. I don't want to know. I think the more important topic of discussion has something to do with your current get-up. Please, don't tell me that you snuck into that army camp."

"Of course," Cael replied with a large smile, pulling a paper out of his jacket. "What else would I be doing the day before the election? Can we find a table or something? I have a lot to show you."

"Yeah, there's a little something nearby," Aydiin said, leading Cael outside the Grand Hall. "I know this isn't the first time I've said this, but don't tell Byanca that I showed you this."

"I'm glad that your relationship with my sister already has a healthy amount of secrets," Cael laughed as the two kept walking through the palace.

After a few minutes, they approached the servants' staircase hiding the entrance to Marcino's secret study. Without an explanation, Aydiin pulled on the baluster and looked at Cael's face to see the young man's reaction as the secret doorway opened.

"Wait, this is your secret? I've known about this little entrance since before I could talk."

"Well, now we know who the favorite is," Aydiin laughed. "Byanca said your father only showed it to her recently."

"Dad never showed it to me," Cael said, leading the way into the study. "He's just not as sneaky as he'd like to believe."

The study was exactly as Aydiin had left it a few weeks ago. Dust hung in the air, and the desk on the far side of the room remained in disarray. Aydiin nodded for Cael to take a seat.

"Okay, I took some time to sketch out a map of Diaz's camp," Cael said, spreading out a paper across the desk.

"You are a brave man," Aydiin said, patting Cael on the shoulder. "What did you find out?"

"Well, they have about ten different supply tents," Cael said, pointing to a few circles spread throughout the map.

"So, trying to hit all of them at once would require a much larger team than just the two of us," Aydiin said. "A repeat of your little fireworks show may not be ideal."

"Exactly," Cael said, pointing to a triangle he'd drawn on the side closest to the city. "Now, interestingly enough, this is where Diaz has his command tent."

"That's practically on the perimeter," Aydiin said, rubbing his chin. "I would have thought he'd keep it near the center."

"I know, but apparently, he wants to keep himself as close to the city as possible."

"What's this right here?" Aydiin asked, pointing to a star on the side of the camp furthest from the city.

"That, my dear brother, is the reason I needed to speak with you. While they're keeping their supplies spread throughout the camp, Diaz has decided to congregate his trucks into a single motor pool."

"If we could sabotage those trucks—"

"Those soldiers would have to march into Palmas on foot," Cael finished for him. "They'd also have a harder time sending in suicide bombers to destroy the forts."

"Any idea how we get in there?" Aydiin asked, a smile spreading across his face.

"Of course," Cael said, an equally large smile plastered across his countenance.

As Cael began going into the details of his plan, Aydiin's eyes caught sight of the book he'd placed on the desk during his last incursion into the office.

The Song of Alarun was an epic poem written in the third century. It was taken from various accounts of those who had survived the devastating War of Divinity. It was possibly the only book written to glorify Alarun. Needless to say, it was not well-received throughout the world.

He opened the book and began flipping through its pages. It had been years since he had read it, and he had mostly done it to spite his father. He opened to the middle—the beginning of the book was rather dry.

The Dark Lord awaits your embrace,
For all those who seek his face

Aydiin stopped. He didn't remember any mention of the Dark Lord in the *Song*. He kept reading.

And life eternal
Comes to those who choose the infernal.

Aydiin began flipping through the rest of the book. There were more similar passages as Cael continued explaining his plan to sabotage the army. A surge of nervous adrenaline rushed through his veins, and Aydiin's hands began to shake as he realized what he held in his hands.

Prophecies of the Return.

He examined the book's binding, and it was now obvious where the leather had been ripped from its original pages. He could see the rough thread used to sew the forbidden pages into the cover of such an innocuous book.

Aydiin's mind began to race about what this meant. Was Marcino a member of the Order? If so, why would he have been kidnapped? In the glimpse he had seen of the man before he had vanished, he had certainly looked distressed. His hands had been bound, his clothing torn.

He knew there wasn't enough here for Aydiin to judge his father-in-law, although the mere possession of this book would be enough to see him executed in many nations. However, Aydiin knew how seductive the Undergods could be—Barrick had proven that. No matter what Marcino had done, he was being held prisoner by members of the Order. That fact alone meant he was worthy of pity, and he knew he had to save the man. Aydiin knew something else—he could never tell Byanca.

"I'm sorry, Cael," Aydiin said, closing the book. "I was a bit distracted. Can you go over that last part again?"

"Come on, Aydiin, this is important," Cael said with a sigh. "Once I sneak past the guards, I'll—"

"How many guards were outside the motor pool?" Aydiin asked.

"Well, that's not important..."

"Because there's a lot of them?" Aydiin said. It wasn't really a question.

"Okay, yes, I think they know how vulnerable it is. There are guards surrounding the entire perimeter all the time," Cael sighed. "But I'm sure we can get past them."

"This doesn't really sound worth it," Aydiin said, unable to fully pull his mind away from what he'd just discovered. "It's just too risky."

"Just think about the possibilities," Cael said. "This could make all the difference in battle."

"Maybe if we had more time to scout out their camp and come up with a plan, I'd be on board," Aydiin said, still trying to pull his mind away from the book sitting on the desk. "But we only have tonight. If something's going to happen, it will be in the aftermath of the election."

"All we need to do is get in without being seen," Cael said. "It can't be that hard."

"There's not a cloud in the sky, and the moon's almost full," Aydiin said. "The only way we could get in past those guards would be on a particularly dark night."

"Please," Cael said, clasping his hands together.

"No," Aydiin sighed. "We really just can't risk it. How about we head out to some forgotten neighborhood and practice combat? We could use some before tomorrow."

"Don't you have a dinner with your wife and some clown from the Senate?" Cael chuckled. "Besides, I think I'll just go to bed. I have a feeling that tomorrow is going to be a long day."

34

Byanca fought to control her hand from shaking as she placed the last morsel of food into her mouth. The tiny, shriveled piece of poultry had been doused in the same white sauce that gave flavor to the pile of noodles that took up the majority of her plate. Overall, it wasn't the finest meal she'd eaten during the past few weeks, but considering the rampant food shortages, it wasn't terrible.

"Byanca, you know that nothing would give me more pleasure than seeing you take up residence in the Doge's Palace," Lady North said from across the table, and Byanca looked up from her plate.

Octavia North was certainly not a young woman anymore. Approaching her seventieth year, her face was graced by wrinkles, and her thin frame seemed to swim in her black gown. Despite her advancing age, the woman sat with head held high, and there was a certain elegance to her movements that Byanca could never hope to emulate.

"Thank you, Octavia," Byanca smiled, setting down her fork to take a sip of the white wine in her glass. "However, we both know that returning to my childhood home has little to do with my desire to be elected."

After spending the past hour in the formal dining room of the North's mansion, Byanca had contented herself with small talk. Despite her desire to discuss politics, she let her hosts guide the conversation. If she wanted to convince Lady North to lend her vote tomorrow, she would have to tread a very fine line this evening.

"As the city's favorite daughter, I could be facing a mob if the vote goes against you," Octavia chuckled, her voice growing raspy. "And now that you have a tall, dark, and handsome husband in tow, you're definitely the most interesting person in town."

"My husband is much more than just an accessory," Byanca said, trying not to look over at Aydiin. She had no idea how he would take the news that the people of Palmas saw him as little more than a noble barbarian pet.

"Oh, I didn't mean any offense," Octavia replied, her gaze never moving toward Aydiin.

"I've been nothing more than an accessory for decades now," Lord North spoke up with a wink at Aydiin, his voice growing weak as he also advanced in age. "It's really not so bad once you get used to it."

"Oh, quiet, Eugene," Octavia snapped, turning back to Byanca. "He's been pouting ever since I was elected to the Senate."

Nearly a decade older than his wife, Eugene North was certainly showing his age. The man sat in a faded tuxedo, his white hair combed to the side in an attempt to cover the bare skin on top. His cheeks and chin were covered in a thin stubble as if shaving every day were just too much of a hassle.

"I'm just glad to see a noble house using its wealth for the betterment of the nation rather than throwing it away on balls and expensive vehicles," Aydiin spoke up for the first time. "You have my respect more than you could ever know."

"Well, someone had to step up and make sure Diaz doesn't bully his way into power," Octavia said, dabbing her lips with a napkin. "Byanca, I really do want to give you my vote. However, I do have some reservations."

"Beyond the massive army camped on our doorstep?" Byanca asked. "That seems to be everyone's concern."

"There's no doubt in my mind that you would make a better leader than the Field Marshal," Octavia continued, ignoring Byanca's comment. "Yet, we have to consider the potential bloodshed that will ensue should you be elected."

"I understand your concerns, and—believe me—I am up at night worrying about the possibility," Byanca said, setting down her fork and knife. "However, I believe the city's fortification network, not to mention the massive swell of new recruits to the city's garrison, will persuade the Field Marshal to keep his troops back."

"And if he doesn't?" Lady North responded, her voice deepening. "Will you sacrifice the blood of thousands to keep your title?"

"While I strongly believe we can avoid battle, I will not shrink away if it is the only recourse," Byanca said, trying to keep her voice firm. "This has nothing to do with a title and everything to do with the long-term good of Genodra. As I'm sure you saw during the Revolution, the price of freedom is often the blood of patriots."

"That, my dear, was my real reservation," Octavia replied with a smile. "I wanted to make sure that if you're elected, you'd have the backbone to stand up to that monster. I'd rather vote for the beast and know what I'm getting into than vote for a puppet."

"People often criticize politicians for sending others to war," Lord North spoke up. "However, knowing that the blood of innocents will be on your hands can be far worse than dying yourself. Whatever happens, you will have to live with it for the rest of your life."

"I fully understand our situation," Byanca said. "If I could stop the bloodshed with my own sacrifice, I would. However, that's just not how things work."

"Madam Byanca, you have my vote," Lady North said, lifting her glass. "And you will have my firm support as we re-forge the Republic."

Footsteps sounded in the hall, not the delicate sound of a butler or maid hurrying to fulfill a request, but the heavy gait of booted soldiers. Byanca raised an eyebrow as the sound grew louder.

The dining room door burst open, and the sound of shattering wood filled Byanca's ears. Her eyes veered to the door in time to see Field Marshal Diaz enter the room, flanked by a dozen soldiers in their signature grey uniforms. Wearing a smile that matched his own perfectly pressed dress uniform, the man approached the table as if he'd been invited as the guest of honor.

"Ah, my dear Lord and Lady North," he said, raising his arms in greeting. "I can't express my pleasure at being invited into your home."

"You know very well that you were not invited," Lord North stood, his hand shaking along with his voice.

"That's no way to treat the savior of Genodra," Diaz said, clicking his tongue. "If I were actually here to speak with you, I'd be terribly offended."

"What brings His Excellency to our home?" Octavia spoke up, rising to her feet and forcing her husband back into his chair.

"I require some time alone with young Byanca and Aydiin," Diaz replied, his smile never wavering. "Finding them absent at their current residence, I had no choice but to follow them here."

"Do you really intend to evict me from my own dining room?" Octavia barked.

"Yes, I thought that was obvious," Diaz replied. With a wave of his hand, two soldiers stepped forward to escort the aging aristocrats from the room. "Don't worry, I won't harm your guests. These men are only here to ensure that no one tries to disturb our discussion."

"Unhand me, you rogue," Octavia snapped, slapping one of the men across the face as he grabbed her by the arm. "I will leave of my own volition, but I will not be dishonored by your filthy hands."

"Thank you for seeing reason, Lady North," Diaz said. "And again, my sincerest apologies."

"Byanca, I will see you first thing in the morning," Octavia said as she shuffled toward the door. "And I want it to be known that this monster will never be the Doge as long as I still breathe."

Lady North grabbed her husband by the hand and led him out the door, followed by two soldiers. Byanca sincerely hoped that they wouldn't be harmed for the simple crime of providing her dinner. Of course, it was impossible to predict what this madman would do.

"Oh, the drama," Diaz chuckled as his men shut the door, leaving the Field Marshal alone with the young couple. "Some people have the hardest time following even the simplest of requests."

"What do you want?" Aydiin asked, his tone conveying the emotions that Byanca also felt.

"I wanted to congratulate you on a hard-fought campaign," he said, taking a seat in the chair that had so recently been occupied by Lord North. "From what my sources can surmise, it appears that the Senate will be announcing your election in the morning."

"It's been a pleasure running against such a fierce competitor," Byanca said with a nod. "However, that information hardly requires you to treat our hosts with such impropriety."

"Oh, but it does. You see, I do so want to offer the services of both myself and the First Army as we restore the Republic and take back the country from the chaos caused by my idiotic predecessor," Diaz said.

"I thank you for the support, Field Marshal," Byanca said. "By your tone, I'm assuming that your loyalty and assistance will come at a price."

"You are a smart one," Diaz said, grabbing the remainder of Lord North's wine and leaning back in his chair. "I can see why you're the one being elected instead of me."

"I can assure you that I will not be your puppet," Byanca said. "You can decide where your loyalties lie, but regardless, I will govern Genodra according to my own conscience."

"I have no desire to control you," Diaz said, taking a sip of the wine. "However, I do control Skraa and the army. So, regardless of any fancy words that come out of that gorgeous little mouth of yours, it would be to our mutual advantage to form a partnership of sorts."

"Your organization has already tried to kill me," Aydiin said, leaning forward in his chair. "It's hard to imagine working with you."

"I'll admit that under Arathorm Fortescue, the Order became bent on creating chaos and releasing the Undergods," Diaz said, waving his hand. "However, I'm cut from a different cloth. I'd much rather rule the world than destroy it. With your help, we could set up an imperial dynasty and unite the squabbling nations."

"Do you really think that Skraa would allow you to do that?" Byanca scoffed. It wasn't really a question.

"I control Skraa, not the other way around," Diaz said, his face darkening as he leaned forward in his chair. "That tormented soul will do as I tell him. If I want him to leave you alone, he will. If I tell him to devour your skin while you scream in agony, he'll do so with pleasure."

"I won't be intimidated," Byanca replied, forcing her voice to remain below a shout. "The world has a way of rewarding tyrants like you, and I won't be a part of it."

"Well then, I can see this little chat was in vain," Diaz said, rising to his feet. "Just as a gesture of goodwill, I promise not to attack tomorrow. This offer will remain on the table for forty-eight hours—I suggest you think it over."

Diaz began moving toward the door. As he grabbed the handle, he turned back around, his smile growing somehow wider.

"Oh, one more thing," he said. "We caught a red-haired little boy sabotaging our trucks about an hour ago."

Byanca felt the blood drain out of her face, and her head grew dizzy. She resisted the desire to look at Aydiin. She should have known that Cael's soldier outfit would lead to nothing good.

"He's currently in the loving care of Skraa," Diaz said before letting out a long laugh. "I can assure you that until my offer expires, his life won't. After that, I offer no such assurances."

At that, Diaz turned and opened the door.

"Wait," Byanca said, holding back tears. "Let's discuss your terms a bit further before retiring for the night."

"I was hoping you'd say that," Diaz said, closing the door and returning to his chair. "Tomorrow, you will be named Doge of Genodra, which I'm sure will be the happiest moment of your young life."

"As you've said," Aydiin cut in.

"For your first official act," Diaz continued, ignoring Aydiin's outburst, "you will magnanimously name your defeated competitor as supreme commander of all Genodran armed forces."

"You realize that the Senate will immediately understand that makes me a puppet," Byanca said, gritting her teeth. "Would it kill you to use at least some subtlety?"

"There's no fun in that. In addition, you will dissolve the militia—with a hearty pat on the back for a job well done, of course."

"Is that all?" Byanca asked. "Do you want me to promise my firstborn as well?"

"Of course not," Diaz laughed, reclining into the chair and placing his hands behind his head. "Children are a nasty, smelly lot. I do, however, want you to name me as your Chief Advisor."

"That's not a thing," Byanca said. "Nobody will even know what I'm talking about."

"These are times for new ideas and—more importantly—new titles. On every decision, you will be required to hear my counsel."

"You're essentially not even hiding the fact that you'll be the one pulling the strings," Aydiin broke in.

"These are my demands," Diaz said, stretching and rising to his feet. "This is not a starting point for negotiations—this is the final list."

"You know these demands are completely unacceptable," Byanca said, also rising to her feet.

"Sleep on it, if you want," Diaz said, striding over to the doorway. "However, I know with the lives of both your brother and your city in my hands, you'll make the right decision."

Before Byanca could respond, Diaz opened the door and exited into the hallway.

35

T hunder rolled in the distance, a most unusual sound for early spring. Considering the perfect weather of the day before, it was even more surprising. With a mental curse, Byanca forced her mind from the weather back to the present moment.

From her position sitting atop the dais at the far end of the Senate Chambers, Byanca could see everything from the raised seating on both sides of the chamber to the crowd gathered on the mezzanine above. The seating reserved for the senators was empty, a sign that their deliberations within the inner halls of the building were not free of contention. Nearly two hours after both she and Diaz had delivered their final arguments, the Senate was still deliberating.

The crowd above represented every rung of the social ladder. Factory workers covered in dust and grime sat next to perfumed ladies and lords. She even noticed a smattering of soldiers in both green and grey uniforms who had come to see how their fates would be directed.

Byanca never really thought that she'd be a candidate for Doge. She most certainly never thought it would be at such a young age and amidst a crisis that threatened to unravel the very fabric of her nation. Of course, she never thought she'd be married to the Heir of Alarun, either. Life had a way of surprising her.

To her right, Diaz leaned back in his chair. Their conversation the previous night still rang in her ears, the consequences of which were hanging over her head like a specter. A restless night did little to help her make the decision.

Diaz looked over and noticed her glare. With a smile, he pulled out a golden pocket watch from his grey jacket and opened it. He lifted it toward her direction as if to say, "you're running out of time."

A hush spread across the room as a small door opened, and Byanca tore her gaze away from the Field Marshal. She looked up to where Aydiin had been sitting for a bit of reassurance, only to find a group of steelworkers. That man was going to be the death of her.

The senators began filing in, their plodding footsteps filling the chamber. It was interesting to think how the fate of Genodra—and perhaps of the world—now sat in the hands of these twenty-five men and women. A vote for Diaz would most certainly mean tyranny. A vote for her could also mean nothing but tyranny with a beautiful facade.

Lord Renault headed the procession, and Byanca couldn't help but think for the hundredth time that he should be the one in her position. Of course, since he didn't have the backbone to actually put his name forward, he would probably have been weak enough to become Diaz's puppet. It was difficult to look on a face that she had held in such high esteem her entire life to now feel only loathing and disgust.

The senators took their seats, and Renault climbed the stairs to the podium. As he drew closer, Byanca could see the look of exhaustion on his face. The bags forming under his eyes spoke of the sleepless nights and the stress he'd endured. A portion of her disgust turned to pity.

"Citizens of Genodra," Renault spoke, his voice hoarse. "It is with a deep sense of solemnity that we gather today to elect one of these two fine individuals to lead our great nation."

He paused for a moment, and the assembled crowd broke out into a quiet applause.

"Let me stress the weight that we have given this decision, knowing the consequences of this outcome," Renault continued once the applause began to die down, his voice growing stronger. "After significant debate, the Senate has decided that the next Doge of the Republic of Genodra will be Byanca of House Cavour."

A much more raucous applause broke out among the crowd, and for a moment, Byanca's heart lifted at the sound. Amid the clapping, she could hear dozens of men whistling in jubilation and shouts of pure joy. Then, her heart fell again at the thought of her impending betrayal in order to save their lives.

"We'd like to invite our new leader to say a few words," Lord Renault said, motioning for Byanca to join him at the pulpit.

She rose to her feet, and her muscles grew stiff. Forcing her legs to move, Byanca winced at the applause now filling the Senate Chambers as she approached Lord Renault. Her stomach yelled out, wanting more than anything to eject the meager breakfast she'd consumed that morning.

"I want to offer my sincere gratitude to the Senate and the people of Genodra for this great honor," she said as the applause died down, the words she'd written out the night before running across her mind's eye. "It is with great solemnity that I accept the office of Doge along with all the authority and duties that come with it."

Another burst of applause came from the audience, although this round was much more subdued. Somehow, Byanca realized they were expecting a bit more from her than memorized words spoken without emotion. Yet she couldn't give them that—not when she was about to hand the reins of power over to Diaz and the Order.

"As my first official act, I am creating the office of Supreme Commander of the Armed Forces," she sighed, and she could almost hear the collective intake of air from the citizens within the sound of her voice. "To this most dignified of offices, I name..."

The words caught in her throat as her eyes made contact with a young girl up in the mezzanine. She couldn't have been more than four years old, her blonde hair pulled back into pigtails as she sat on her father's shoulders. Massive blue eyes widened as Byanca's words died down—even such a young girl knew she was witnessing a pivotal moment in history. Mentally, Byanca threw away the speech she'd written the night before.

"I name General Luka Marzio," she finally said, the new name leaping from her throat with a mixture of joy at resisting the Order and despair at condemning her brother to death. "And I further denounce Field Marshal Diaz as a traitor to the Republic and demand his immediate arrest."

"You little whore," Diaz shouted, rising to his feet as green-clad militiamen stormed the dais. "You've doomed this city and everyone in it."

"You really shouldn't use such words when addressing your Doge," Byanca said as two soldiers grabbed the Field Marshal by the arms while three others pointed bayonets at his chest. "It's simply not polite."

"You think you've cut your strings?" Diaz growled, grinding his teeth. "You've only ensured a harsher puppet master."

Byanca could feel the hair on her arms and neck begin to rise. Underneath the man's grey uniform, she could see a brilliant blue light emanating, and her heart began to pound in her ears.

With a shout, Diaz lifted his hands and bolts of electric-blue energy sprang from the Field Marshal's fingers. The five green-clad soldiers flew in all directions, the sound of their bones slamming into the marble walls lost amid the screams that overcame the massive hall. The air filled with the smell of burning hair and clothing, and Byanca held in another wave of nausea.

"Let's take a moment to talk about manners," Diaz growled, moving toward Byanca and ignoring the shouts as the crowd scattered like a toppled ant hill.

Under Diaz's clothing, Byanca could see the glow emanating from the man's Markings grow stronger. As he approached, the illumination grew brighter, a sure sign that he was building up energy for a single, horrifyingly powerful burst. Byanca commanded her legs to move, to do something. They refused, locked in fear.

Diaz lunged, and Byanca's muscles finally responded. Rolling to the side as the Field Marshal soared through the air, Byanca could feel the grey coat brush against her cheek as she fell to the ground. Tucking in her arms, she rolled along the cold marble floor.

The screams throughout the chamber began to diminish as both the senators and spectators cleared the building. The sharp sound of soldiers' boots hitting the polished marble began to replace the screams, and Byanca looked up to see a half-dozen of her soldiers filing into the room.

Diaz—now at the bottom of the dais after his botched lunge—rose to his feet. Raising his hands, he unleashed a chain of lighting on his attackers. The smell of burning flesh and uniforms filled the air as the Field Marshal turned back to Byanca.

"You should have just taken the deal," Diaz spat as he climbed the dais.

"You don't understand what my country means to me," Byanca responded, pushing herself up onto her hands and knees.

"And you should be exalted for your courage—but damned for your naiveté," Diaz said, launching a kick at Byanca's ribs. She grunted as the man's boot connected, sending her sprawling back onto the floor. "Now, I'll have to take the city by force. Your acts today have ensured that thousands of your compatriots will suffer and die."

"It's better than living under a petty tyrant," Byanca gasped, trying again to rise up.

"I should probably keep you around to witness the complete destruction of Palmas," Diaz shouted, lifting his hands as the glow underneath his jacket grew stronger. "But I've grown tired of you."

Diaz closed his eyes, and Byanca could feel her hair begin to stand. The smell of a summer thunderstorm filled her nostrils, and she knew nothing could stop it. Yet she forced herself to keep her eyes locked on the Field Marshal's, refusing to cower in death.

The man's eyes bulged as a rope formed from water appeared around his neck. The electric-blue glow disappeared as Diaz's face began to turn purple and his hands flailed. The water rope tightened, lifting the Field Marshal a span off the ground.

A gurgling escaped the man's throat as another band of water appeared around his wrists, slamming both arms down to his side. Like a snake rising from an afternoon slumber, another thin band of water began wrapping itself around the immaculate uniform.

"One move, and I'll slice through you like a cured meat," Aydiin's voice sounded from the floor. With a small gesture from his hand, the binding around Diaz's neck loosened.

"This isn't a fight you can win," Diaz gasped, turning his head to look at Aydiin.

"I've been told that before," Aydiin responded, his footsteps echoing through the empty chamber as he approached the dais. "So far, I feel like I've done a good job at defying the odds."

"You forget that I control Skraa," Diaz replied. "For now, he is held back from destroying you. If I'm gone...well, that's another story."

Footsteps sounded from the chamber's entrance, accompanied by shouts. Byanca turned her gaze away from Diaz to see a young man in a green uniform sprinting through the open doors. With a frenzied look in his eyes, the young man didn't even stop at the sight of his dead and injured comrades.

"The forts are under attack," the soldier cried out as he drew closer. "Fort Savoy is on the brink of destruction, and General Marzio begs for reinforcements."

"This is impossible," Diaz stammered, his face losing several shades of color. "I control Skraa and the army—unless..."

"Unless what?" Aydiin's voice sounded as he climbed the dais to stand by Byanca.

"He must have found it," Diaz said, his eyes growing sharp again.

"What did he find?" Byanca asked, her brow lowering.

"The only thing that could free him from my control—one of the lost Great Stones," Diaz replied, his eyes widening at the words. "I'm a dead man."

Diaz began to howl, his muscles straining to break free from the water binding his limbs. His face again grew purple, and he looked as if he were descending into apoplexy. A vein on his forehead began to pulse as his shouting grew louder.

"Get a hold of yourself," Byanca shouted, moving toward the frantic prisoner. With a grunt, she slapped the Field Marshal square in the face. The sound rang throughout the marble walls, and the man's howling grew silent as his gaze turned to Byanca.

"Around my necks is a golden chain," Diaz whimpered. "Please, lift it out."

Byanca ripped open the Field Marshal's top button and clasped her fingers around the chain. Yanking it free, her mouth dropped open as she withdrew an electric blue stone the size of her palm.

"The Great Stone of Perun," Aydiin said, the awe evident in his voice as he moved closer to inspect the Stone.

"My life is already forfeit," Diaz said. Byanca removed the Stone from around the man's neck and handed it to her husband.

"Why would you just give this to me?" Aydiin asked, his grip firmly around the chain and not the Stone. Now would not be a good time for her husband to enter the vision-filled trance that would overtake him once he touched the Stone.

"Skraa has been telling me for months that once he's free, I'll be the first to die," Diaz whispered. "Take the Stone and end him."

The dome above shook, as if lightning had struck the Senate Chamber's roof, and the green-clad messenger shouted. Byanca looked up as another crash sounded to see a hole in the dome. A massive black hand reached through the opening, ripping away the man-made structure.

"He's coming," Diaz yelled. "Flee!"

Byanca saw Aydiin stuff the Great Stone of Perun into his pocket as the dome above began to give way. Grabbing Aydiin by the arm, Byanca pulled her husband off the dais as wood and plaster rained down. A thick dust hung in the air, accompanied by a shrill cry from above.

A massive creature formed of pure shadow leapt through the hole in the dome and glided down on enormous wings. A smile formed on its otherwise blank face, white teeth contrasting sharply with the dark, ephemeral skin. With a howl of delight, the monster grabbed Diaz in one of its giant hands.

"Flee!" Diaz shouted as the claws wrapped around his abdomen. The water ropes collapsed, leaving a puddle on the dais.

With a push from its powerful legs, the creature leapt into the air, its wings creating a vortex within the chamber. With a final, soul-piercing cry, the shadow creature slipped through the demolished dome and into the open air.

36

The glow of the morning sun on white canvas walls greeted Gamila as her eyes fluttered open. For a moment, she could imagine that today would be like any other over the past weeks—filled with riding in the hot sun and terrible food, but overall uneventful. However, she knew that would not be the case this day, and her stomach squirmed at the thought.

Lifting herself up from the bedroll, she forced her legs toward the opposite end of the tent and her washbasin. Picking up a small cloth, she disrobed and began to wash. The water—chill from the night air—soothed her skin, and more importantly, alerted her mind.

It had been two days since she'd seen her uncle, and she had the feeling he was avoiding her. He knew the only way forward was to accept the constitution that Bayram had drafted, but the man's pride was likely getting in the way. Grabbing a dress of deep blue, Gamila tried to calm her stomach as she dressed.

Without poking her head outside, she knew the sight that awaited her. After a week of trudging through the desert and coastal plain at a snail's pace, the behemoth of a camp had finally arrived. Placing the veil over her face and taking a deep breath, Gamila opened the tent flap.

The white walls of Maradon shone in the sunrise, an unmistakable sign that her entire world would be different by sunset. Today would likely never be forgotten by anyone present, whether for good or for ill. The thought sent yet another shiver up her spine.

Brightly dressed soldiers filed past her in an unending line, rifles in hand. It was still difficult for her mind to comprehend what a hundred thousand armed men would look like assembled in a single place. Were they not intent on destroying her home, Gamila would very much like to witness it with her own eyes.

"Well, are you ready to re-make Salatia?" Agha's voice—laced with exhaustion—sounded, and Gamila jumped. The man stood at her side, the stub of a cigar hanging lazily in the corner of his mouth. The usual smile was absent, and Gamila hoped that he felt at least a fraction of the anxiety that assaulted her mind.

"That depends," Gamila sighed. "Have you decided on your course of action?"

"After a few rather sleepless nights, I have made up my mind," Agha said, taking a long draw on the cigar before tossing the butt to the ground. "And I believe you are correct—the next chapter of Salatian history can't begin with a bloodbath in the streets of Maradon."

"Oh, thank the Divines that you've come to your senses," Gamila said, letting out a breath as her anxiety began melting away.

"I would greatly appreciate your company this morning," Agha said, offering his arm with a wan smile. "This task requires strength that I don't have. I'll need some of yours."

"I'll gladly lend you my strength," Gamila said, taking her uncle's arm. "I'm just glad you made the right decision. Divines willing, we'll all sleep well tonight."

"Hard to imagine it being any worse than last night," Agha replied. "One way or another, this ends today."

The two descended into silence as soldiers continued trotting past them to the assembly point outside of camp. Most held stony expressions, unaware that their emperor had decided against an all-out assault. Gamila wondered how many lives her uncle was saving.

After a few minutes of silence, the two reached a pair of horses—a fierce steed of midnight black for Agha and a grey mare with gentle eyes for Gamila. Agha offered his hand to help his niece ascend, and the princess climbed onto the horse.

"Thank you again for accompanying me," Agha said, climbing onto his own mount. "It certainly wouldn't look good if I were to approach the Surion Gate with armed soldiers."

"The optics of that would probably be less than perfect," Gamila laughed as she directed her horse forward. "Besides, if things do go poorly, my presence should provide more protection than an entire battalion."

"I would very much prefer it if you didn't reveal your identity," Agha smiled as the two rode through the camp. "After all, I went to a lot of effort to fake your death. If the tribal elders somehow decide that the entire royal family needs to go along with my brother, your life would be in danger."

"I know," Gamila nodded. "I plan on keeping back. No need to worry about me."

The two rode through camp, quickly outpacing the soldiers filing toward the edge. From horseback, the camp felt much smaller than it had on foot. It was still impressive in nearly every aspect, but moving through it in a matter of minutes gave her a whole new perspective.

"Get ready to be amazed," Agha called out, turning in his saddle with a smile as they reached the camp's perimeter.

Gamila couldn't help but gasp at the sight of soldiers lined up in their ranks. Standing in blocks, the army stretched in an arch that matched the circular walls of Maradon. With the lack of uniforms, the multi-colored mass of humanity was almost painful to Gamila's gaze, but she forced herself to not look away.

Throughout the ranks, artillery pieces sat ready to fire, the bronze canisters glistening in the morning sun. The heavy projectiles that the guns belched would cover the half-league to the walls, leaving them little more than rubble in no time. If Agha and her father couldn't make this deal work, then Maradon really wouldn't stand a chance.

Riding through the no man's land, Gamila had to force herself to stay focused on the city walls ahead. It was more than disconcerting to have that many guns at her back, but she knew that turning around constantly wouldn't make any difference. Of course, riding toward a wall manned by potentially hostile soldiers wasn't exactly comforting either.

The road was still muddy from recent rains, although it wasn't the quagmire that it so often became during monsoon season. The horses didn't seem to mind the sticky clay as she and Agha neared Surion Gate, the largest and most-trafficked entrance into the city. For the first time in her life, Gamila saw the portcullis closed.

Gamila pulled up on her mare's reins, coming to a stop just shy of the closed gate. In the gatehouse over the portcullis, she assumed a group of soldiers sat looking out through narrow arrow slits. However, she had no way of knowing for sure.

"I come to speak with Oosman the Third," Agha cried out, his voice ringing in the silence. "It's time we settle this without the bloodshed of open battle."

The words died in the air, suffocated by the silence. Gamila's heart began pounding in her ears, marking the passage of seconds and then minutes. The beating grew louder and faster as time passed without a response.

"I am Agha, Emperor of Salatia," her uncle again called out, apparently hoping that a bit of bravado would pay off. "As the legitimate ruler of this land, I demand to speak with the usurper currently sitting on the throne."

Again, silence was the only reply from the walls. Gamila couldn't even see soldiers standing at the battlements. Was something wrong? Or were the city's defenders just purposefully ignoring this half-crazed bandit?

"Well, I tried, Gammy," Agha sighed, turning his horse around. "If they won't—"

The heavy moan of ill-used chains sounded from the gatehouse as the portcullis began to inch upward. Behind the steel bars, the massive hardwood doors opened, the hinges wailing in protest.

"I hear your request," a familiar voice cried out over the noise, and Gamila held back a gasp as her father appeared in the opening gate. "And I am here to discuss peace as the rightful and lawful sovereign of Salatia."

Dressed in robes of pure violet and a white turban, her father certainly looked every bit the ruler he claimed to be. Yet, the grey pallor that had recently taken over his skin had grown worse since she'd seen him last. The bags under his eyes were more pronounced, giving him the look of a man who was crumbling under the pressure of recent months.

"We are at a crossroads, dear brother," Agha said, turning his midnight black steed around before descending. "I know that neither of us would like to see the death of so many strong and noble Salatians."

"I'm glad we can agree for once in our lives," Oosman said, stepping toward his estranged brother. "I assume that you've had plenty of time to think about Bayram's proposal."

"I have, indeed," Agha nodded, coming within two spans of Oosman.

"With two paths forward, we can either choose war or compromise," Oosman said, his eyes drifting behind Agha, toward the massive army assembled in the distance. "The lack of thundering cannon—not to mention your presence at this moment—leads me to believe you are choosing the latter."

"Sometimes at a crossroads, you see only two paths, both of which lead to undesirable destinations," Agha said, pulling two long, wicked knives from his belt. "In this particular situation, I'm choosing to take neither of them.

"Are you challenging me to a *kavga*, dear brother?" Oosman smiled as Agha threw one of the knives into the dirt at the Sultan's feet. "A barbaric practice for barbaric times."

"I'm glad to see you respect the old ways," Agha replied as his brother grabbed the thrown knife by the hilt and yanked it from the damp soil.

"I cannot say that I am upset by this challenge," Oosman said, cleaning the mud-covered knife on his robes. "I find it far preferable to die in honorable combat than to live as nothing more than a figurehead. Between brothers, just because I allowed Bayram to go ahead with his constitutional reforms doesn't mean that I liked any of it."

"I had a feeling that your endorsement of any change was made under at least some level of duress," Agha said as he tightened his grasp on the long knife. "I have already written a proclamation that is being read to my troops at this very moment. They know that I'm risking my own life so that they don't have to. It is possible that if you are victorious, the tribal elders will still order an attack. However, they—more than anyone else—should hold respect for the old ways."

"Rebels have no honor," Oosman replied, inspecting the knife blade. "However, even with that knowledge, I gladly accept your challenge."

Oosman pulled off his violet robes, revealing simple cotton underclothing. A fire came into the old man's eyes, and the grey pallor of his skin seemed to fade as he took a wide stance. A smile spread across his face, adding fuel to the fire, and the bags under his eyes grew less prominent.

Agha gripped his own knife before ambling closer to his brother and taking the same stance. The bandit didn't remove any of his clothing, choosing instead to maintain the robes of white that he'd worn almost without variation since Gamila had been brought to the rebel camp.

Without even so much as a grunt, Oosman slashed at his brother's neck, his blade moving in a blur to Gamila's eyes. Steel crashed onto steel as Agha parried the blow with the back of his blade, letting the force of his push put him into a spin. He slashed at Oosman's stomach, catching some of the loose cotton material but failing to make contact with the skin.

The move left Agha extended, and Oosman brought his blade careening down toward the thief's head. Agha dove to his right, and Oosman's blade sliced through the thin air. With a shout, Agha sent a blow toward the Sultan's face, but Oosman brought his blade up just in time to stop the blow.

With a shout, Agha pushed his weight into the Sultan, and the two fell to the ground. Gamila couldn't help but squeal as Oosman's knife fell from his hand, the blade landing on the wet dirt next to the two men. With a smile spreading onto his face, Agha placed the blade against his brother's throat.

"Do it," Oosman hissed, the words struggling to reach Gamila's ears. "You've been threatening to kill me for years—let's see if you have what it takes."

Agha's hand trembled as he pressed the blade closer to Oosman's throat, the blade making contact with the old man's skin. Gamila's heart pounded in her ears, and she rushed forward, ripping off her veil.

"Don't do it," Gamila cried out as if she were no longer in control of her own voice. "Please show him mercy."

"Gamila," Oosman and Agha both gasped, the latter lowering his knife.

Oosman's gaze shot back toward his brother, anger replacing the shock and surprise. A fiery red light began to emanate from the Sultan's hands, the Markings of Power coming alive. Agha turned back to his brother, bringing the knife up to his throat as Oosman's Markings grew brighter.

Fire erupted from the Sultan's fingertips, filling the air with a rage-fueled inferno. Agha rolled off his younger brother, the directionless flames brushing his clothing instead of slamming into him. With a shout, the thief rose to his feet and readied himself for the next attack.

"You let me believe my own daughter was dead," Oosman growled, leaping to his feet and raising his hands to conjure up more of the divine power he held within him.

"I was protecting her," Agha shouted back. "Something that you were unable to do."

Oosman's face grew crimson as a howl erupted from his throat and flames burst from his hands. With wide eyes, Agha leapt aside, the hem of his white robes smoldering. Rolling to his feet, the thief charged Oosman, knife in hand. A growl rising from his chest, Oosman began conjuring more flames as his brother charged. With a final roar, Oosman let out an inferno.

Agha disappeared into thin air, and Oosman dropped his hands, the rage dying in his throat as confusion took its place. For a moment, the world grew silent.

"I knew you weren't a naturally talented thief," Oosman cried out, his hoarse shout disturbing the air as he turned in circles to catch a glimpse of his brother's imperfect invisibility. "I should have realized you were nothing more than a Creep."

The sound of footsteps from the gate took Gamila's attention from the fight, and she looked over to see Bayram flanked by blue-clad soldiers. Running up behind, she recognized General Tartlan. The newcomers stood in silence, obviously unsure of how to respond.

"Come out and fight like a man," Oosman roared, summoning a flame, letting it dance in between his fingers.

"If you're going to fight like a Divine, then why shouldn't I?" Agha's voice called out from behind Oosman, and the aging monarch dodged as the sound of a knife slicing through the air announced his position.

Oosman fell to the ground in a roll, leaping to his feet in one swift motion. Gamila had no idea her father still possessed such agility—it was as if the thrill of battle took decades away from his age.

"You're pathetic," Oosman shouted into the air, his gaze shifting in yet another attempt to find his invisible attacker.

"I should never have hesitated to cut your throat," Agha said, his voice moving as the words came out. "You have no honor—you pay lip service to tradition, but once it doesn't suit your purposes, it's okay for you to be above the law."

"The blood on your hands should preclude you from lecturing any-one about honor," Oosman growled, unceasing in his search for any sign of Agha.

"Maybe you're right," Agha's voice again sounded. "Yet no man can rule innocently. Blood will stain my hands just as it has yours—what I do now, I do for the good of my country and—"

Thunder rolled in the distance, and Gamila looked up to see nothing but clear skies. Agha appeared, the knife falling from his grip onto the dirt at his feet. Far from looking at his brother, Oosman looked up toward the rebel camp.

The scream of flying steel filled the air, and Gamila dove the ground. The wall exploded in a flash of brilliant white, and Gamila's world became nothing but dust and the sulfurous stench of burning gun-powder.

Bayram lifted himself up off the ground with trembling arms, his ears ringing in the new-found silence. Taking in a breath, his lungs seized control of his entire body, and he collapsed back to the ground in a fit of coughing. Every muscle in his being tightened as the smoke and dust were ejected.

"What happened?" Gamila's voice—hoarse and dry—sounded through the dust. "Agha, don't your gunners know we're here?"

"Of course they do," Agha coughed, his form becoming visible as the dust began to settle. "I gave explicit instructions to hold their fire until told otherwise."

"Some emperor you are," Oosman's voice sounded from the dust. "Can't even keep your own soldiers from shooting at you."

"You'd better hold your tongue," Agha shot back. "You're the one who lost his grip on power, you—"

The pounding of horses at full gallop penetrated the dust, and Agha's words died on his lips. Sensing that things were about to go from bad to worse, Bayram pulled on the powers within his chest, magnified by the Great Stone of Vindred around his neck. The world grew brighter, his vision cutting through the dust that still hung in the air. The sound of approaching horses grew louder and somehow more distant. Without looking at himself, he knew that nobody would be able to see him.

"Lord Agha," a voice cried out from the lead rider, whose face was indiscernible at this distance, although the riders were approaching quickly. "I'm glad to see you are safe, and that you have brought us the Usurper."

Bayram rose to his feet and drew closer to the approaching riders. Pulling harder on the powers of Vindred, he recognized the relatively youthful face of Yusef, the youngest of the tribal elders. His mind drifted back to that evening peace negotiation in Agha's tent. The man looked even more unstable this morning than he had that night.

"Oosman the Usurper, in the name of the revolution, I order your arrest," Yusef said, his gaze focused on Oosman. The man snapped his fingers, and a dozen men descended from their horses. Two of the men grabbed Oosman while the others merely stood at the ready, rifles raised.

"You have already been found guilty for treason and high crimes against Salatia," Yusef continued as Oosman was brought before him. "I am pleased to say that your execution will be at sunset."

"What is the meaning of this?" Agha scoffed, striding toward Yusef and his guards. "I sent an official order that no shots were to be fired until I gave the go-ahead. In case you didn't notice, the initial volley almost killed your sovereign."

"Yes, it's a pity that you survived," Yusef chided, nodding his head for two more soldiers to grab the thief. "I'm afraid that the Council has also found you guilty of crimes against Salatia, for which the punishment is death."

"You forget your place," Agha shouted, shaking off the men attempting to grab him.

"No, you forget yours," Yusef barked before a smile spread onto his bearded face. "Or rather, your place is no longer needed."

The two soldiers again moved in, grabbing Agha by the arms as another soldier slapped iron manacles on the deposed emperor's wrists.

"You've just made a massive mistake," Agha growled. "One which you will live to regret."

"That may be true, but it's not one that you'll live to see me regret," Yusef said, motioning for the guards to take Agha away. "I do look forward to your execution, standing side by side with your brother."

"Lord Yusef," a voice called out behind Bayram, and he turned to see the last person he expected.

"Yes, General Tartlan?" Yusef replied, motioning for the blue-clad commander to continue.

"Don't forget the two other members of the royal family," Tartlan said, pointing to Gamila, who was still prostrate on the ground. "Agha's supposed mistress was just Princess Gamila in disguise."

"Ah, I should have guessed as much," Yusef sniffed, nodding for two guards to grab the girl. "They certainly didn't act much like lovers. Who is the other?"

"I have the Crown-Prince here," Tartlan said, looking around, and Bayram held in a laugh at the man's confusion.

"Oh, really?" Yusef scoffed, looking around. "You really should keep a better eye on your charges."

"He was just here," Tartlan said, placing a hand on his forehead. "Standing right next to me before the artillery struck. Men, check under the rubble from the wall."

"The sickly young man is not much of a worry," Yusef said, dismissing the soldiers. "There are few enough men who would rally to the Sultan, let alone his son. We already have what we need. I assume the youngest prince has been taken care of?"

"Yes, sir," Tartlan nodded. "He's already in the dungeons, awaiting his family. It will be good for someone besides the guards to hear his screams."

"Good work, General," Yusef said, tossing the man a sack. "It's been a pleasure working with you, and I wish you all the best in your luxurious retirement."

"Thank you, sir," Tartlan said, saluting the rebel elder before turning to his men. "I would say it's been a pleasure working with you, but that cannon barrage was unexpected. You could have warned me first."

"It was unavoidable," Yusef said, waving his hand. "Now, take our prisoners to their new quarters. They deserve a day to reflect on their crimes and the just punishment that awaits."

37

G unfire and explosions reverberated throughout the city, and if he were closer, Bayram felt positive that he would hear the screams coming from women and children as the rebels inflicted their revenge on Maradon. Even with the Great Stone of Vindred, making his way through the city had been difficult with all the chaos. Fire burned in the streets, roving bands of rebels fought with the few regular army units yet to surrender, and the civilian population was hunkering down as best they could.

Shaking himself, the former prince brought his mind back to his own situation, which was just as precarious. Heart beating from exertion, he surveyed his surroundings from a crouched position in the shadows of late afternoon.

Ahead of him, a group of rebel soldiers—the most elite warriors held back from looting the city—stood guard outside the palace's main gate. The portcullis and heavy wooden doors stood open as people streamed in and out of the palace grounds. He'd recognized at least a dozen members of the city's aristocracy entering, most in chains.

Bayram lifted a hand to feel again at the Great Stone of Vindred hanging around his neck. It was a reminder that all was not lost. It was also a reminder of how much was being placed on his shoulders.

Pulling on the power of the Great Stone, Bayram partially removed himself from the world. The tangy scent of burning buildings in the air attacked his nose with new force while the late-afternoon sun's heat intensified. Moving toward the palace, he didn't bother sneaking in the shadows—the guards would be able to neither see nor hear him approach.

With sweat pouring down his face, Bayram moved past the guards standing watch, the rifle-toting brutes completely oblivious to his presence. Even with his normal abilities, he wouldn't be so brazen. Grabbing the Stone, Bayram gave it a quick kiss as he entered the main courtyard.

Evidence of violence was strewn throughout the palace—blood stains dotted the paving stones, gunpowder burns marred several tile mosaics, and the stench of death mingled with the perfumed flowers and burnt vegetation. Bayram did his best to ignore all of that as he made his way to the dungeons. Descending a set of stairs, Bayram grabbed onto the handle that led to the nearest block of cells.

Locked.

Grabbing the door, Bayram pulled with all his might. His brain told him that no amount of effort would open the door. At the moment, he could not think of a better idea.

"Something tells me that's not going to work," a deep, melodic voice sounded from behind, and Bayram jumped, slamming his head into the stone door.

Taking in a deep breath and placing a hand to his pounding head, Bayram turned around to see a tall, dark-skinned man dressed in white robes. His head was shaved completely bald, and his wide smile shone brightly as the sun. Bayram felt confident the stranger had not been there even a moment ago.

"Let me guess—you're Gamila's mystery man," Bayram said, letting go of the heavy door handle. Of course, he would be able to see through Bayram's powers. Gamila should have been trying much harder to find this man.

"My name is Rashad," the man said with a bow. "It is an honor to make the acquaintance of Salatia's crown-prince."

"Former crown-prince," Bayram sighed. "I don't know if you heard, but my father was deposed a few hours ago."

"Yes, and that's why I'm here," Rashad said, his face growing serious. "We need to rescue your family and get all of you to Genodra."

"Genodra?" Bayram asked. "I know we need to get out of here, but...wait, does this have something to do with Aydiin?"

"Yes, I'm afraid your brother will need everyone's help if we are to succeed," Rashad nodded.

"I have at least a hundred questions for you, but right now, we should probably focus on getting that door open."

"Ah yes, I am glad you are able to concentrate on the task at hand," Rashad replied, his bright smile shining through.

"You're a big guy, can't you just kick it down?"

"Unfortunately, no," Rashad said, shaking his head. "This door was made by a master Stone-weaver in Margella, and it has the strength of the Great Stone of Okuta."

"So, a key then?" Bayram asked. "I'm assuming the rebels didn't just leave one lying around."

"Well, it wasn't just 'lying around,'" Rashad said as he withdrew an ornately carved bronze key. "I did have to take it from around the neck of the one they call Yusef. That man is lucky I didn't take his head at the same time."

"What are you doing just sitting around here?" Bayram gasped. "You could be half-way to Palmas by now."

"I knew—or at least hoped—that you would be coming," Rashad said, placing the key into the door and turning it. The satisfying clicks of a locking mechanism met their ears, and Rashad turned to Bayram, his gaze boring into the young man's soul. "After all, our escape would be rather pointless without that Great Stone hanging around your neck."

Gamila's cell smelled like nothing she had ever before experienced—a mixture of unwashed bodies, bowel movements, and decay. She had already retched more times in the past hour than she would like to admit.

The stone walls, cold and unforgiving, met with the ceiling at a point far too low for her to stand up straight, and she felt as if they were slowly collapsing in on her. The iron bars separating her from the others were covered in rust, and she feared that even a single touch would result in some horrific malady.

Gamila could hardly believe her father had sent people to rot in such a horrible place as this. Then again, that was probably part of the reason there had been such a strong movement to overthrow him. How long would it be before someone else rose up to overthrow the tribal elders. Would this be their same fate?

Uncle Agha sat in the cell across from hers, just visible through the iron bars in the dim light of the room's solitary lantern. The former emperor now sat huddled in the corner of his cell, completely motionless. Perhaps he had snapped? Or maybe he was just despondent.

"Gamila," her father's voice whispered from the cell next to hers, and she jumped, hitting her head against the wall. "Gamila, can you hear me?"

The stone wall blocked him from her view, but she could easily hear his voice. She hadn't been aware that he was being kept in the same block of cells. For a moment, she couldn't decide if she wanted to respond or not.

"Gamila," her father whispered again, his voice growing hoarse.

"She's fine," Agha's voice called from his cell. Gamila raised her eyebrow—her uncle's still form hadn't moved with the words.

"You had better keep your divine-forsaken mouth shut," Oosman shot back, his voice gaining strength. "If I only have a few hours left in mortality, the least you can do is spare me the sound of your voice."

"You think I want to spend my last hours listening to your caterwauling?" Agha scoffed, his body again not moving.

"Why don't both of you shut up?" a fourth voice sounded from the cell next to Agha's, and Gamila sat up. She hadn't been aware of another prisoner in their midst.

"Now, Jabari, that's no way to speak to your father," Oosman shouted at the young man.

"Why should I care about that?" Jabari snarled. "You fool of an old man—it's your fault we've ended up in a dungeon."

"Shut up, all three of you," Gamila shouted before calming herself down. "I can hardly hear myself think. Father, yes, I'm okay—although none of us will be if we can't figure a way out of here. Jabari, you're a prepubescent twit, and you know it. And Uncle Agha, are you invisible in there?"

Agha materialized, a sheepish grin on his face just visible in the low light as he stood pressed against his cell bars, dressed only in his small clothes.

"Very clever," she said, looking away from the rather disturbing image. "May I ask what your actual plan was?"

"Well, pretty soon, the guards will be coming to open my cell," Agha said, a shrug obvious from his tone. "I figured it wouldn't be too hard to slip out during the confusion."

"That's a dumb plan," Jabari said, his voice as irritating as ever. "You'd probably need to at least incapacitate the guard so he doesn't just chase you down."

"There's no use either way," Oosman said, tears obvious in his voice. "No one has ever escaped from these dungeons. Even if you could get out from behind these bars, there'd still be an entire city full of rebel soldiers at your heels."

A silence settled in as the words hung in the air. Gamila wanted to contradict her father, but she knew he was right. The city was swarming with a hundred thousand soldiers. Anyone with the desire to help them escape was likely either dead or on the run.

The clang of metal on stone reverberated through the dungeon as someone on the outside unlocked the heavy stone door separating them from the outside world. The hinges groaned as the door was pushed, and a stream of light flooded in. Blinking, Gamila looked up to see who had come for them—apparently, it was time.

Two figures—one short and trim, the other tall and muscular—entered the dungeons, the light at their backs leaving their faces in shadow. The taller of the two grabbed the lantern on the wall, casting a pale orange light onto a beautifully dark complexion.

"Rashad?" Gamila cried out before she could stop herself.

"It would be well to keep your voice down," Rashad responded in his beautiful baritone. Her heart leapt at the sound, and she immediately picked herself up off the floor, careful to not smack her head on the ceiling.

"Well, you've certainly gotten yourself into quite the pickle," Bayram wheezed, his smiling face appearing in the lantern light.

"Oh, Bayram, I should have known you would come," Gamila whispered, this time trying to keep her voice from being overheard outside the dungeon. She could see her uncle perk up in his cell, and she assumed her father and Jabari had done the same.

"I'm just lucky that I ran into your mystery man," Bayram said as Rashad increased the flame on the lantern and the room flooded with light. "Now we need to get you out of here, quickly."

Bayram pulled a key from his pocket and began to unlock Gamila's door.

"Bayram, how did you get past all the soldiers?" Gamila asked.

"Oh, I have my ways," Bayram said, a smirk on his face.

"There is much more to your brother than meets the eye," Rashad added, a grin spreading onto his own face. There was certainly something that they weren't telling her.

"I've always said that everyone underestimates you, my dear boy," Oosman called from his cell.

"I've never—not even once—heard you say that," Bayram responded, opening Gamila's cell. "Maybe you were saying it during all those meetings I wasn't invited to."

"Oh, Father's just worried you won't let him out, too," Gamila said, moving to give Bayram a hug.

"Well, I guess you can come along," Bayram said, moving to unlock Oosman's cell. "But you'll have to remember that you're no longer Sultan. From now on, I expect to hear plenty of 'please' and 'thank you.'"

"Alright, please let me out," Oosman said, his tone not agreeing with the words. "But you forget that I am still Sultan, even if those idiots out there don't recognize it."

"No, you've been deposed by a rebellion caused by your own inability to adapt. I'm not going to let you out if you have delusions of getting your throne back," Bayram said as he opened Oosman's cell.

"Well, you've already let me out," Oosman said, moving into the corridor.

"Bayram is right," Rashad cut in, his voice silencing Bayram's response. "There are more important tasks at hand than seizing control from the rebels."

"What could be more important—hey, don't let *him* out," Oosman shot back, stopping mid-sentence as Bayram moved to unlock Agha's cell. "That man's the reason we're all here in the first place."

"I have a feeling that Agha's going to be rather helpful in getting us out of here," Bayram said, unlocking the man's cell before moving onto Jabari's.

"If you're referring to my remarkable powers, you may be disappointed," Agha said, moving out into the hallway, his posture stooped. "I fear that even after we escape, my life as a successful thief is over."

"Well, that's probably for the betterment of the world," Gamila said, trying to keep her gaze from lingering on Rashad for too long.

"I fear that Yusef could be the one who has—" Agha began, but Bayram cut him off.

"Actually, I believe this is what you're looking for," Bayram said, pulling out a dark green stone attached to a chain around his neck.

"You?" Agha sputtered, his eyes bulging out from the sockets. "How? When?"

"I'll explain later," Bayram responded. "For now, I need your help with it. After I found this, all of the rumors about your daring feats began to make sense. It's obvious that you know some of this old girl's secrets that I don't."

"We'll discuss your impudence at a later point," Agha said, a sincere smile on his face. "But for now..."

The old thief closed his eyes and extended his hand toward the Great Stone. Gamila reflexively grabbed for Rashad as the Stone began to glow a magnificent, deep green. Looking up at the man she'd spent the past few months dreaming about, her jaw dropped to find that he was gone.

Except, she was still touching him. The hem of his wool robe was thick and rough in her hands, and she gingerly put out a finger, making contact with a hardened abdomen. Yet, he wasn't there.

"Gamila, where did you go?" Oosman's voice called out, and Gamila turned to her father.

He was gone, too. She had just heard his voice. Looking around, she was alone. Not one of her companions remained.

"Well, the cat's out of the bag," Agha's voice sounded, although she couldn't see the man. "I was never really the greatest or most brilliant thief of all time. I was just an old Creep with the Great Stone of Vindred."

"Well, without further delays, we should really get going before anyone realizes what's happened," Bayram's voice called out in the empty room. "Onward and upward."

38

T he day's heat had yet to dissipate as Barrick made his way
through the now-familiar palace grounds in search of the Great
Stone. Sweat beaded at his forehead as he crouched, darting in between the shadows. Even after his years spent in the sweltering heat
of Maradon, he was still built for the rain and fog of his homeland.

He could tell the wrappings on his shoulder were growing filthy
after a week in the Pit. The few mirrors he had come across during his
time spent searching for the Great Stone of Hermnes showed that the
rest of him didn't look any better. With thoughts of a bath and new
bandage occupying his mind, he descended the hallway toward the
kitchens for a quick meal. Sobs caught his attention, and he stopped
outside the door.

Two small figures sat against one of the walls, across the room from
the sleeping laborers. As he drew closer, he made out a woman—the
source of the sobbing—and a man, his arms around the woman's
shoulders.

"I know she didn't do it," the woman moaned. "Our little girl would
never steal food—we raised her better than that."

"I know, I know," the man said, scooping the woman up into an
embrace and rocking her.

"I think the Protector is wrong," the woman said flatly.

"Don't say that," the man scolded her, pulling back from his embrace. "The Protector can't be wrong—it's impossible. I know you're
upset, but you'd best be back to yourself by morning, or..."

"We'll be next," the woman whimpered. "I don't have any idea who's
stealing food, but I know it wasn't our little girl."

Barrick pulled back, his stomach groaning in hunger. He had no idea his theft would cause such a problem in such a luxurious palace. The woman resumed her moaning, and Barrick leaned forward to listen.

"I know I'm not alone in this," the woman said, gaining control of herself again. "Lynn is positive her Abigail didn't steal anything either."

"I'll tell you what—tomorrow night, I'll stay up and keep watch," the man said, again wrapping up the woman in another embrace. "No more food will be stolen. No one else will have to die."

Barrick's heart skipped a beat. Did he just hear that right? Not only were a few missing loaves noticed, but there were dire consequences for innocent people. He'd always heard how scarce food was in Gorteo, but he assumed that would be outside the palace. Was the famine really that bad? Or was the Protector just that much of a tyrant?

Shaking, both from hunger and emotion, Barrick headed back up the corridor. Yes, he wanted more bread. No, he didn't want anyone else to die.

I just need ter find that Stone, he thought, stopping in his tracks at the soft hum from his goddess.

Turning to look in the courtyard with the three golden fountains, his eyes latched onto the woman with midnight-black hair and impossibly elegant features. Despite the knowledge that she shared the same genes as the man who killed servants because food went missing, he still couldn't help but think of her as his goddess.

Unable to resist, he crept through the shadows, making his way into the courtyard. Such beauty was difficult to admire from afar, and he needed something to give him strength before another night of searching. If he couldn't fill his stomach with food, he would have to fill his heart with something else.

She sat humming a beautiful tune as she had every night for the past week. Sometimes she would spend half the night in this courtyard, and Barrick would take breaks to come and admire her. Perhaps if she weren't here, he would have already found the Stone.

"I really am quite flattered," her voice sounded as she turned around, her eyes locking onto Barrick's. "But at some point, it's rude to stare."

Barrick's jaw dropped, and his heart immediately began pounding as the adrenaline rushed through his veins. The eye contact she'd made on the first night must not have been a mere coincidence. Still, he sat in silence, hoping that his ears had deceived him.

"Yes, I'm talking to you," she continued, her gaze boring into him. "You're a sneaky one, but I can't really let this go on."

"I'm sorry to disturb yeh, lass," Barrick said, trying to stop his heart from breaking through his ribs as he stepped out of the shadows. He could almost feel himself become visible in the lantern light, the powers of his jacket being negated.

"It's no disturbance at all," she said, a smile spreading across her face. "Oh my, I didn't know my little shadow was going to be so handsome."

"Oh, well...I..." Barrick sputtered, unsure of how to respond, and she rewarded him with a peel of laughter, sweeter than the chiming of a crystal bell. He could feel color rising in his cheeks, and he wished he could be anywhere else. After spending a week in the Pit, he was positive that he looked anything but handsome.

"I've been thinking of you as 'my little shadow,'" she said. "However, I would like to know what you prefer to be called."

"Meh name's Barrick Fortescue," he said, offering a bow, which precipitated another peel of soft laughter. "And besides your position as the Protector's sister, I don't know anything else about yeh."

"Well, Mr. Fortescue, you may call me Mirna," she said, offering an exaggerated curtsy. "And there's no need to be so nervous—I mean you no harm."

"Well, from my experience, women don't often take kindly to strange men watching them in secret," Barrick said, hearing just how terrible the words sounded in his ears. "Not that I have much experience in watching women without their knowledge, of course."

"Well, I'm glad to know that I'm the first," Mirna responded, her smile fading. "Would it be improper to ask how you were able to hide so well in the shadows?"

"Well, I wouldn't call it 'improper,' but I do consider mehself a man of mystery," Barrick responded, flashing the best smile he could muster. "You can't go around asking men to reveal all of their secrets. Life would be so dull if you knew everything about everybody."

"Alright then. May I ask how you came to find yourself wandering around the Divine Palace? I'm assuming you're one of the prisoners who washed up on shore the other day. Escaping the Pit isn't exactly something I'm used to seeing."

"Oh, so that's what you call it, eh?" Barrick said, taking another look around the palace. "Divine Palace is quite the lofty title."

"This is the very heart of Gorteo," Mirna said. "From here, my dear brother governs our nation, protecting the people. And since you didn't answer my second question, I'll just assume that you're a Traveler—something that shouldn't be found outside Gorteo."

"Well, we are pretty rare," Barrick said, guessing that the term "Traveler" was her way of saying "Lurcher". He decided it was pointless to deny something so obvious. "I've never met another one...that is, until about a month ago. I saw two funny little men rummaging through a storeroom in Naerdon."

"The foraging crews have been busy," Mirna sighed. "Gorteo is an unforgiving land. We're completely dependent on the river, and it's been three years since we've had a decent flood. Food is scarce all over the country."

"If the situation is so bad, why don't you trade with the outside world instead of stealing?" Barrick asked. "From what I can see, your people are starving. You could have foreign grain coming in by the shipload."

"It's not that simple," Mirna said, rising to her feet.

"Mirna, people are being killed because I stole a few loaves of bread," Barrick said, giving her space. "Doesn't that seem crazy to you?"

"Yes, it is crazy," she replied, her eyes darting around. Barrick had the impression that she wanted to say something else.

"You can trust me," Barrick said, placing his right hand over his heart.

"Well, my brother wasn't always so bad," Mirna responded, the words coming out slowly. "But the years have been hard on him."

"Being worshipped by those you rule can do strange things to a man's mind," Barrick said. "Constant praise can go to your head."

"You don't understand the half of it," Mirna replied, looking up at the sky. "I just wish we could go back and change a few things."

"Do you think Gorteo would be better off without your brother?" Barrick asked, placing his hand on the woman's arm.

"Of course not," she said, shaking her head and bringing her gaze to meet Barrick's. "It's only by his power that we survive at all."

"What power?" Barrick asked.

"He gives his power to the scavenger crews. They leave and come back with food. It's not quite enough, but it keeps everyone alive."

"Mirna, that power is nothing more than the Great Stone of Hermnes," Barrick said, not letting his gaze leave hers. "I don't know what your brother has been telling everybody, but—"

"Great Stone?" Mirna interrupted, a harsh laugh leaping from her throat. "Oh Barrick, you don't know as much as you think."

"I know less than most," Barrick said with a smile, "but more than some. I would love for you to enlighten me."

"Barrick, what do you know of the Creation and the Final Battle?" Mirna whispered, her voice shaky.

"What everyone knows," Barrick responded with a shrug. "The Divines created the world, then they sacrificed themselves to seal the Undergods in their prison. I'm sure there's more to it than that, but that's the gist of it."

"You're right," Mirna whispered. "There is much more to it than that."

Mirna rose to her feet and took in a deep breath. Barrick got the feeling he was about to hear a sermon and settled into his spot on the fountain's edge.

"In the beginning, there weren't just nine Divines—there were hundreds of them, and they used their powers to do wonderful things. They created the rivers and the mountains. They created the plants and the animals. Everything in the world, both the good and the bad, is from of them."

"They lived here for millennia, perfecting their creations," Mirna said, turning back to face Barrick. "Until Alarun began to grow restless. He wanted to create something intelligent—something with a spark of divinity. I don't know how he did it, but he succeeded in a creation that matched the Divines in both appearance and intelligence—only they lacked the lifespan and some other powers."

"It was only natural that the men and women they created began to worship the Divines. In turn, the Divines continued to perfect the world, often to the delight of their most recent creation."

"While not inherently good or evil, there were Divines who tended to give in to their destructive tendencies more than the others. Some didn't seem to care that their powers caused misery to humans. Alarun didn't like that his greatest creation was mistreated by some of his brother and sisters, and he devised a plan to rid some of the Divines of their powers."

"He failed, beginning the War of Divinity," Mirna said, tears welling up in her eyes. One fell down her cheek. "Many of the Divines rebelled against him, upset that he had chosen humans over their own kind. Others joined him in the war that consumed all they had worked so hard to create."

"Wait a second," Barrick said, unable to hold back his skepticism any longer, despite the conviction in Mirna's words. "You're telling me that the Undergods—the foul creatures of blackness that every child is taught to fear—they were themselves Divines?"

Even after all his time spent in the Order, he'd never once heard that the Undergods had been Divine. They were separate and different creatures, that much had been understood. Of course, there may have been additional secrets awaiting him upon ascending to the rank of Knight, had he not betrayed them.

"Unfortunately, yes," Mirna said. "Although those creatures that you mortals think of as the Undergods are nothing more than minions created by the Raven."

"I'm sorry to have interrupted," Barrick said, trying to get the story back on track. "What happens in the Gorteon version of the war?"

"When all was lost, Alarun devised a plan—an imperfect, implausible plan," Mirna said, apparently oblivious to Barrick's voiced skepticism. "Yet it was enough to save what he had created—for a time. He and seven other Divines sacrificed themselves, locking the rebels away. That sacrifice resulted in the Divinity Stones that give mortal men such magnificent power."

"So, you say that Alarun and *seven* Divines sacrificed themselves," Barrick challenged. "I've always been taught there were eight. How do you explain the eight types of Divinity Stones?"

"That is a very astute question that I will answer with one of my own," Mirna said, fixing her gaze onto Barrick. "How do you explain the rarity of the Travelling stones?"

"Are you telling me that Hermnes wasn't at the Last Battle?"

"Oh, he was there," Mirna responded. "He lent his power—or at least, most of it—to Alarun in order to imprison the Undergods. However, he failed to give up his life."

"So, if he survived—what happened to him?" Barrick responded.

"He lives on," Mirna said. "The Gorteons are not deceived when they say their Protector is Divine."

"How can you believe that?" Barrick asked. "You're the man's sister. You grew up with him. How could he be Hermnes?"

"Believe what you want," Mirna said, turning her back to him.

"Look, I believe that you believe this," Barrick said, rising to his feet and placing a hand on Mirna's shoulder. "I get that this is your religion, but how can you be so sure? How do you know Hermnes didn't sacrifice himself at the Final Battle?"

"Because," Mirna said, her voice cracking as she turned to face Barrick with tearful eyes. "I was there."

39

Aydiin filled his lungs with the cold morning air as he looked down on the battle raging below. From his vantage point atop this lonely knoll, he could see every aspect of the fighting. At the moment, his stomach wished he couldn't.

Soldiers in bright armor and long pikes stood against a raging river of creatures with skin dark as the night. Screams pierced his ears as shadowy flesh met with hard steel. They were joined by the howling of men as incorporeal teeth tore through armor.

Reaching for the well of energy within, Aydiin lifted his hands into the air and commanded the clouds above. A smile crept onto his face as the dark clouds—a tool used by those damned fools—began to swirl. Letting more of his power loose, the swirling turned into a vortex.

He could feel the particles above begin to charge, the energy begging to be let loose. The clouds continued in their movements, the power building. Below, the creatures of shadow continued their onslaught, oblivious to the fate that awaited them.

With an ever-widening grin, Aydiin commanded a bolt to crash into the chaos below. His ears were immediately met by howls from the foul creatures of shadow and cheers from his soldiers. Launching another bolt into their midst, the ground shook as a massive hole appeared in their ranks.

Further cheers erupted from the soldiers' throats, and the sound mixed with the cries of agony from their foes. With renewed strength, the pikemen began surging forward to crush their foe. Aydiin's grin grew even wider as he launched a chain of lightning into the mass of shadows.

The black mass that marred the landscape was moving backward despite the fierce howls emanating from below. Aydiin launched another bolt into the very center, and shadow bodies flew into the air, scattering in all directions. Within moments, Aydiin knew that panic would overtake the tortured creatures. Today would be his.

A shriek pierced the sky from above, echoing on the clouds and barren landscape. Without looking up, Aydiin knew what he was about to face, and his blood turned to ice in his veins.

Out of the swirling vortex, a dark shape swooped down, its wings flapping in the wind. Without looking, Aydiin could picture the eyeless face boring into his very soul. He could feel the gaping maw with endless rows of teeth about to encompass his body. He knew it was all over.

With a surprisingly soft thud, the creature landed on all fours atop the grassy knoll. Aydiin turned to face his death as the monster's wings retracted into the dark body. Rising to stand on its hind legs, the beast's eyeless gaze met Aydiin's.

The creature's massive head began to shrink, its gaping mouth—with its row upon row of teeth—diminished and began to take on a human appearance. Its curved back began to straighten, and its claws transformed into hands and feet.

Aydiin blinked, and the creature of shadow now sported the blond hair and pale face he still remembered with nausea. The eyes of pure darkness continued to bore into him, daring the young prince to defy this creature of pure power. Even without his characteristic uniform of grey, Aydiin now knew why Skraa had told him to look within his memories to find his identity.

"Well done, Perun," Skraa said, clapping his hands. "Your little powers over lightning are still enough to cause quite the disturbance."

"They're capable of more than you might imagine," Aydiin said, lifting his hands and feeling for the vast reserves within.

"I wouldn't be so hasty," Skraa said, lifting the black stone in his hand. Even from this distance, Aydiin could feel it pulse, waiting to absorb his powers.

"Your little tricks won't work forever," Aydiin said, his voice so much more powerful than he could have ever imagined.

"You always were so confident in yourself," Skraa chuckled, his slow gait bringing him closer to Aydiin. "Imagine what your confidence could accomplish if you were to only join the winning side."

"I'd die before helping you destroy what we've created," Aydiin shouted.

"It's not really up to you, now is it?" Skraa laughed. "Do you think that I joined up willingly?"

"Let me take you to Alarun," Aydiin said. "I'm sure we could figure out a way to undo this."

"Death is my only escape," Skraa whispered, his face now just inches from Aydiin's. "You have no idea what has been done to me."

"Well, my friend, if death really is the only escape, I will have to oblige," Aydiin said, and despite the black stone, he unleashed the well of energy.

Aydiin could feel the energy gushing from him. Yet, no lighting came from the sky, the characteristic blue glow was absent. Instead, he channeled divine power in its purest form into his old friend—the sensation was both exhilarating and terrifying at the same moment.

He could feel the black stone absorbing his powers, could feel it moving to block him like a dam trying to block a raging torrent. Yet Aydiin kept pushing, the water unwilling to let itself be bottled up. A crack began to form in the black stone, and Skraa's eyes grew wide. Aydiin pushed, forcing his power into the stone, even as he could feel the reservoir beginning to empty.

With a scream, Aydiin could feel the last of his power be absorbed into the stone. If only he had more. If only.

"Ah, Perun—always the hot-headed little boy," Skraa laughed, rising to his feet. "Once the Raven arrives, your temperament might have to change."

Aydiin didn't respond—couldn't respond—as he fell to the ground. His energy was completely spent, and for the first time, he felt truly powerless. He tried to block out the words spoken by Skraa, but even that took too much effort.

As Skraa approached, a deep rumble emanated from the ground below. The clouds above began to part, with rays of sunshine breaking through for the first time in months. One slammed down into Skraa, and Aydiin's nose was immediately assaulted by the scent of burning flesh.

Knowing this was far from ordinary sunlight, Skraa let out a scream and leapt into the air, transforming himself back into the winged beast of shadows. As the rays of light began to burn brighter, Skraa flew away, dodging the beams that were deadly only to him.

Aydiin let himself fall back to the ground, offering thanks to his brother-Divine. Once again, the power of Alarun had saved him when his own had proved to be insufficient.

The ground once again shook as the artillery bombardment entered into its second hour. Byanca's head pounded as she wrapped clean bandages around the burnt arm of an unconscious corporal. Until only moments ago, his screams had filled the room, now silenced by a heavy dose of morphine from the room's only doctor.

"Those bastards," the young doctor mumbled as he stitched a gash running across a young girl's forehead. "They're shelling an unforti-fied city filled with civilians."

"That army is taking orders from some of the most insidious crea-tures imaginable," Byanca said to the young man. "From here on out, we can expect only devastation and crimes against humanity."

"It was horrible," said a young soldier sitting on a nearby cot, his right eye covered in bandages. The majority of his face was burned, although not terribly. Yet the look in his remaining eye told Byanca that his internal scars may never heal.

"I know," Byanca said moving to help the wounded soldier lie back down on his cot.

"Those teeth," he whimpered. "They cut men in two like they were nothing."

Byanca stopped, realizing this young man had somehow survived an attack from the same creature that taken Diaz. Her mind's eye went to Aydiin, lying unconscious in the next room. The sooner he awoke from taking the Stone of Perun, the sooner they could figure a way out of this mess.

It was the third time she'd had to watch her husband endure the process of a Great Stone absorbing into his body. At this exact mo-ment, he was experiencing moments from the life of Perun, God of

Thunder. She knew that the extra power would be absolutely essential for the difficulties ahead, but she still didn't like the feeling of helplessness that engulfed her while Aydiin was unconscious.

"It's okay, soldier," Byanca said easing the man back down and ignoring her own sense of despair. "You just need some rest."

"We're all going to die," the man said, the words lacking any emotion. It was simply a fact.

"We'll find a way through this," Byanca said, patting the man's shoulder.

"You weren't there," the soldier shouted, trying again to sit up. "That thing slaughtered children and women. It didn't care if you were holding a rifle or not—it simply...destroyed."

The rumbling of trucks outside the building reached Byanca's ears, and her heart fell into her stomach. There wasn't a single vehicle in the city with a motor powerful enough to make that much noise. They had all been requisitioned by Diaz.

"We need to get these people out of here," Byanca said, moving to the window.

Looking up from the basement window, she could only see tires and the underside of vehicles. It was impossible to tell if they were here for her, or if they were simply moving in to invade the city proper.

Boots landed on the broken asphalt, and Byanca could see the grey trousers belonging to the regular soldiers. More hit the ground as the soldiers left their transports. Heavy footsteps pounded the street, and Byanca moved away from the window.

"There's no back way out," the young doctor said, the blood absent from his face.

"You're telling me the only way out of this basement is through a dozen enemy soldiers?" Byanca asked, and the doctor only nodded.

"I told you—we're all going to die," the wounded soldier said, sitting up from his cot.

Ignoring the man's words, Byanca rushed to the back room holding her husband. He was still prostrate, completely still except for the nearly imperceptible rise and fall of his chest. With tears in her eyes, Byanca fell to her knees at his bedside.

"Aydiin, I know you're probably in the middle of something important," she said, clasping his hands. "But if you don't wake up, we're all going to be killed."

Her husband's breathing didn't change as the basement door slammed open. Shouts from both the grey-clad soldiers and the conscious wounded filled Byanca's ears, and she gave Aydiin's hands one final squeeze. Rising to her feet, she grabbed a small revolver from the nightstand and strode into the infirmary.

A dozen soldiers had filed in, bayonets fixed on their rifles. The young doctor she'd been assisting was on his knees, a rifle pointed at his head as the other soldiers inspected the wounded. Byanca lifted her revolver, took aim at the nearest soldier and pulled the trigger.

The man fell to the ground as the bullet collided with his chest. Her ears still ringing from the sharp crack of exploding gunpowder, Byanca took aim at the next soldier. She squeezed the trigger, and the grey uniform fell to the ground.

Shouting, the remaining soldiers rushed to bring her down. One raised his rifle, and before she could squeeze off another round, a bullet slammed into her leg.

Hand clenched around her revolver, Byanca fell to the ground. Supporting herself against the wall, she found another approaching soldier and fired. The man doubled over with a bullet in his abdomen.

A strong hand grabbed her wrist and pulled the gun away. Her head tilted to the side as a fist collided with her temple, and the world grew fuzzy. She screamed as the butt of a rifle smashed into her face, and she could feel blood stream down her cheek.

"Stop it," a voice barked. "That one's for the Field Marshal."

Byanca opened her eyes to see an officer enter the room, his back ramrod straight as he strode through the maze of beds toward her. His grey uniform was immaculate, as if he were expecting a victorious parade rather than a fight through city streets.

"Ah, Byanca, the 'Princess of Palmas,'" the officer said, a smile coming across his face. "I wonder what the people of this fair city would say if they saw you now."

Byanca launched spittle onto his face in response.

"Tie her up," the officer said, straightening back to his perfect posture. "I think we should let Skraa have some fun with her."

A thin ray of molten fire crackled in the air, hitting the officer in his back and boring a hole through his chest. Without a sound, the man fell to the ground, and Byanca heard shouts from the remaining soldiers.

Another blast shot through the air, boring through the chest of another grey-clad attacker. Before Byanca could react, three more soldiers fell to similar flames, smoking holes in their chests the only sign of what had happened to them. Four others were caught by a lasso formed from water. The room filled with an electric blue light, and Byanca saw the men fall to the ground.

Without a word, Aydiin moved into Byanca's field of vision, his hands probing her body for wounds. Even in her state of semi-consciousness, Byanca could tell his hands were shaking. No matter what she'd just been through, she knew that Aydiin had just passed through something potentially worse.

"I'll be alright," she managed to say, grabbing Aydiin's hands and pushing them away. The young doctor, his face now sporting a fine bruise, fell to his knees and began examining her wounds.

"The gunshot will be fine," he said, looking at her leg. "It's only grazed the muscle. We'll get it bandaged up, but you should heal quite nicely."

"That's assuming we survive the next few hours," Byanca smiled, turning to face her husband. "Aydiin, what are we going to do?"

"I need to find Skraa," Aydiin sighed.

"I'm not sure that's wise," Byanca said. "I was thinking we could try to escape. The city is lost, and this is one time that I don't think a captain should go down with the ship."

"I know how to kill him," Aydiin said, bringing his wife's gaze up to meet his own. "We take him down, then maybe we can stop the fighting."

"There's no way I can convince you to stay, is there," Byanca said, tears coming to her eyes. It wasn't a question.

"There's no point in running anymore," Aydiin breathed out. "It's time to face that beast."

"Please be careful," Byanca whispered, a smile coming to her face as the tears rolled down her cheeks. "I can't always come to your rescue."

She felt his arms wrap around her head, could feel tears spilling onto her hair. Aydiin knew where his priorities were meant to be, but Byanca knew that didn't make it any easier. She loved him for that. She always would.

40

Y ou're…Divine?" Barrick stammered, his eyes bulging. He had mentally referred to Mirna as his "goddess" because he didn't think any mortal woman could be so beautiful. He couldn't believe he had been right.

"I'm afraid so," Mirna said. "Although it's a horribly inaccurate term."

"And your brother really is Hermnes, the Messenger of the Gods?"

"Unfortunately," she whimpered.

"So, there is no Great Stone," Barrick said, letting his shoulders fall. Then a question came to his mind. "Wait, how are there any Lurchers at all? I *remember* seeing the Divinity Stone. I held it in my hand before it became part of me."

"Hermnes hasn't always been mad, but has always been selfish," Mirna said, the words coming out slowly, as if she were still trying to decide how much to tell him. "At the Last Battle, he withheld part of his power, leaving him weakened but alive. Driven by guilt, he eventually learned how to make his own Divinity Stones to help Gorteo. However, he learned—too late to be of any good—that the Stones don't just contain his powers, but part of what makes him who he is."

"You're saying he's not exactly the same man he used to be?" Barrick asked.

"Deep down, he's still the same old Hermnes…I hope. But he's lost what made him my brother—empathy and love. He's still immortal, but that alone doesn't make one Divine."

"That's why he rules like a crazed tyrant? That's why there are the random executions?" Barrick probed.

"He's completely lost his ability to think about how his actions affect others. His only thoughts are of keeping Gorteo itself alive and atoning for his sins."

"I'm right pleased you're telling me this," Barrick began, choosing his words carefully. "But what do we do? Yeh can't just be fine livin' like this."

Mirna looked down at her feet in silence while Barrick kept his gaze on her. He'd obviously picked too hard a question for this moment in time.

"What about you?" Barrick said, trying to break the silence. "I've never been much for studying history, but I have a hard time believin' I missed the part talking about the Goddess Mirna."

"Hermnes told Alarun that I had already died," Mirna kept her gaze at her feet.

"Why would he do that?"

"I was afraid, Barrick," Mirna said, her voice choking. "Mirna, Goddess of the Hunt. Mirna the Fearless. I couldn't bring myself to answer his call to sacrifice ourselves. No matter how selfish my brother was, I will forever be worse."

Barrick stepped forward, grabbing Mirna's chin and lifted her face up to meet his. Her flawless dark eyes were swimming with moisture, and a tear spilled out onto her smooth cheek.

"No, you are perfect," he whispered.

"You see me through the eyes of an adoring mortal," she said, pulling away from him. "You do not see me for who I am. Do you not realize that if I had gone that day, the world would not be such a terrible place?"

Barrick opened his mouth to answer, but she continued on.

"My brother blames himself, but if I had gone, Alarun would have had enough power to imprison the rebels forever," Mirna cried out, multiple tears now running down her face. "The prison would have been perfect. Instead, it had flaws, cracks. Because of my selfishness, the world is doomed."

The tears turned into sobs, and Barrick moved to wrap her up in his arms, ignoring the filth that clung to him. He rocked her gently as her body shook, the emotion taking over. After a moment, she let her head rest softly on his shoulder, and he winced as she did so. He could feel his wound open up, the filthy and torn remnants of his bandage doing little.

"I apologize," she said, lifting her head and wiping the tears away. "I've been living with that weight for a thousand years."

"It's not a weight you should have to live with," Barrick said, standing up. It somehow felt sacrilegious to keep touching her, but it also felt so incredibly right.

"You're bleeding," she yelped, pointing at his arm.

"Oh, it's just a wee little cut," Barrick said, covering the wound with his hand. The blood was starting to soak through onto the shadowy material of his jacket.

"I'm the Goddess of the Hunt—I know a thing or two about wounds, and that looks serious," Mirna said, grabbing his arm.

"No, really, it's nothing," Barrick said, struggling to keep her away from the wound caused by the shadow blade.

"Don't be such a silly little mortal," she scolded him, slapping his free hand away and removing the jacket.

"No, I just have this thing about being undressed by a goddess," Barrick said as Mirna's eyes widened.

"I haven't seen a wound like this in a thousand years," Mirna said, looking into Barrick's eyes. "Who gave it to you?"

"I'm not quite sure, exactly," Barrick lied, lifting a hand to scratch the back of his head. "You see, I'm always getting into tough scrapes. Coulda gotten it anywhere."

"Yes, you've made it rather clear that you're quite the brigand," Mirna said, a smile on her face, but her eyes overtaken by concern. "But we both know you didn't get this in a tavern fight."

"Fine, if you have to know—a feller with a shadow blade got me," Barrick said. "If it helps, he's dead now."

"That doesn't help your situation. Barrick, this is serious—I saw hundreds of such wounds in the War of Divinity."

"So, how do we stop your brother?" Barrick asked, trying his best to distract the frantic Divine.

"I helped Ninazu heal a couple of wounds like that," Mirna ignored his feeble attempt to change the subject. "They nearly drained her—the Goddess of Healing herself could barely handle them. Those wounds came from dark blades created by...*her*."

"Her?" Barrick gulped.

"Foscora—the Goddess of the Night. Even before the war, I could barely stand that woman. During the war—well, I don't want to think about the things she did. While none of the Divines can truly be called 'evil,' she certainly comes close to fitting the description."

Mirna's words slowed as her gaze redirected toward Barrick's jacket. Blushing, he removed it completely, stowing the shadowy fabric behind his back.

"You're really not as sneaky as you believe," Mirna said, reaching behind Barrick. "Let me see that jacket."

"I'll show it to yeh later," he said, moving to keep it out of her grasp. "After I've had a chance ter wash it. Right now, it's covered in blood and grime—the Pit isn't exactly the cleanest place to sleep."

"Barrick, I want to help you, but I can't do so if you refuse to be honest with me," Mirna said, her tone of voice like any mother he'd ever heard.

With a sigh, Barrick pulled the dark coat from behind his back and handed it to her. He knew that she would need a good explanation as to why he was in possession of something from the Undergods. He began choosing his words carefully, his eyes downcast.

"This jacket—is this how you have been able to avoid the guard patrols?" Mirna gasped, her eyes wide. "Is this why I couldn't see you in the shadows?"

"I—uh..."

"This was made from her powers," Mirna continued, ignoring Barrick's attempt to speak. "How could you use such a thing? How did you even obtain such an item? Unless—oh, no. You're not one of *them*, are you?"

"I can explain," Barrick began, but the words wouldn't come.

The problem was that Barrick didn't really know where to begin. He technically was a member of the Order, since he had been initiated as a Squire, but he was also the reason that hundreds of the Undergods' followers were now dead. He had used this shadow jacket for both good and evil purposes. His past wasn't exactly pure, but he had gone to great lengths to atone for it.

A clock tower in the distance chimed. As the bell echoed through the courtyard, Mirna's mouth opened in shock.

"You have to leave," she said, throwing the jacket at Barrick's face. "Now."

"Mirna, wait," Barrick said, grabbing at Mirna's arm. "I won't be leaving until I explain myself."

"You can explain yourself tomorrow," she said, pushing his arm away and shoving him toward the edge of the courtyard. "But at this exact moment, you can't be here."

"Look, I know you're stubborn," Barrick said, planting his feet into the ground. "But so am I."

"This isn't a question of who is more stubborn, Mr. Fortescue," Mirna gasped. "And right now, you have to trust me when I say you need to leave."

Barrick opened his mouth to argue further, but the look on her face silenced him. There really was something Divine about her. Already, he was looking forward to tomorrow night.

"Mirna, are you going to introduce me to your friend?" a voice sounded at Barrick's rear, and he turned away from his beautiful goddess.

Hermnes—Lord Protector of Gorteo and Messenger of the Gods—stood less than a span away. He wore a tunic of pure white, the collar open to show his inhumanly muscular build. The Divine's long, silver hair practically glowed in the moonlight, framing a strong jaw, large nose, and high cheekbones. The mouth was nothing but a tight line, his eyes shining with anger.

"Hermnes, I—" Mirna began, but her brother raised his hand for silence.

"I know you've been lonely, but to spend your time with a human," he began, his gaze drifting over to Barrick. "Wait, you're one of the criminals who attempted to infiltrate my realm."

"Well, I, uh—" Barrick began an explanation, but the words failed to form. He barely knew what to say in front of one Divine, let alone two.

"Mortals—especially criminals—are not allowed to be in the presence of Gorteo's most beloved goddess," he said, his deep voice scouring Barrick like a wave of ice.

"Wait, you don't understand—" Mirna began, but Hermnes launched a glare that shut her mouth. Hermnes turned his gaze back to Barrick.

"It pains me to do this, but instead of a life in prison, you've earned yourself a public execution at first light," Hermnes said, turning his back and heading out of the garden. "I truly did expect better from you, Mirna."

The words hung in the air—execution, for nothing more than speaking with his sister. Barrick ran toward Hermnes, grabbing the Divine by the shoulder.

"I've come as an emissary from the Heir of Alarun," Barrick said as the Divine turned to face him, his eyes little more than a thin veneer of ice over a blazing inferno.

"You dare use his name in my presence?" Hermnes shouted, the ice in his eyes melting, giving way to the deluge of fiery madness. Before Barrick could blink, the backside of the Divine's hand slammed into his cheek, and the Albonan flew across the courtyard.

Barrick's wounded shoulder slammed into the stone of a pathway, and he could feel the blood now pouring out of the cut. His face already beginning to swell, he used his good arm to lift himself up. Shaking, his muscles struggled to hold his weight.

"I know you've been tormented by what happened at the Last Battle," Barrick shouted, the words slurring with the pain. "But now you have the chance to make things right again."

"You know not of what you speak," Hermnes roared, the insanity gripping him completely. "My sins are unforgivable."

"Deep down, you know that's not true," Barrick panted, finally rising back to his feet. "Please, come speak with Aydiin. As the Heir of Alarun, he'll know what to do."

"There is nothing that anyone can do," Hermnes shouted, launching a kick at Barrick's torso.

Closing his eyes, Barrick lurched a few spans away, and Hermnes' foot hit nothing but air. Barrick could feel his Markings of Power glowing as he reappeared. For the first time, he could sense the raw energy emanating from Hermnes as if the Divine himself were a Great Stone. With renewed energy, Barrick opened his eyes to see the Divine's face gripped by an anger that made his previous outbursts appear tame.

"You dare to use my powers," Hermnes growled. "None but my own Chosen are allowed to do so. For this crime, I will kill you with my own hands."

Hermnes pounced, the weight of his frame slamming into Barrick's body before he could lurch. The Divine's powerful hands wrapped around Barrick's throat, the divine muscles squeezing against those of a mere mortal. Barrick gurgled, clawing at Hermnes to get some air.

"May you find redemption from your sins," Hermnes whispered in Barrick's ear. "For me, there is no forgiveness."

Barrick's vision began to close, the darkness taking over. Drawing on the power deep within him, he placed a hand on Hermnes' arm. Drawing in the extra power from the Messenger of the Gods, Barrick lurched.

41

Images of red rock, sand, and green rivers flashed before Barrick's vision as his powers propelled him away from the Divine Palace. He could feel the energy coursing through his body, threatening to tear him apart. Yet, he also knew it was taking him away from certain death.

Panting, Barrick collapsed onto cold stone, a harsh wind pounding him with snow. The air here felt thin, and he struggled to fill his lungs. Unable to lift his head, he had no idea where he had gone, but the relief washing over him was stronger than the fear of what was next. He would have to move soon before the cold got him.

His mind was reeling from his first—and hopefully, only—encounter with divinity. He could believe that Mirna had helped create the world. In fact, it somehow made more sense than finding her level of perfection in a mortal. However, he couldn't wrap his mind around the insanity he'd seen in the eyes of Hermnes.

"Why did you bring me here?" Hermnes' voice sounded through the wind, and Barrick looked over to see the Divine standing a few spans away, mouth and eyes wide open.

"I didn't mean for you to come along," Barrick responded, trying to roll onto his hands and knees. Some of his ribs were definitely bruised and possibly broken.

"Please, don't lie to me," Hermnes responded, his voice growing weak and hoarse. "I know you must desire to punish me by making me face the past."

With shaking muscles, Barrick pushed himself to his feet, and his vision began to swim. Looking around for the first time, his foggy mind was just able to comprehend his surroundings.

Standing at a cliff's edge, behind him sat a high-mountain meadow, covered in snow. Several peaks jutted into the sky like a giant's fingers swiping at the clouds. Looking down the cliff, however, brought the most majestic sight.

A vast plain stretched on to his left and right. Straight ahead, his eyes caught sight of the ocean, far in the distance. There was only one place he knew of in the entire world where such a sight could be seen.

"We're in the Pharone Mountains," Barrick muttered, realizing that the sight he was seeing below him was Genodra. He supposed that somewhere in the distance was Palmas. Despite the cold and danger, his mind went to Aydiin and Byanca. Somewhere on that coastal plain, Aydiin was enduring his own struggles. Barrick hoped they weren't as desperate as his own.

"I promise yeh, mate," Barrick panted. "I've got no idea how we got here."

"Stop lying," Hermnes shouted, and a strong hand grabbed the collar of Barrick's jacket before tossing him through the air like a rag doll. Landing in a field of white powder, Barrick gasped as the cold cut through his rags. With a surge of adrenaline, he shot out of the snow and onto his feet. Ignoring the pain in his ribs and shoulder, he caught sight of a large boulder near the cliff's edge and lurched behind it.

"You know, I was wondering how things were going missing in the Palace," Hermnes' voice called out as the Divine prowled through the boulder-strewn cliff edge. Barrick prayed that he would have a moment to catch his breath before the Divine found him. "I killed a dozen servants for your sins. Come out so I can give their families peace."

"Hermnes, you don't understand," Barrick gasped. "Alarun has returned. If you don't go to help him, then the world is doomed."

"Alarun has no heir, and the prison is sound," Hermnes said, appearing at Barrick's side and grabbing the young man by the throat. "The traitors will never be freed. Their fate is even worse than mine."

Hermnes shoved Barrick to the ground before grabbing a large stone and lifting it above his head.

"As Protector of Gorteo, I sentence you to death for defiling a Divine with your presence and the wrongful usurpation of divine power."

Barrick closed his eyes, preparing for the end to come. At least he would be free from the pain. At least the fight would be over. At least he would be reunited with his lost love.

A tremor rippled through the ground, the sensation reverberating in Barrick's chest. Opening his eyes, he saw Hermnes standing above him, the rock still clutched in his powerful hands. Yet the tremor had apparently rattled him more than it had the ground.

"No, it can't be," Hermnes whispered, dropping the rock at his feet. Barrick looked into the Divine's eyes, and he could see something there. The fire was gone, replaced by something else. Was it sanity?

"No, this cannot be happening," Hermnes said, his gaze turning to the coastal plain, toward Palmas. "The prison is indestructible."

Far in the distance, a ray of violet light shot up into the air, reaching high above the mountain peaks before dissipating and casting its glow on the world. A shiver ran down Barrick's spine, and he had a feeling that it had little to do with the cold.

"Do you feel that presence?" Hermnes gasped, falling to his knees.

"What presence do you feel?" Barrick said, rising to his feet and moving over to the Divine.

"It's... Her."

Aydiin raced out onto the street, making for one of the now-empty trucks. Pulling up a mental image of a city map, he knew that making it there in time on foot would be impossible. As he opened the door to one of the trucks and got behind the wheel, he wished he'd taken his driving lessons more seriously.

"Okay, I just pull on this," he said to himself, trying to remember everything Byanca had taught him. "I push my foot on this pedal..."

He felt the engine roar, and he let his foot off the clutch while continuing to push on the accelerator. Spinning the massive steering wheel, Aydiin turned the truck around. The truck shuddered as he switched gears, and the engine began to sputter. Slamming his foot onto the clutch and shifting the gearstick into place, the engine again roared to life.

Not too bad for how little practice I've put in, Aydiin thought to himself as the truck lumbered through the city streets.

"Hey, learn how to drive," a voice from the truck bed called, and Aydiin's stomach fell.

Stones! Why didn't these soldiers get out with the others? Aydiin thought. A dozen men had come into the basement hospital. What possible reason could these men have had to stay in the trucks?

"Uh, just got word we're needed back at camp," Aydiin called back, trying his best to sound like a Genodran soldier.

"Hey, that doesn't sound like Sergeant Willis," one of the men said. "What's going on?"

Aydiin swerved in the large, empty avenue and was rewarded by the thud of bodies hitting the inside canvas of the truck, followed by groans. Luckily, there was no direct way from the canvas-covered truck bed to the cabin. He slammed his foot onto the accelerator, focusing his gaze on the road ahead.

Movement in the left side mirror caught his eye, and Aydiin did a double-take to see a grey-clad soldier climbing out along the side. Aydiin spun the steering wheel, and the vehicle swerved. The soldier stopped, hugging the canvas to avoid being dislodged. As Aydiin straightened out, the man continued his slow side steps, each one bringing him closer to the cabin.

Aydiin looked in his other mirror to see two more men on the opposite side. He had no doubt he could beat these men in combat, but strange things could happen in close quarters. He may have the power of three Divines, but a collision at high speeds into the side of a building would kill him just like anyone else.

He turned around and sent a marble-sized ball of fire at the man climbing on his side. The fire sailed past the soldier, hitting the canvas covering the truck. Smoke began to curl up from the oil-soaked fabric as flames began to devour the cover.

With a variety of screams, the three soldiers leapt from their climb. Their shouts were joined by the others still inside the truck along with the muffled sounds of men diving from the bed. Breathing a sigh of relief, Aydiin switched gears and slammed his foot onto the accelerator.

Sweat trickled down his forehead as the fire raged behind him. The flames were already feeling their way toward the cabin—it was only a matter of time before they found the petrol tank. While focusing on the road ahead, Aydiin began collecting the humidity in the air, preparing to douse the fire with a blanket of water.

Wait—the flames might be...advantageous, Aydiin thought, a smile coming to his face, despite the sweat now pouring down his skin. The very edge of the army's camp was already in view. He just needed this piece of junk to hold on for a little bit longer.

Ahead, a checkpoint had been assembled on the road. Sandbags were piled up, creating a wall that could only be bypassed through a set of mechanical arms. About a dozen soldiers stood at the gate, their rapid movement indicating concern over the advancing inferno on wheels.

Aydiin shouted as the soldiers dove out of the way and the truck careened through the mechanical arms with a crash that reverberated through his entire frame. Sand flew into the air, the bags shredded to pieces, and the truck's engine rattled. Metal began to grind on metal as he guided the truck through the camp, the map that Cael had drawn for him imprinted on his mind.

The truck limped through the streets, the fire growing stronger as the machine itself began to break apart. Soldiers and couriers leapt out of the way as Aydiin focused on his destination—the command tent that was already visible. The truck sputtered to a stop, the whine of the engine giving way to the roar of the fire.

Shoving the door open, Aydiin leapt onto the damp grass, already stoking the divine powers within his chest. Looking around, he saw the large command tent, although the flap was closed. The few soldiers in the area were running or hiding behind various debris.

"Skraa," Aydiin bellowed, advancing toward the tent. "Come out here and face me. We all know what you want."

Aydiin rolled up his sleeves and elevated his arms, revealing the shifting Markings that seemed to intertwine but never mix. A few soldiers looked out from their hiding spots, eyes wide.

"Are you afraid?" Aydiin shouted again as no answer came. A heavy silence had settled in over the camp, broken only by the fire, which Aydiin was quickly leaving behind. Striding over to the tent, the young prince threw open the flap.

The room was set up with what he would have expected from a command tent—a table with a map of Palmas dominating the center, with other maps and reports hanging on boards that had been set up along the perimeter. However, the tent lacked the officers and aides running in every direction expected during a battle.

In fact, there were only three figures in the tent. Diaz and Cael sat with hands and feet bound to wooden chairs on the far end. Next to them stood Skraa, arms folded in anticipation.

"Congratulations, Prince Aydiin," Skraa shouted. "I'm glad to see that the Heir of Alarun is just as predictable as his predecessor."

"Who were you?" Aydiin asked, ignoring Cael and Diaz, focusing his attention on Skraa. "Before the Raven turned you into his puppet."

"You finally figured it out," Skraa laughed. "Would you like a special prize? It must not have been easy looking into your memories for that little gem."

"I saw you from Perun's point of view," Aydiin smiled, drawing closer to the beast. "You two were close at one point."

"We were inseparable," Skraa said, ignoring Aydiin's revelation that he now controlled the Stone of Perun. "But that was long ago. And I'm glad to hear you've taken the Great Stone of Perun—that only makes this easier."

"Aydiin, you must flee," Diaz shouted from his chair. "Get far away from here before—"

Skraa rounded on the bound man, slamming his fist into the Field Marshal's head. With a crash, Diaz fell to the ground, the chair going with him as the cords stood strong. Cael's eyes grew large at the sight, but the young boy had the good sense to remain silent—good sense, or possibly the fear of death.

Aydiin could feel the power of three different Divines raging within his chest, each vying to escape. Thinking back to his vision, he focused his gaze on Skraa and the black stone that hung around his neck. The blackness pulsed, matching the pounding of his heart in his ears.

Moving to unleash the power within him, Aydiin couldn't help but gasp as he felt the familiar dam already put into place. The tactic he'd learned from Perun wouldn't work if he couldn't get the power to flow at all. As if all strength had fled, Aydiin fell to his knees.

"It's far too late to flee, I'm afraid," Skraa said, his smile growing even more wolf-like as the tent's flap flew open. "Besides, you can't run away from your destiny."

Several black-robed Squires drifted into the tent, hoods shadowing their faces. Two of the figures grabbed Diaz's unconscious form while another began dragging Cael to the corner of the tent. Without a word, the others began forming a circle around Aydiin.

"We are yours, Master Skraa," one of the figures—a very feminine voice—cried out as the group completed the circle.

"Aydiin, have you ever thought about what it takes to form a Blood Altar?" Skraa said, ignoring the black-robed servants as he crossed the tent, his gaze focused solely on the Heir of Alarun. Aydiin refused to look at the man's fiery eyes.

"Have we decided to go mute?" Skraa chuckled, coming within a span of Aydiin. "Well, let's just say the process is rather...messy. You see, it's quite easy to *enter* the Underworld as a creature of this realm—it's another thing entirely to leave it once bound there."

Skraa lifted his hand, and each one of the black robes withdrew a knife. Aydiin's eyes widened at the sight—the blades were forged in the Underworld to be used for unspeakable evils. He'd used one before, and the memory still haunted his dreams.

"I believe you're rather familiar with a Blood Circle," Skraa continued, again ignoring the figures surrounding them, "which I'm sure you've guessed by now is how we took Marcino to face punishment."

Still on his knees, Aydiin's head began to spin. He didn't remember seeing Skraa that day. Although everything had happened so quickly, it was more than possible the strange man had been there. Aydiin kept his mouth shut, determined not to give the evil creature any satisfaction.

"That circle required the blood of one willing follower of the Great Lord. However, to create a Blood Altar—a portal that allows passage *from* the Underworld—we require the blood of eight willing sacrifices."

Aydiin didn't have to count the robes surrounding him to know how many there were. He couldn't suppress the shiver that ran down his spine. Skraa noticed the involuntary action and smiled.

"You're not as dim as I thought you were. Maybe the Great Lord will have use for you when this is over."

Aydiin's mind began to race. According to Rashad, the Order needed all the Great Stones in order to release the Raven. With the addition of the Stone of Perun, he now held four of the nine, including that of Alarun. Diaz had seemed sure that Skraa had found a Great Stone.

Was it really possible that Skraa had found all of them? Sure, he could probably waltz right into Margella and take the Great Stone of Okuta, but the others were lost. It didn't seem likely, but it was certainly possible.

"You don't expect me to believe you have all the Stones, do you?" Aydiin scoffed, deciding that now was the time to keep Skraa talking. "Killing me now would do you no good."

"I'm not going to kill you," Skraa said, bringing his face close to Aydiin's and lowering his voice to a whisper. "But you don't know as much as you think."

Skraa lifted his hand, and each of the robed figures placed the dark blades to their skin, filling the tent with the smell of blood. The figures began drawing a circle around Aydiin, the blood soaking into the dirt. His heart pounded in his ears as the circle was closed around him, containing the blood from each robed figure. As the Squires straightened back to attention, Aydiin could see their bodies shaking.

"Do you have faith the Great Lord will reward your sacrifice this day?" Skraa called out to the robed figures, taking his gaze away from Aydiin for the first time.

"We do," the mix of masculine and feminine voices cried out as one.

"Then your sacrifice is accepted," Skraa shouted. "Life Eternal awaits you."

Skraa snapped his fingers, and the eight figures collapsed. Aydiin held in his scream—even knowing what was going to happen couldn't have prepared him for it.

As he had seen so many months ago, the blood began to bubble, turning black and thick as tar. The circle grew stronger, the blackness expanding inward, filling the interior. The room grew dim as the darkness began absorbing the light of the setting sun.

The dirt and grass beneath his feet began to harden, a black stone taking its place. As if carved by a master artisan, a sunburst appeared, surrounded by three ravens. The carved stone began to shift as it rose into the air, lifting Aydiin and Skraa a few spans above the unaffected ground.

"There is no greater honor for a mortal than to be part of forming a Blood Altar," Skraa hissed in Aydiin's face, reaching into his pocket and pulling out a large stone of milky white. "However, the honor you are about to be given surpasses even theirs."

"The Stone of Ninazu," Aydiin gasped, unable to help himself. The Great Stone of the Goddess of Healing was unmistakable. Its color matched perfectly the Markings he'd seen on those blessed with the gift of health. Healers more than anyone else liked to show off their Markings.

"She was such a pitiful creature," Skraa croaked, holding the Great Stone in the air. "It's hard to imagine spending my life in the service of the sick and afflicted—ironic that now she'll find her greatest purpose in bringing death and destruction to this world."

Skraa grabbed Aydiin's wrist and lifted an ordinary blade, slicing through the skin. The pain shot through Aydiin's arm, awakening his mind. As the blood began to run down his skin and onto the Great Stone, Skraa dropped it to the altar.

"You have no idea how long I have waited for this moment," Skraa hissed, turning his gaze away from Aydiin, focusing on the blood-covered Stone of Ninazu now lying on the Altar.

Aydiin reached again for his powers, feeling the weight of the three Divines pushing against the barrier blocking them as the black stone around Skraa's neck continued to pulse. Aydiin's blood began to boil with frustration. A howl launched from his throat, and Aydiin grabbed Skraa by the shoulders, crashing his forehead into the monster's face.

A horrific crunch filled the air as blood began to gush from the man's nose. Doubling over, Skraa howled in pain, although Aydiin knew from experience that it wouldn't last for long. Deep within his chest, the dam holding his powers in place felt weakened, if only just. Aydiin stoked the powers, and like a river breaking free, the divine powers burst from their prison.

Skraa howled again, still holding his bloodied nose as Aydiin focused the raw energy of three Divines into the black, pulsing stone. He didn't summon lightning or fire or water—it was simply divine energy in its purest form. The powers rushed out of him like a torrent, filling the black stone as its pulsations grew stronger.

As the energy flooded from him, memories rushed in to take its place—memories of a young Divine with an innocent face. Aydiin remembered sunny days on the beach and nights spent under the stars. He remembered an ever-ready smile that could melt the iciest of hearts. Yet at this moment, that face now howled in agony, bearing little resemblance to the one in his memories.

A clap of thunder filled the tent, nearly knocking Aydiin backward. Regaining his footing, a smile spread onto his face as his eyes made contact with the black stone around Skraa's neck.

A single crack had appeared on the black stone. Aydiin forced the dwindling energy out of its reservoirs, willing the crack in the stone to grow larger, to finally split the despicable object. Yet he could tell the powers were running low. Somehow, they would have to be enough.

A light broke through the crack, shining straight up into the air. The ray of light expanded, filling the entire tent, and the black stone began to spiderweb like a frozen lake in spring. Bringing his focus back to the stone, Aydiin forced the last of his energy into it. The stone exploded, launching both Aydiin and Skraa off the Blood Altar in separate directions.

A dull ringing hung in his ears, and the stench of burnt sulfur clung to his nose. Opening his eyes, Aydiin could only tell that the world around him was spinning uncontrollably, and he closed his eyes to avoid vomiting.

As the spinning diminished, Aydiin forced himself onto his hands and knees. Looking over to his side, Aydiin saw a wide-eyed Cael sitting silently. The young man looked largely unhurt from the blast, other than a few potential burns on his face.

"We need to get you out of here," Aydiin gasped, using the fumes of power still within him to summon a needle-thin blade of water.

"I won't fight you on that," Cael muttered, the words hardly intelligible. Whatever he'd gone through with Skraa over the past twenty-four hours would take some time to heal. Focusing his gaze back onto the thin stream of water, Aydiin commanded the blade to sever the cords that bound Cael's hands.

"Aydiin, look," Cael gasped, pointing one of his newly liberated hands toward the Blood Altar.

The Great Stone of Ninazu sat on the Blood Altar, still covered in Aydiin's blood—blood that contained the power of four Divines. The red liquid had begun to boil, and steam was now rising into the air. The prince held in a scream as the blood began to turn black, staining the altar. The three ravens surrounding the sun began to glow an intense violet, and the tent grew dark as the altar began sucking in light from the setting sun.

Aydiin and Cael fell backward as a pillar of violet light burst out of the altar's center, ripping a hole in the tent's roof before continuing into the sky above. Propping himself onto his elbows, Aydiin had to partially shut his eyes against the intensity, and his skin began to prickle from a cold unlike any he'd ever experienced.

Within the violet light, the puddle of goo that had once been Aydiin's blood began to solidify and shape itself into a lump, like a stalagmite forming in a cave. The bubbling and sizzling darkness began to expand, reaching toward the tent ceiling. Unable to react, Aydiin just sat as the mound of what used to be blood stopped a few spans short of the ripped canvas.

Squinting harder against the light, Aydiin could see the mass of goo forming into something beyond a simple stalagmite—first, he saw a hand begin to take shape, followed by delicately crafted arms. Two legs formed, supporting a lithe torso and ample bosom. As the bubbling died down, a head began to form from the boiled blood, with details appearing as if sculpted by an invisible hand. The sizzling ceased completely, although the violet light emanating from the Blood Altar remained.

While his senses were focused on the pillar of light and the accompanying dark statue, Aydiin was able to sense other events around him. To his left, a whimpering Skraa crawled around the Blood Altar, his face even paler than usual as all four limbs struggled to propel him forward. His grey uniform was nothing but half-burnt rags, and there was pain in his foe's eyes that Aydiin could hardly fathom.

At the base of the dark figure sat the Great Stone of Ninazu, completely clean and unaffected by the events that had taken place. As if Aydiin's blood had never even touched it, the milky-white Stone sat, a soft glow emanating from its depths. Even surrounded by the violet light, it resisted the darkness.

Yet, even as his brain registered what was happening around him, he couldn't bring himself to care. All of his senses were focused on the solitary figure now emerging from the pillar of violet light—the most beautiful woman Aydiin had ever seen.

Black, silky curls cascaded down onto her shoulders. Full red lips contrasted with a face that was sculpted from the whitest marble by a master artisan. A voluptuous body was covered by nothing more than a thin, black dress. As if awakening from a deep slumber, the woman opened her eyes, revealing obsidian orbs.

"After a thousand years of imprisonment, you free me inside a tent?" the woman scoffed, glaring unapprovingly at the writhing Skraa.

"Please forgive me, Great Mistress," Skraa quivered, his voice barely audible as he grabbed the Blood Altar and pulled himself to his feet.

"Oh, please don't tell me you allowed this mortal to defeat you," the woman laughed, descending from the Blood Altar with all the grace of a swan in flight.

"My deepest apologies, Mistress," Skraa gasped, using the Altar as a crutch, moving toward Aydiin and Cael. "It is, of course, an honor to die in your service."

"Yes, it is. However, you will not be given that honor this day," the woman said, turning her attention to Aydiin. "Now, who is this delicious young creature?"

"This is the Heir of Alarun, Mistress," Skraa groveled, his body trembling as he joined the woman.

"Oh, I am so pleased to see that the Sun God chose such a handsome specimen as a replacement," she said, advancing toward Aydiin, and lifting his face to meet her gaze. "You don't know it yet, but you will love me more than life itself."

As he stared into those obsidian eyes, Aydiin found himself agreeing with her. His body began to tremble, both with fear and desire. At this moment, there was nothing beyond those eyes and a need to please them.

"Yes, you will do just fine," she said, moving her hand to cup Aydiin's cheek. "Tell me, mortal, what do you know of your new goddess?"

"Nothing, Mistress," Aydiin stammered, the trembling in his bones growing stronger.

"I thought so," the woman sighed, removing her hand from Aydiin's cheek. "I've seen your world, and I've seen what you mortals are taught. You think of us as shadows, nightmares, stories to scare children. Your priests use us to keep the masses in line, and your artists depict us as nameless, faceless shadows. For a thousand years, I have seen my name forgotten by men."

"This is a tragedy," Aydiin muttered, unsure how any amount of time could erase this beauty from the collective mind of humanity.

"Well, now you know that I'm not nameless," the woman said, moving to wrap an arm around his shoulders, bringing her perfect lips to Aydiin's ears. "I am Foscora—Goddess of the Night."

The name jostled memories inside him, and more images of her beauty flashed in front of his mind's eye. Yet with that beauty came other memories—scenes where her heart proved to be cold as her beauty.

"You know, Alarun was once my lover, before he spurned me," she said, bringing her lips close to Aydiin's own. "Tonight, I take him back...in a way."

Fear and longing battled within him as her lips grazed his own. Her breath was sweet and cool on his face as if an evening breeze had rolled in from the mountains. Yet the memories within him cried out that he was in danger. A voice deep within screamed at him to flee. Yet, all he could do was stare at the porcelain face.

"Skraa, you will return to the Underworld," she said, pointing to the column of violet light still emanating from the Blood Altar.

"Mistress?" he asked, daring for the first time to question her. "Am I not needed here?"

"No," Foscora responded. "Without your Stone, you are useless to me."

Skraa hesitated, his hands still resting on the Blood Altar.

"Quickly now," Foscora shouted, gesturing again to the Altar without turning her gaze away from Aydiin. "The energy that brought me here is quickly dissipating."

Aydiin looked toward the Blood Altar, the violet column still illuminating the tent as the twilight grew dim. However, he could tell that it was indeed growing faint, the color fading. He still didn't understand exactly what had taken place, but he knew that the column of light acted as a sort of gateway between this world and the prison binding the Undergods.

As he stared at the dying light, another voice sounded in Aydiin's head. This one contrasted sharply with the voice that now filled the tent. Where the voice of this goddess before him was cold and cutting, the voice in his mind was warmer than a summer's evening.

Aydiin, please be careful. I can't always come to your rescue.

A face—infinitely more beautiful and flawed than that of Foscora's—charged into his mind. Red hair, the color of a sunset contrasted with the midnight black. Soft skin and cheeks seemed almost child-like compared to the razor-sharp features of the Divine standing before him. Eyes greener than emeralds outshone the obsidian orbs now facing him.

Those eyes lacked the ferocity, the anger, and the lust for power that filled the eyes of the Goddess. As he allowed the emerald eyes to fill his mind, the trembling that had overtaken him began to diminish. The beauty of the woman facing him—while intense and undeniable—suddenly became increasingly...less.

Her skin was too perfect and flawless. Her overly-styled hair felt fake and empty. Most of all, her eyes lacked the depth of those belonging to the woman in Aydiin's memory.

You already have come to my rescue, Byanca, he thought to himself. *I promise to come back for you.*

Aydiin grabbed Cael's hand, and—with a shout to give himself courage—he dove for the Great Stone of Ninazu still sitting on the Blood Altar. The familiar joy and sorrow, pleasure and agony filled his entire body as he rolled onto the hard surface of the Altar, his hands firmly clenching the milky-white Stone. It began to dissolve immediately, melding into his skin, filling his entire being with emotions and sensations he couldn't comprehend. Looking around, he and Cael were surrounded by the violet pillar of light, and a sensation began to overcome him—a sensation completely unrelated to the Great Stone melding into his being.

A scream launched from Foscora's throat, and her marble face grew red as one of those delicate hands snatched at him. Aydiin cringed as it approached, but her fingers passed right through him as if he were incorporeal.

Skraa arose, a weak yet sincere smile spreading onto his face. The pale, sickly face topped with blond hair lacked the usual malice. The smile that was now taking over held genuine joy. Most of all, his dark eyes seemed to shine.

Both figures grew hazy, and Aydiin's stomach began to tighten. Turning to look away, he saw the Great Stone of Ninazu finish breaking apart, the last of the fine dust soaking into his skin. The pain began to rack his body, and he squeezed Cael's hand to keep focused.

I'll come back for you, he thought, hoping Byanca could somehow hear the words as he felt both the mortal world and his own consciousness slipping away.

I promise.

The adventure continues in...

The Return

Glossary

The following glossary has been lovingly prepared by the author to help readers of all interest levels in understanding the world in which this story takes place. Broken out in three different sections, the reader will find a pronunciation guide and helpful facts for all major types of magic, countries, and characters.

Glossary: Magic

A t the Final Battle, the Divines sacrificed themselves to save the world they had worked so hard to create. In the process, the essence of each Creator was spread throughout the world in the form of Divinity Stones. While each Divine made thousands of these stones, they each created a single Great Stone.

Ordinary Divinity Stones—if such a word can be applied to them—are absorbed by human beings, giving them a spark of divine power. However, the Great Stones serve to enhance those powers like a battery. A Fire-dancer who could normally burn a house to the ground can lay waste to city blocks when drawing on the Great Stone of Surion. Stone-weavers close to the Great Stone of Okuta are able to build structures unlike anywhere else in the world.

After finding the Stone of Alarun, Aydiin is now able to absorb the Great Stones, giving him powers beyond anything believed possible. As he takes the Great Stones, he grows increasingly powerful; however, the prison binding the Undergods also breaks down as the Great Stones disappear.

For those who need help remembering the powers from the Divines, please see the following summaries and pronunciation guide:

Alarun (Ahl-ah-RUNE)
The God of the Sun and chief of all the Divines sent to this particular world, Alarun's powers are little understood. The Great Stone taken by Aydiin hasn't given any direct powers beyond the ability to absorb the other Great Stones. Aydiin is able to feel a well of power within him that is somehow distant and unavailable.

Dogodal (Doh-goh-DAHL)

The Goddess of the Wind, her Stones are most common in the nation of Lusita. Those who have taken her Divinity Stones are given the ability to manipulate the air around them and are called Wind-walkers.

Hermnes (HERM-knees)
The Messenger of the Gods, his Stones are the rarest of all. Those who have taken his Divinity Stones are given the ability to travel short distances, regardless of barriers and are called Creeps.

Katala (Kah-TAHL-uh)
The Goddess of Water, her Stones are common throughout the entire world. Those who have taken her Divinity Stones are given the ability to manipulate water and are called Waver-crafters.

Ninazu (Knee-NAH-zoo)
The Goddess of Healing, her Stones are somewhat common throughout the entire world. Those who have taken her Divinity Stones are given the ability to heal wounds and diseases (although knowledge of the human body and its functions plays a role) and are called Healers.

Okuta (Oh-KOO-tuh)
The God of Craftsmen, his Stones are most common in Margella. Those who have taken his Divinity Stones are given the ability to manipulate stone and are called Stone-weavers.

Perun (Pear-OON)
The God of Thunder, his Stones are common throughout the world. Those who have taken his Divinity Stones are given the ability to generate electricity (often in the form of lightning bolts) and are called Jolts.

Surion (SIR-ee-ahn)
The God of Fire, his Stones are most common in Salatia. Those who have taken his Divinity Stones are given the ability to manipulate fire and are called Fire-dancers.

Vindred (VIN-dread)

The Goddess of Thieves, her Stones are somewhat rare and found throughout the world. Those who have taken her Divinity Stones are given the power of invisibility and are called Creeps.

Glossary: Nations

Albona (Al-BONE-uh)
   Capital City: Somerset
Form of Government: Monarchy
Population: 4,369,000
Nationality: Albonan (Al-BONE-uhn)
Summary: A rainy nation on the northern reaches of the continent, Albona specializes in international trade, agriculture, and manufacturing.

Genodra (Jen-OH-druh)
Capital City: Palmas
Form of Government: Republic
Population: 10,543,000
Nationality: Genodran (Jen-OH-druhn)
Summary: A southern nation with a Mediterranean climate, Genodra specializes in finance, agriculture, and manufacturing.

Ghindi (GIN-dee)
Capital City: Ghindi
Form of Government: Monarchy
Population: 3,574,000
Nationality: Albonan (Al-BONE-uhn)
Summary: An agriculturally based economy to the north of Salatia, Ghindi also specializes in shipbuilding.

Gorteo (Gore-TAY-oh)
Capital City: Unknown
Form of Government: Theocratic Dictatorship

Population: Unknown
Nationality: Gorteon (Gore-TAY-uhn)
Summary: A small, isolated nation bordering Genodra and Pilsa. There are no relations with the outside world.

Lusita (Loo-SEE-tuh)
Capital City: Lusita
Form of Government: Monarchy
Population: 7,544,000
Nationality: Lusitaan (Loo-see-TAHN)
Summary: A large nation with a mild climate, Lusita is filled with wooded hills and forests. The nation's main export consists of lumber and minerals.

Margella (Mar-JELL-uh)
Capital City: Silvino City
Form of Government: Empire
Population: 8,699,000
Nationality: Margellan (Mar-JELL-uhn)
Summary: A northern nation with varied geography—hot coastal plains and a mountainous interior. The economy is largely focused on mining, timber, and fishing.

Naerdon (Nye-EAR-done)
Capital City: Naerd (NAY-erd)
Form of Government: Monarchy
Population: 9,755,000
Nationality: Naerdic (Nye-EAR-dik) as an adjective, Naerd (NAY-erd) as a noun
Summary: A tundra island nation far to the north, Naerdon lacks significant natural resources and arable land. As the epicenter of the industrial revolution, Naerdon's skyline is filled with smokestacks.

Pilsa (PILL-suh)
Capital City: None
Form of Government: Anarchy
Population: Unknown
Nationality: Pilsan (PILL-suhn)

Summary: After falling into anarchy during its wars of revolution, Pilsa is now split among a myriad of warlords and petty kingdoms.

Salatia (Sah-LAY-shuh)
Capital City: Maradon (MARE-uh-dawn)
Form of Government: Monarchy
Population: 3,328,000
Nationality: Salatian (Sah-LAY-shuhn)
Summary: Only recently unified under Oosman the Great, Salatia's economy is largely focused on agriculture and mining.

Glossary: Characters

Agha (AH-guh)
Nationality: Salatian
Appearance: Olive skinned, dark hair, mustache, generally wears a white robe with a cigar hanging from his mouth
Helpful Facts: Lord Agha is the brother of Oosman III and uncle to Aydiin, Bayram, Gamila, and Jabari. He is first introduced in *Rise of the Forgotten Sun* as the bandit lord Aydiin was sent to stop near the mining town of Oltu.

Alise (AH-lease)
Nationality: Genodran
Appearance: Light skin with dark brown hair and eyes
Helpful Facts: Alise Marzio is the sister of Luka Marzio, both of whom are first introduced in *Rise of the Forgotten Sun* at the only ball Aydiin and Byanca attend together. Her only contribution to the first volume of the series is a disparaging remark about Aydiin's homeland.

Askari (Ah-SCAR-ee)
Nationality: Salatian
Appearance: Green and scaly, with a long tale powerful enough to kill people. Just imagine a velociraptor, and you're not too far off the mark.
Helpful Facts: Askari is a powerful kerton (KEAR-tuhn) belonging to Aydiin. As the prince's most loyal (non-human) friend, the two have traveled the world together in search of adventure. While unable to speak, he can make his inner thoughts understood to Aydiin through a mere glance.

Aydiin (Eye-DEAN)
Nationality: Salatian
Appearance: Olive skin with black, curly hair and brown eyes. Slender frame
Helpful Facts: Aydiin is the presumed heir to the throne of Salatia and second son of Oosman III. While in the Soulless Desert, he found the Great Stone of Alarun, beginning both the story and the end of the world.

Barrick (BEAR-ick)
Nationality: Albonan
Appearance: Dirty-blond hair with a ruddy complexion atop a moderately sized frame
Helpful Facts: After losing his true love to illness, Barrick began serving the Undergods to get her back. When Aydiin found the Great Stone of Alarun, Barrick began to feel conflicted between what he wanted and what he knew to be right. In the end of *Rise of the Forgotten Sun*, he saves Aydiin and knocks out a good chunk of the Order's personnel in Salatia.

Bayram (BYE-rum)
Nationality: Salatian
Appearance: Black curly hair with a slender frame
Helpful Facts: Bayram is Aydiin's oldest brother and heir to the throne; however, he has been in poor health since childhood, and everyone seems to forget that he's still alive. He is first introduced in *Rise of the Forgotten Sun* when Aydiin returns to the palace from the Soulless Desert. He plays a very minor role in the first volume of this series, but the reader will note he comes into his own during *The Impending Night*.

Byanca (Bee-AHN-kuh)
Nationality: Genodran
Appearance: Auburn hair with green eyes that never cease to captivate her husband
Helpful Facts: Byanca is the daughter of Marcino and Lissandra, sister to Cael, and wife of Aydiin. She is ambitious, patriotic, and fiercely loyal to those she loves. As the daughter of an elected leader,

she doesn't inherit any titles or positions, but her eventual rise to power would be a smart bet.

Cael (Kai-EL)
Nationality: Genodran
Appearance: Messy red hair and green eyes, a large nose, and a generally awkward teenage body
Helpful Facts: Cael is Byanca's younger brother, and he's always ready to crack a joke. He is first introduced in *Rise of the Forgotten Sun* when Aydiin meets the entire family at a rather awkward dinner in the Doge's Palace.

Diaz (DEE-ahz)
Nationality: Genodran
Appearance: Light skin with dark hair and eyes. He wears a flashy grey uniform, which is covered in medals.
Helpful Facts: Field Marshal Armando Diaz has been leading the Genodran First Army for decades, ensuring that warlords from neighboring Pilsa don't spread their chaos into peaceful Genodra. He is first introduced in *The Impending Night*, although he is mentioned in *Rise of the Forgotten Sun* as the leader of the rebel army marching on Maradon.

Ferdinand (FUR-dih-nand)
Nationality: Margellan
Appearance: Dark brown hair, darker eyes, a thin frame.
Helpful Facts: Ferdinand is an admiral in the Margellan Imperial Navy and one of the first supporter of Silvino in the civil war. He is first introduced in *The Impending Night* when he mocks both Seb and the deposed Queen Isbyl. For his impudence, Sebastian smashes the man's face and knocks him into the Palmas harbor.

Gamila (Gah-MEE-luh)
Nationality: Salatian
Appearance: Dark hair with olive skin, a thin frame
Helpful Facts: Gamila is the sister of Aydiin and the only princess in Salatia. She is first introduced in *Rise of the Forgotten Sun* when

Aydiin returns to the palace from the Soulless Desert. She is saved from assassination by Rashad, with whom she becomes infatuated.

Harlin (HAR-lin)
Nationality: Margellan
Appearance: Dark hair, beard, and a very plump figure
Helpful Facts: General Harlin is the head of the Imperial Guard and former subordinate of Seb during Margella's civil war. While in command of the Segre—an ancient fortress that acted as the Royalist headquarters—Harlin betrayed his comrades to Silvino, ending the war.

Jabari (Jah-BAR-ee)
Nationality: Salatian
Appearance: Olive skin with dark hair. He generally wears a turban and crimson cape, despite the latter being out of fashion.
Helpful Facts: Jabari is the youngest brother of Aydiin, Gamila, and Bayram. First introduced in *Rise of the Forgotten Sun* when Aydiin returns to the palace from the Soulless Desert. He desires nothing more than to be the next Sultan, despite being last in line for the throne.

Joon
Nationality: Gorteon
Appearance: Short with red hair and beard
Helpful Facts: Joon is the leader of the small group of Gorteons living in the sewers of Palmas. He has an unexplained ability to track people, which he simply calls "the ability." He is first introduced in *Rise of the Forgotten Sun* when Byanca recruits him to help her find Aydiin.

Lissandra (Lee-SAHND-ruh)
Nationality: Genodran
Appearance: Auburn hair and brown eyes
Helpful Facts: Lissandra is the mother of Byanca and Cael. She is first introduced in *Rise of the Forgotten Sun* when Aydiin arrives in Palmas. Generally seen as a harmless socialite more concerned with

gossip and fashion than politics, Lissandra has a quick mind and sharp tongue that she keeps hidden.

Luka (LOO-kuh)
Nationality: Genodran
Appearance: Brown hair, pale skin, and blue eyes
Helpful Facts: Luka Marzio is the brother of Alise Marzio, both of whom are first introduced in *Rise of the Forgotten Sun* at the only ball Aydiin and Byanca attend together. His only contribution to the first volume of the series is his warm welcome to Aydiin, marking him as the only young aristocrat to show kindness to the foreign prince.

Marcino (Mar-SEE-no)
Nationality: Genodran
Appearance: Dark, greying hair with a strong face and green eyes
Helpful Facts: Doge Marcino is the elected executive of the Genodran Republic. While the office's term is for life, his children do not inherit the position, and there are plenty of checks on his power from the Senate. He is first introduced in *Rise of the Forgotten Sun* when Aydiin first arrives in Palmas. He is last seen near the end of that same book when members of the Order take him away using a Blood Circle. His current whereabouts are unknown.

Oosman (OOS-mahn)
Nationality: Salatian
Appearance: Olive skin with a dark yet greying beard
Helpful Facts: Sultan Oosman III is the monarch of Salatia and father of Bayram, Aydiin, Gamila, and Jabari. He is first introduced in *Rise of the Forgotten Sun* when Aydiin returns from the Soulless Desert. He is a renowned Fire-dancer and very proud of his Salatian heritage.

Rashad (Rah-SHAHD)
Nationality: Unknown
Appearance: Dark skin with a shaved head and strong physique
Helpful Facts: Rashad was the High Priest of Alarun before the Final Battle and now leads the few disciples of the Sun God that are spread throughout the world. He is first introduced in *Rise of the Forgotten Sun* when Gamila is nearly assassinated.

Sanborn (SAHN-born)
Nationality: Albonan
Appearance: Pale skin with light brown hair
Helpful Facts: Sanborn is first introduced in Rise of the Forgotten Sun on Barrick's return trip to Salatia. A fiercely loyal member of the Order, Sanborn is a crafty snake who blames Barrick for the demise of Arathorm Fortescue.

Sebastian (Seb-ASH-tuhn)
Nationality: Margellan
Appearance: Aging yet strong with a shaved head
Helpful Facts: Sebastian Montague (generally known simply as "Seb") is the exiled First Champion of the Queen's Guards and former Disciple of Alarun. After his queen was killed, Seb left his homeland and faith, wandering the world in search of meaning. That meaning was found when he met Aydiin on their voyage to Genodra in *Rise of the Forgotten Sun*. Seb saved the young prince from the Order and together they traveled to the monastery at Mount Pietra. Near the end of the first volume, Seb, Joon, and Askari part ways from Aydiin and Byanca in the streets of Palmas.

Silvino (Seal-VEE-no)
Nationality: Margellan
Appearance: Trim with dark hair and sun-damaged skin
Helpful Facts: Emperor Silvino is the current ruler of Margella, taking the throne after a bitter civil war against Queen Isbyl.

Skraa (Skrah)
Nationality: Unknown
Appearance: Pale face with even paler hair and dark eyes
Helpful Facts: Skraa is an immortal beast from the Underworld. First introduced in the prologue to *Rise of the Forgotten Sun*, Skraa takes a much larger role in *The Impending Night* as one of Aydiin's main foes.

Sophie (SO-fee)
Nationality: Margellan
Appearance: Light skin with soft brown hair and blue eyes

Helpful Facts: Sophie is first introduced in *The Impending Night* as a kitchen maid with a penchant for breaking curfew. An astute reader will have no doubt guessed that despite her humble beginnings, she is destined for greatness.

Tartlan (TART-luhn)
Nationality: Salatian
Appearance: Olive skin with a black beard
Helpful Facts: General Tartlan is the commander of Maradon's regular army garrison.

Tomas (Toe-MAS)
Nationality: Margellan
Appearance: A long, sharp face with shockingly dark hair
Helpful Facts: Tomas is the heir to the Empire of Margella and son of Silvino. While he shares his father's genes, he does not share his love of power. He is first introduced in *The Impending Night* in the gardens of the Imperial Palace.

About the Author

Jon Monson is happiest when completely engrossed in his writing, creating characters, worlds, and plots that surprise even himself. When he's not crafting stories, Jon enjoys spending time outdoors in southern Utah where he lives with his wife and two daughters.

To see more from Jon, visit JonMonson.com

Made in the USA
Columbia, SC
05 September 2024